PANTOMIME™

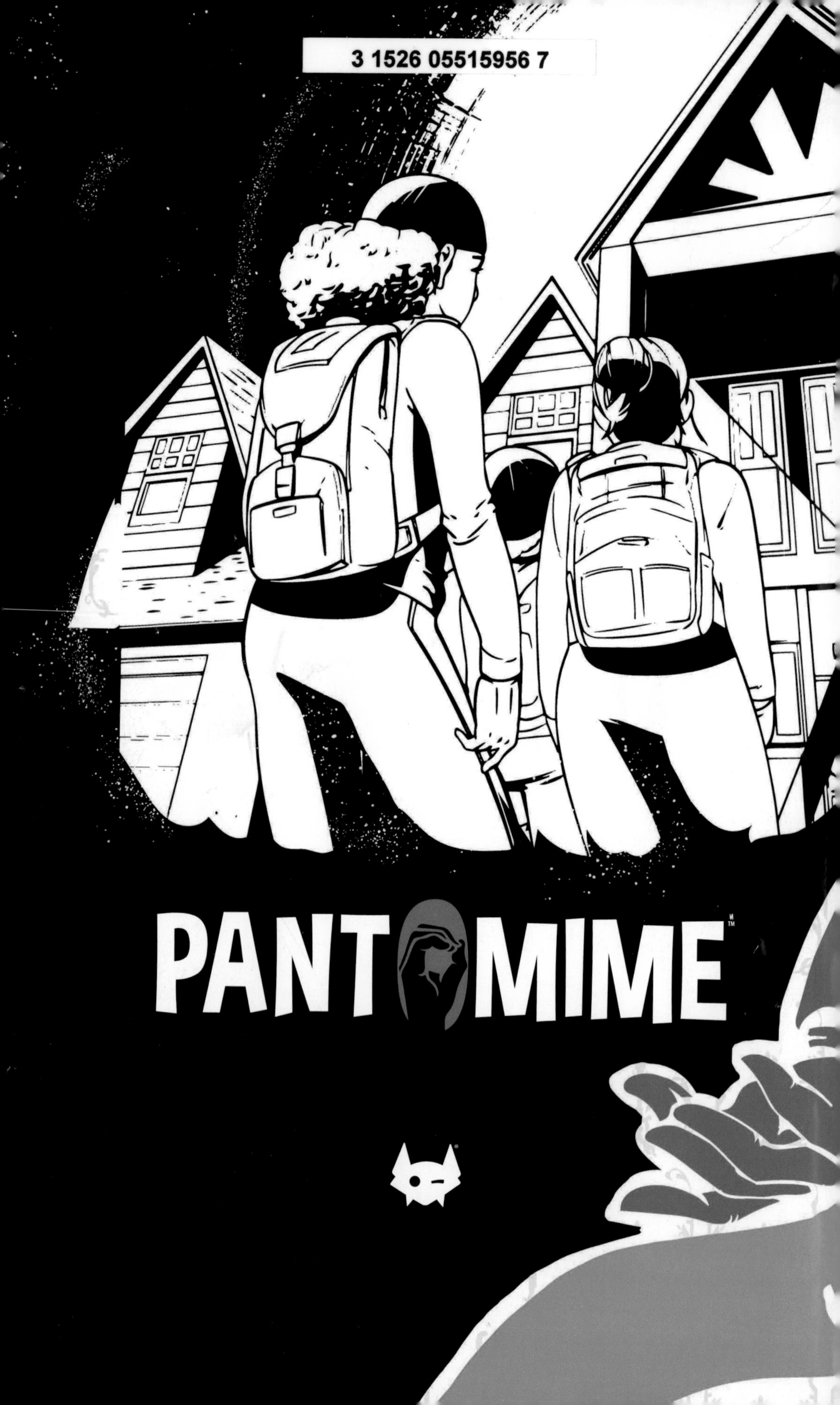
PANTOMIME

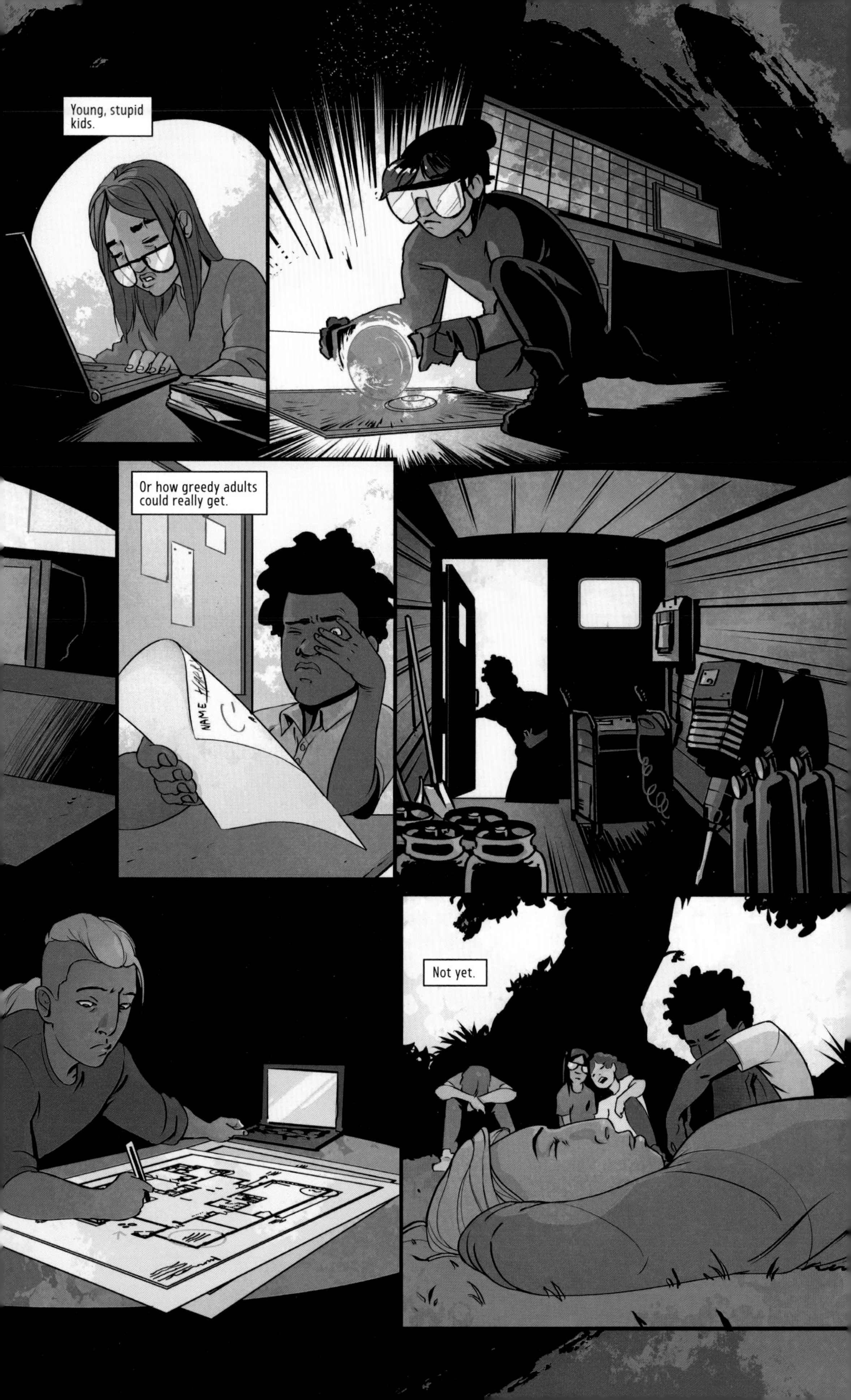
Young, stupid kids.
Or how greedy adults could really get.
NAME
Not yet.

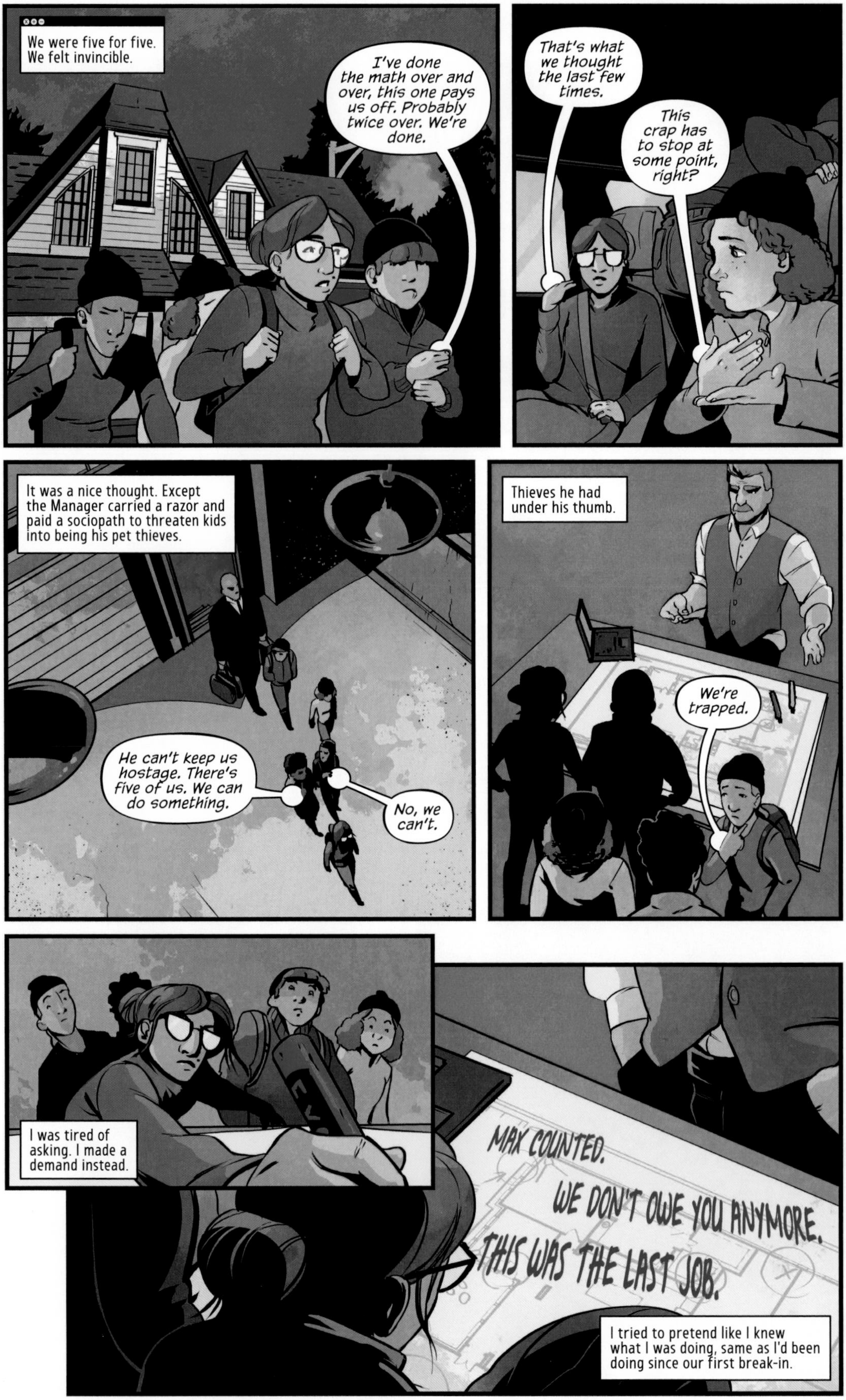
We were five for five. We felt invincible.
I've done the math over and over, this one pays us off. Probably twice over. We're done.
That's what we thought the last few times.
This crap has to stop at some point, right?
It was a nice thought. Except the Manager carried a razor and paid a sociopath to threaten kids into being his pet thieves.
He can't keep us hostage. There's five of us. We can do something.
No, we can't.
Thieves he had under his thumb.
We're trapped.
I was tired of asking. I made a demand instead.
MAX COUNTED.
WE DON'T OWE YOU ANYMORE.
THIS WAS THE LAST JOB.
I tried to pretend like I knew what I was doing, same as I'd been doing since our first break-in.

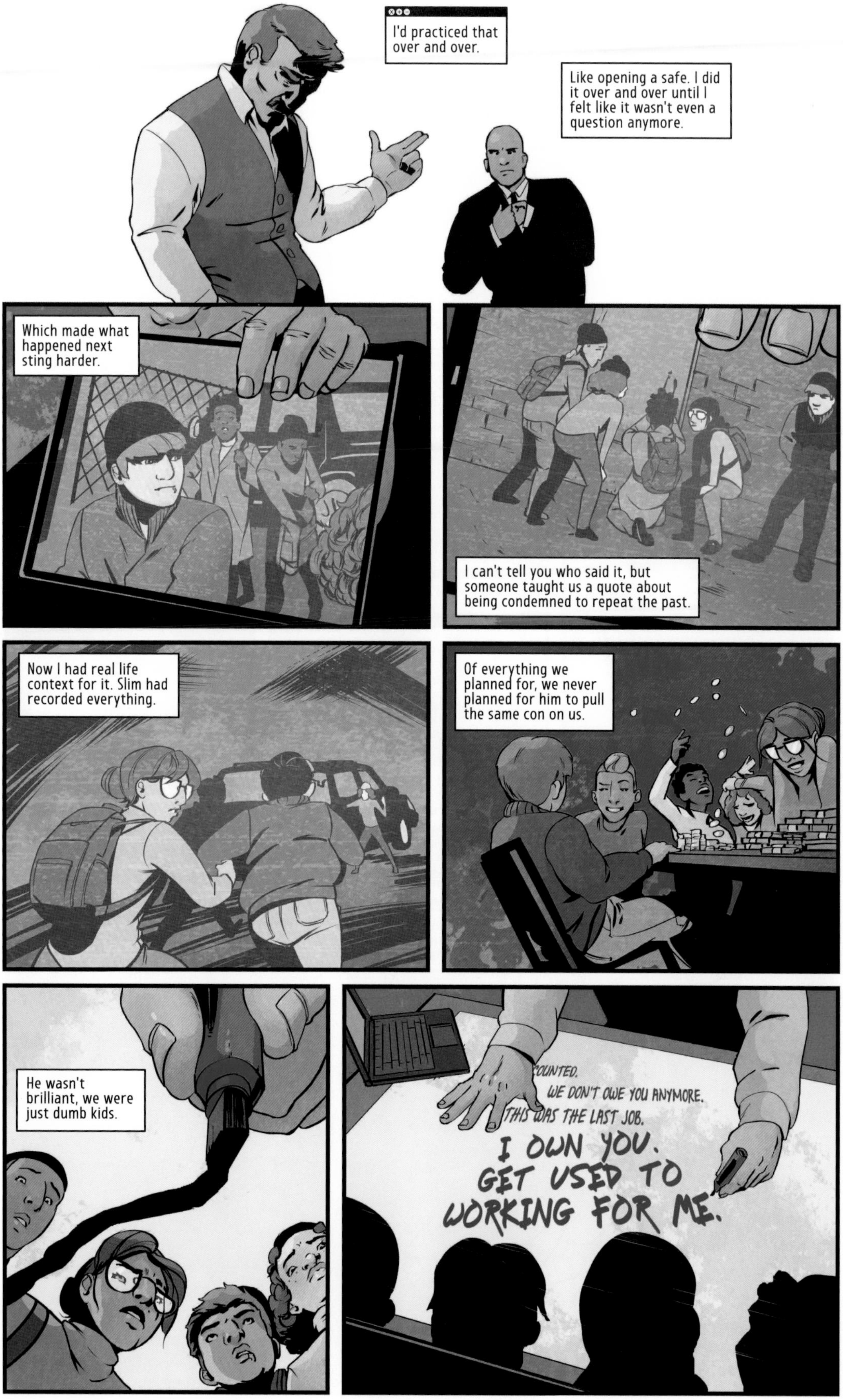
I'd practiced that over and over.
Like opening a safe. I did it over and over until I felt like it wasn't even a question anymore.
Which made what happened next sting harder.
I can't tell you who said it, but someone taught us a quote about being condemned to repeat the past.
Now I had real life context for it. Slim had recorded everything.
Of everything we planned for, we never planned for him to pull the same con on us.
He wasn't brilliant, we were just dumb kids.
WE DON'T OWE YOU ANYMORE.
THIS WAS THE LAST JOB.
I OWN YOU.
GET USED TO WORKING FOR ME.

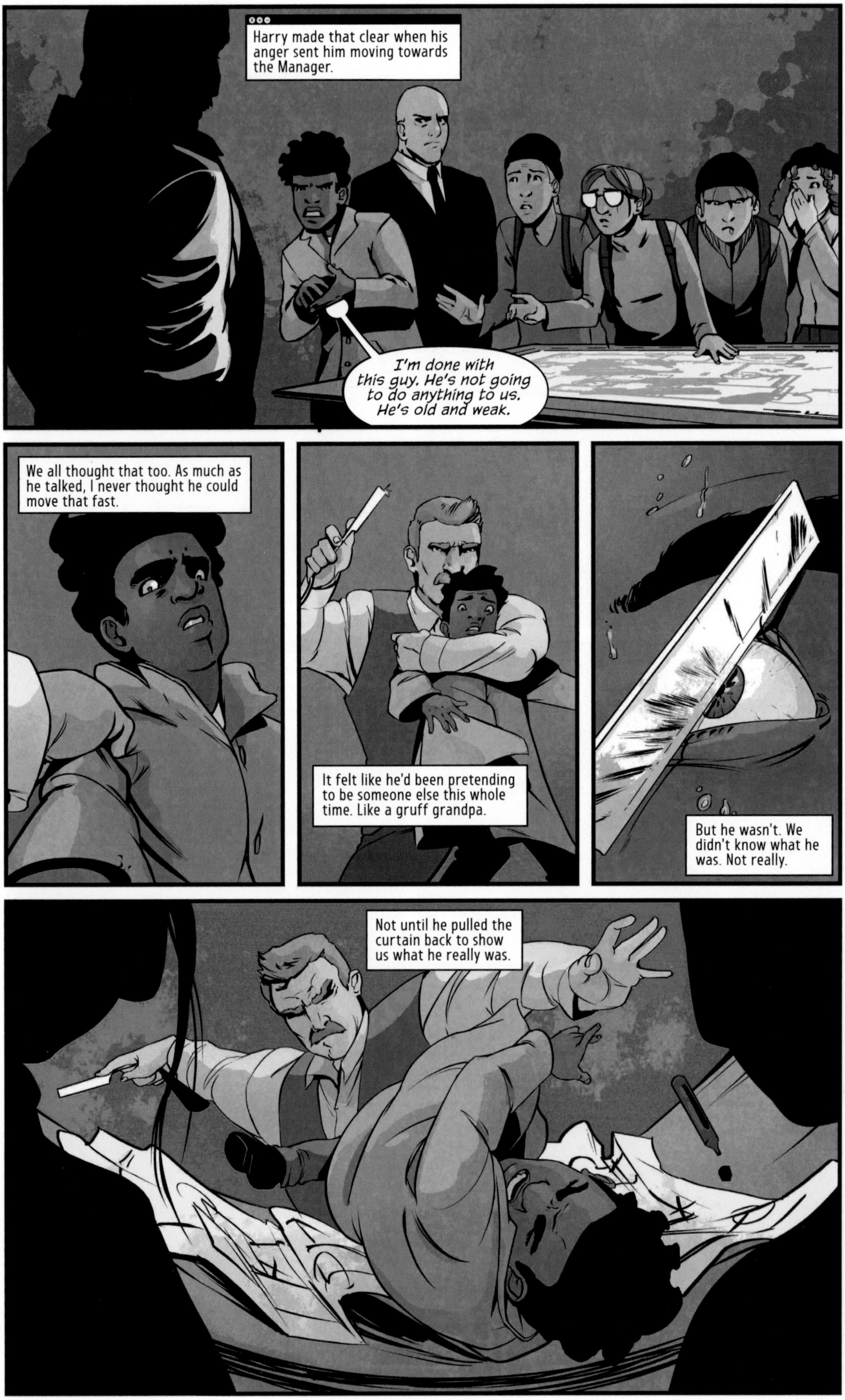
Harry made that clear when his anger sent him moving towards the Manager.
I'm done with this guy. He's not going to do anything to us. He's old and weak.
We all thought that too. As much as he talked, I never thought he could move that fast.
It felt like he'd been pretending to be someone else this whole time. Like a gruff grandpa.
But he wasn't. We didn't know what he was. Not really.
Not until he pulled the curtain back to show us what he really was.

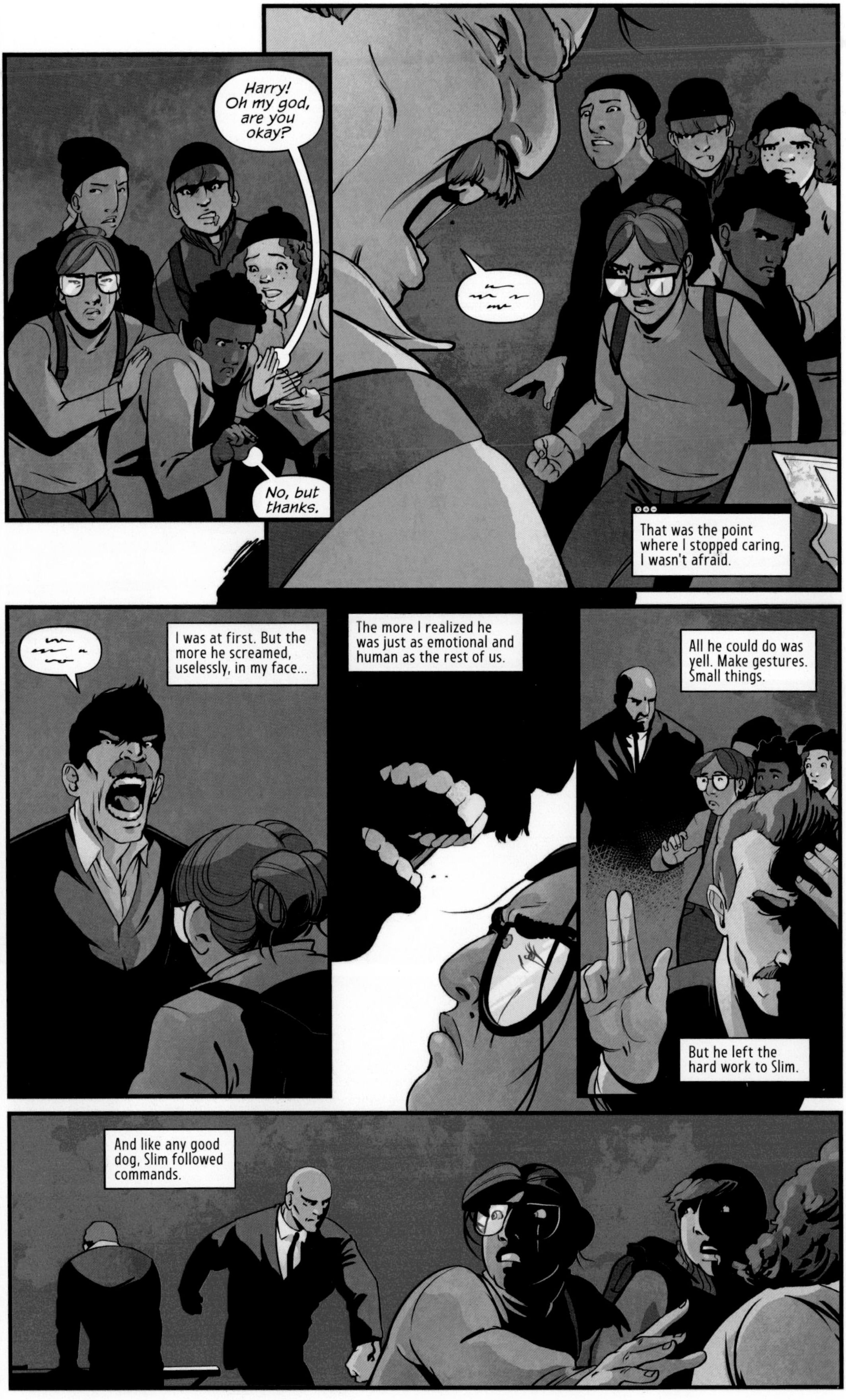
Harry! Oh my god, are you okay?
No, but thanks.
That was the point where I stopped caring. I wasn't afraid.
I was at first. But the more he screamed, uselessly, in my face...
The more I realized he was just as emotional and human as the rest of us.
All he could do was yell. Make gestures. Small things.
But he left the hard work to Slim.
And like any good dog, Slim followed commands.

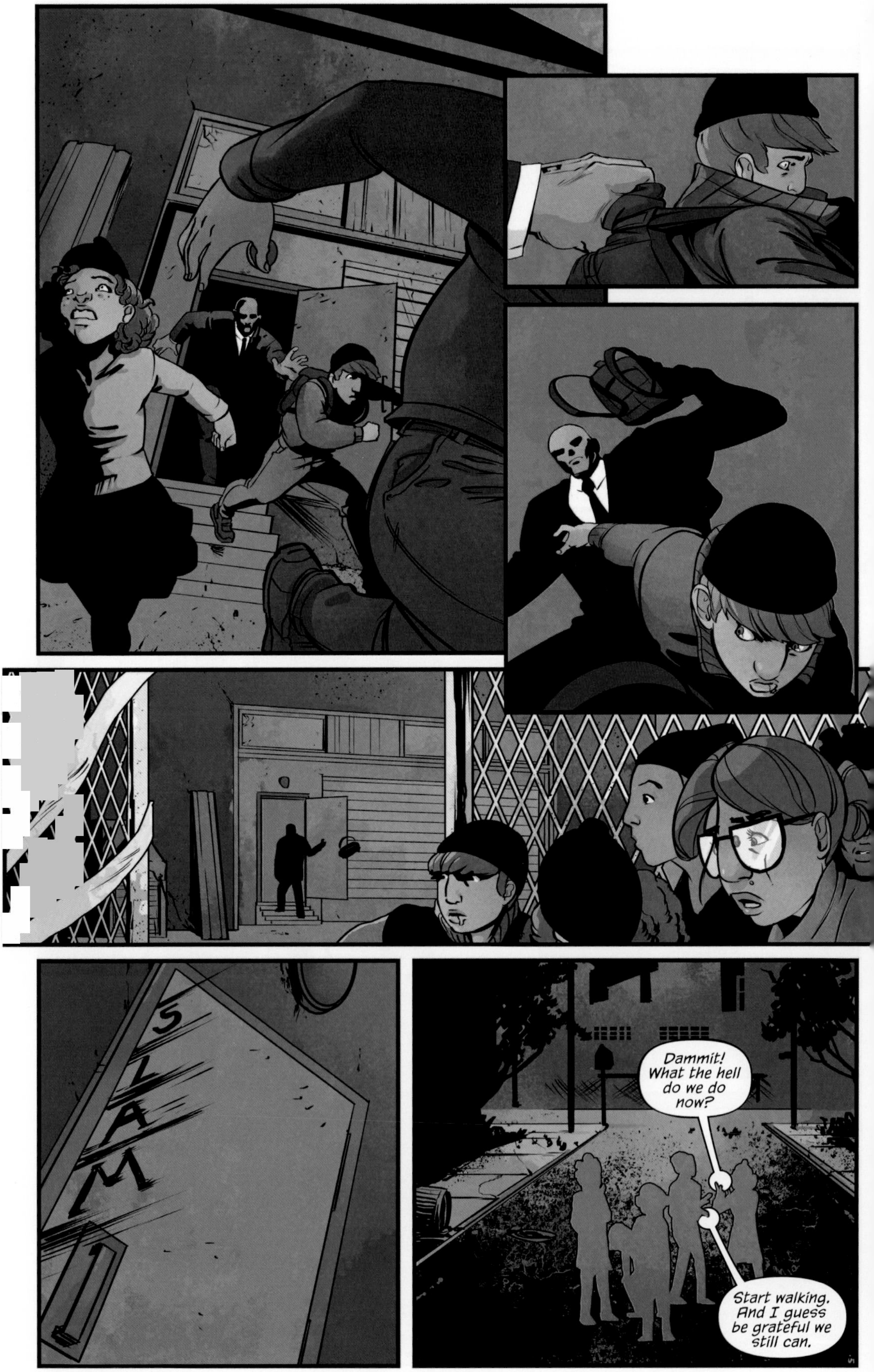
SLAM
Dammit! What the hell do we do now?
Start walking. And I guess be grateful we still can.

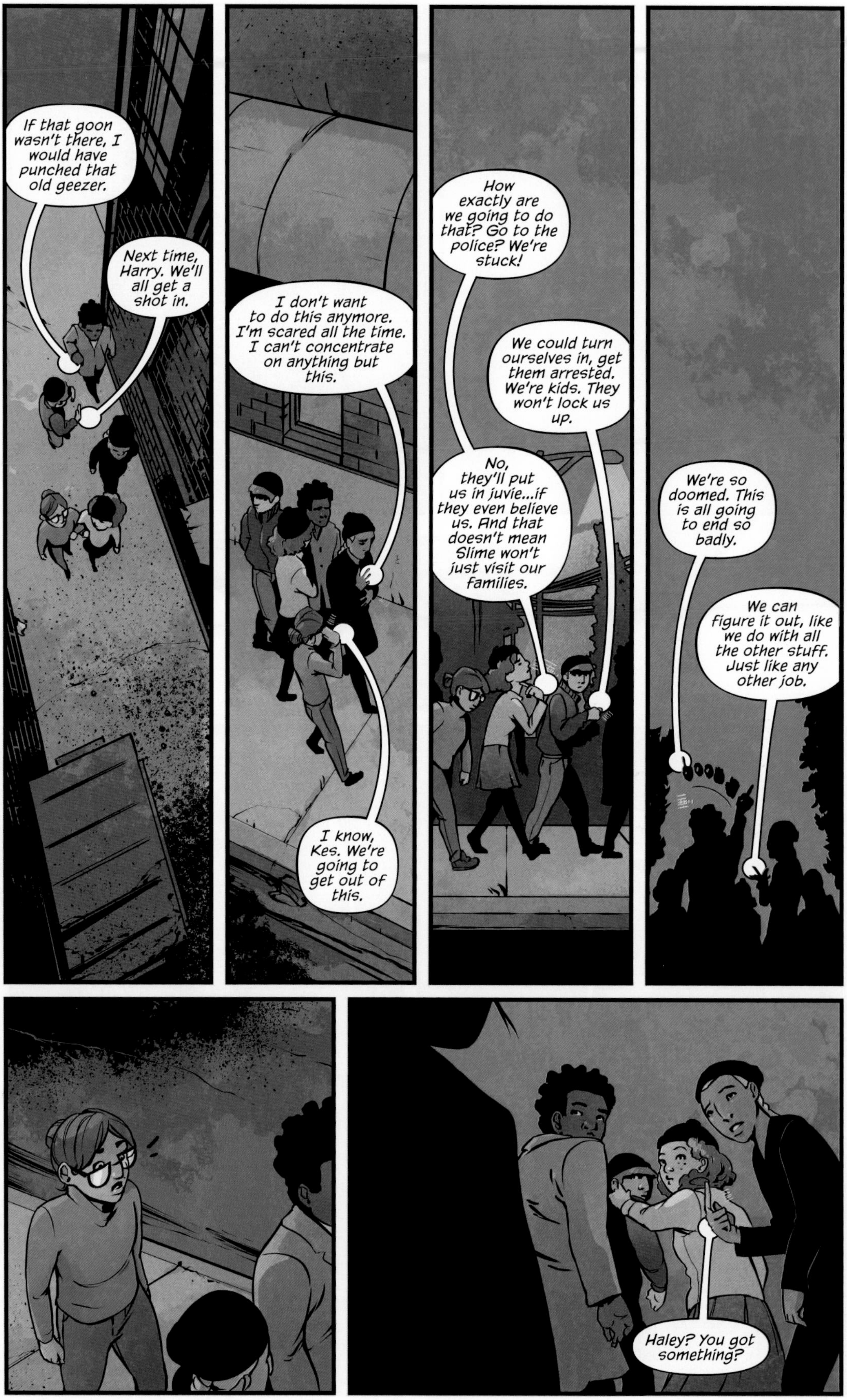
If that goon wasn't there, I would have punched that old geezer.
Next time, Harry. We'll all get a shot in.
I don't want to do this anymore. I'm scared all the time. I can't concentrate on anything but this.
I know, Kes. We're going to get out of this.
How exactly are we going to do that? Go to the police? We're stuck!
We could turn ourselves in, get them arrested. We're kids. They won't lock us up.
No, they'll put us in juvie...if they even believe us. And that doesn't mean Slime won't just visit our families.
We're so doomed. This is all going to end so badly.
We can figure it out, like we do with all the other stuff. Just like any other job.
Haley? You got something?

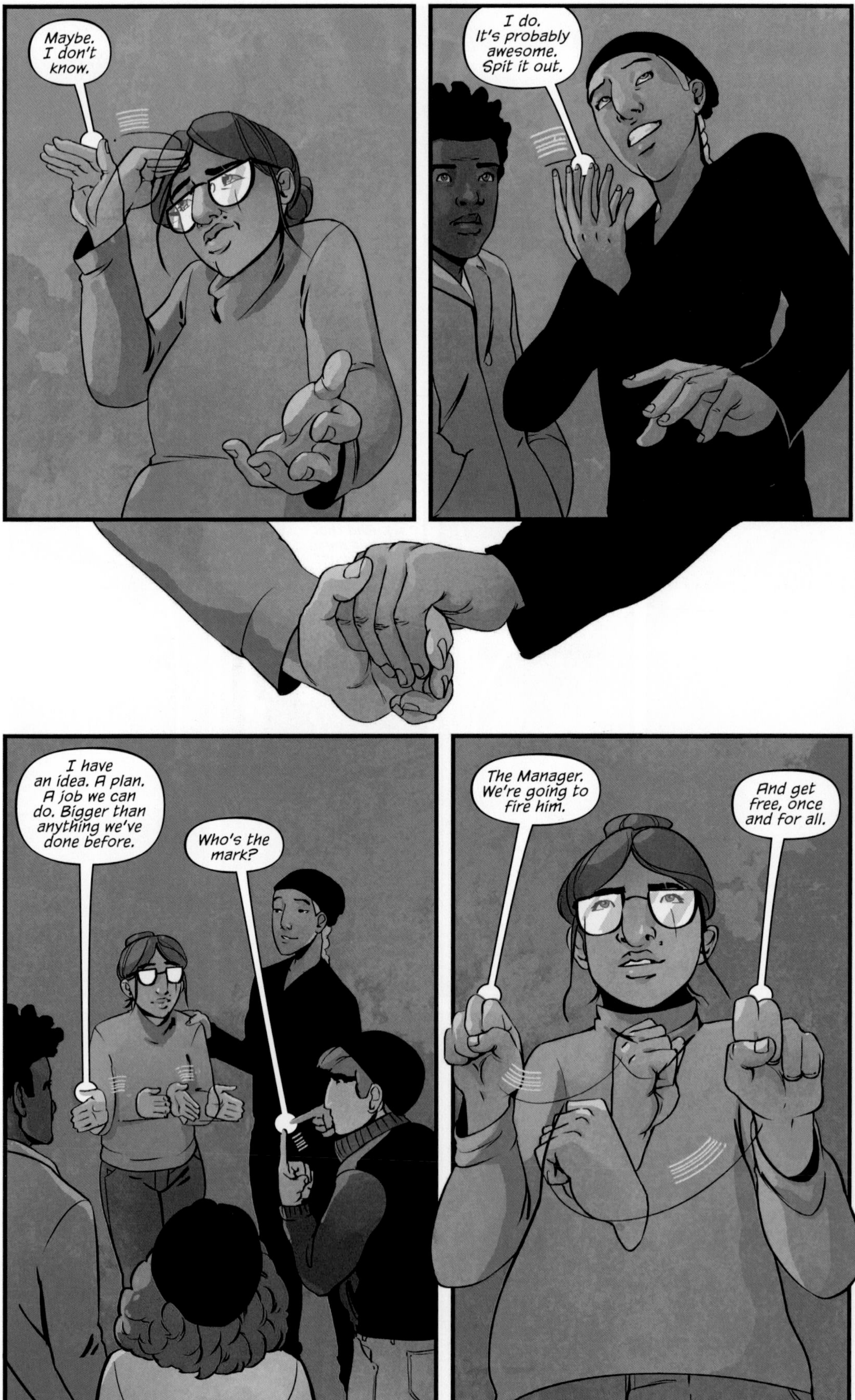
Maybe. I don't know.
I do. It's probably awesome. Spit it out.
I have an idea. A plan. A job we can do. Bigger than anything we've done before.
Who's the mark?
The Manager. We're going to fire him.
And get free, once and for all.

CHAPTER THREE

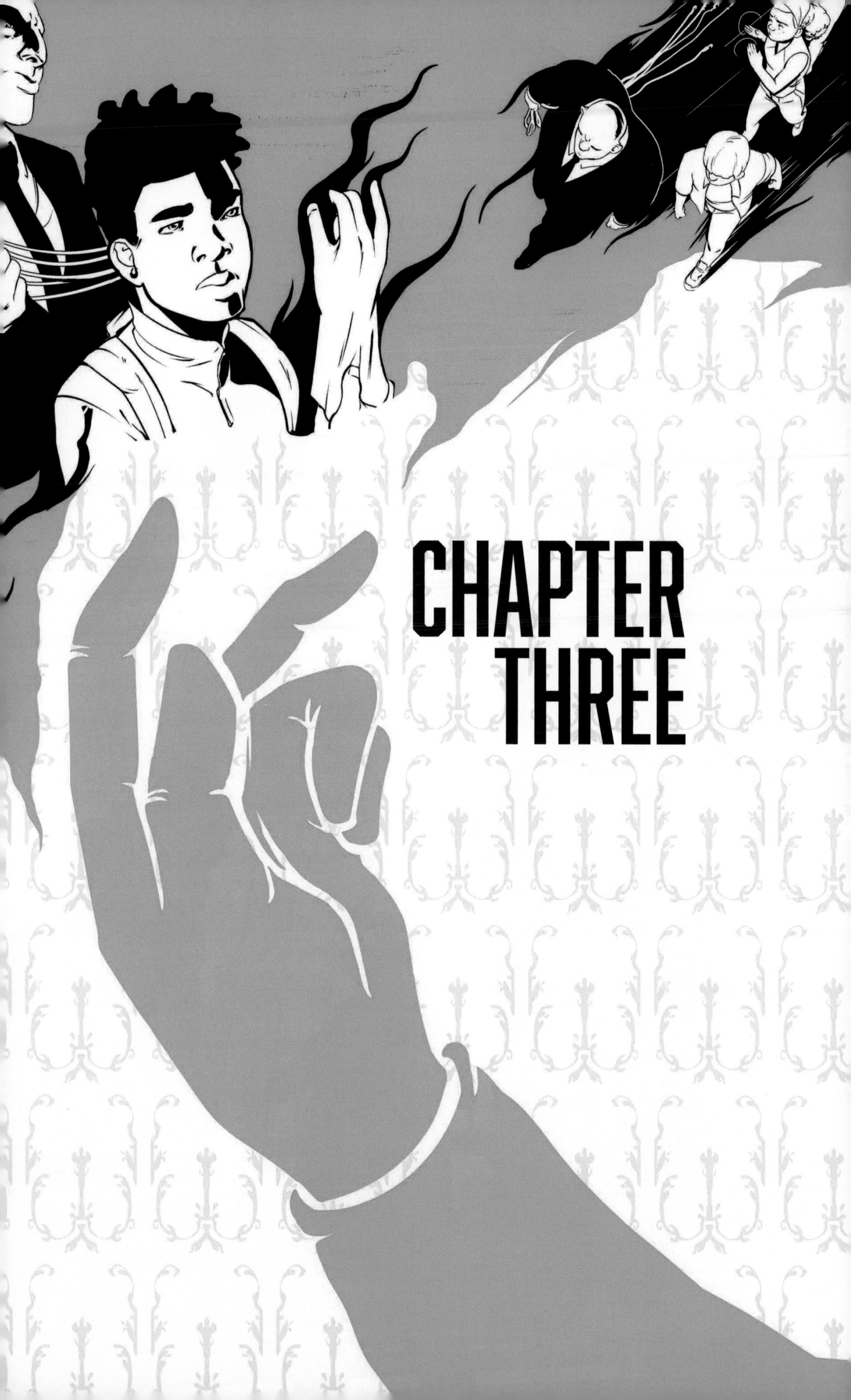

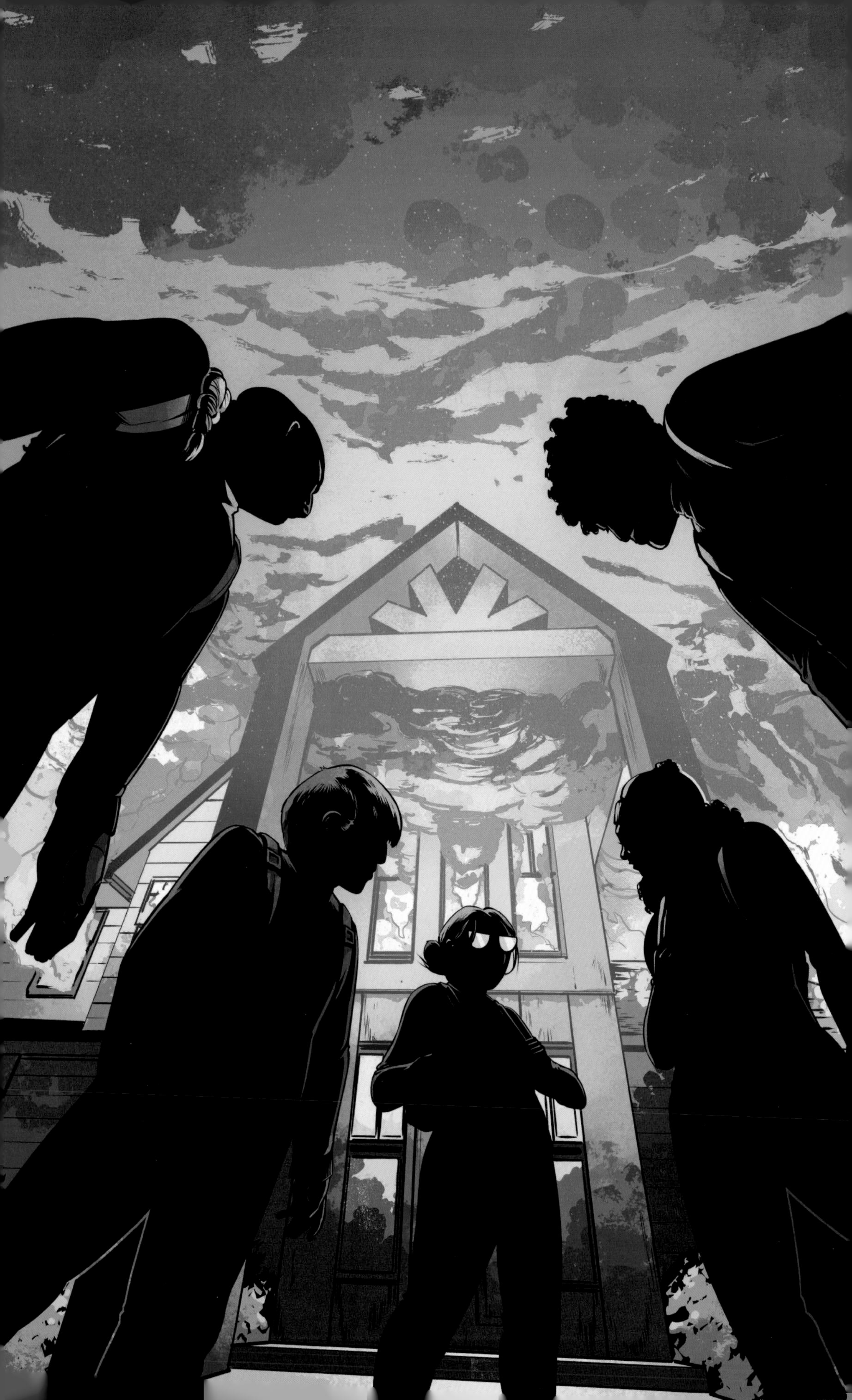

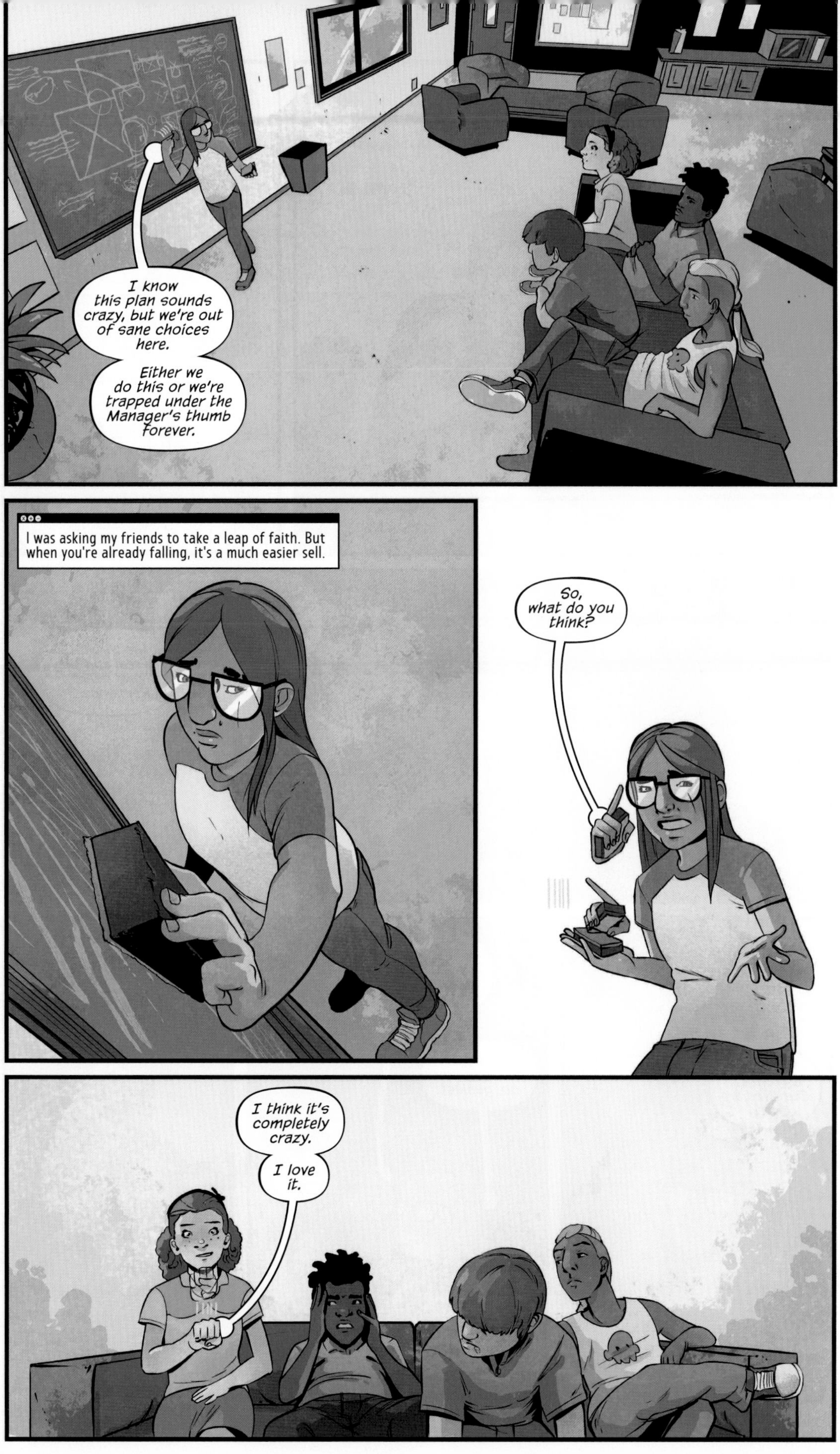
I know this plan sounds crazy, but we're out of sane choices here.
Either we do this or we're trapped under the Manager's thumb forever.
I was asking my friends to take a leap of faith. But when you're already falling, it's a much easier sell.
So, what do you think?
I think it's completely crazy.
I love it.

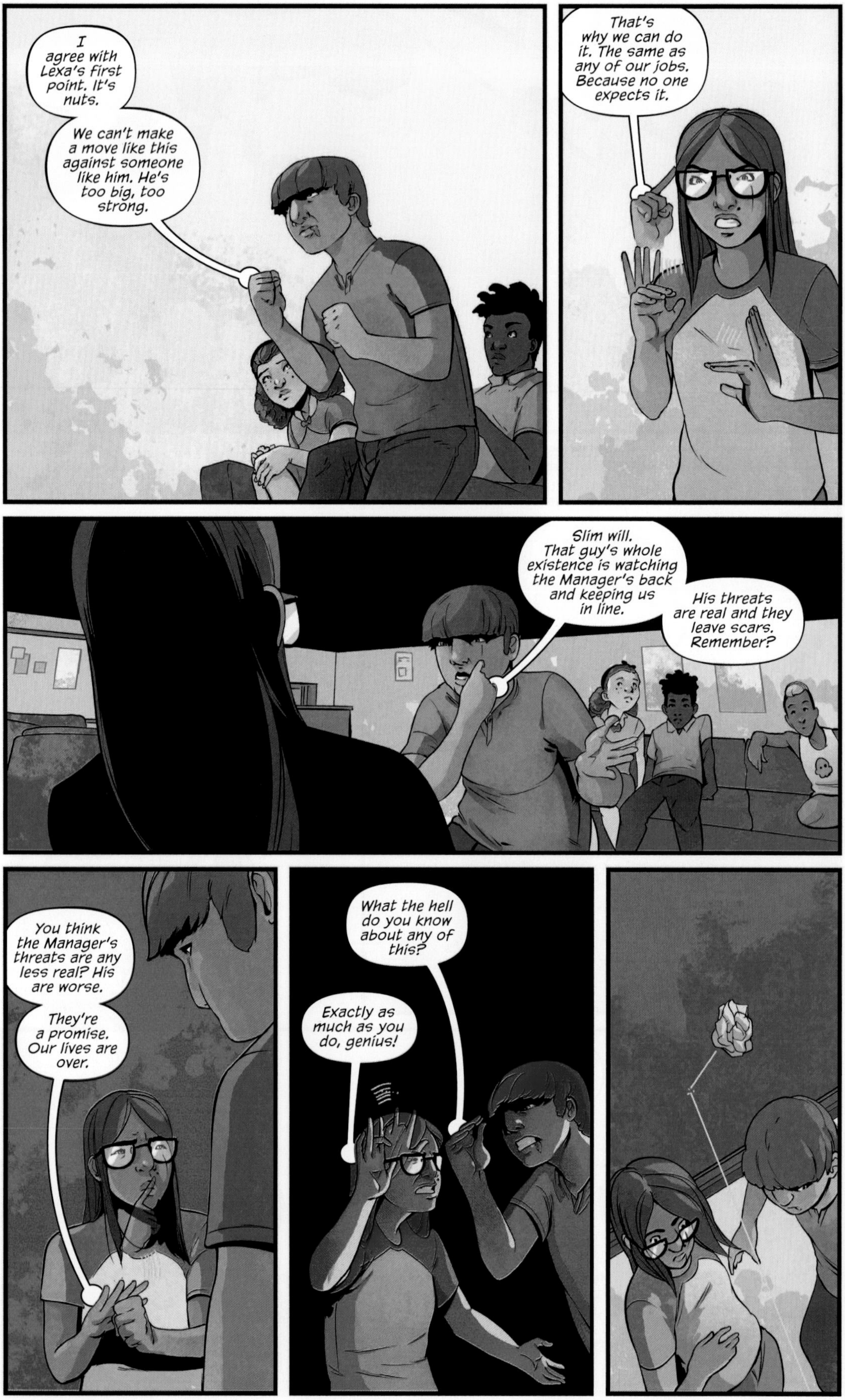
I agree with Lexa's first point. It's nuts.
We can't make a move like this against someone like him. He's too big, too strong.
That's why we can do it. The same as any of our jobs. Because no one expects it.
Slim will. That guy's whole existence is watching the Manager's back and keeping us in line.
His threats are real and they leave scars. Remember?
You think the Manager's threats are any less real? His are worse.
They're a promise. Our lives are over.
What the hell do you know about any of this?
Exactly as much as you do, genius!

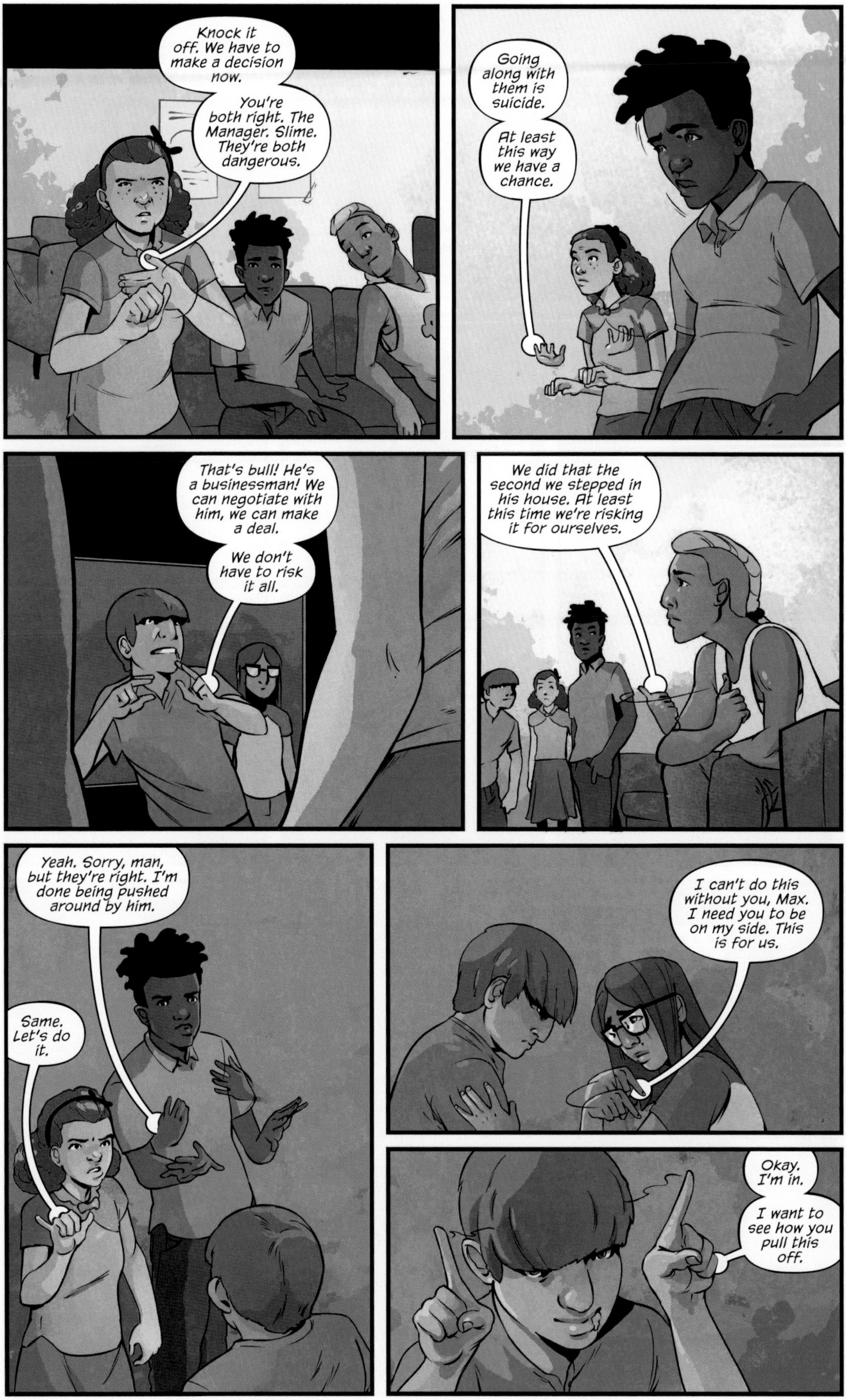
Knock it off. We have to make a decision now.
You're both right. The Manager. Slime. They're both dangerous.
Going along with them is suicide.
At least this way we have a chance.
That's bull! He's a businessman! We can negotiate with him, we can make a deal.
We don't have to risk it all.
We did that the second we stepped in his house. At least this time we're risking it for ourselves.
Yeah. Sorry, man, but they're right. I'm done being pushed around by him.
Same. Let's do it.
I can't do this without you, Max. I need you to be on my side. This is for us.
Okay. I'm in.
I want to see how you pull this off.

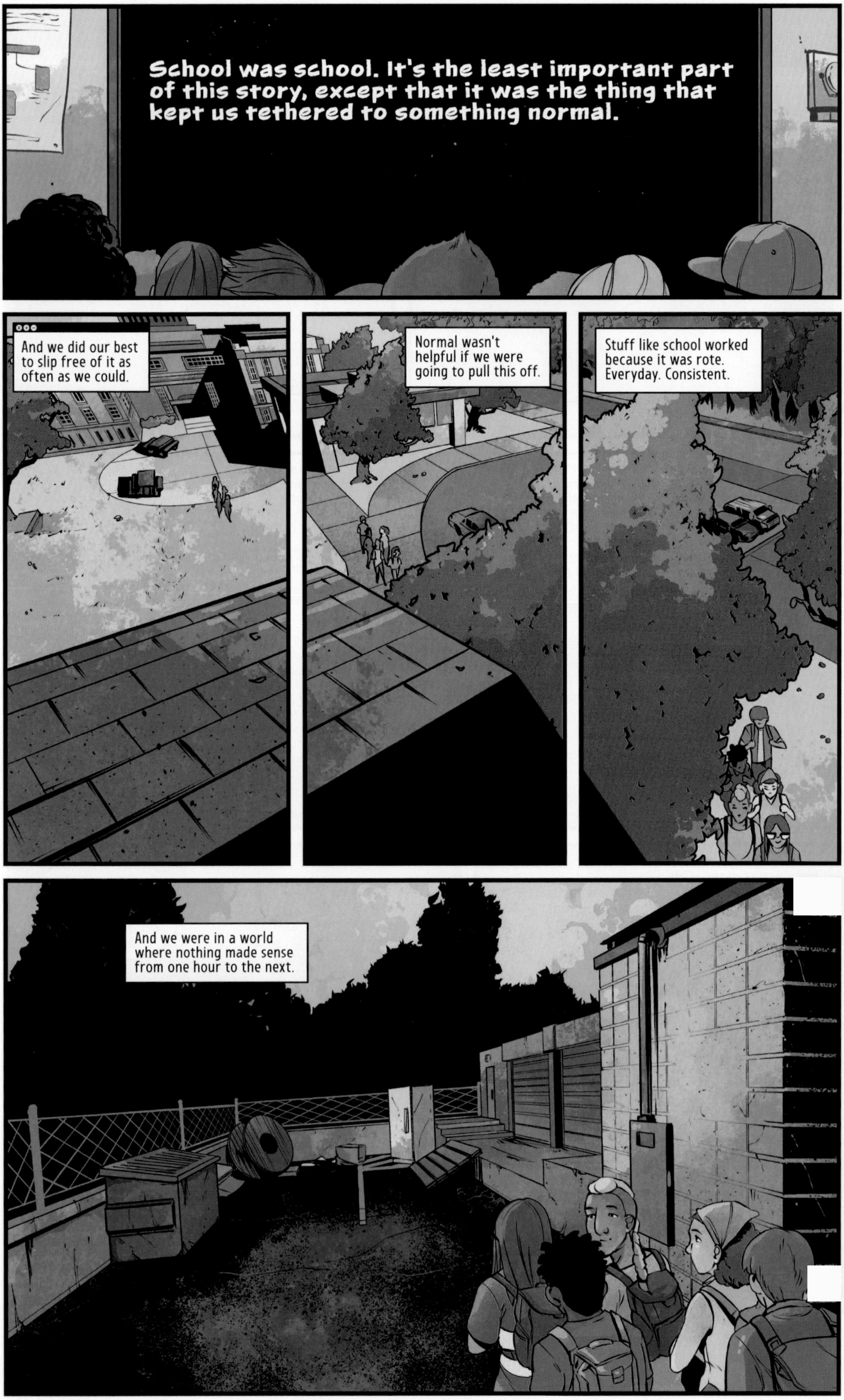
School was school. It's the least important part of this story, except that it was the thing that kept us tethered to something normal.
And we did our best to slip free of it as often as we could.
Normal wasn't helpful if we were going to pull this off.
Stuff like school worked because it was rote. Everyday. Consistent.
And we were in a world where nothing made sense from one hour to the next.

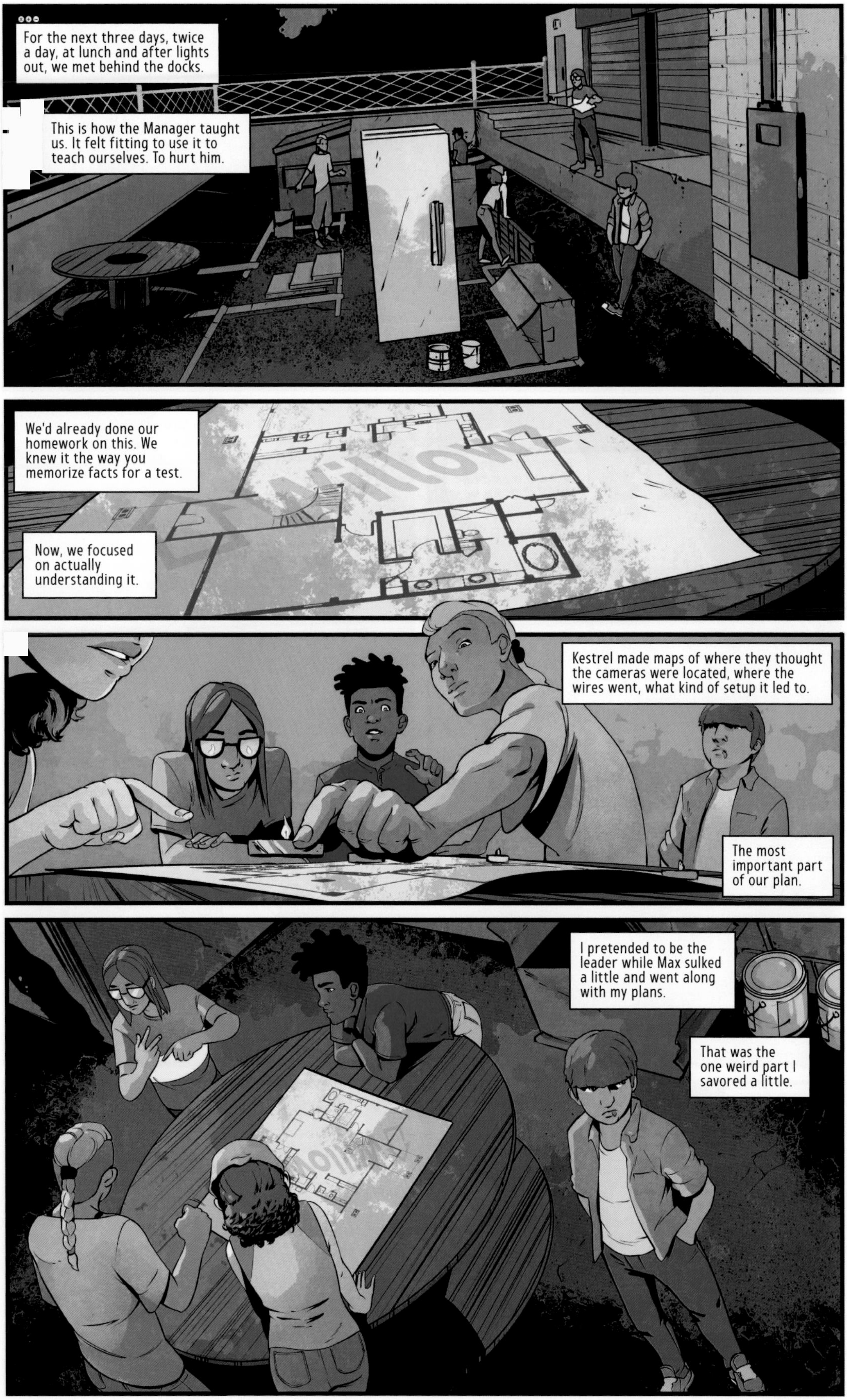
For the next three days, twice a day, at lunch and after lights out, we met behind the docks.
This is how the Manager taught us. It felt fitting to use it to teach ourselves. To hurt him.
We'd already done our homework on this. We knew it the way you memorize facts for a test.
Now, we focused on actually understanding it.
Kestrel made maps of where they thought the cameras were located, where the wires went, what kind of setup it led to.
The most important part of our plan.
I pretended to be the leader while Max sulked a little and went along with my plans.
That was the one weird part I savored a little.

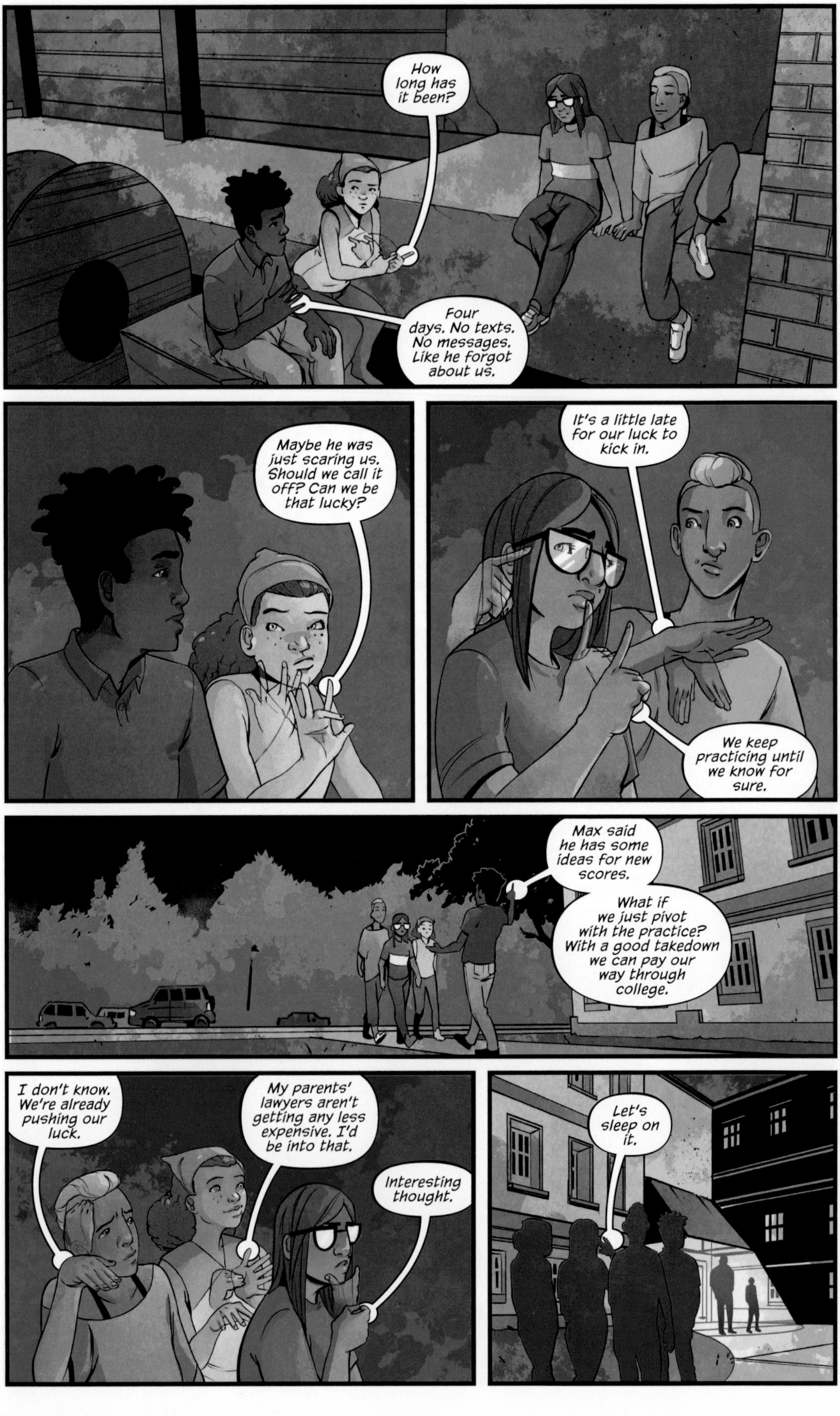
How long has it been?
Four days. No texts. No messages. Like he forgot about us.
Maybe he was just scaring us. Should we call it off? Can we be that lucky?
It's a little late for our luck to kick in.
We keep practicing until we know for sure.
Max said he has some ideas for new scores.
What if we just pivot with the practice? With a good takedown we can pay our way through college.
I don't know. We're already pushing our luck.
My parents' lawyers aren't getting any less expensive. I'd be into that.
Interesting thought.
Let's sleep on it.

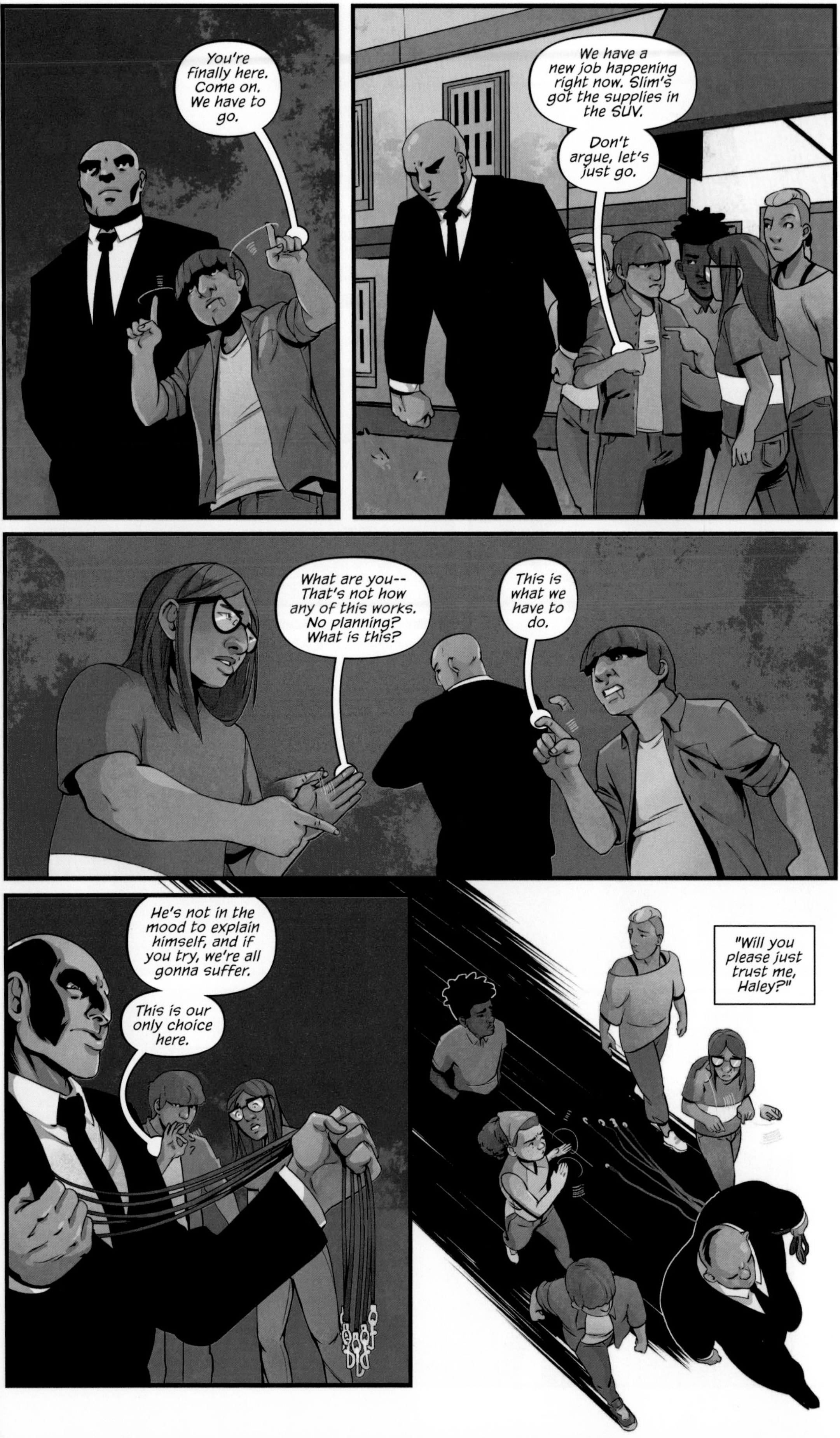
You're finally here. Come on. We have to go.
We have a new job happening right now. Slim's got the supplies in the SUV.
Don't argue, let's just go.
What are you-- That's not how any of this works. No planning? What is this?
This is what we have to do.
He's not in the mood to explain himself, and if you try, we're all gonna suffer.
This is our only choice here.
"Will you please just trust me, Haley?"

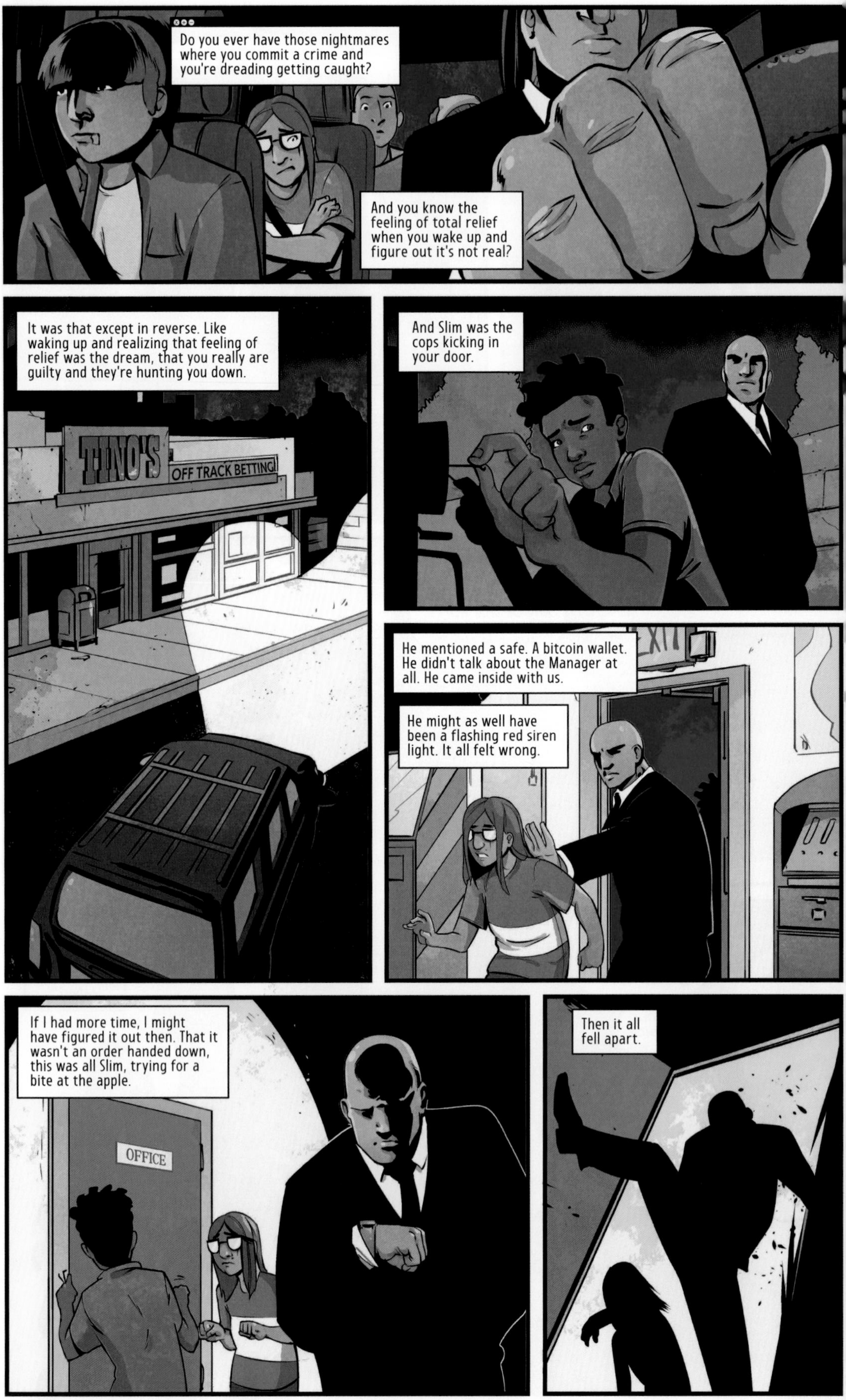
Do you ever have those nightmares where you commit a crime and you're dreading getting caught?
And you know the feeling of total relief when you wake up and figure out it's not real?
It was that except in reverse. Like waking up and realizing that feeling of relief was the dream, that you really are guilty and they're hunting you down.
TINO'S
OFF TRACK BETTING
And Slim was the cops kicking in your door.
He mentioned a safe. A bitcoin wallet. He didn't talk about the Manager at all. He came inside with us.
He might as well have been a flashing red siren light. It all felt wrong.
If I had more time, I might have figured it out then. That it wasn't an order handed down, this was all Slim, trying for a bite at the apple.
OFFICE
Then it all fell apart.

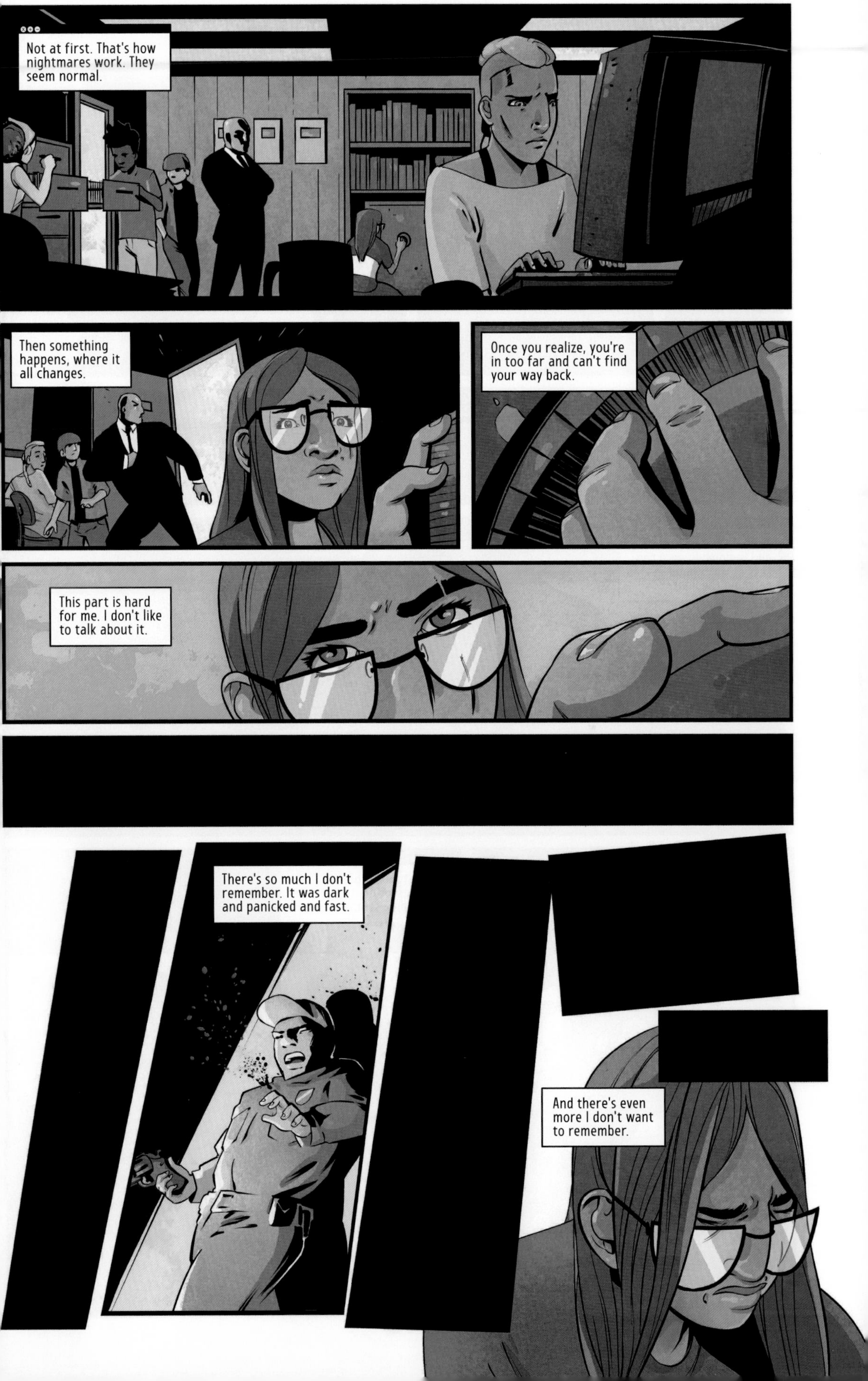
Not at first. That's how nightmares work. They seem normal.
Then something happens, where it all changes.
Once you realize, you're in too far and can't find your way back.
This part is hard for me. I don't like to talk about it.
There's so much I don't remember. It was dark and panicked and fast.
And there's even more I don't want to remember.

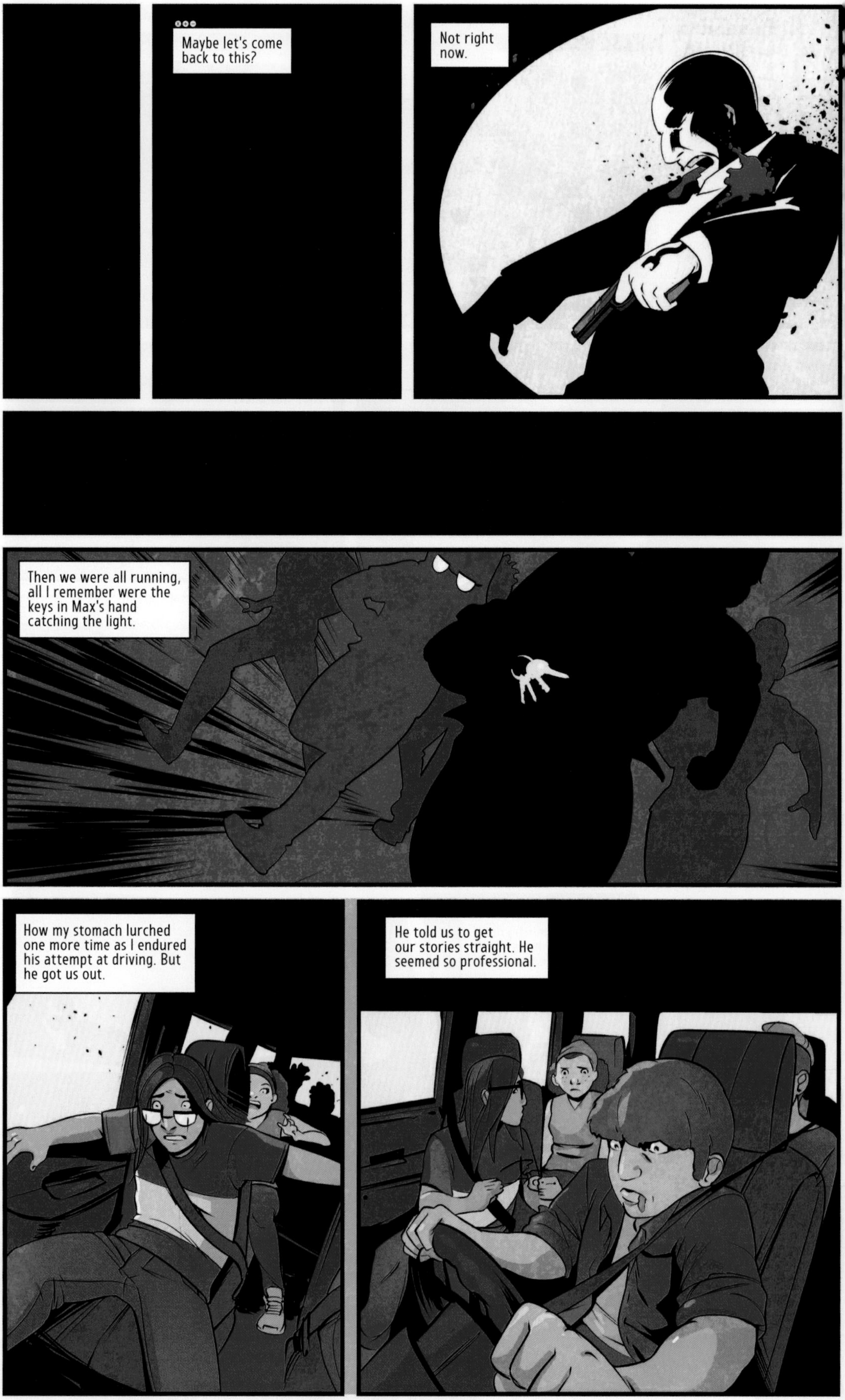
Maybe let's come back to this?
Not right now.
Then we were all running, all I remember were the keys in Max's hand catching the light.
How my stomach lurched one more time as I endured his attempt at driving. But he got us out.
He told us to get our stories straight. He seemed so professional.

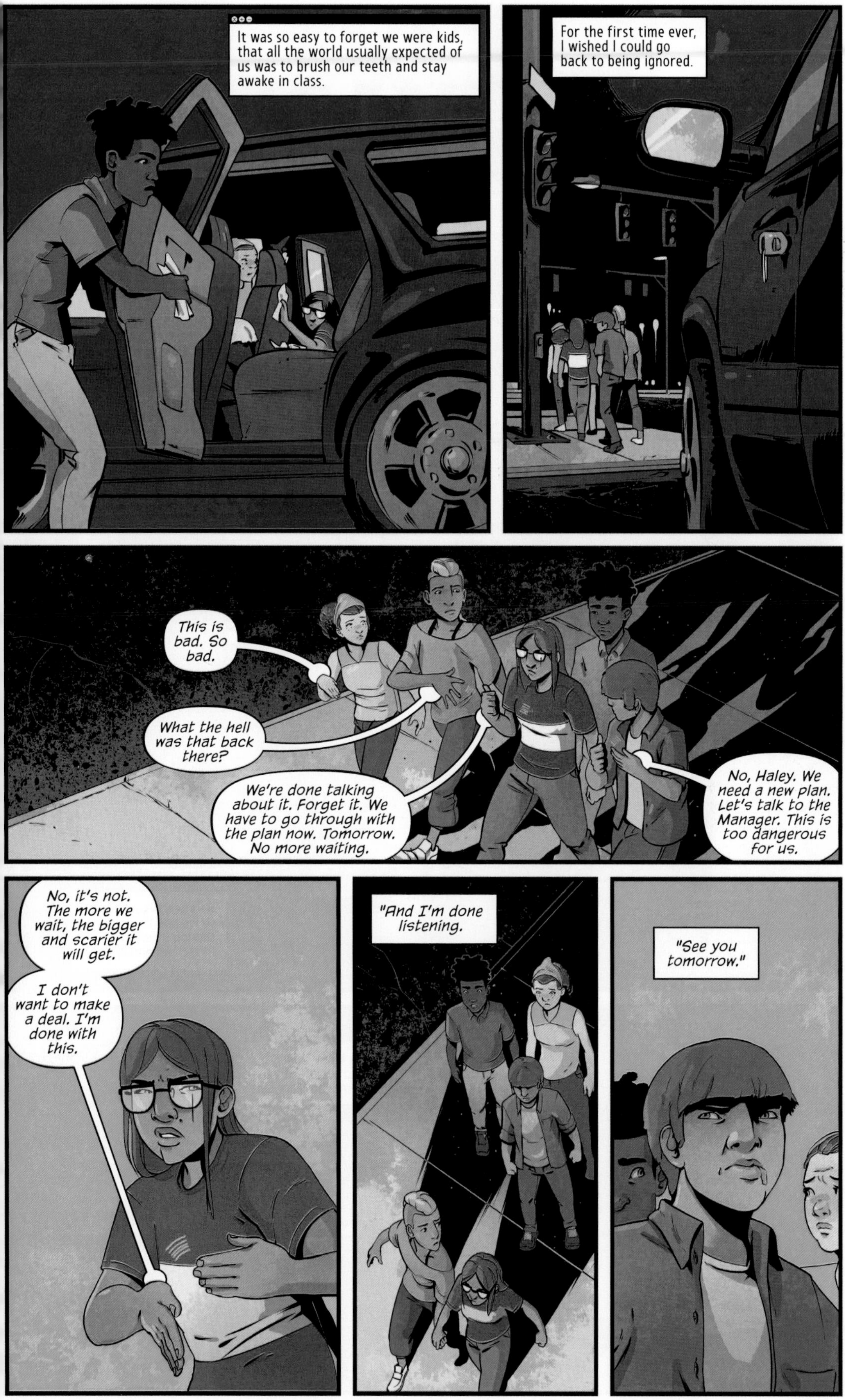
It was so easy to forget we were kids, that all the world usually expected of us was to brush our teeth and stay awake in class.
For the first time ever, I wished I could go back to being ignored.
This is bad. So bad.
What the hell was that back there?
We're done talking about it. Forget it. We have to go through with the plan now. Tomorrow. No more waiting.
No, Haley. We need a new plan. Let's talk to the Manager. This is too dangerous for us.
No, it's not. The more we wait, the bigger and scarier it will get.
I don't want to make a deal. I'm done with this.
"And I'm done listening.
"See you tomorrow."

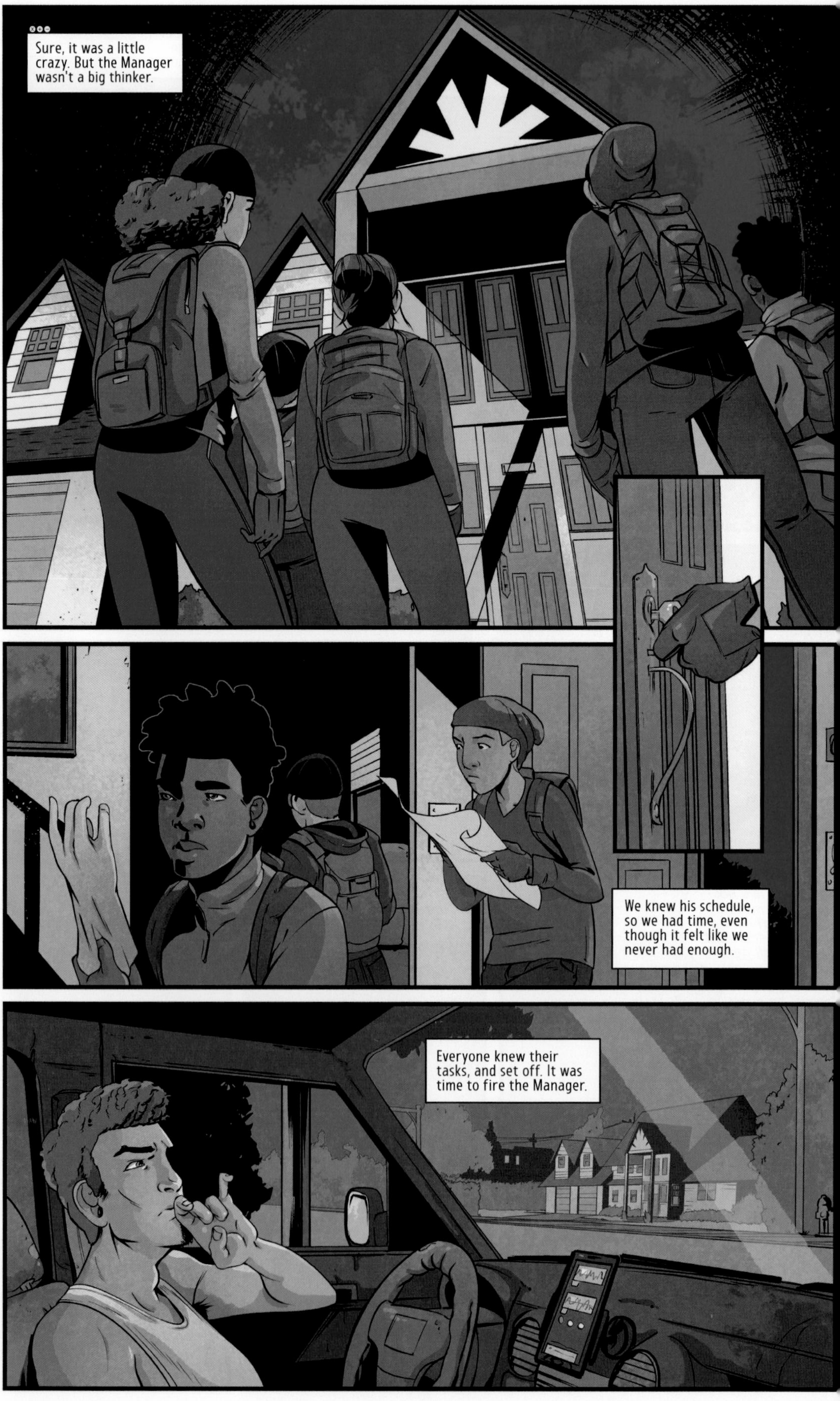
Sure, it was a little crazy. But the Manager wasn't a big thinker.
We knew his schedule, so we had time, even though it felt like we never had enough.
Everyone knew their tasks, and set off. It was time to fire the Manager.

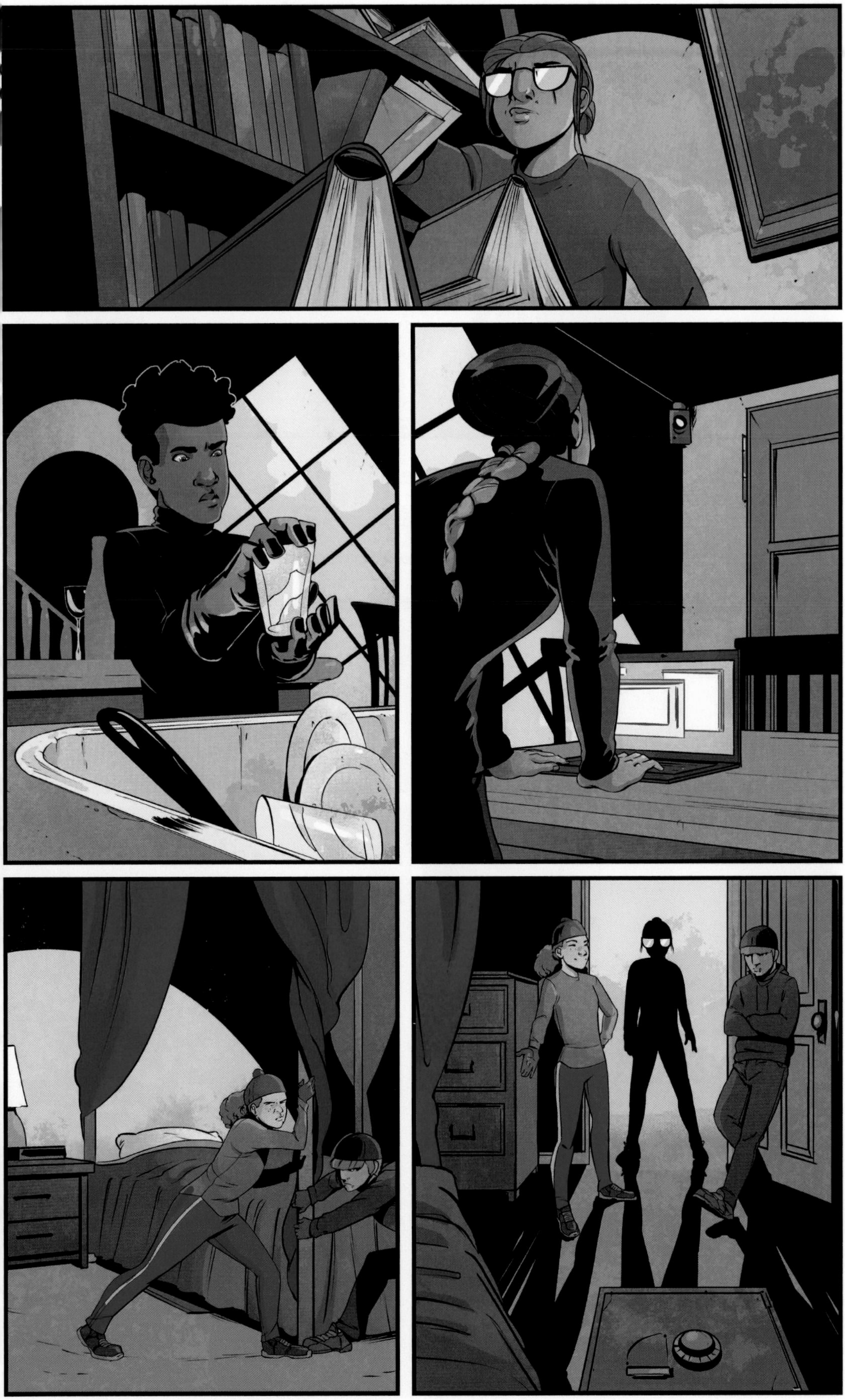

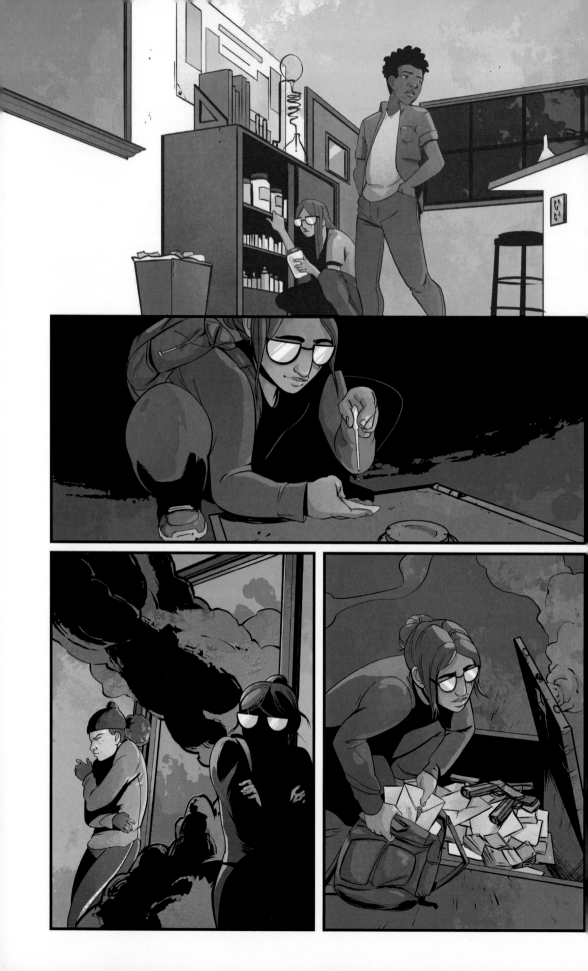

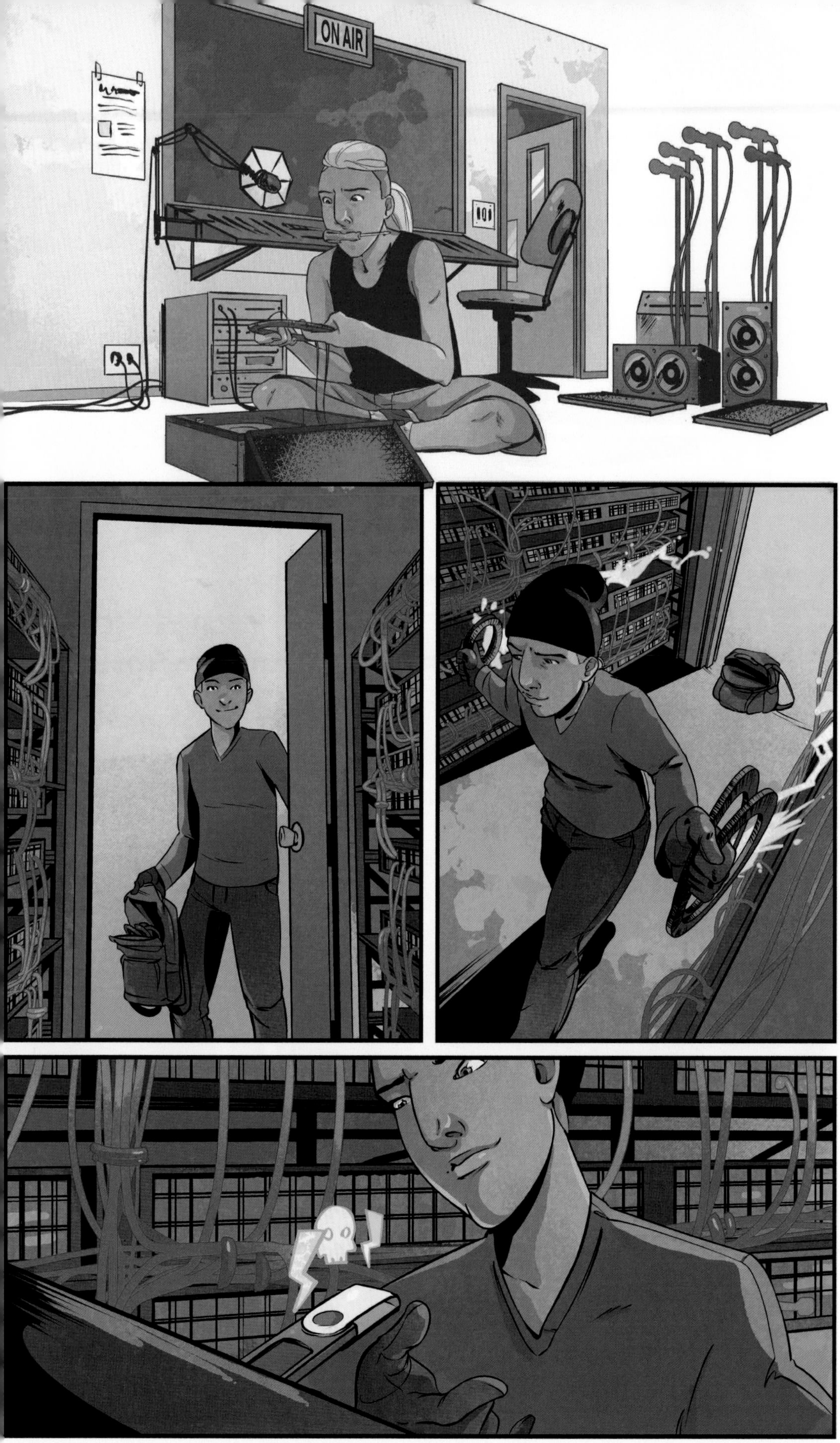
ON AIR

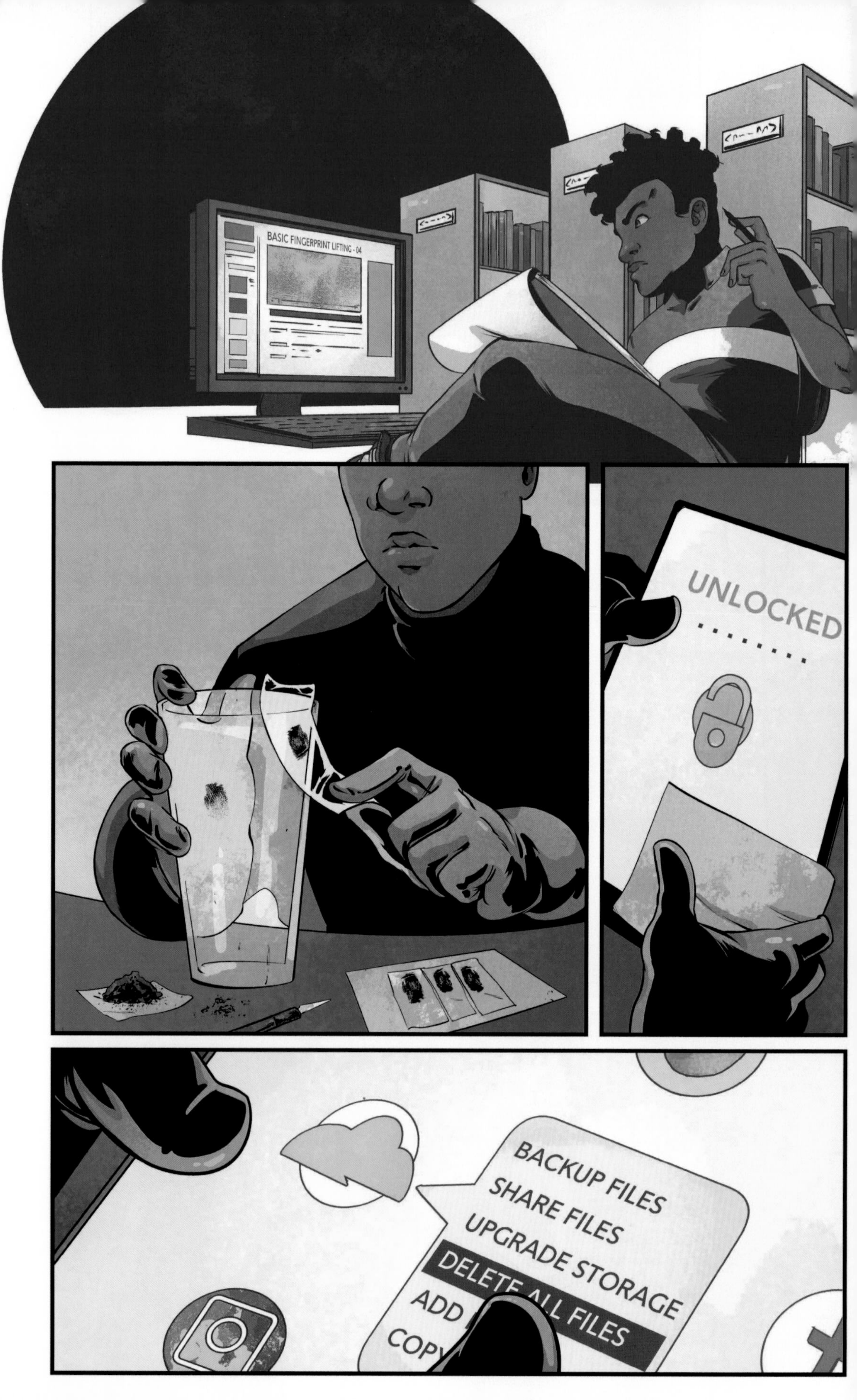
BASIC FINGERPRINT LIFTING - 04
UNLOCKED
BACKUP FILES
SHARE FILES
UPGRADE STORAGE
DELETE ALL FILES
ADD
COPY

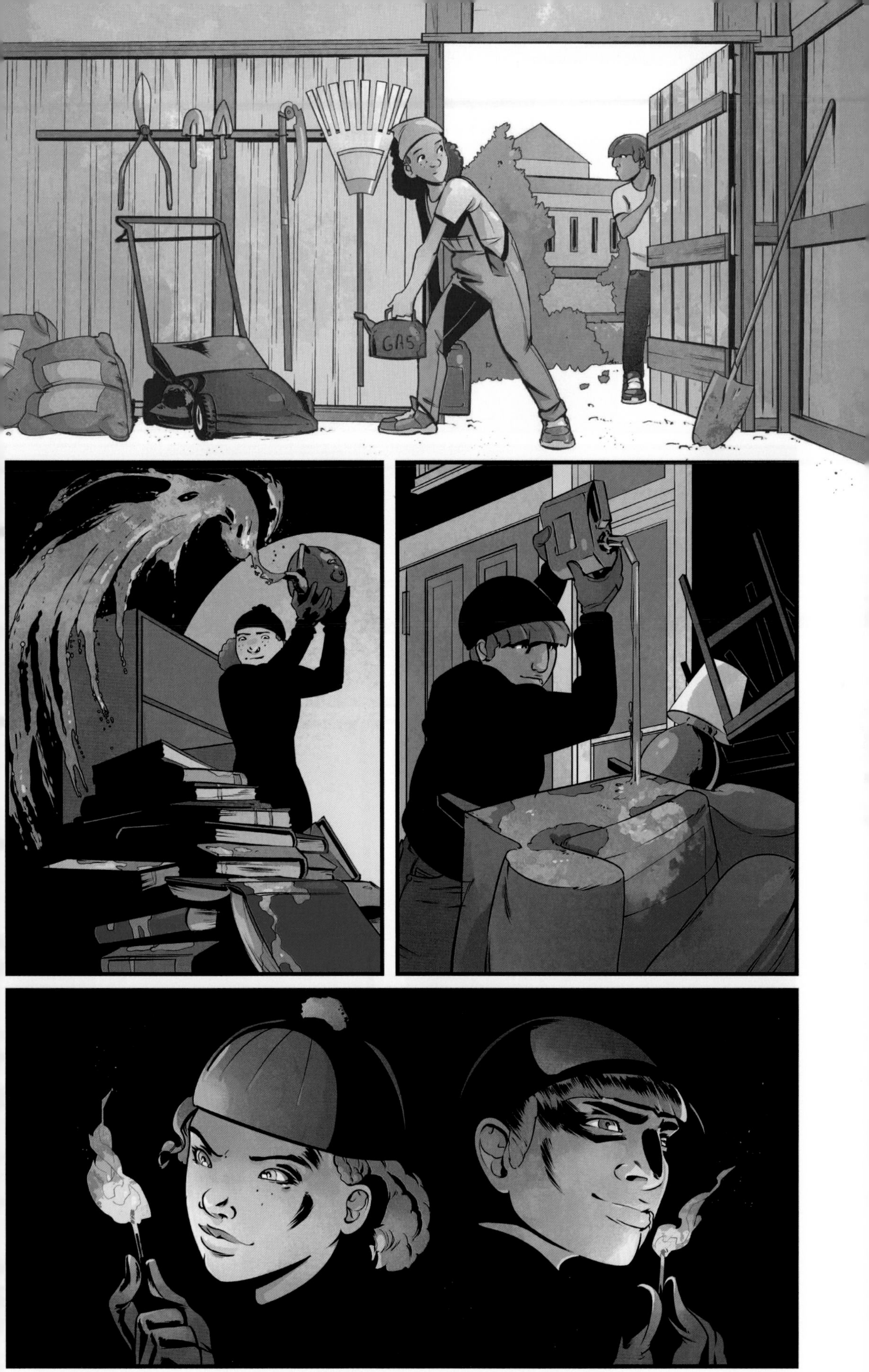
GAS

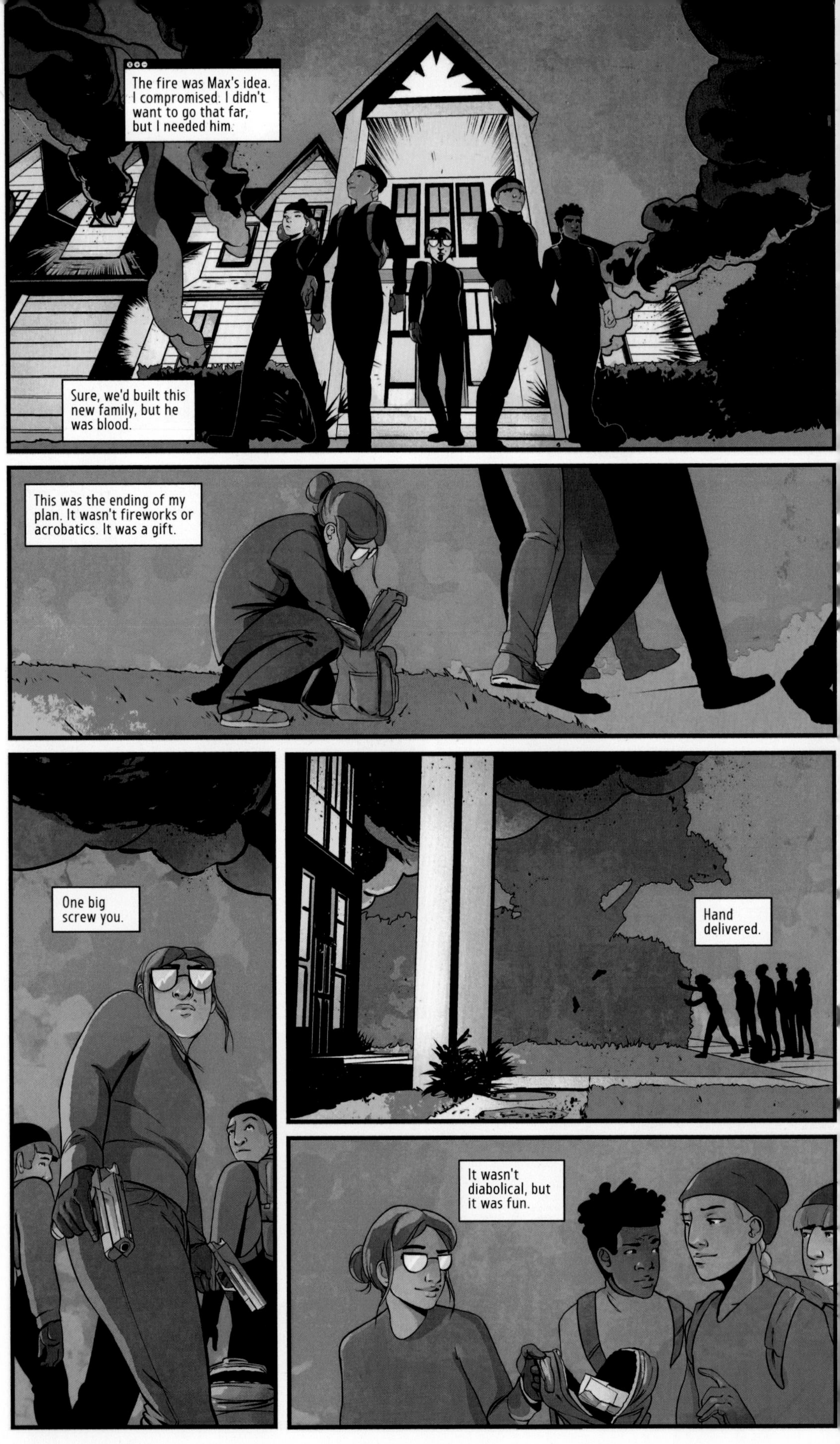
The fire was Max's idea. I compromised. I didn't want to go that far, but I needed him.
Sure, we'd built this new family, but he was blood.
This was the ending of my plan. It wasn't fireworks or acrobatics. It was a gift.
One big screw you.
Hand delivered.
It wasn't diabolical, but it was fun.

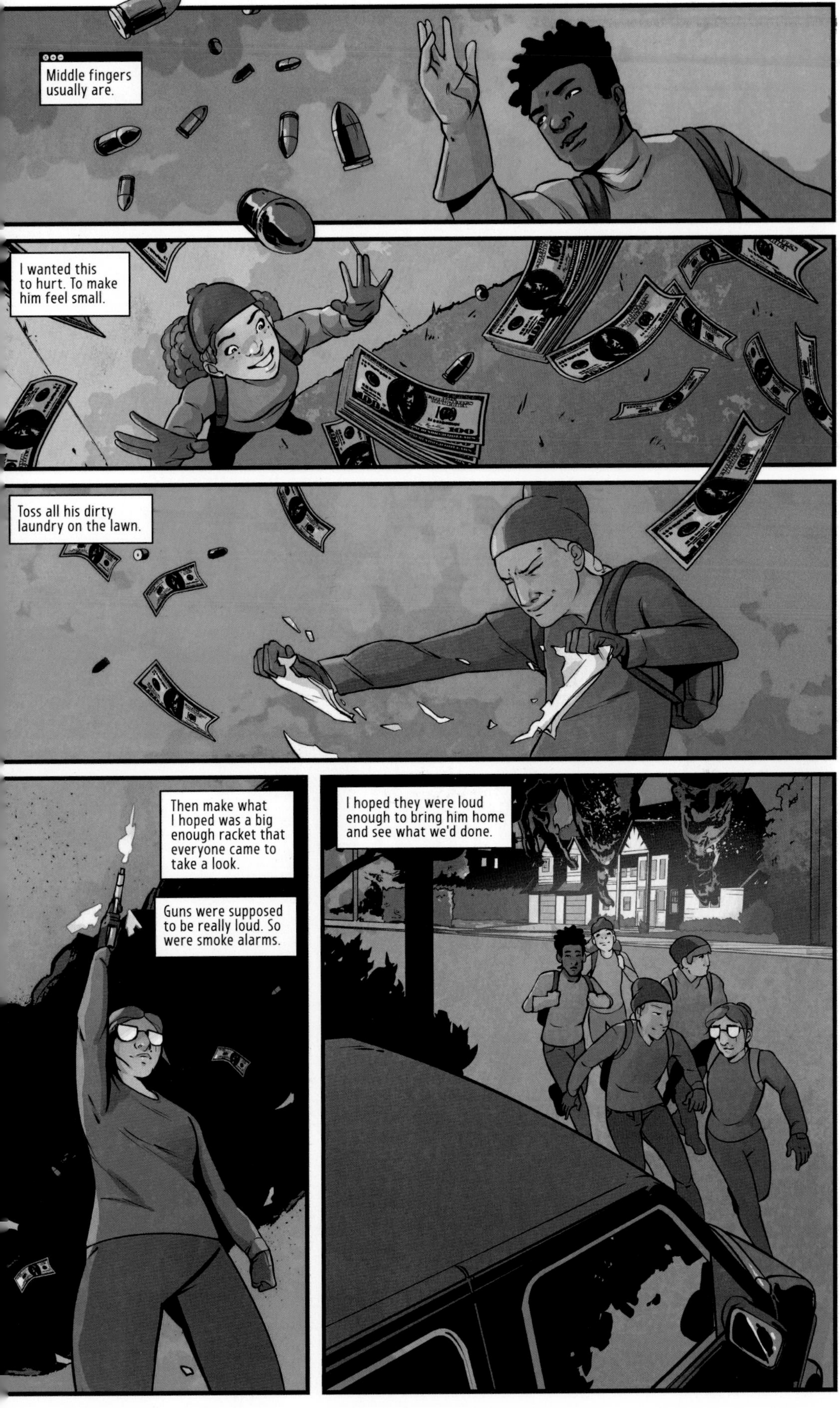

Middle fingers usually are.
I wanted this to hurt. To make him feel small.
Toss all his dirty laundry on the lawn.
Then make what I hoped was a big enough racket that everyone came to take a look.
Guns were supposed to be really loud. So were smoke alarms.
I hoped they were loud enough to bring him home and see what we'd done.

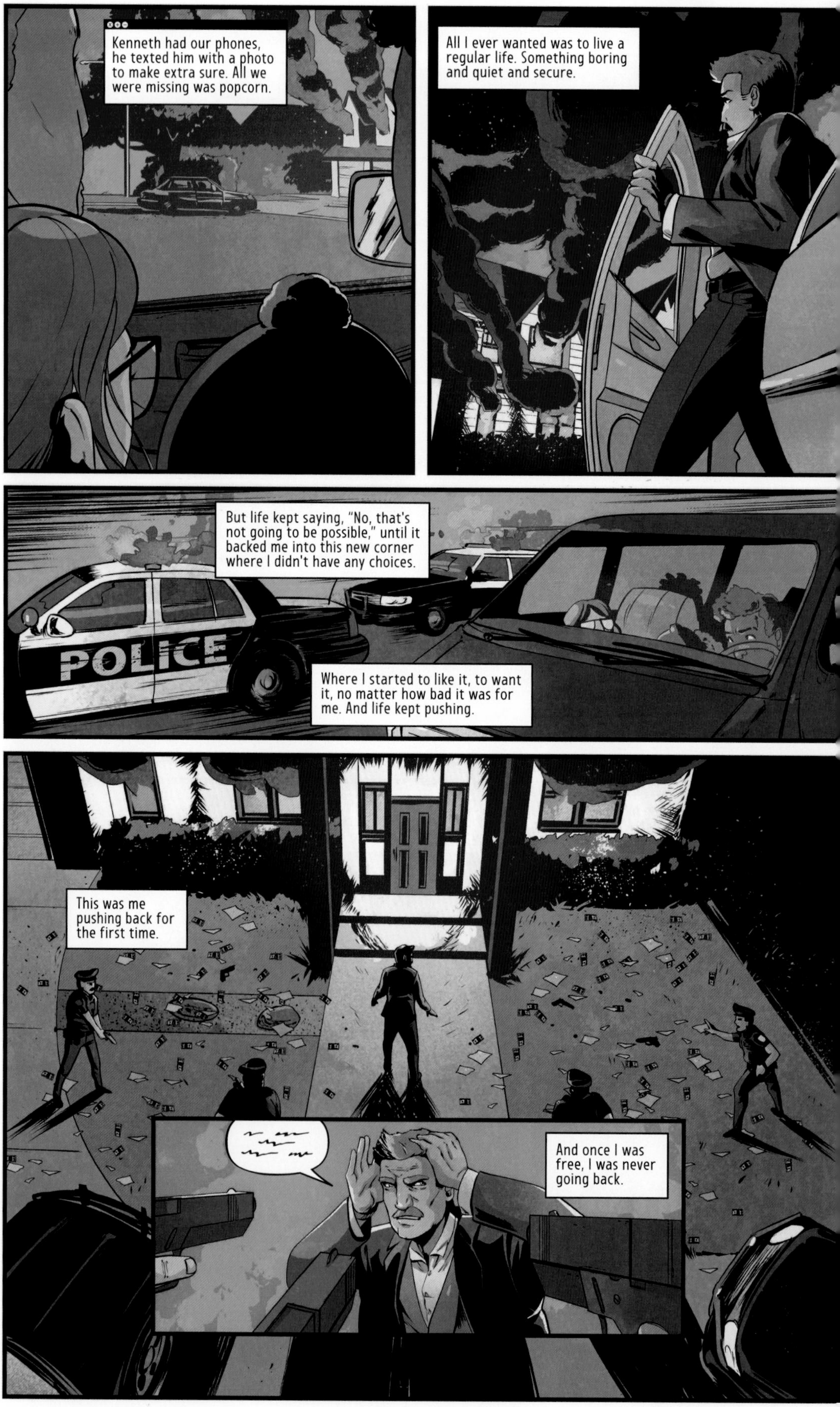
Kenneth had our phones, he texted him with a photo to make extra sure. All we were missing was popcorn.
All I ever wanted was to live a regular life. Something boring and quiet and secure.
But life kept saying, "No, that's not going to be possible," until it backed me into this new corner where I didn't have any choices.
POLICE
Where I started to like it, to want it, no matter how bad it was for me. And life kept pushing.
This was me pushing back for the first time.
And once I was free, I was never going back.

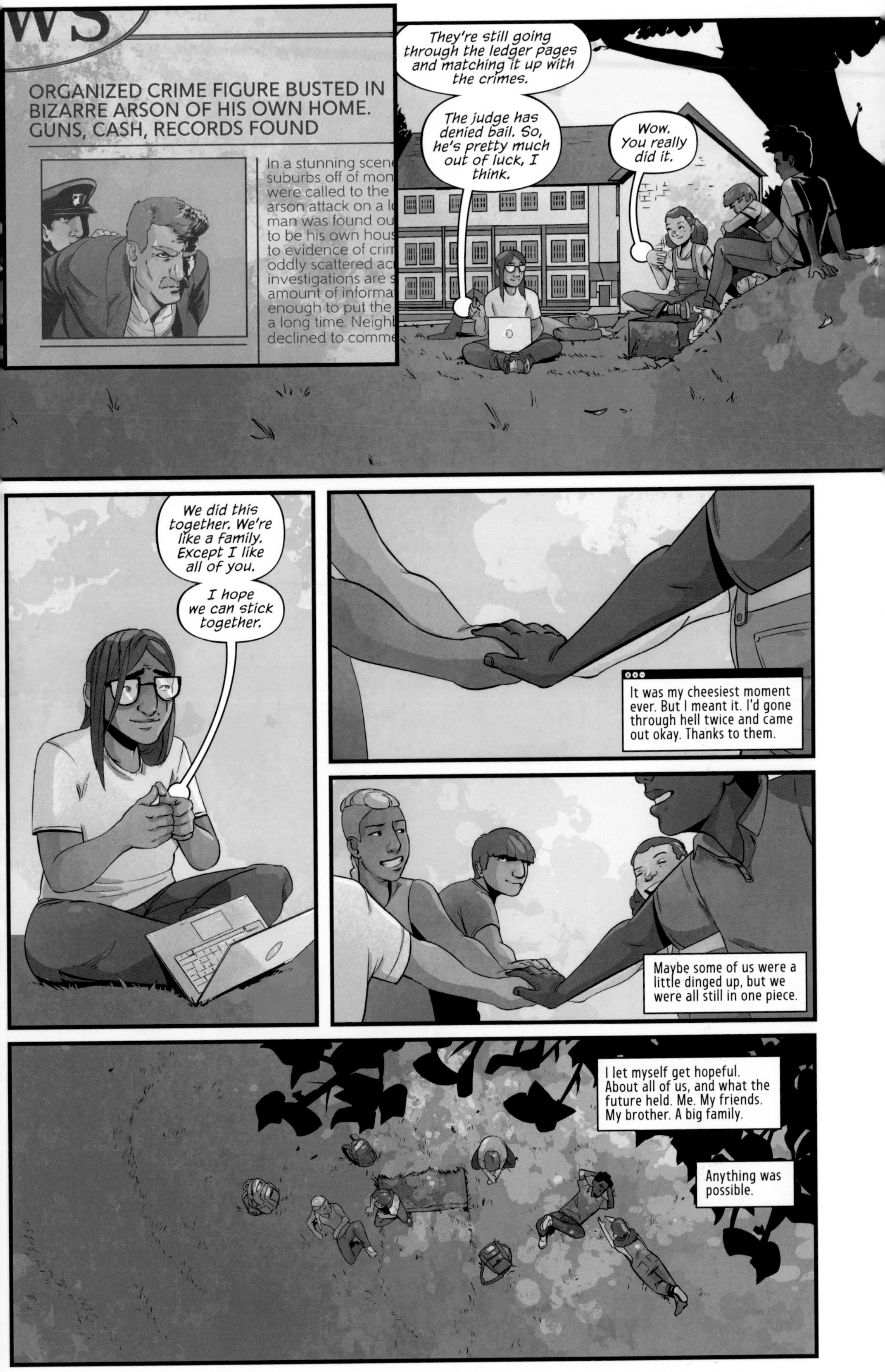
WS
ORGANIZED CRIME FIGURE BUSTED IN BIZARRE ARSON OF HIS OWN HOME. GUNS, CASH, RECORDS FOUND
In a stunning scen
suburbs off of mon
were called to the
arson attack on a l
man was found ou
to be his own hous
to evidence of crim
oddly scattered ac
investigations are s
amount of informa
enough to put the
a long time. Neigh
declined to comm
They're still going through the ledger pages and matching it up with the crimes.
The judge has denied bail. So, he's pretty much out of luck, I think.
Wow. You really did it.
We did this together. We're like a family. Except I like all of you.
I hope we can stick together.
It was my cheesiest moment ever. But I meant it. I'd gone through hell twice and came out okay. Thanks to them.
Maybe some of us were a little dinged up, but we were all still in one piece.
I let myself get hopeful. About all of us, and what the future held. Me. My friends. My brother. A big family.
Anything was possible.

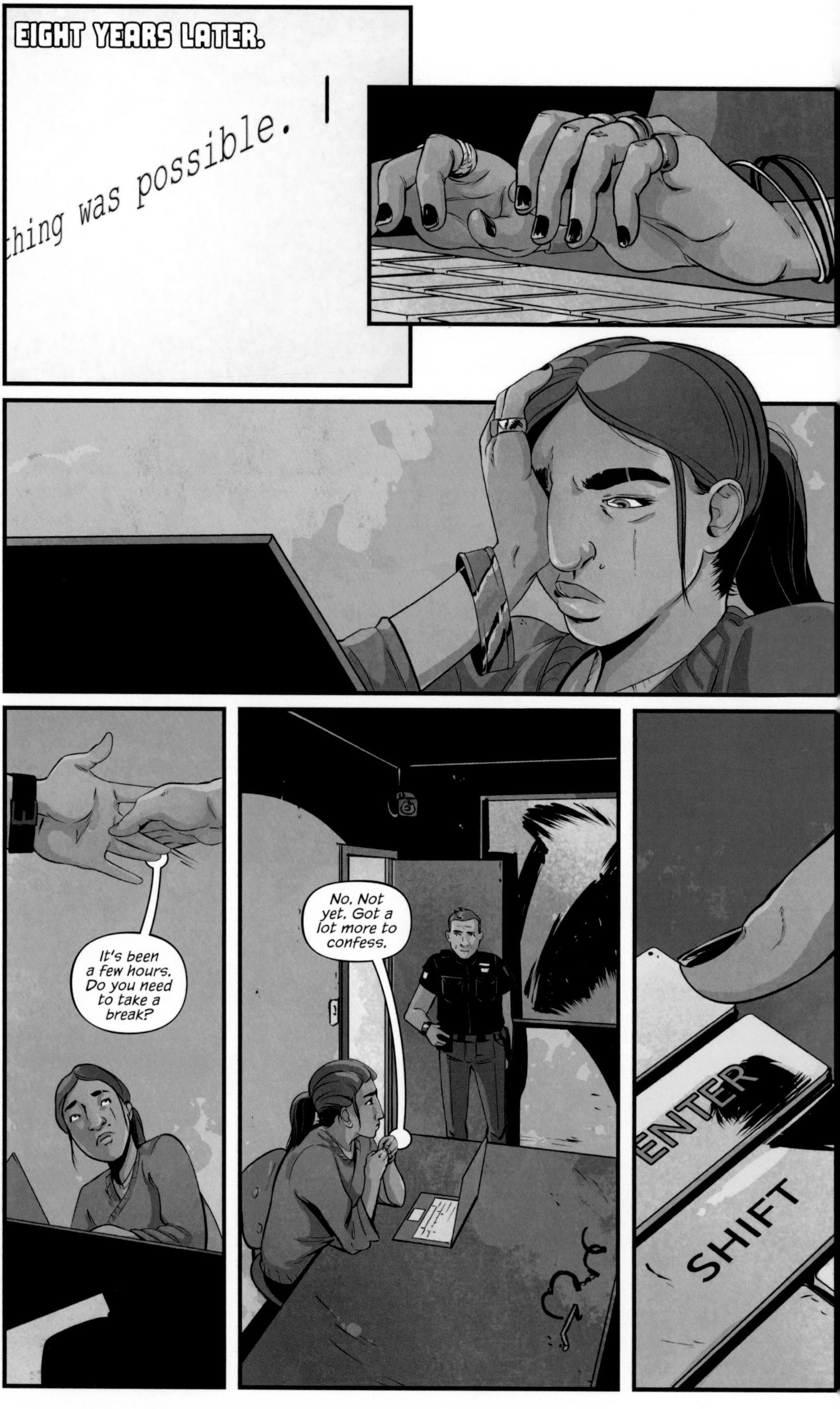
EIGHT YEARS LATER.
thing was possible.
It's been a few hours. Do you need to take a break?
No. Not yet. Got a lot more to confess.
ENTER
SHIFT

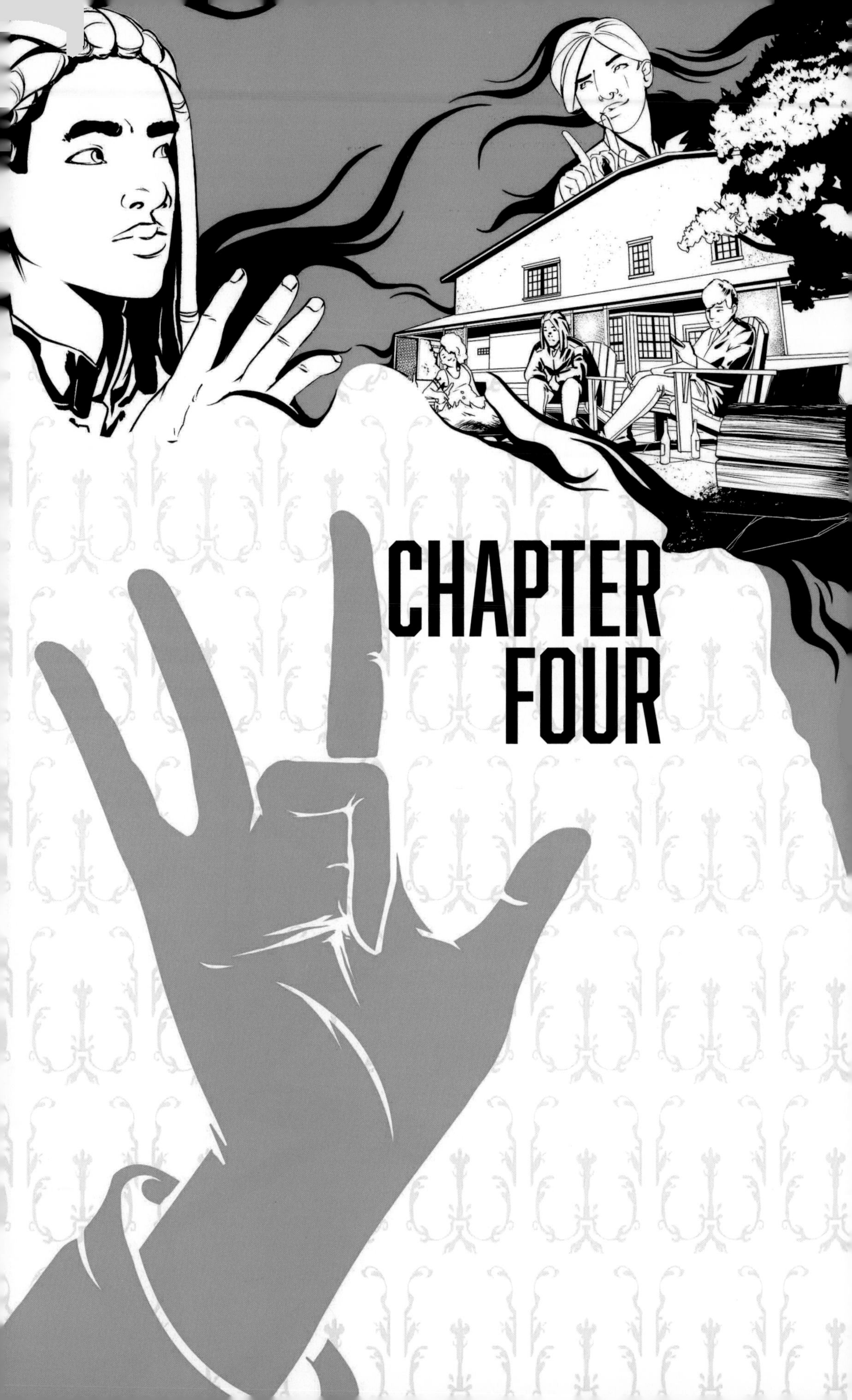

CHAPTER FOUR

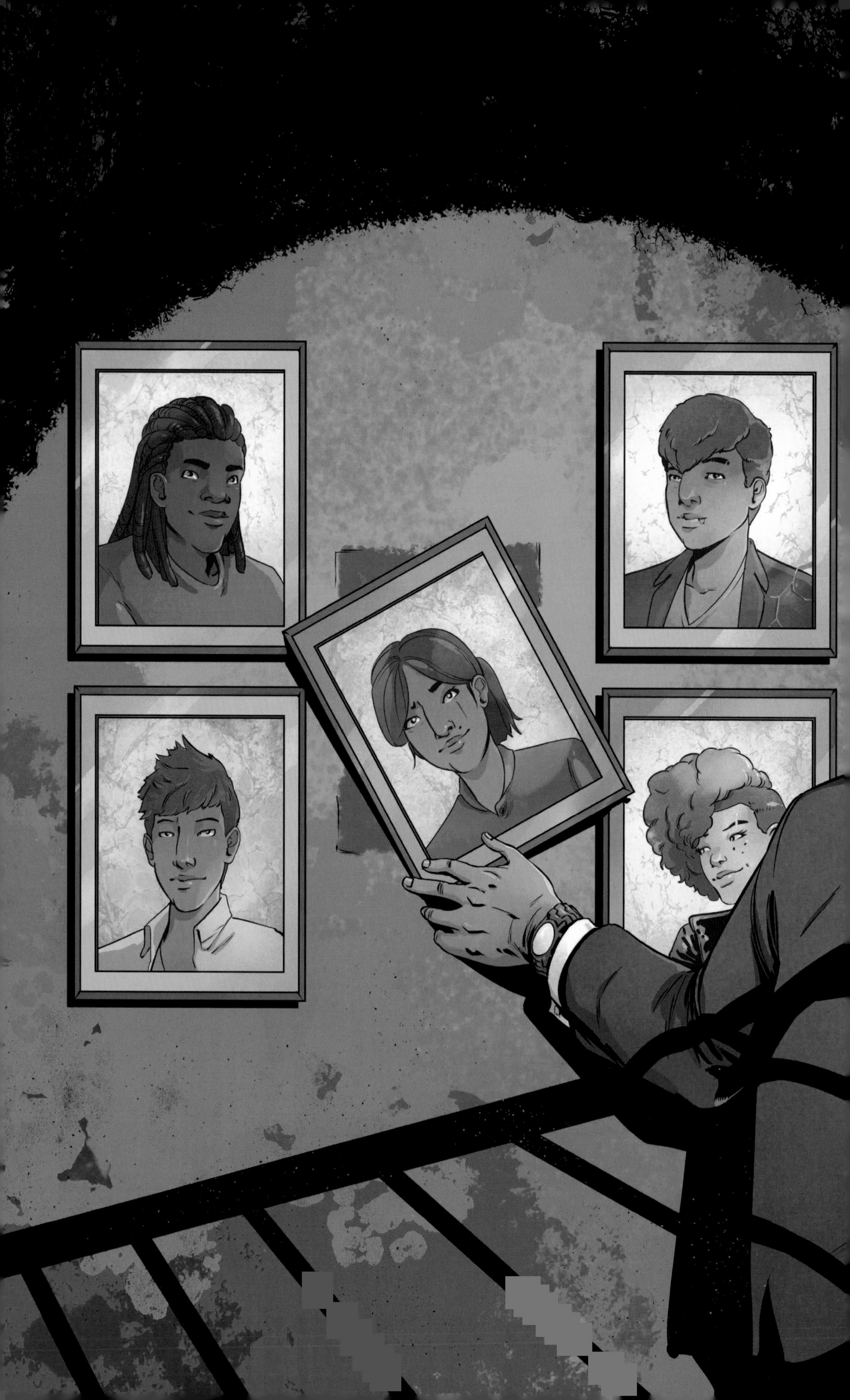

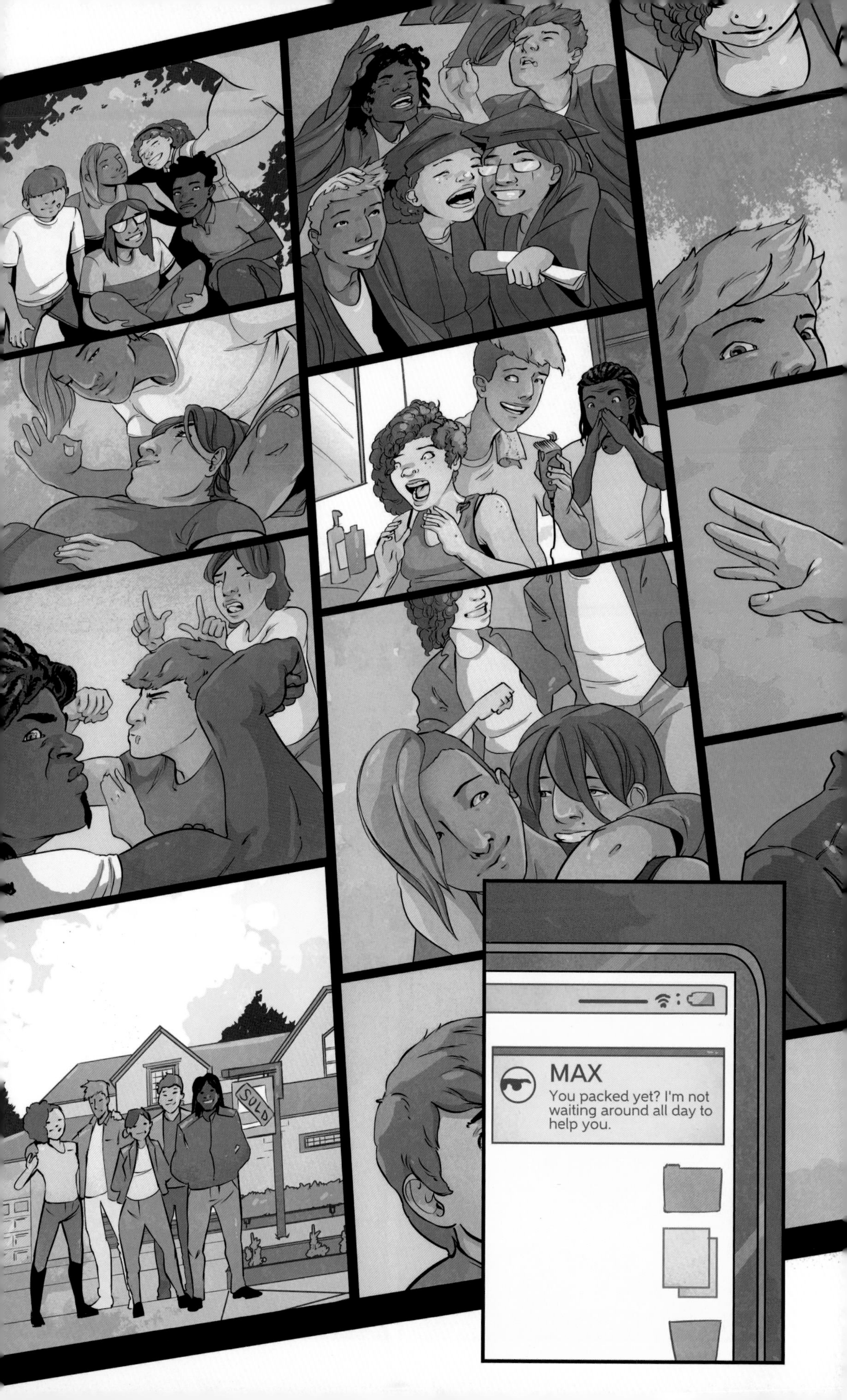
MAX
You packed yet? I'm not waiting around all day to help you.
SOLD

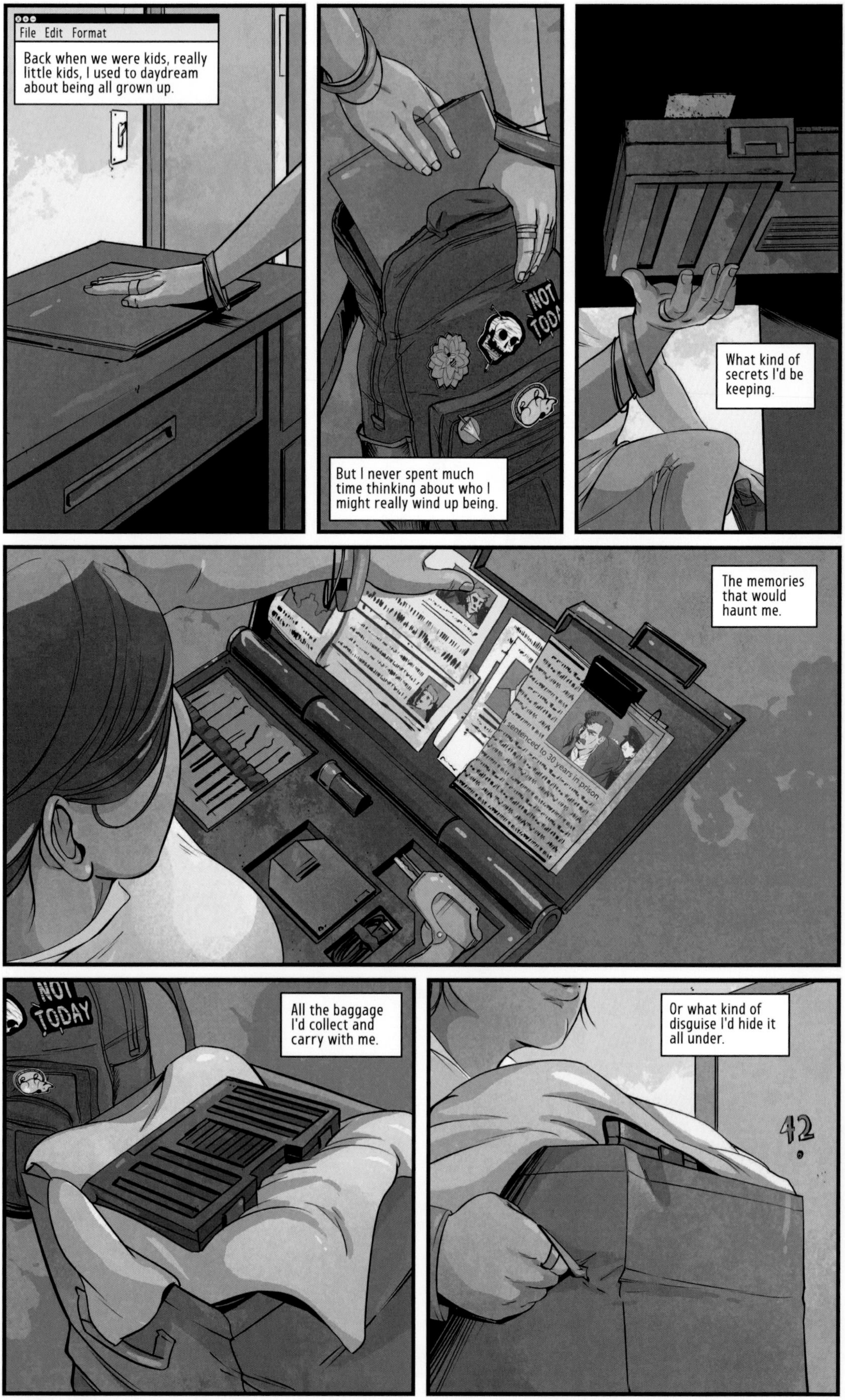
File Edit Format
Back when we were kids, really little kids, I used to daydream about being all grown up.
But I never spent much time thinking about who I might really wind up being.
NOT TODAY
What kind of secrets I'd be keeping.
The memories that would haunt me.
sentenced to 30 years in prison
NOT TODAY
All the baggage I'd collect and carry with me.
Or what kind of disguise I'd hide it all under.
42

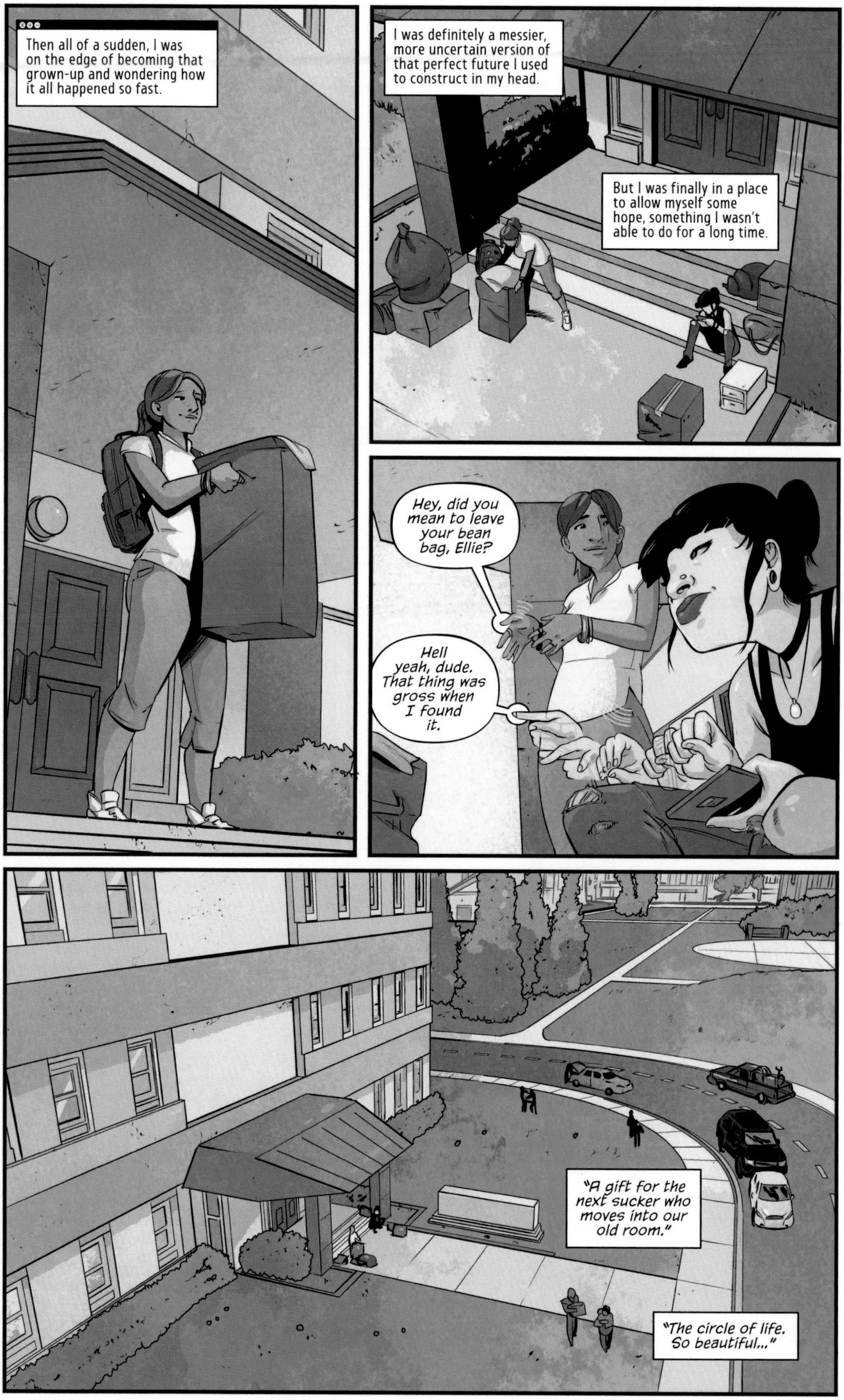
Then all of a sudden, I was on the edge of becoming that grown-up and wondering how it all happened so fast.
I was definitely a messier, more uncertain version of that perfect future I used to construct in my head.
But I was finally in a place to allow myself some hope, something I wasn't able to do for a long time.
Hey, did you mean to leave your bean bag, Ellie?
Hell yeah, dude. That thing was gross when I found it.
"A gift for the next sucker who moves into our old room."
"The circle of life. So beautiful..."

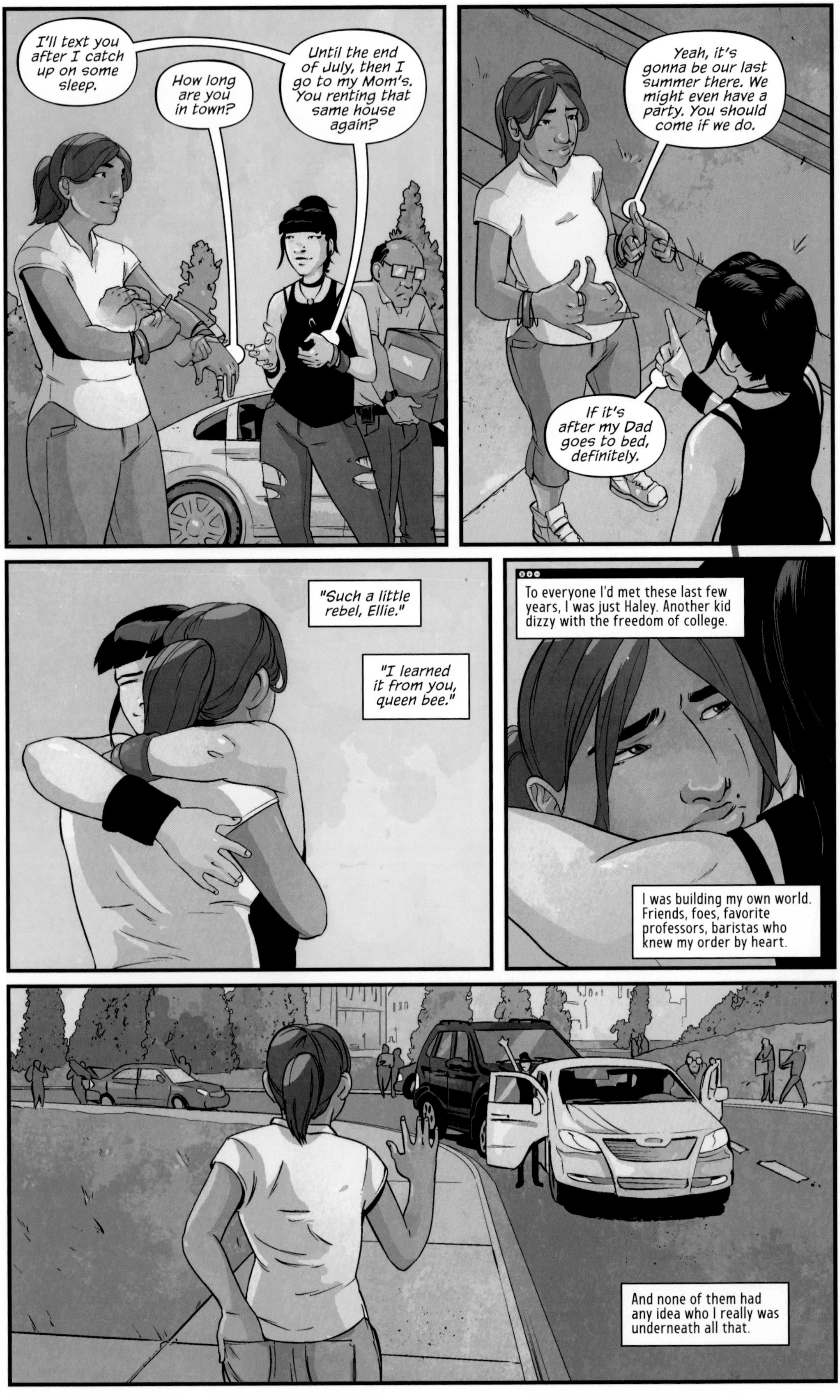
I'll text you after I catch up on some sleep.
How long are you in town?
Until the end of July, then I go to my Mom's. You renting that same house again?
Yeah, it's gonna be our last summer there. We might even have a party. You should come if we do.
If it's after my Dad goes to bed, definitely.
"Such a little rebel, Ellie."
"I learned it from you, queen bee."
To everyone I'd met these last few years, I was just Haley. Another kid dizzy with the freedom of college.
I was building my own world. Friends, foes, favorite professors, baristas who knew my order by heart.
And none of them had any idea who I really was underneath all that.

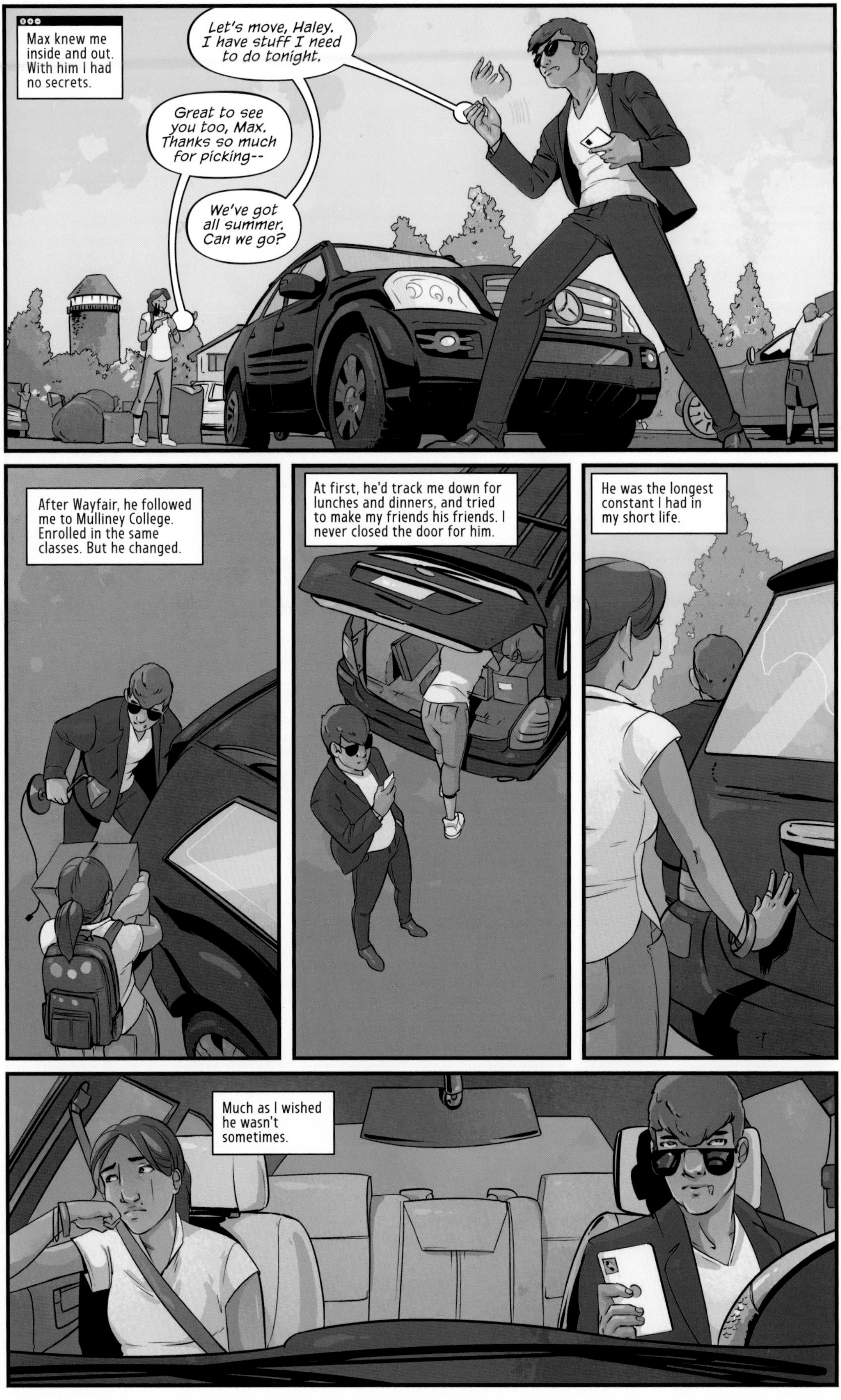

Max knew me inside and out. With him I had no secrets.
Let's move, Haley. I have stuff I need to do tonight.
Great to see you too, Max. Thanks so much for picking--
We've got all summer. Can we go?
After Wayfair, he followed me to Mulliney College. Enrolled in the same classes. But he changed.
At first, he'd track me down for lunches and dinners, and tried to make my friends his friends. I never closed the door for him.
He was the longest constant I had in my short life.
Much as I wished he wasn't sometimes.

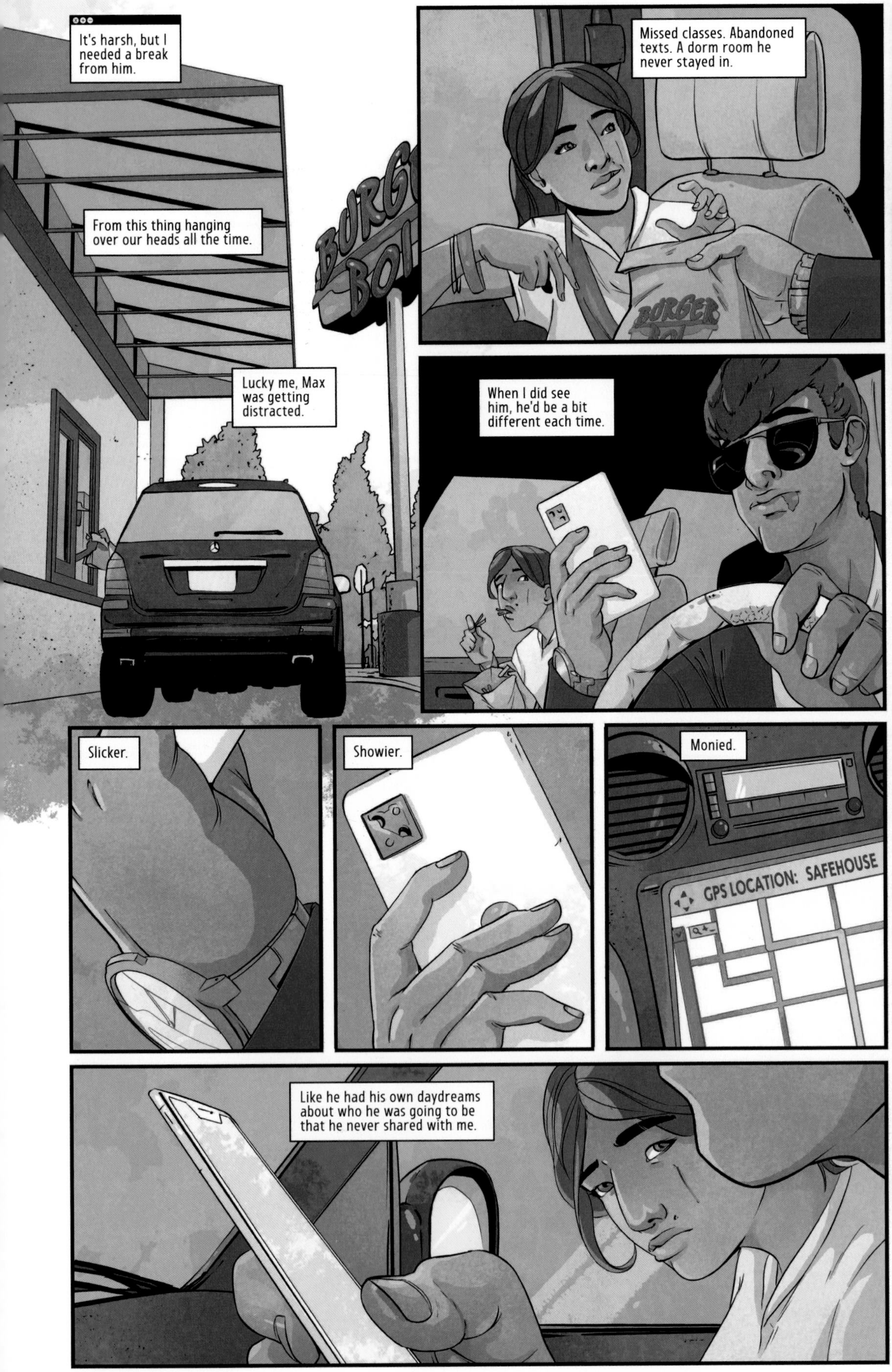
It's harsh, but I needed a break from him.
From this thing hanging over our heads all the time.
Lucky me, Max was getting distracted.
BURGER BOI
Missed classes. Abandoned texts. A dorm room he never stayed in.
BURGER BOI
When I did see him, he'd be a bit different each time.
Slicker.
Showier.
Monied.
GPS LOCATION: SAFEHOUSE
Like he had his own daydreams about who he was going to be that he never shared with me.

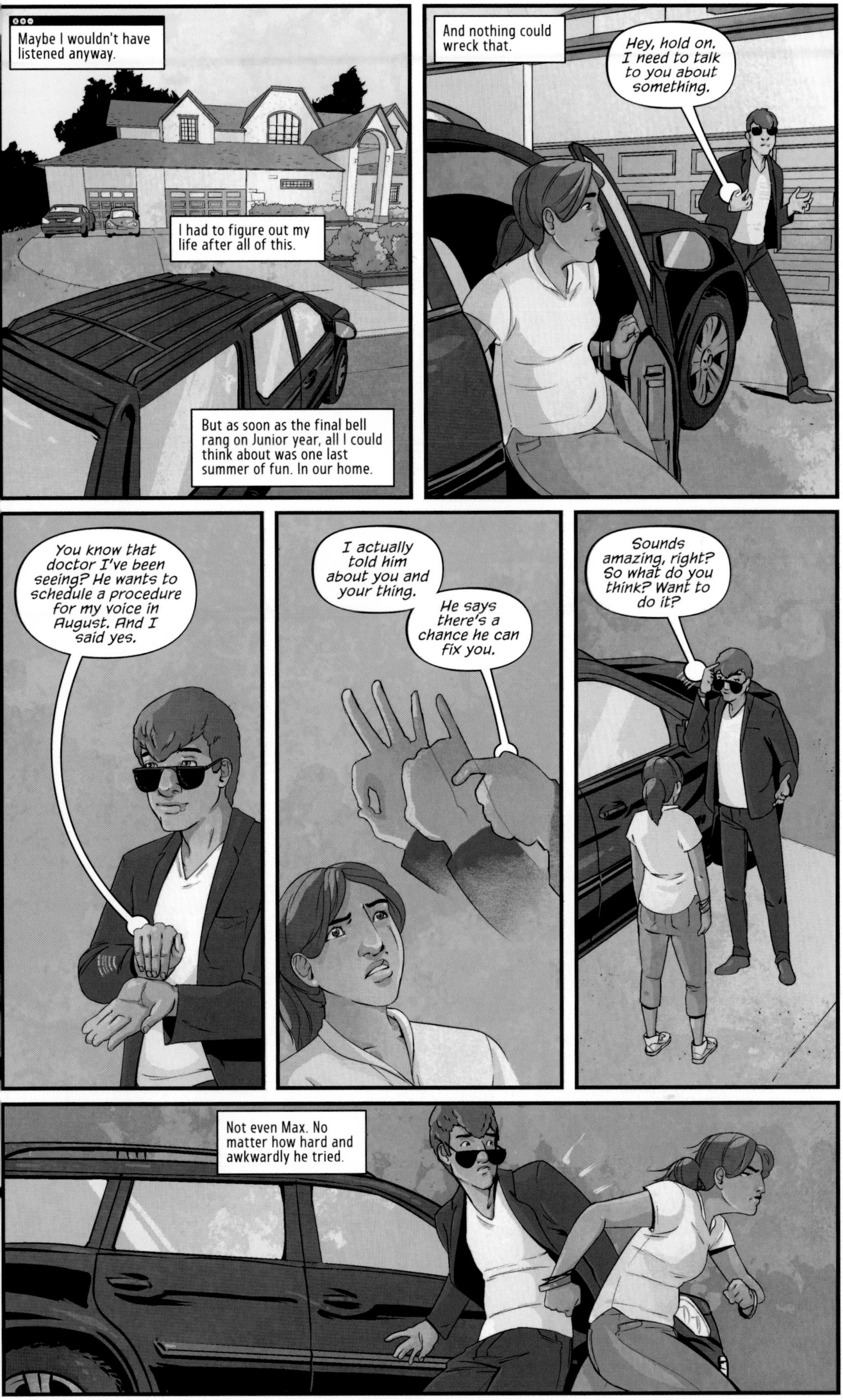
Maybe I wouldn't have listened anyway.
I had to figure out my life after all of this.
But as soon as the final bell rang on Junior year, all I could think about was one last summer of fun. In our home.
And nothing could wreck that.
Hey, hold on. I need to talk to you about something.
You know that doctor I've been seeing? He wants to schedule a procedure for my voice in August. And I said yes.
I actually told him about you and your thing.
He says there's a chance he can fix you.
Sounds amazing, right? So what do you think? Want to do it?
Not even Max. No matter how hard and awkwardly he tried.

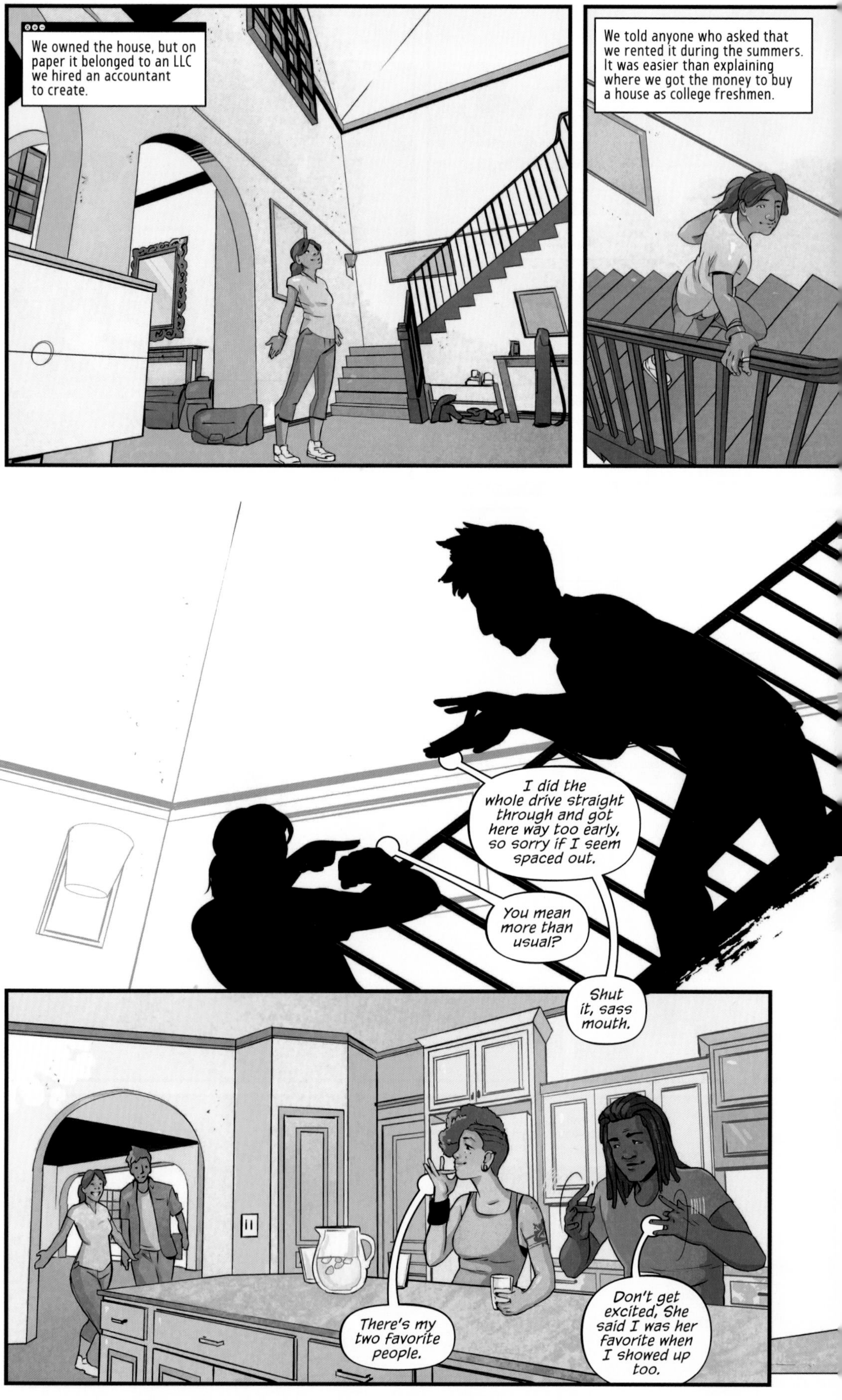
We owned the house, but on paper it belonged to an LLC we hired an accountant to create.
We told anyone who asked that we rented it during the summers. It was easier than explaining where we got the money to buy a house as college freshmen.
I did the whole drive straight through and got here way too early, so sorry if I seem spaced out.
You mean more than usual?
Shut it, sass mouth.
There's my two favorite people.
Don't get excited, She said I was her favorite when I showed up too.

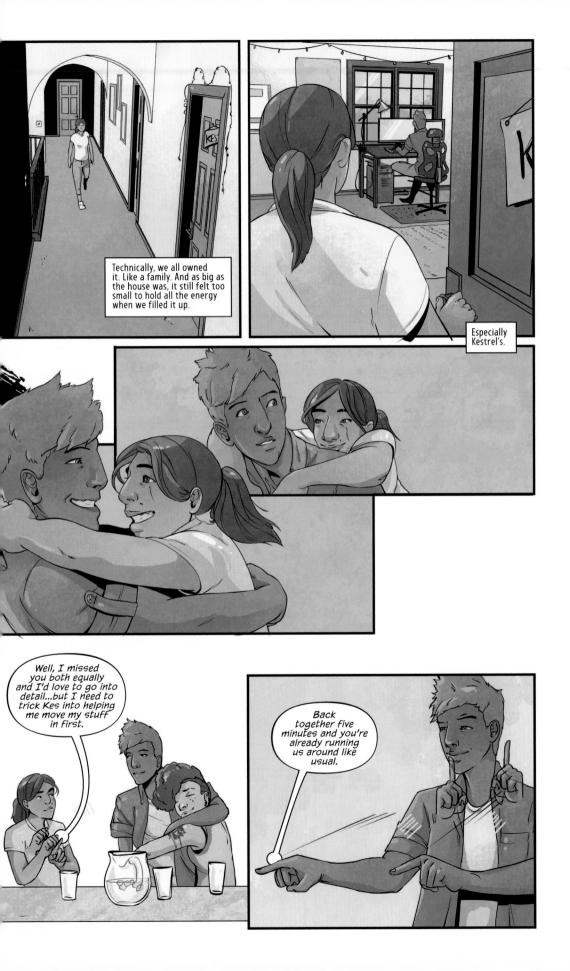

Technically, we all owned it. Like a family. And as big as the house was, it still felt too small to hold all the energy when we filled it up.

Especially Kestrel's.

Well, I missed you both equally and I'd love to go into detail...but I need to trick Kes into helping me move my stuff in first.

Back together five minutes and you're already running us around like usual.

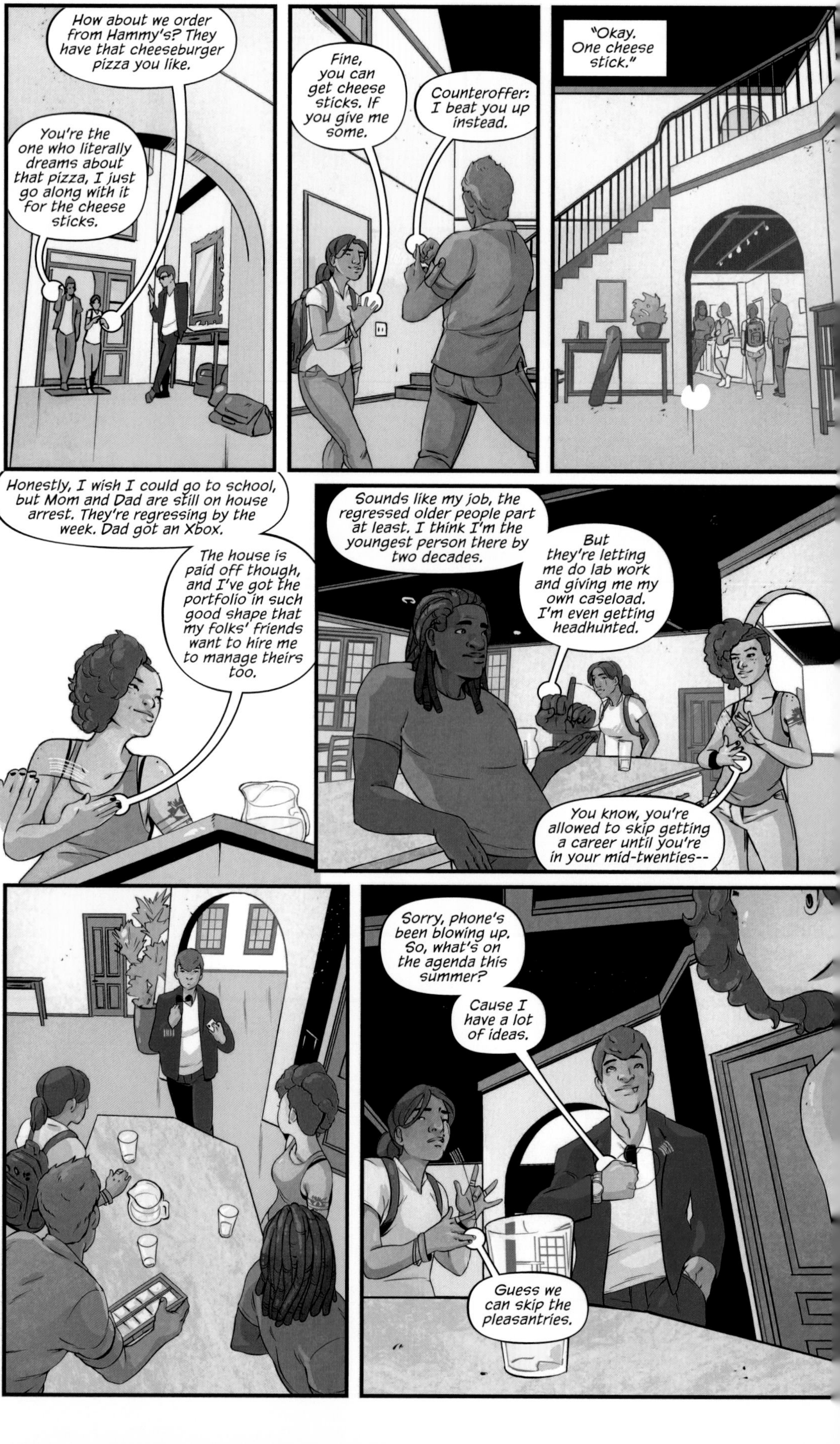
How about we order from Hammy's? They have that cheeseburger pizza you like.
You're the one who literally dreams about that pizza, I just go along with it for the cheese sticks.
Fine, you can get cheese sticks. If you give me some.
Counteroffer: I beat you up instead.
"Okay. One cheese stick."
Honestly, I wish I could go to school, but Mom and Dad are still on house arrest. They're regressing by the week. Dad got an Xbox.
The house is paid off though, and I've got the portfolio in such good shape that my folks' friends want to hire me to manage theirs too.
Sounds like my job, the regressed older people part at least. I think I'm the youngest person there by two decades.
But they're letting me do lab work and giving me my own caseload. I'm even getting headhunted.
You know, you're allowed to skip getting a career until you're in your mid-twenties--
Sorry, phone's been blowing up. So, what's on the agenda this summer?
Cause I have a lot of ideas.
Guess we can skip the pleasantries.

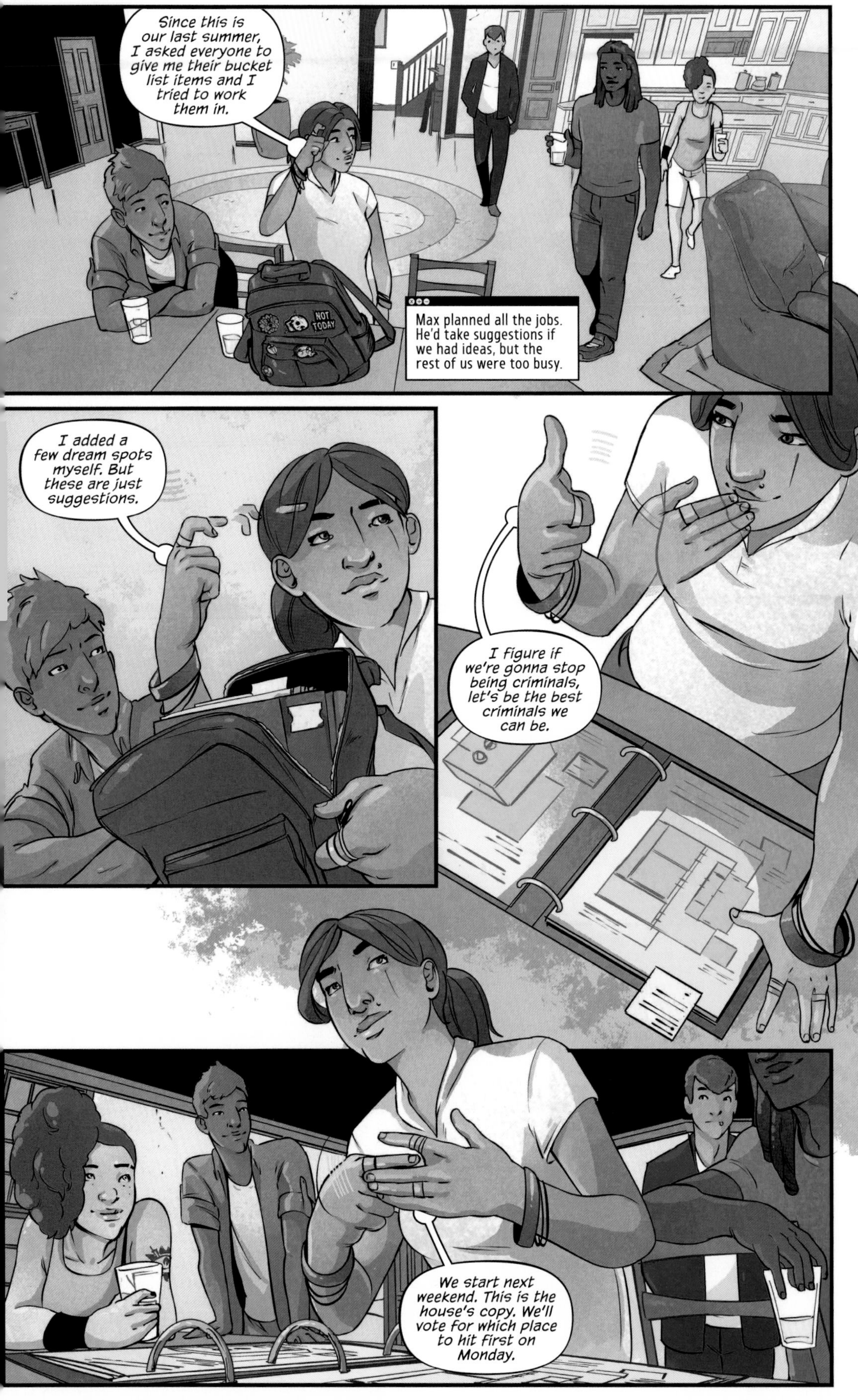

Since this is our last summer, I asked everyone to give me their bucket list items and I tried to work them in.
NOT TODAY
Max planned all the jobs. He'd take suggestions if we had ideas, but the rest of us were too busy.
I added a few dream spots myself. But these are just suggestions.
I figure if we're gonna stop being criminals, let's be the best criminals we can be.
We start next weekend. This is the house's copy. We'll vote for which place to hit first on Monday.

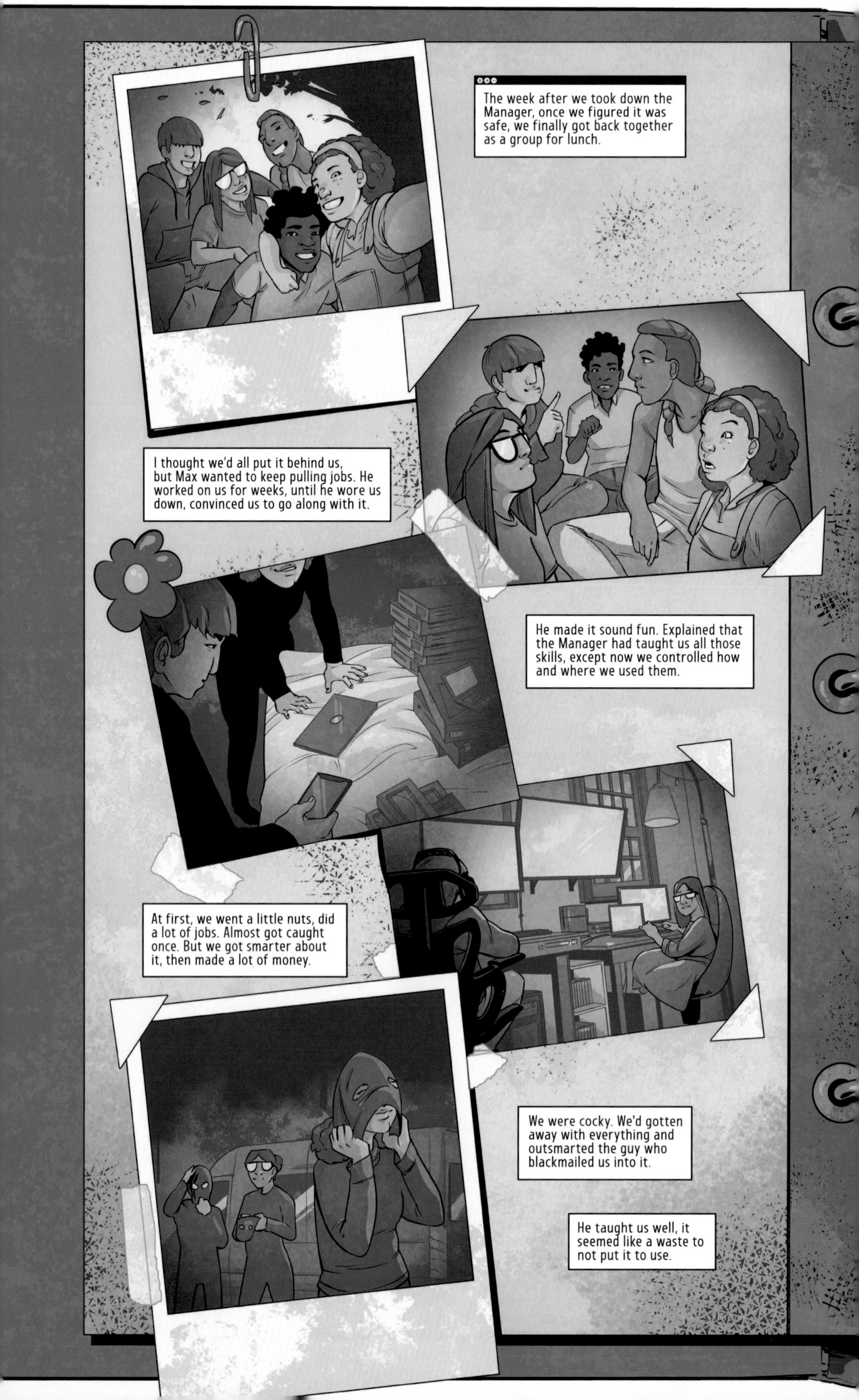
The week after we took down the Manager, once we figured it was safe, we finally got back together as a group for lunch.
I thought we'd all put it behind us, but Max wanted to keep pulling jobs. He worked on us for weeks, until he wore us down, convinced us to go along with it.
He made it sound fun. Explained that the Manager had taught us all those skills, except now we controlled how and where we used them.
At first, we went a little nuts, did a lot of jobs. Almost got caught once. But we got smarter about it, then made a lot of money.
We were cocky. We'd gotten away with everything and outsmarted the guy who blackmailed us into it.
He taught us well, it seemed like a waste to not put it to use.

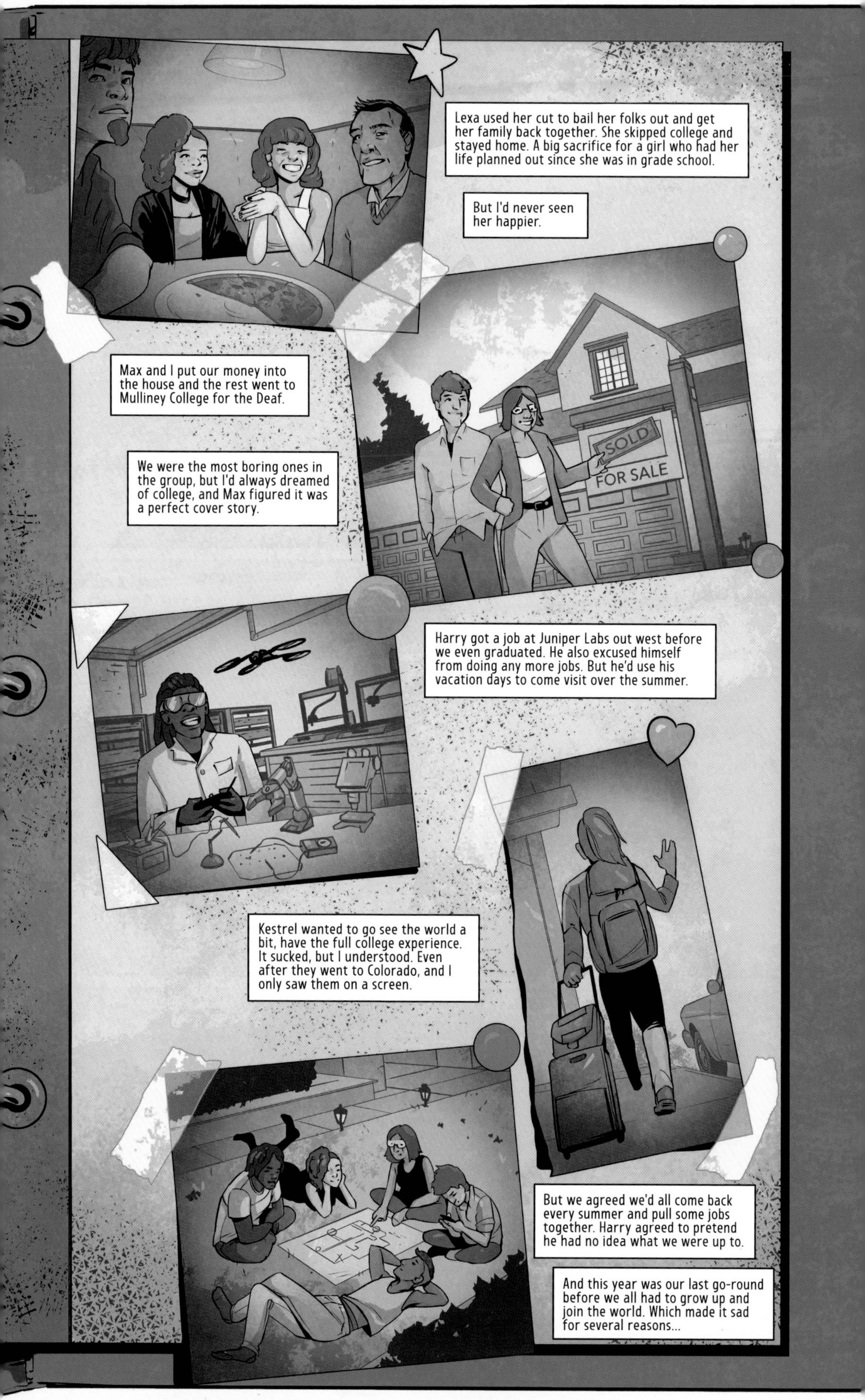
Lexa used her cut to bail her folks out and get her family back together. She skipped college and stayed home. A big sacrifice for a girl who had her life planned out since she was in grade school.
But I'd never seen her happier.
Max and I put our money into the house and the rest went to Mulliney College for the Deaf.
We were the most boring ones in the group, but I'd always dreamed of college, and Max figured it was a perfect cover story.
SOLD
FOR SALE
Harry got a job at Juniper Labs out west before we even graduated. He also excused himself from doing any more jobs. But he'd use his vacation days to come visit over the summer.
Kestrel wanted to go see the world a bit, have the full college experience. It sucked, but I understood. Even after they went to Colorado, and I only saw them on a screen.
But we agreed we'd all come back every summer and pull some jobs together. Harry agreed to pretend he had no idea what we were up to.
And this year was our last go-round before we all had to grow up and join the world. Which made it sad for several reasons...

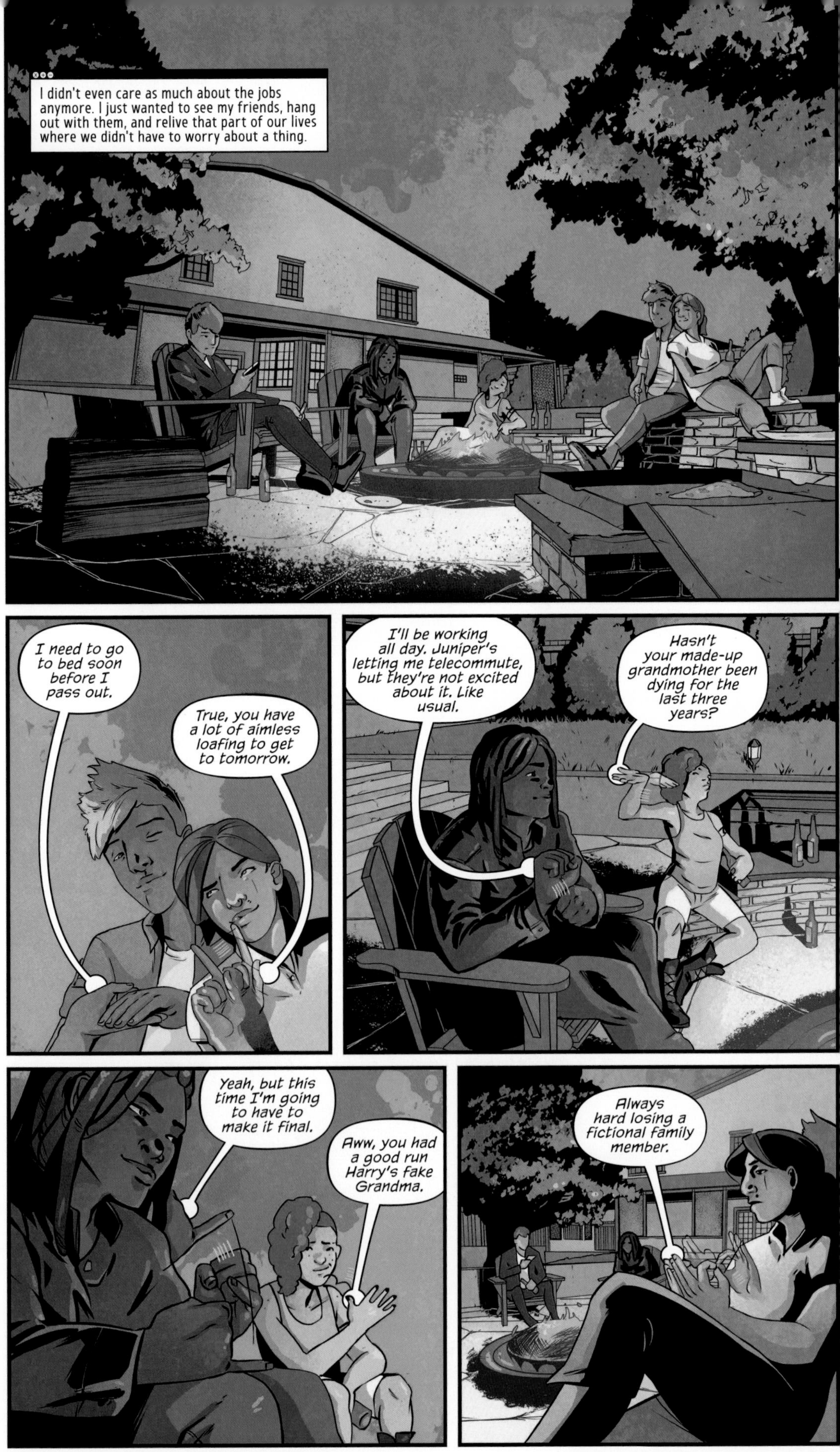
I didn't even care as much about the jobs anymore. I just wanted to see my friends, hang out with them, and relive that part of our lives where we didn't have to worry about a thing.
I need to go to bed soon before I pass out.
True, you have a lot of aimless loafing to get to tomorrow.
I'll be working all day. Juniper's letting me telecommute, but they're not excited about it. Like usual.
Hasn't your made-up grandmother been dying for the last three years?
Yeah, but this time I'm going to have to make it final.
Aww, you had a good run Harry's Fake Grandma.
Always hard losing a fictional family member.

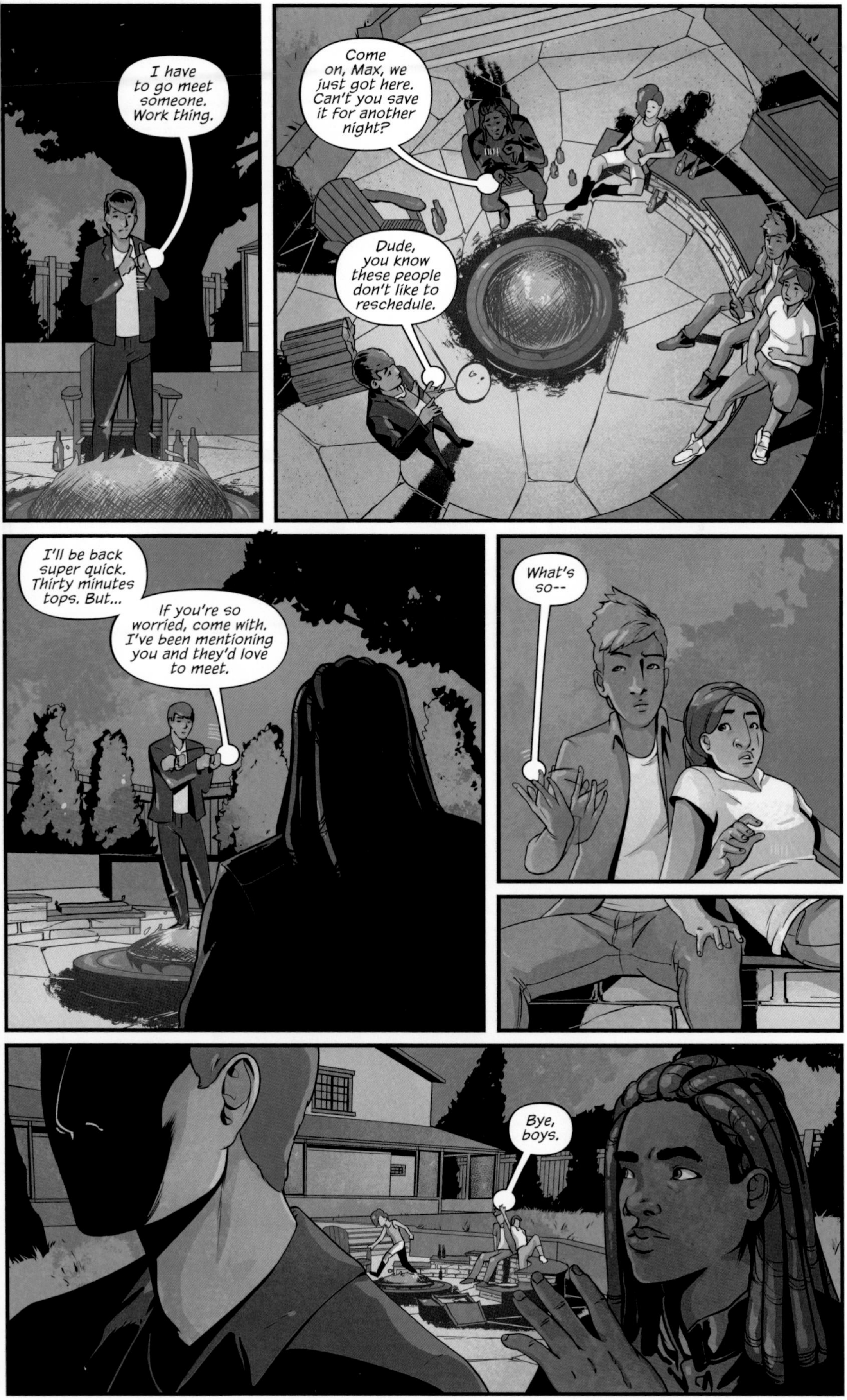

I have to go meet someone. Work thing.
Come on, Max, we just got here. Can't you save it for another night?
Dude, you know these people don't like to reschedule.
I'll be back super quick. Thirty minutes tops. But...
If you're so worried, come with. I've been mentioning you and they'd love to meet.
What's so--
Bye, boys.

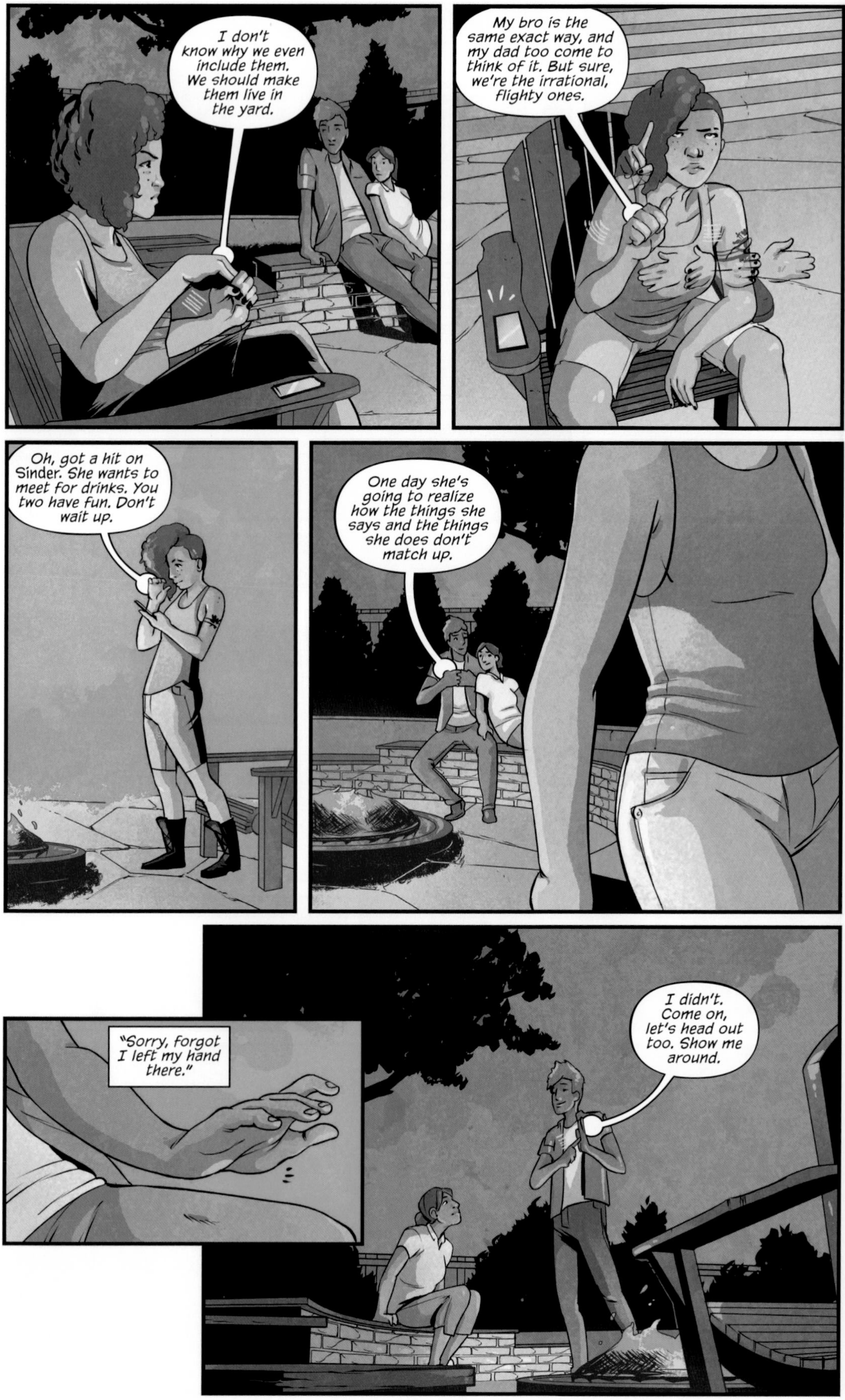
I don't know why we even include them. We should make them live in the yard.
My bro is the same exact way, and my dad too come to think of it. But sure, we're the irrational, flighty ones.
Oh, got a hit on Sinder. She wants to meet for drinks. You two have fun. Don't wait up.
One day she's going to realize how the things she says and the things she does don't match up.
"Sorry, forgot I left my hand there."
I didn't. Come on, let's head out too. Show me around.

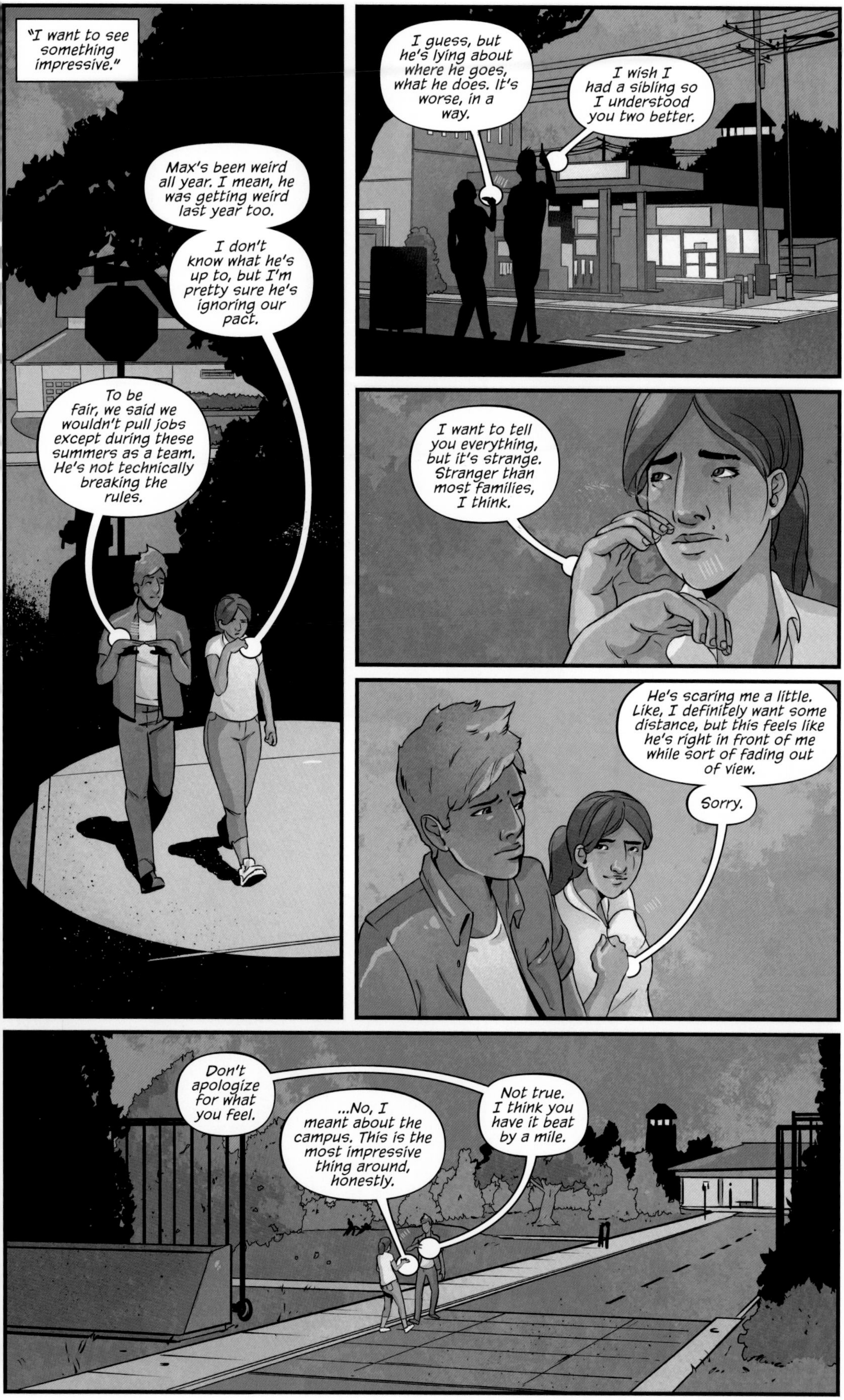
"I want to see something impressive."
Max's been weird all year. I mean, he was getting weird last year too.
I don't know what he's up to, but I'm pretty sure he's ignoring our pact.
To be fair, we said we wouldn't pull jobs except during these summers as a team. He's not technically breaking the rules.
I guess, but he's lying about where he goes, what he does. It's worse, in a way.
I wish I had a sibling so I understood you two better.
I want to tell you everything, but it's strange. Stranger than most families, I think.
He's scaring me a little. Like, I definitely want some distance, but this feels like he's right in front of me while sort of fading out of view.
Sorry.
Don't apologize for what you feel.
Not true. I think you have it beat by a mile.
...No, I meant about the campus. This is the most impressive thing around, honestly.

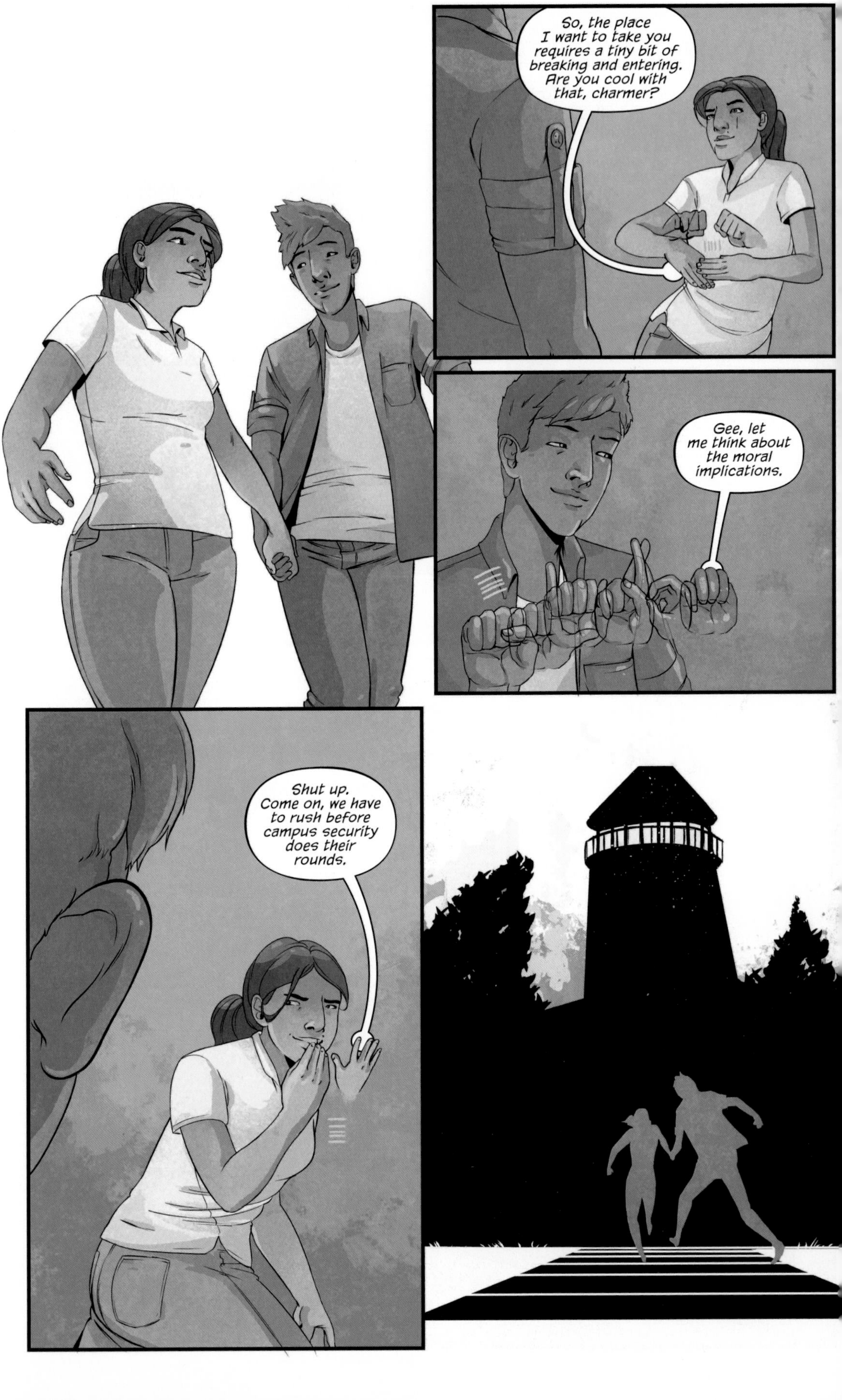
So, the place I want to take you requires a tiny bit of breaking and entering. Are you cool with that, charmer?
Gee, let me think about the moral implications.
Shut up. Come on, we have to rush before campus security does their rounds.

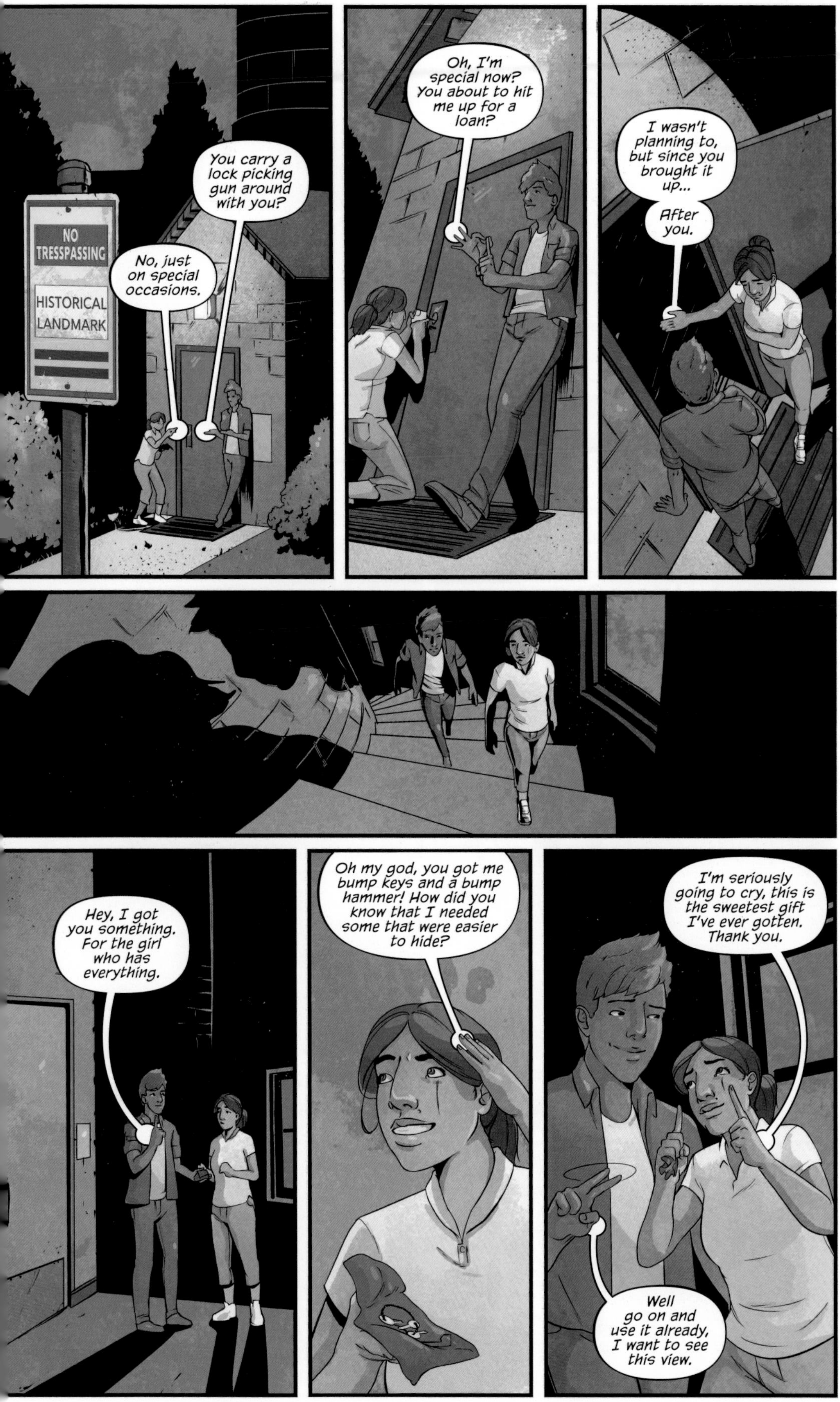
NO TRESSPASSING
HISTORICAL LANDMARK
You carry a lock picking gun around with you?
No, just on special occasions.
Oh, I'm special now? You about to hit me up for a loan?
I wasn't planning to, but since you brought it up...
After you.
Hey, I got you something. For the girl who has everything.
Oh my god, you got me bump keys and a bump hammer! How did you know that I needed some that were easier to hide?
I'm seriously going to cry, this is the sweetest gift I've ever gotten. Thank you.
Well go on and use it already, I want to see this view.

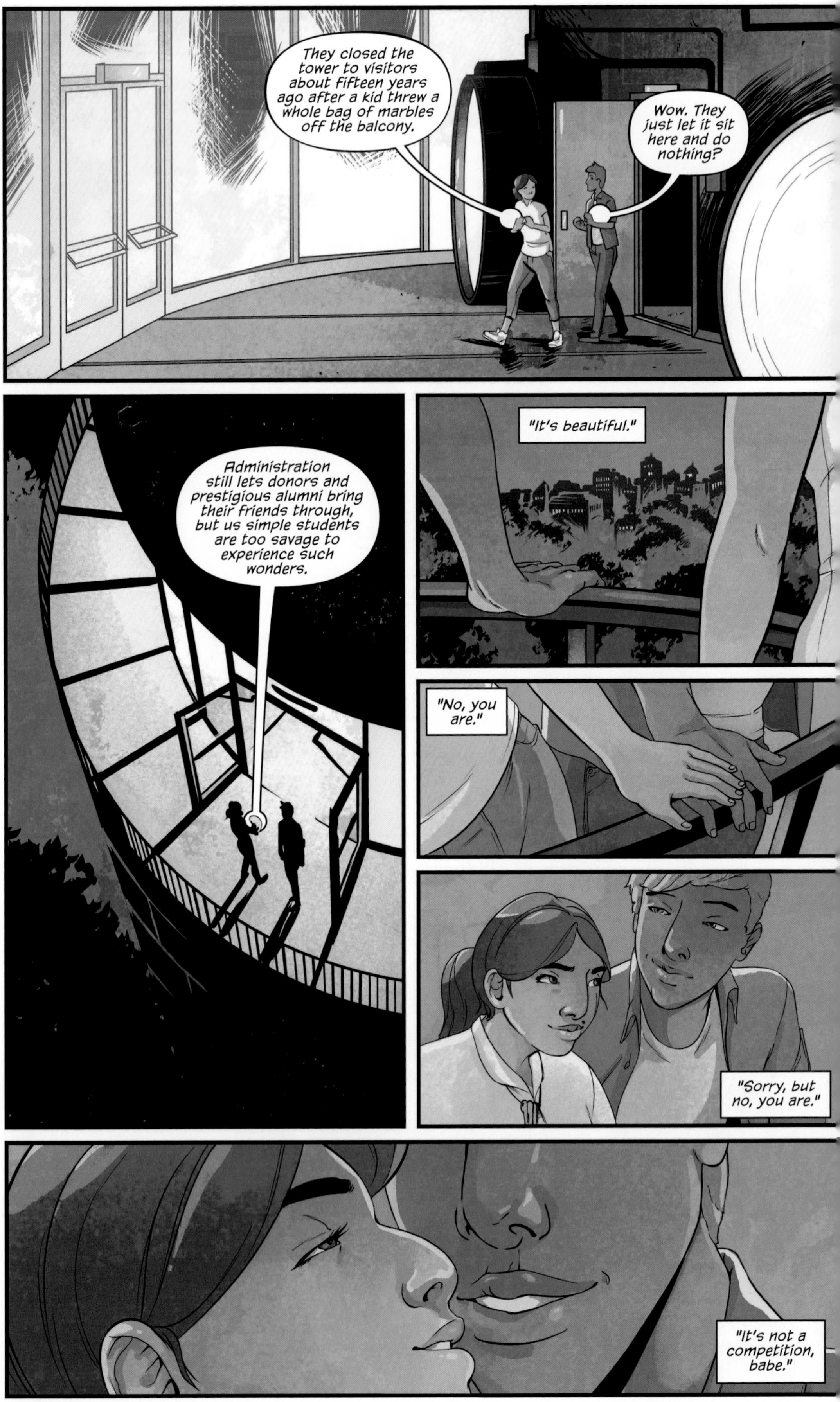
They closed the tower to visitors about fifteen years ago after a kid threw a whole bag of marbles off the balcony.
Wow. They just let it sit here and do nothing?
Administration still lets donors and prestigious alumni bring their friends through, but us simple students are too savage to experience such wonders.
"It's beautiful."
"No, you are."
"Sorry, but no, you are."
"It's not a competition, babe."

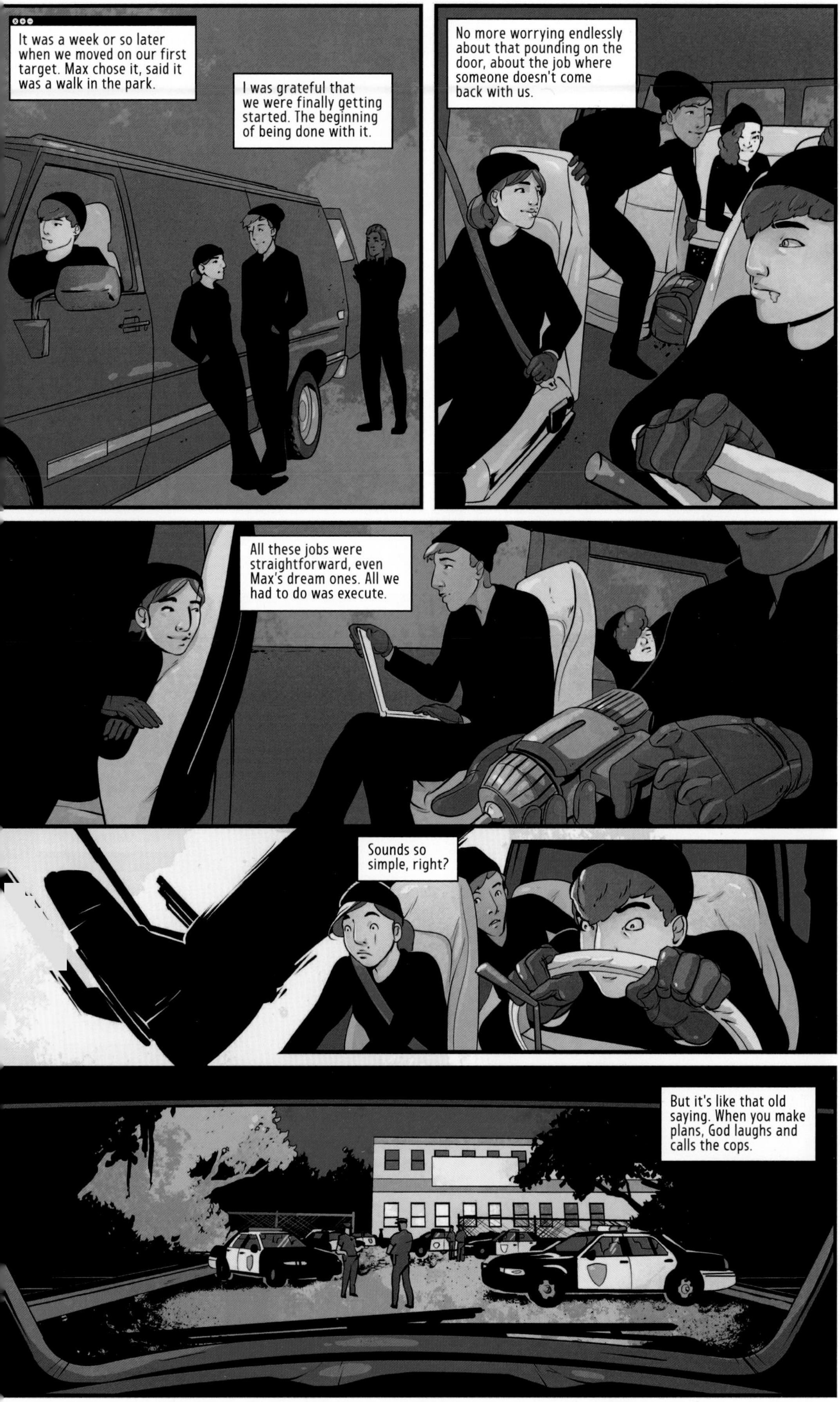
It was a week or so later when we moved on our first target. Max chose it, said it was a walk in the park.
I was grateful that we were finally getting started. The beginning of being done with it.
No more worrying endlessly about that pounding on the door, about the job where someone doesn't come back with us.
All these jobs were straightforward, even Max's dream ones. All we had to do was execute.
Sounds so simple, right?
But it's like that old saying. When you make plans, God laughs and calls the cops.

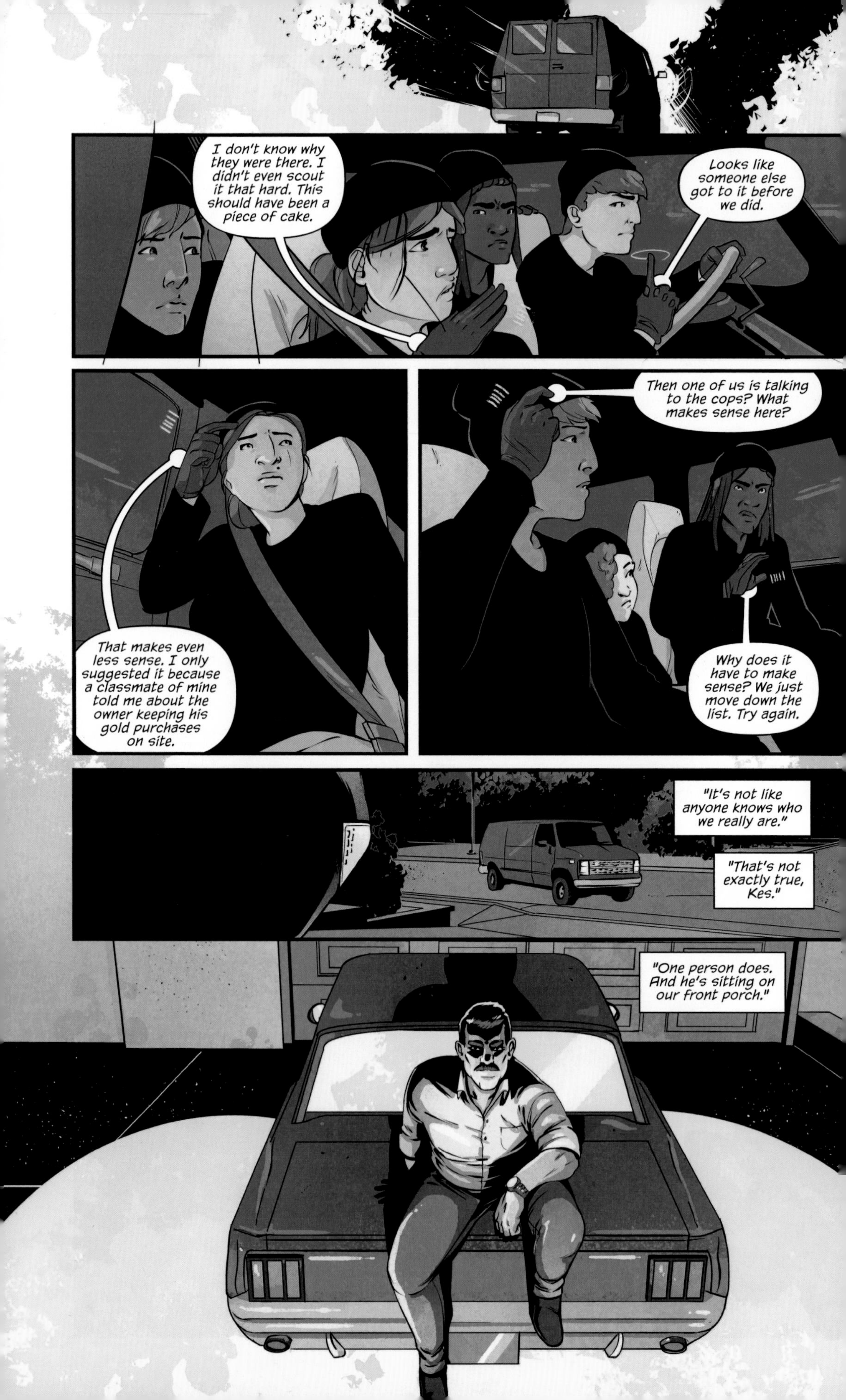
I don't know why they were there. I didn't even scout it that hard. This should have been a piece of cake.
Looks like someone else got to it before we did.
That makes even less sense. I only suggested it because a classmate of mine told me about the owner keeping his gold purchases on site.
Then one of us is talking to the cops? What makes sense here?
Why does it have to make sense? We just move down the list. Try again.
"It's not like anyone knows who we really are."
"That's not exactly true, Kes."
"One person does. And he's sitting on our front porch."

CHAPTER FIVE

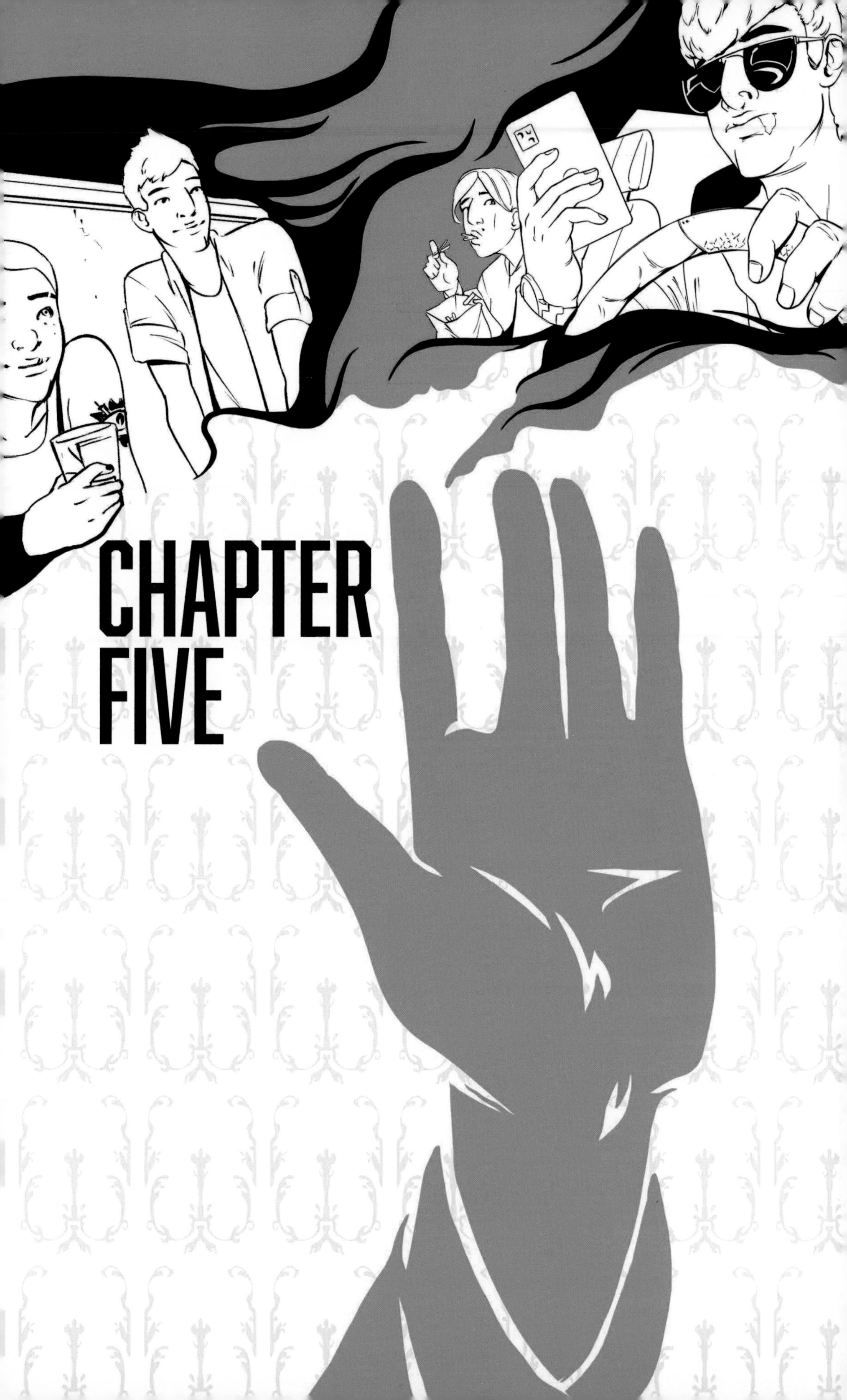

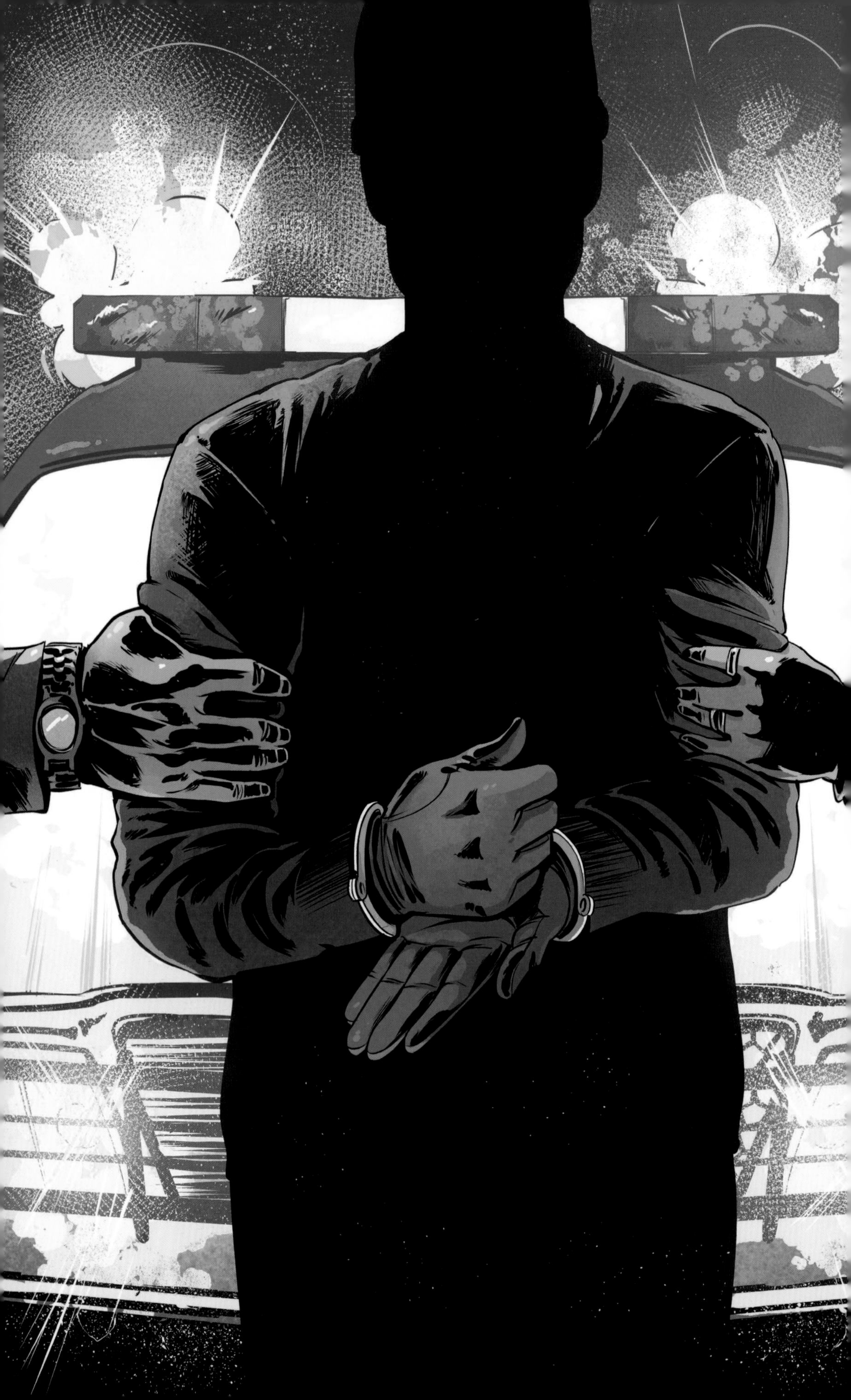

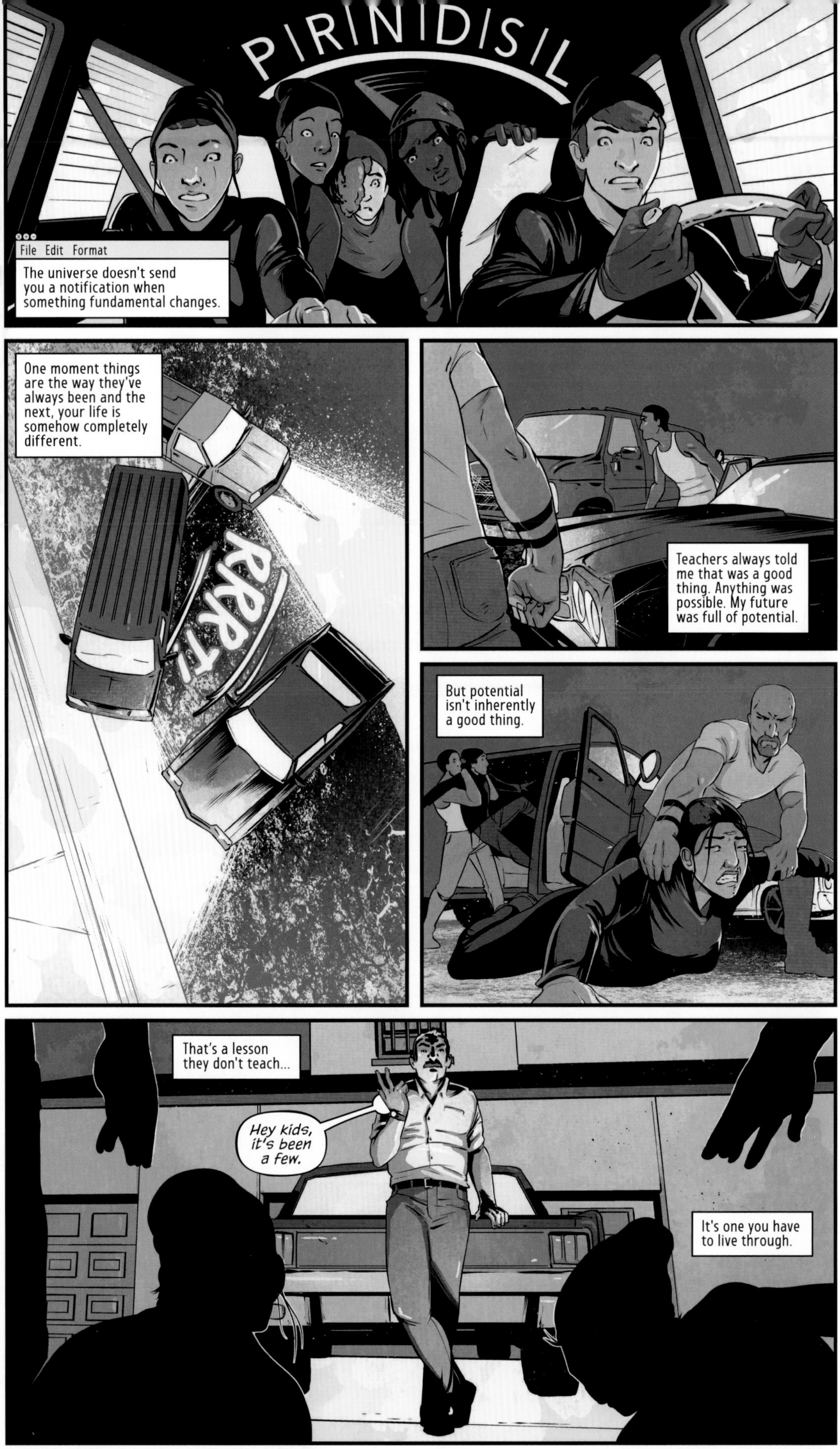
PIRINIDISIL
File Edit Format
The universe doesn't send you a notification when something fundamental changes.
One moment things are the way they've always been and the next, your life is somehow completely different.
RRRT!
Teachers always told me that was a good thing. Anything was possible. My future was full of potential.
But potential isn't inherently a good thing.
That's a lesson they don't teach...
Hey kids, it's been a few.
It's one you have to live through.

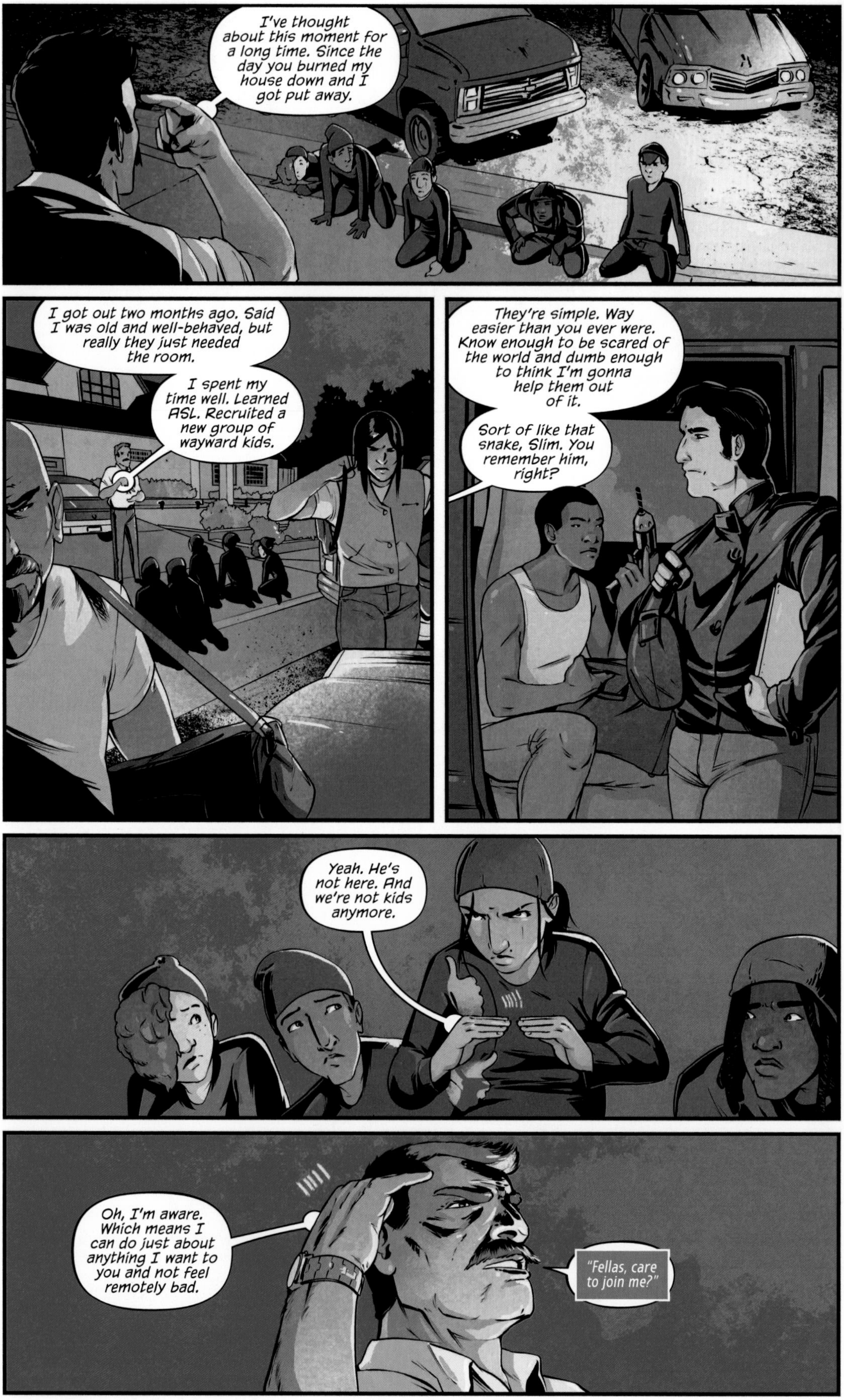

I've thought about this moment for a long time. Since the day you burned my house down and I got put away.
I got out two months ago. Said I was old and well-behaved, but really they just needed the room.
I spent my time well. Learned ASL. Recruited a new group of wayward kids.
They're simple. Way easier than you ever were. Know enough to be scared of the world and dumb enough to think I'm gonna help them out of it.
Sort of like that snake, Slim. You remember him, right?
Yeah. He's not here. And we're not kids anymore.
Oh, I'm aware. Which means I can do just about anything I want to you and not feel remotely bad.
"Fellas, care to join me?"

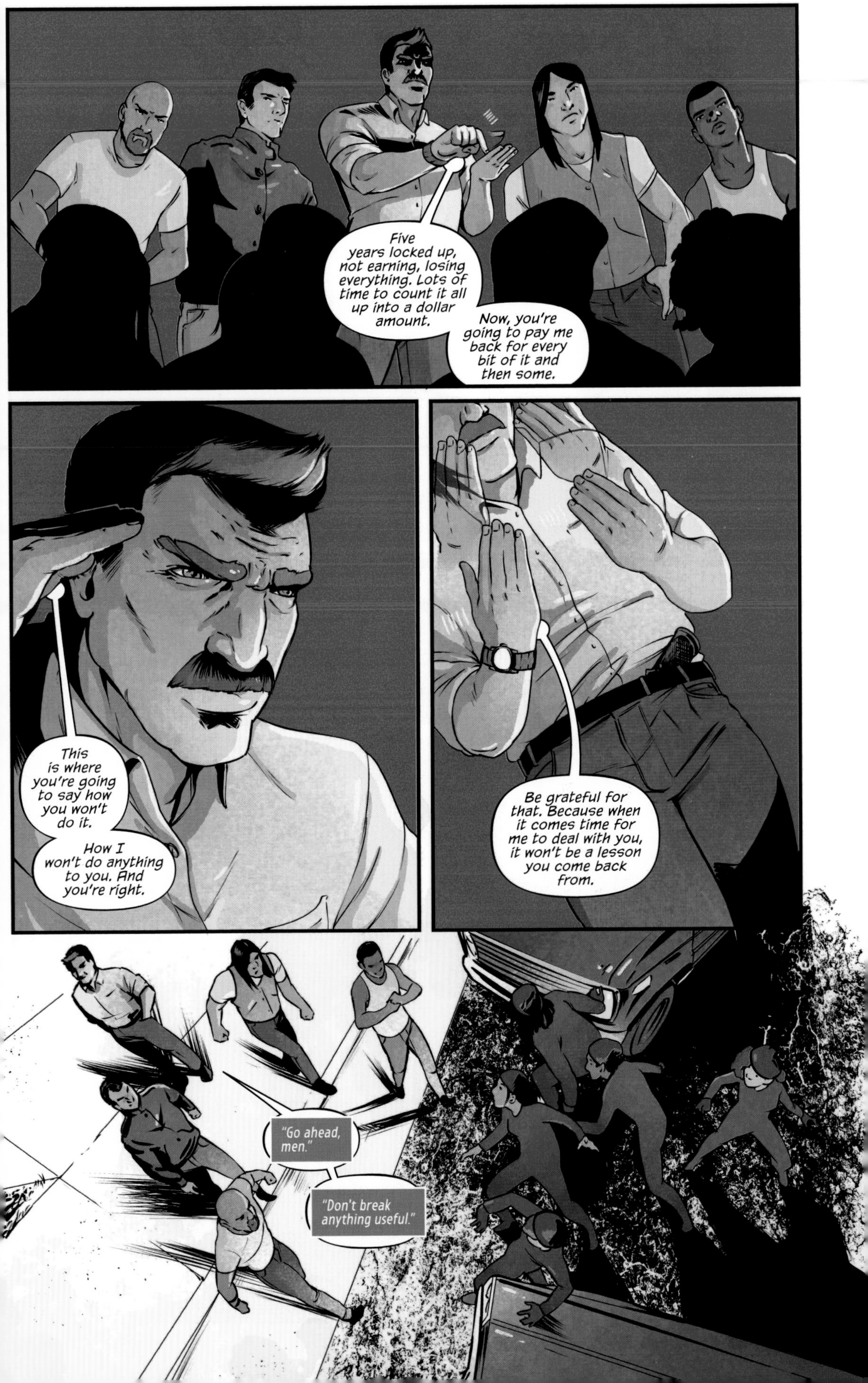
Five years locked up, not earning, losing everything. Lots of time to count it all up into a dollar amount.
Now, you're going to pay me back for every bit of it and then some.
This is where you're going to say how you won't do it.
How I won't do anything to you. And you're right.
Be grateful for that. Because when it comes time for me to deal with you, it won't be a lesson you come back from.
"Go ahead, men."
"Don't break anything useful."

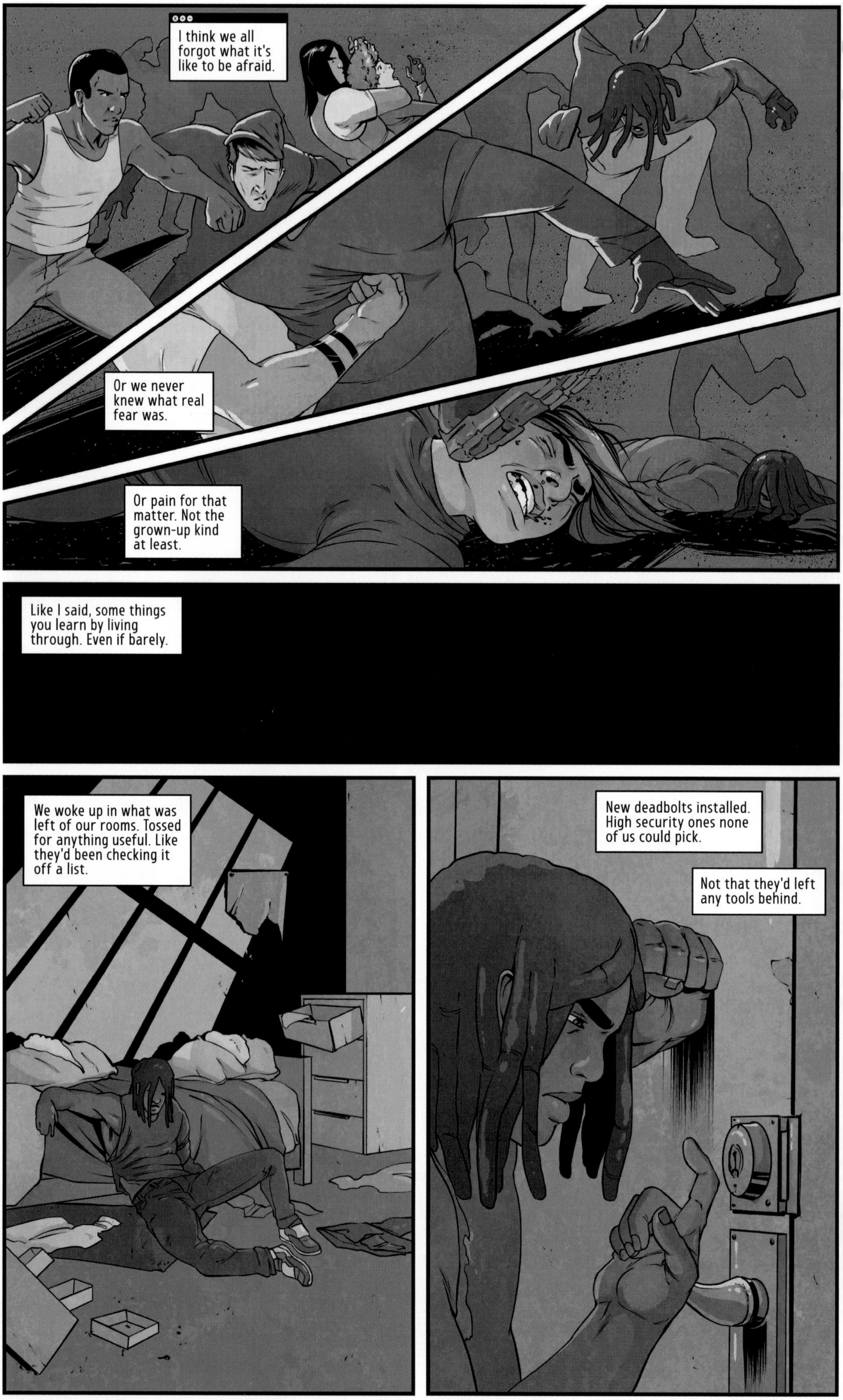
I think we all forgot what it's like to be afraid.
Or we never knew what real fear was.
Or pain for that matter. Not the grown-up kind at least.
Like I said, some things you learn by living through. Even if barely.
We woke up in what was left of our rooms. Tossed for anything useful. Like they'd been checking it off a list.
New deadbolts installed. High security ones none of us could pick.
Not that they'd left any tools behind.

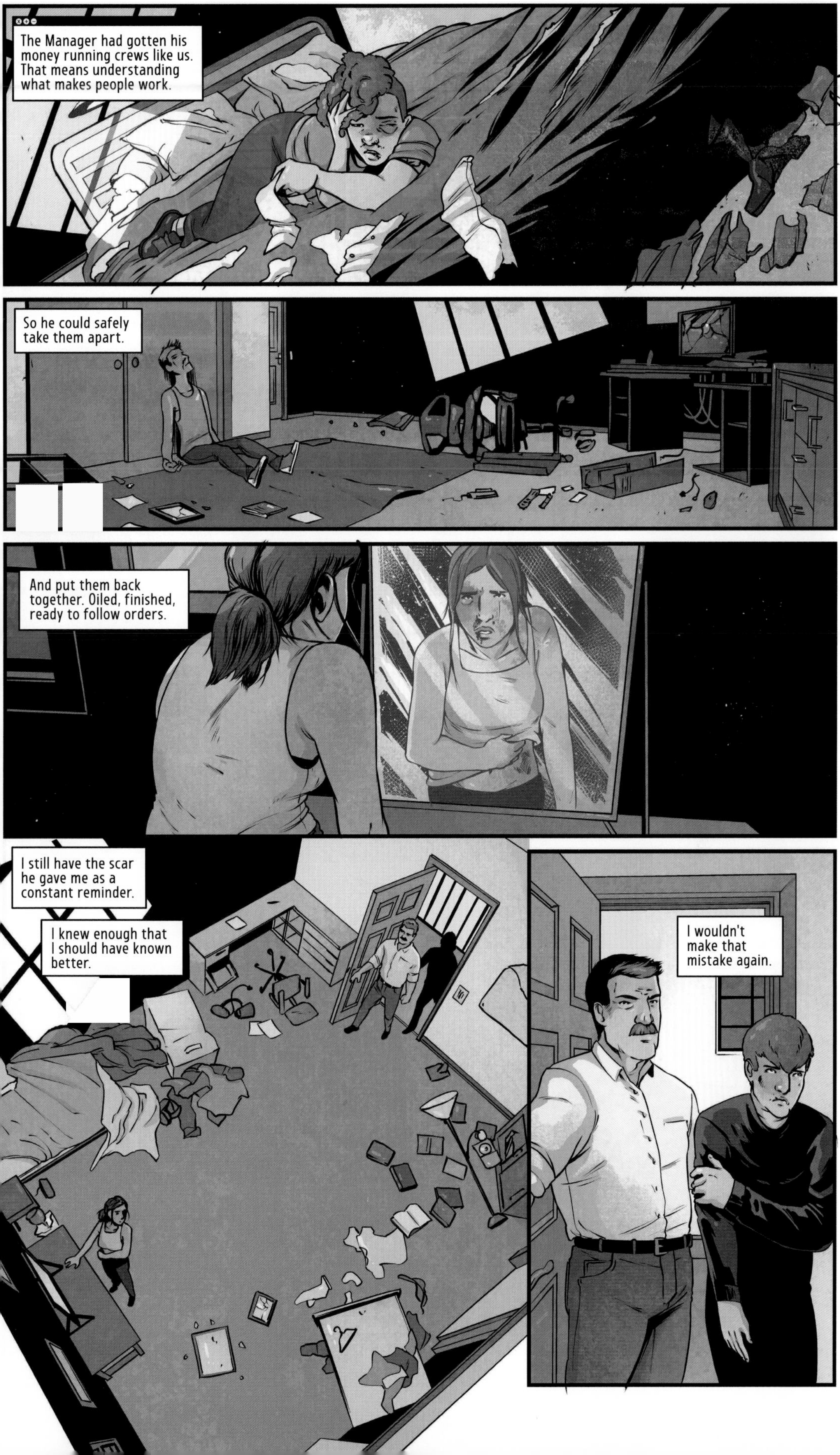
The Manager had gotten his money running crews like us. That means understanding what makes people work.
So he could safely take them apart.
And put them back together. Oiled, finished, ready to follow orders.
I still have the scar he gave me as a constant reminder.
I knew enough that I should have known better.
I wouldn't make that mistake again.

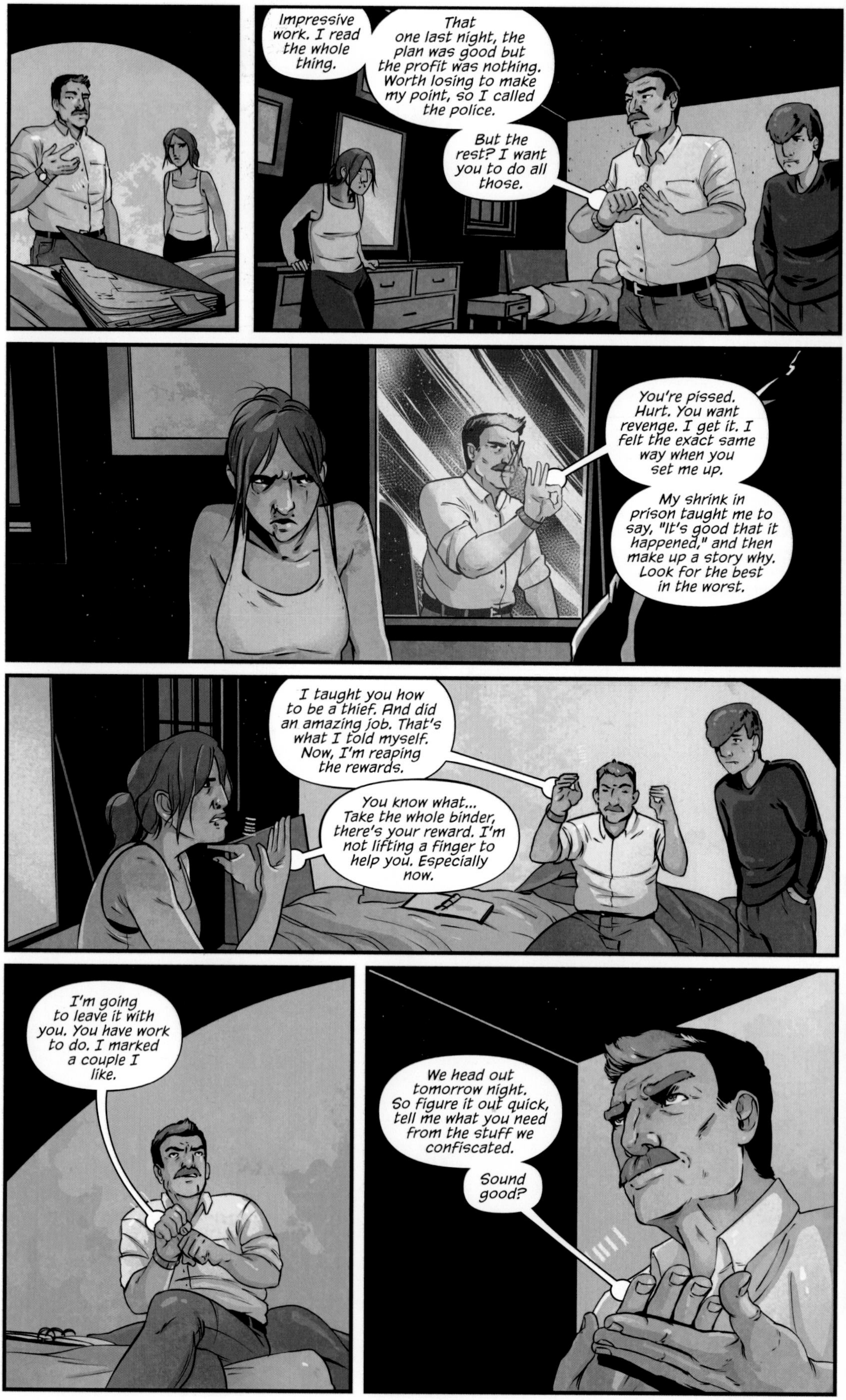
Impressive work. I read the whole thing.
That one last night, the plan was good but the profit was nothing. Worth losing to make my point, so I called the police.
But the rest? I want you to do all those.
You're pissed. Hurt. You want revenge. I get it. I felt the exact same way when you set me up.
My shrink in prison taught me to say, "It's good that it happened," and then make up a story why. Look for the best in the worst.
I taught you how to be a thief. And did an amazing job. That's what I told myself. Now, I'm reaping the rewards.
You know what... Take the whole binder, there's your reward. I'm not lifting a finger to help you. Especially now.
I'm going to leave it with you. You have work to do. I marked a couple I like.
We head out tomorrow night. So figure it out quick, tell me what you need from the stuff we confiscated.
Sound good?

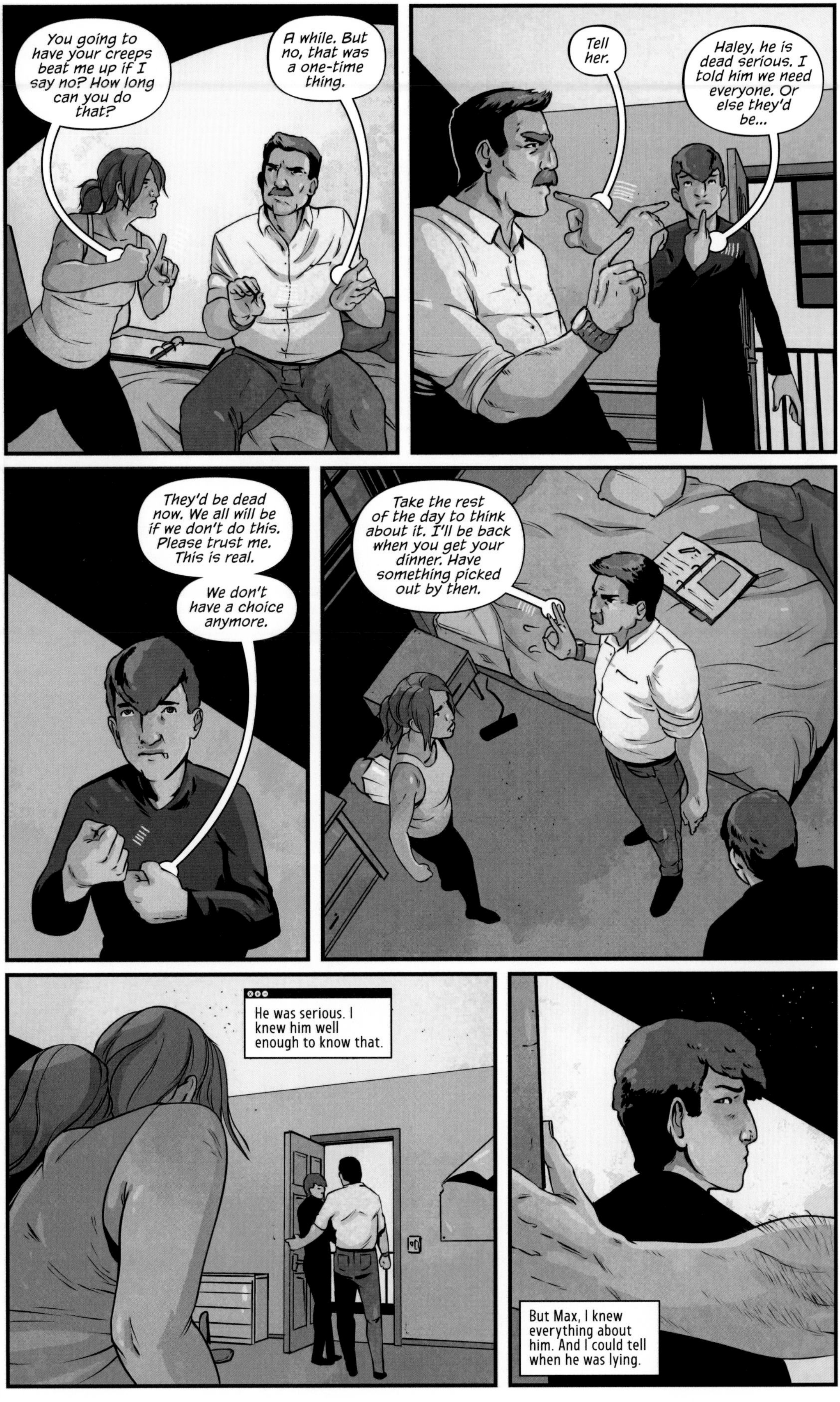
You going to have your creeps beat me up if I say no? How long can you do that?
A while. But no, that was a one-time thing.
Tell her.
Haley, he is dead serious. I told him we need everyone. Or else they'd be...
They'd be dead now. We all will be if we don't do this. Please trust me. This is real.
We don't have a choice anymore.
Take the rest of the day to think about it. I'll be back when you get your dinner. Have something picked out by then.
He was serious. I knew him well enough to know that.
But Max, I knew everything about him. And I could tell when he was lying.

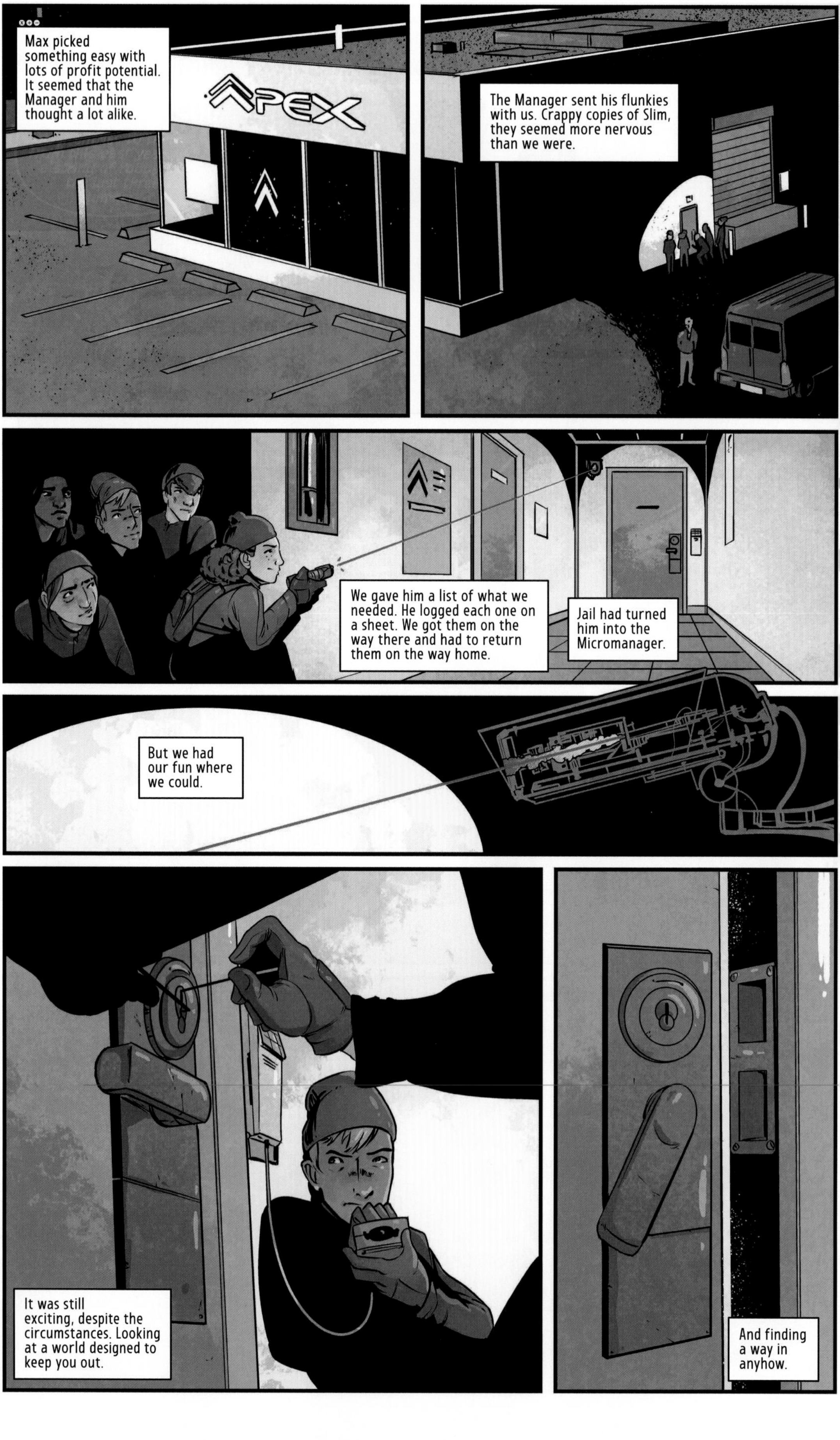
Max picked something easy with lots of profit potential. It seemed that the Manager and him thought a lot alike.
The Manager sent his flunkies with us. Crappy copies of Slim, they seemed more nervous than we were.
We gave him a list of what we needed. He logged each one on a sheet. We got them on the way there and had to return them on the way home.
Jail had turned him into the Micromanager.
But we had our fun where we could.
It was still exciting, despite the circumstances. Looking at a world designed to keep you out.
And finding a way in anyhow.

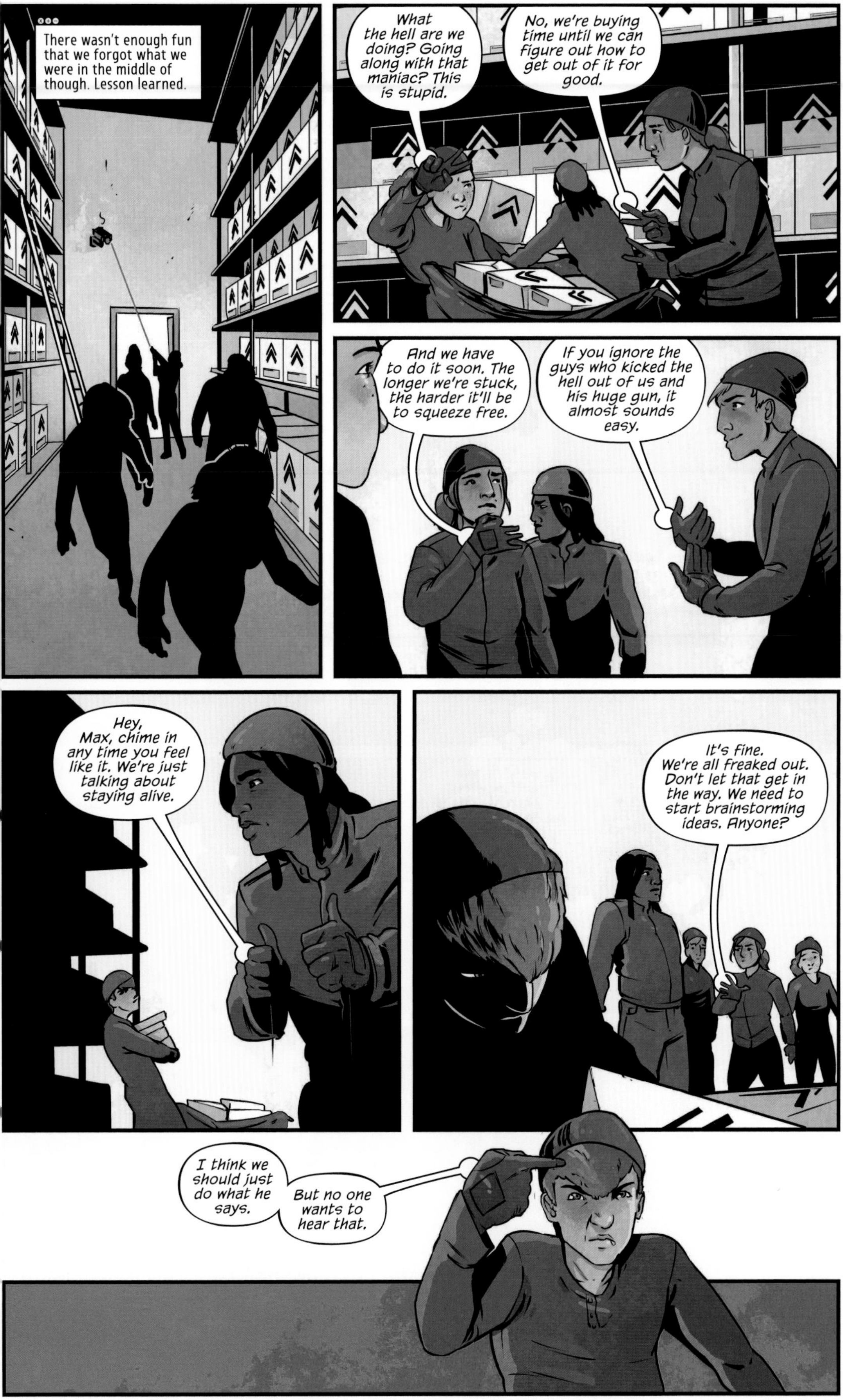
There wasn't enough fun that we forgot what we were in the middle of though. Lesson learned.
What the hell are we doing? Going along with that maniac? This is stupid.
No, we're buying time until we can figure out how to get out of it for good.
And we have to do it soon. The longer we're stuck, the harder it'll be to squeeze free.
If you ignore the guys who kicked the hell out of us and his huge gun, it almost sounds easy.
Hey, Max, chime in any time you feel like it. We're just talking about staying alive.
It's fine. We're all freaked out. Don't let that get in the way. We need to start brainstorming ideas. Anyone?
I think we should just do what he says.
But no one wants to hear that.

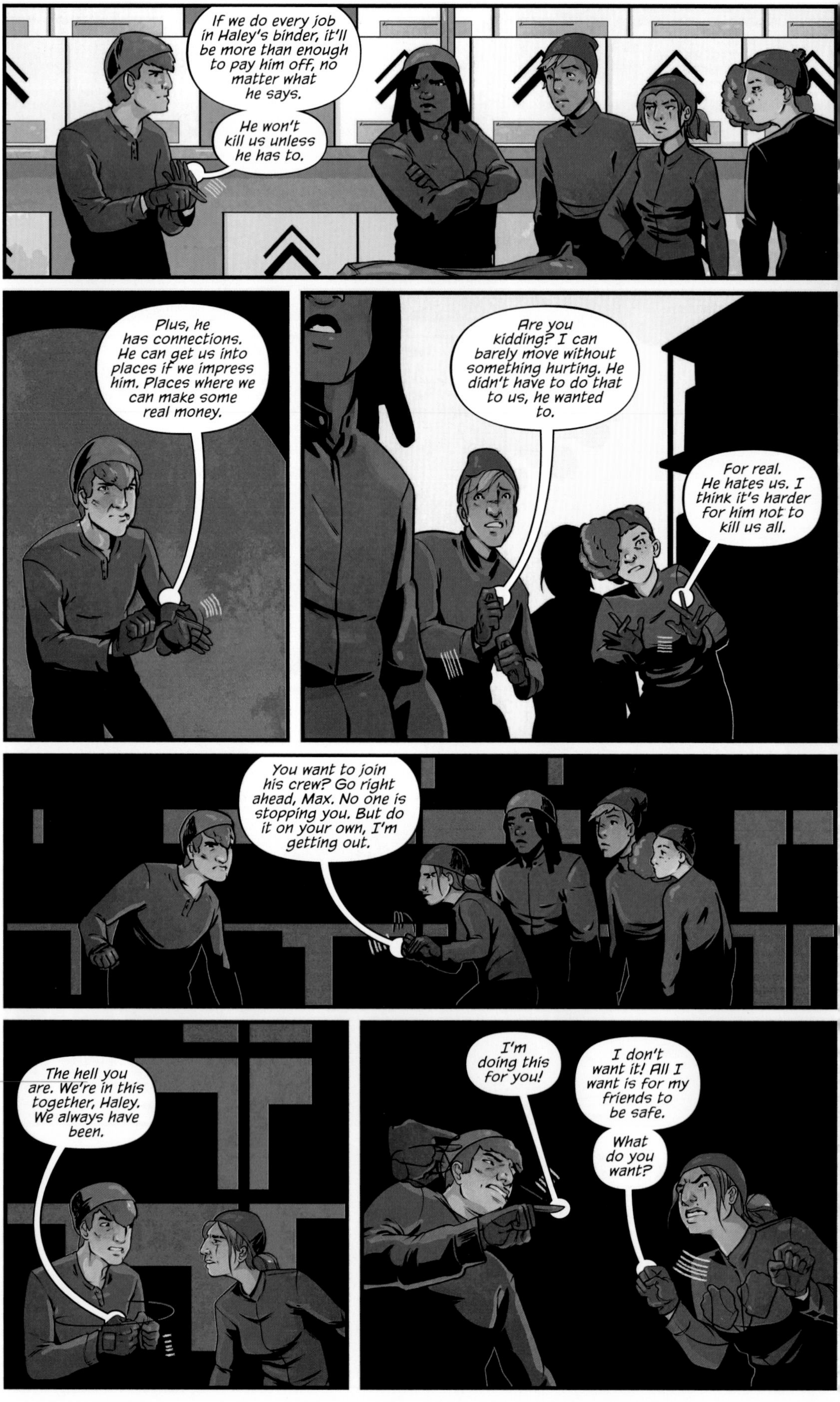
If we do every job in Haley's binder, it'll be more than enough to pay him off, no matter what he says.
He won't kill us unless he has to.
Plus, he has connections. He can get us into places if we impress him. Places where we can make some real money.
Are you kidding? I can barely move without something hurting. He didn't have to do that to us, he wanted to.
For real. He hates us. I think it's harder for him not to kill us all.
You want to join his crew? Go right ahead, Max. No one is stopping you. But do it on your own, I'm getting out.
The hell you are. We're in this together, Haley. We always have been.
I'm doing this for you!
I don't want it! All I want is for my friends to be safe.
What do you want?

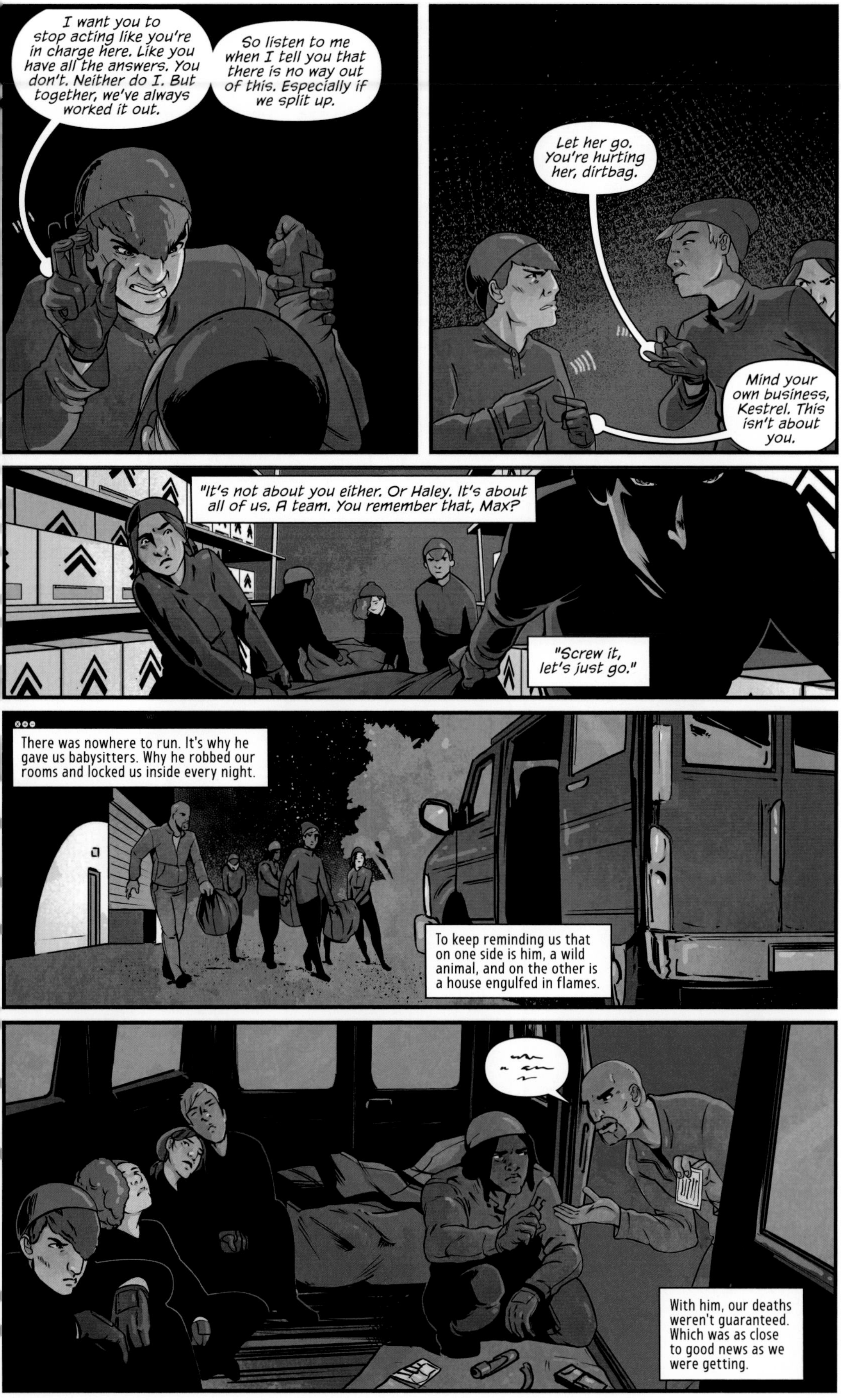
I want you to stop acting like you're in charge here. Like you have all the answers. You don't. Neither do I. But together, we've always worked it out.
So listen to me when I tell you that there is no way out of this. Especially if we split up.
Let her go. You're hurting her, dirtbag.
Mind your own business, Kestrel. This isn't about you.
"It's not about you either. Or Haley. It's about all of us. A team. You remember that, Max?
"Screw it, let's just go."
There was nowhere to run. It's why he gave us babysitters. Why he robbed our rooms and locked us inside every night.
To keep reminding us that on one side is him, a wild animal, and on the other is a house engulfed in flames.
With him, our deaths weren't guaranteed. Which was as close to good news as we were getting.

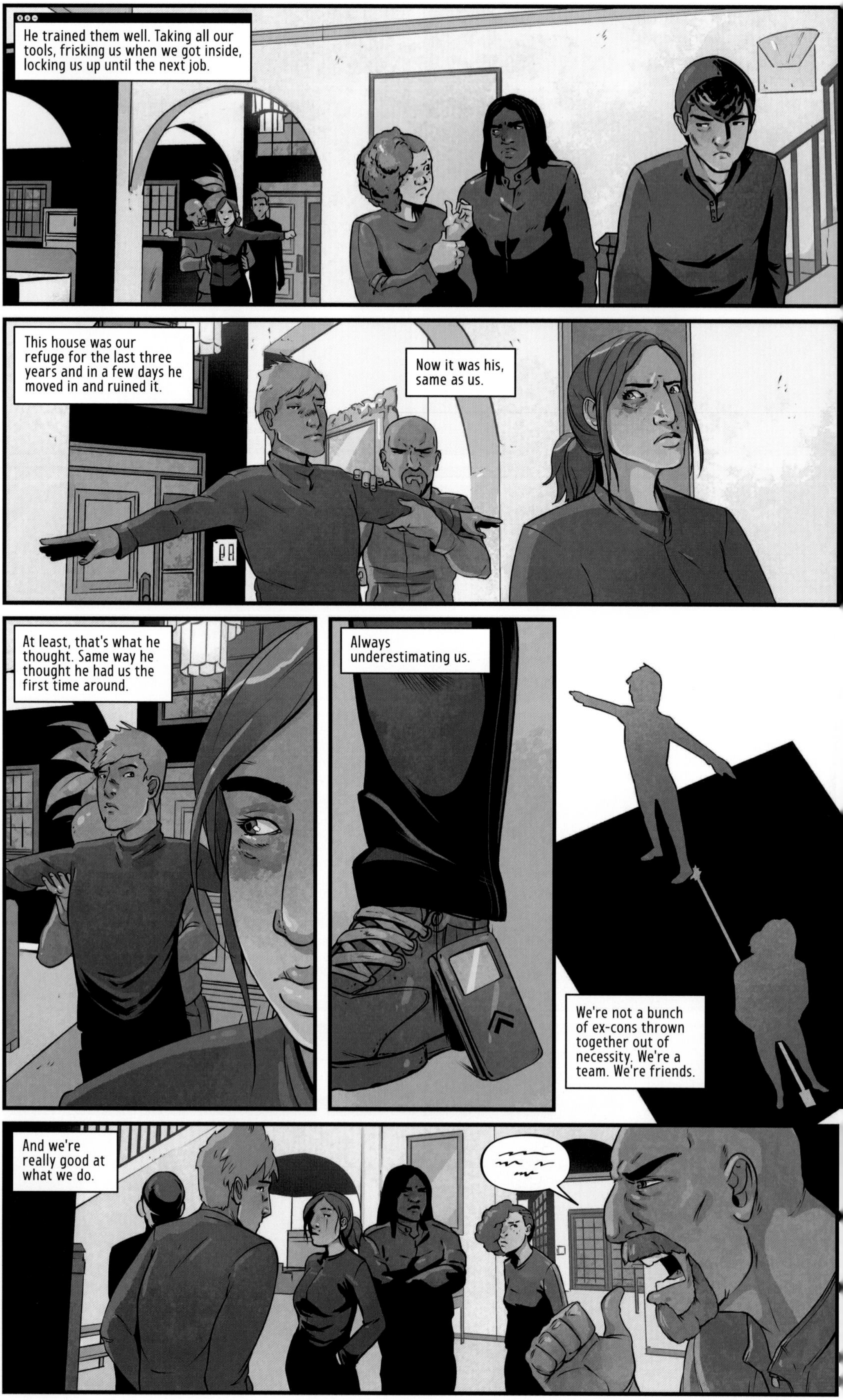
He trained them well. Taking all our tools, frisking us when we got inside, locking us up until the next job.
This house was our refuge for the last three years and in a few days he moved in and ruined it.
Now it was his, same as us.
At least, that's what he thought. Same way he thought he had us the first time around.
Always underestimating us.
We're not a bunch of ex-cons thrown together out of necessity. We're a team. We're friends.
And we're really good at what we do.

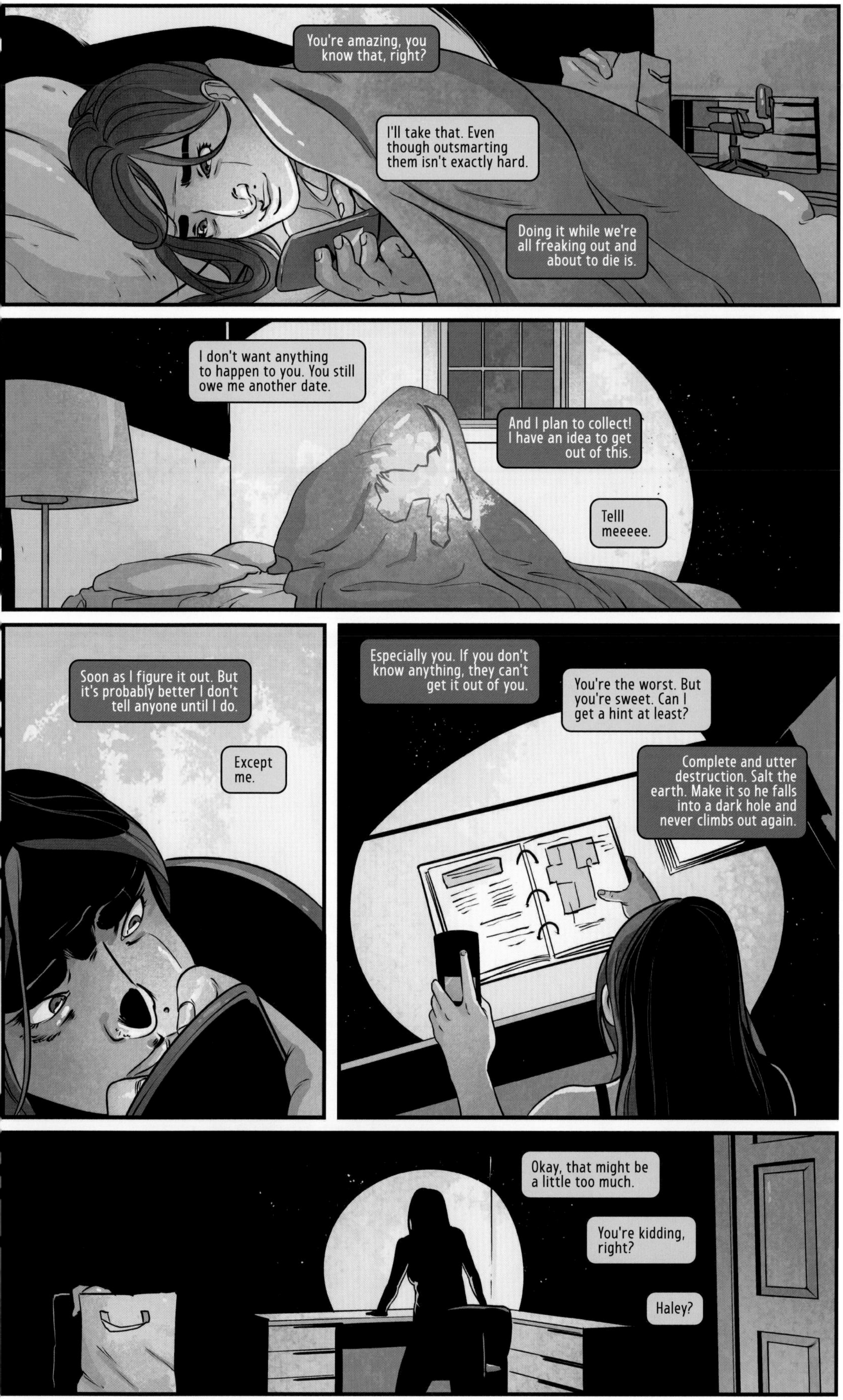
You're amazing, you know that, right?
I'll take that. Even though outsmarting them isn't exactly hard.
Doing it while we're all freaking out and about to die is.
I don't want anything to happen to you. You still owe me another date.
And I plan to collect! I have an idea to get out of this.
Telll meeeee.
Soon as I figure it out. But it's probably better I don't tell anyone until I do.
Except me.
Especially you. If you don't know anything, they can't get it out of you.
You're the worst. But you're sweet. Can I get a hint at least?
Complete and utter destruction. Salt the earth. Make it so he falls into a dark hole and never climbs out again.
Okay, that might be a little too much.
You're kidding, right?
Haley?

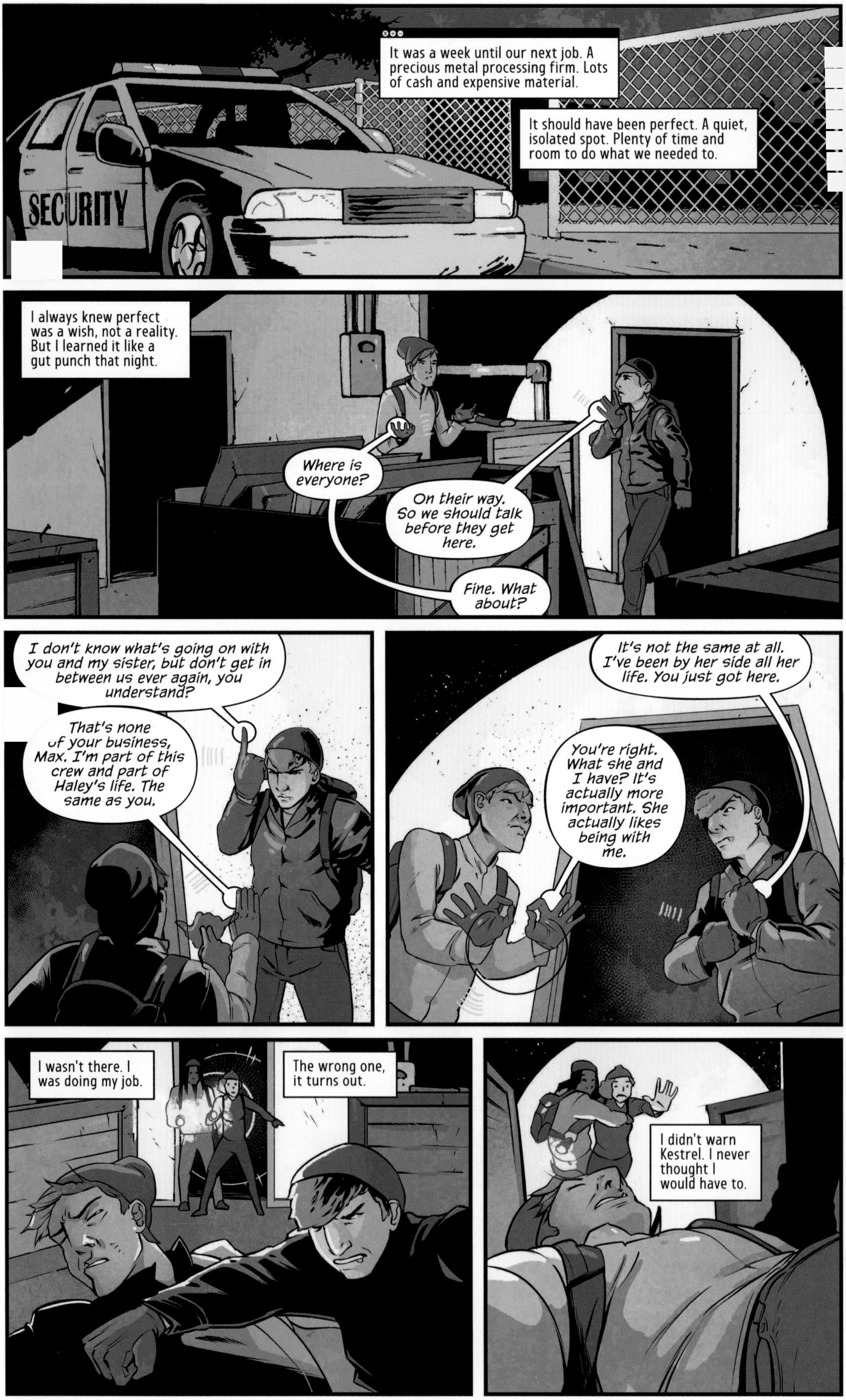

It was a week until our next job. A precious metal processing firm. Lots of cash and expensive material.
It should have been perfect. A quiet, isolated spot. Plenty of time and room to do what we needed to.
SECURITY
I always knew perfect was a wish, not a reality. But I learned it like a gut punch that night.
Where is everyone?
On their way. So we should talk before they get here.
Fine. What about?
I don't know what's going on with you and my sister, but don't get in between us ever again, you understand?
That's none of your business, Max. I'm part of this crew and part of Haley's life. The same as you.
It's not the same at all. I've been by her side all her life. You just got here.
You're right. What she and I have? It's actually more important. She actually likes being with me.
I wasn't there. I was doing my job.
The wrong one, it turns out.
I didn't warn Kestrel. I never thought I would have to.

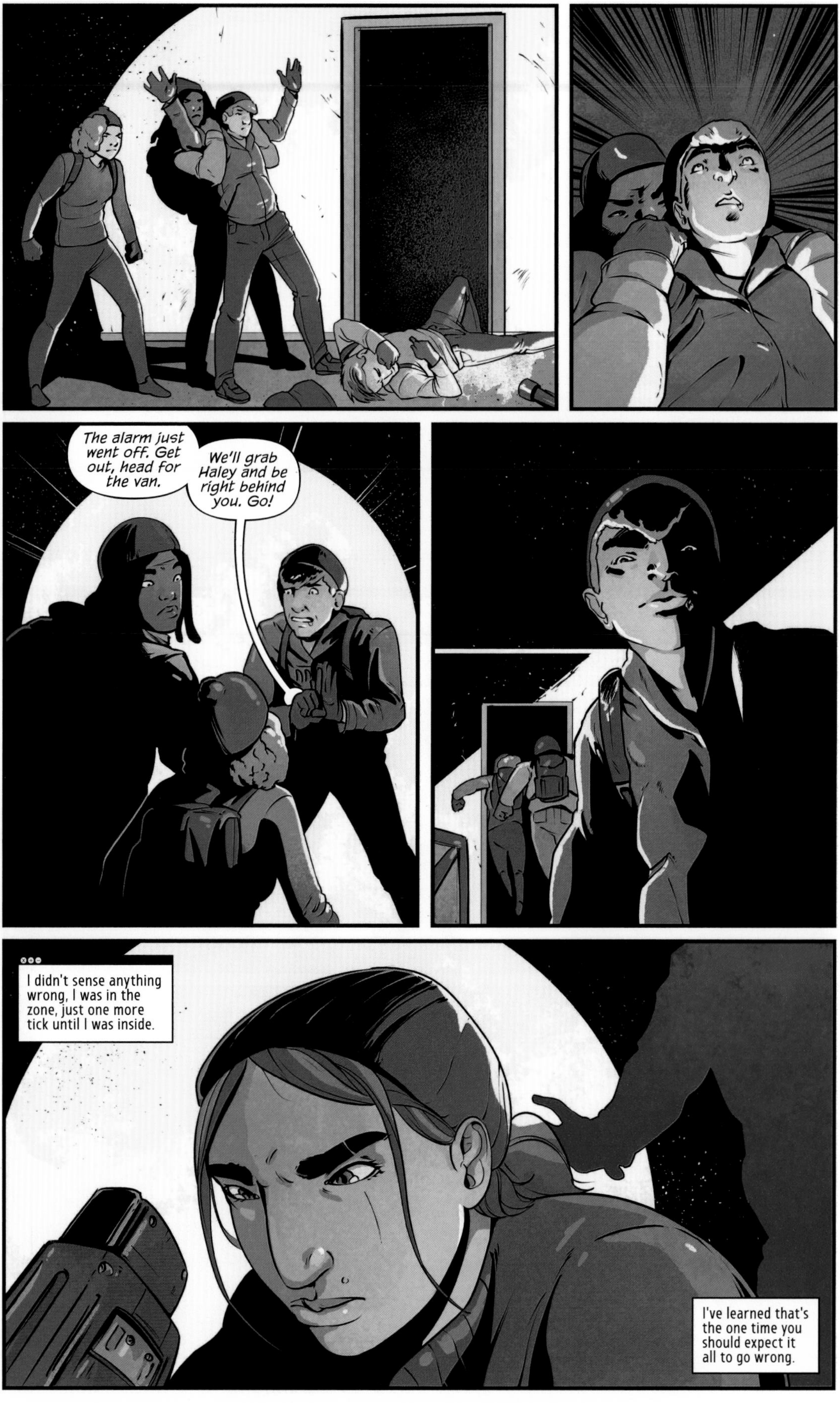
The alarm just went off. Get out, head for the van.
We'll grab Haley and be right behind you. Go!
I didn't sense anything wrong, I was in the zone, just one more tick until I was inside.
I've learned that's the one time you should expect it all to go wrong.

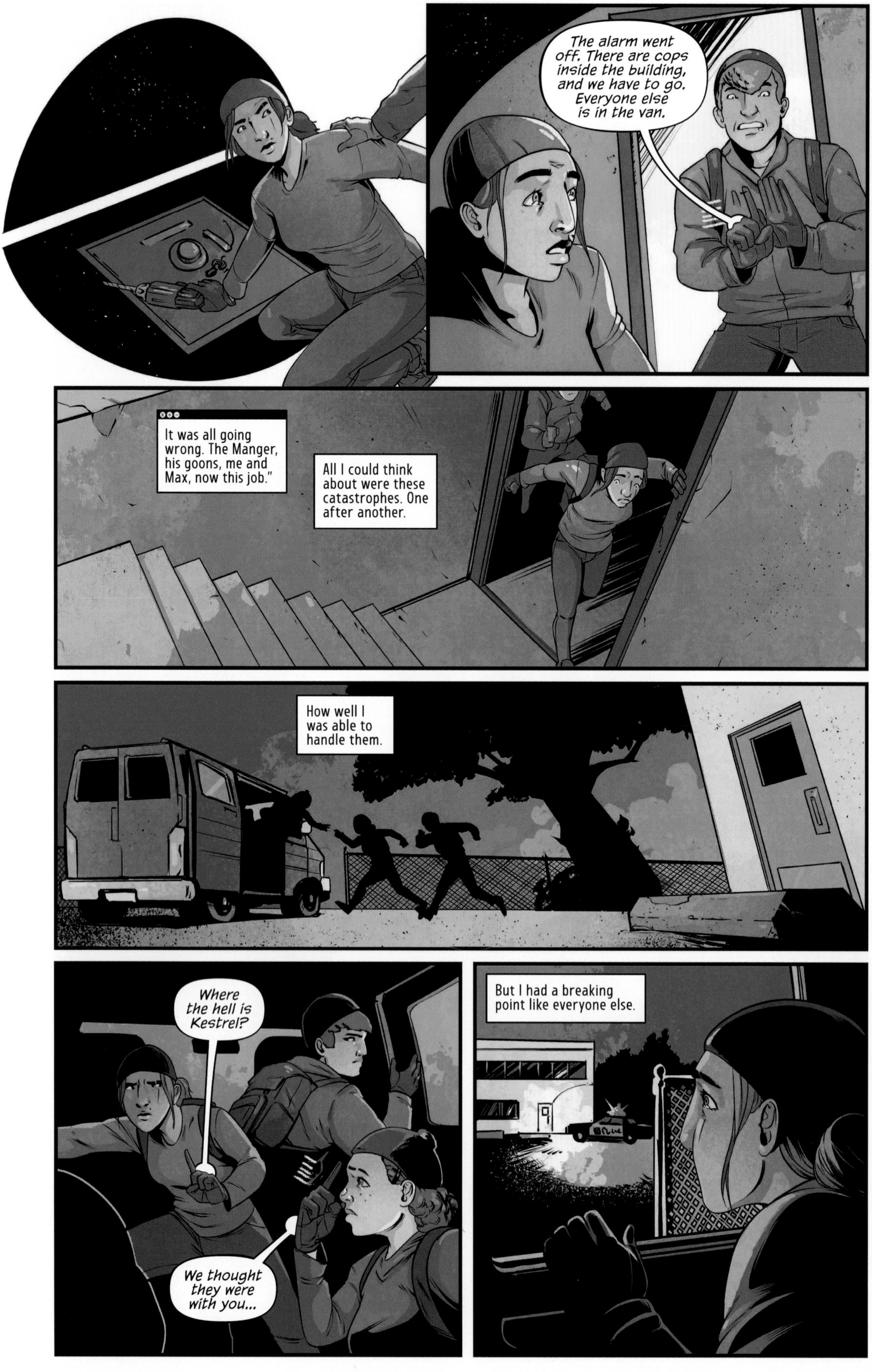
The alarm went off. There are cops inside the building, and we have to go. Everyone else is in the van.
It was all going wrong. The Manger, his goons, me and Max, now this job."
All I could think about were these catastrophes. One after another.
How well I was able to handle them.
Where the hell is Kestrel?
We thought they were with you...
But I had a breaking point like everyone else.

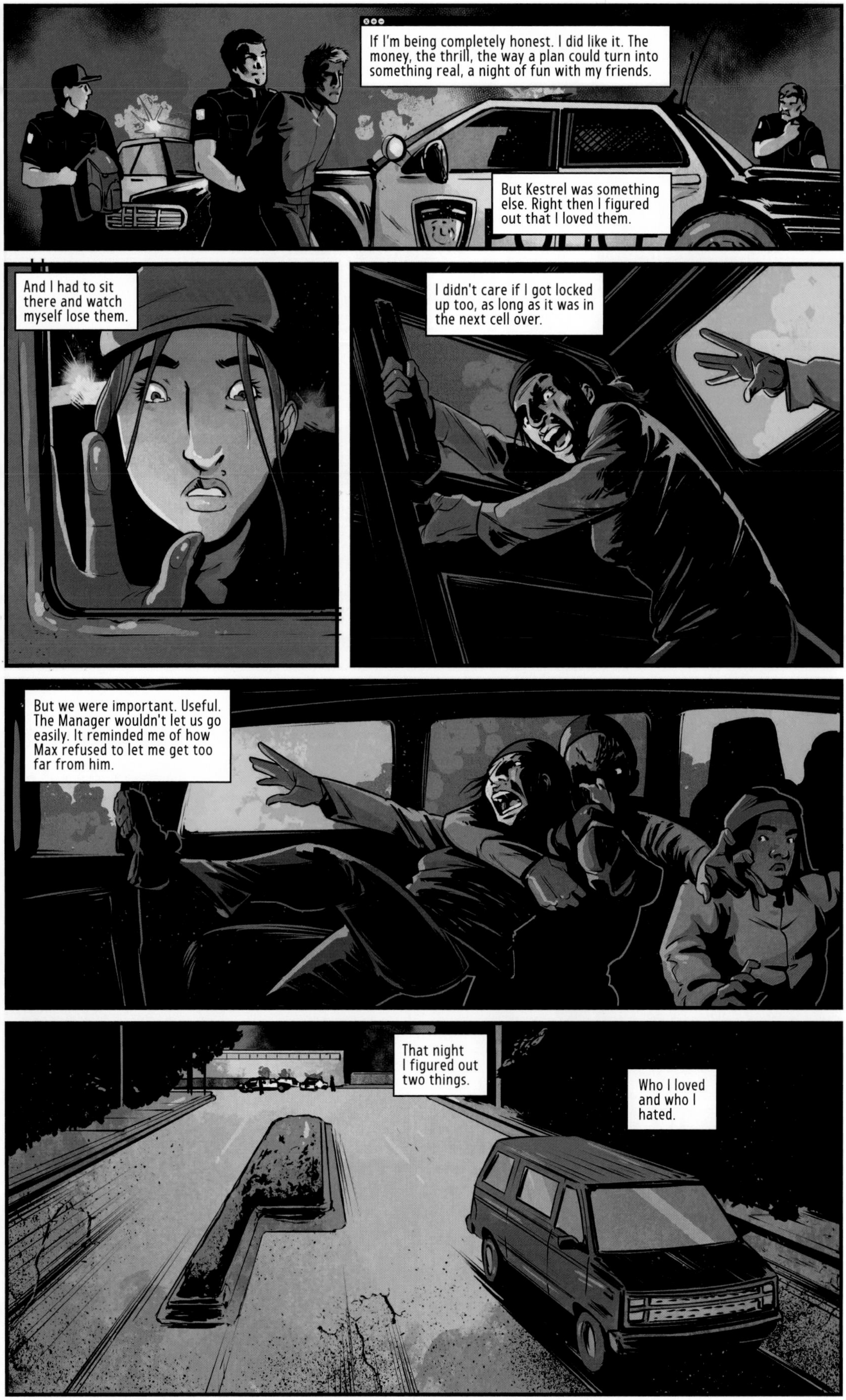
If I'm being completely honest. I did like it. The money, the thrill, the way a plan could turn into something real, a night of fun with my friends.
But Kestrel was something else. Right then I figured out that I loved them.
And I had to sit there and watch myself lose them.
I didn't care if I got locked up too, as long as it was in the next cell over.
But we were important. Useful. The Manager wouldn't let us go easily. It reminded me of how Max refused to let me get too far from him.
That night I figured out two things.
Who I loved and who I hated.

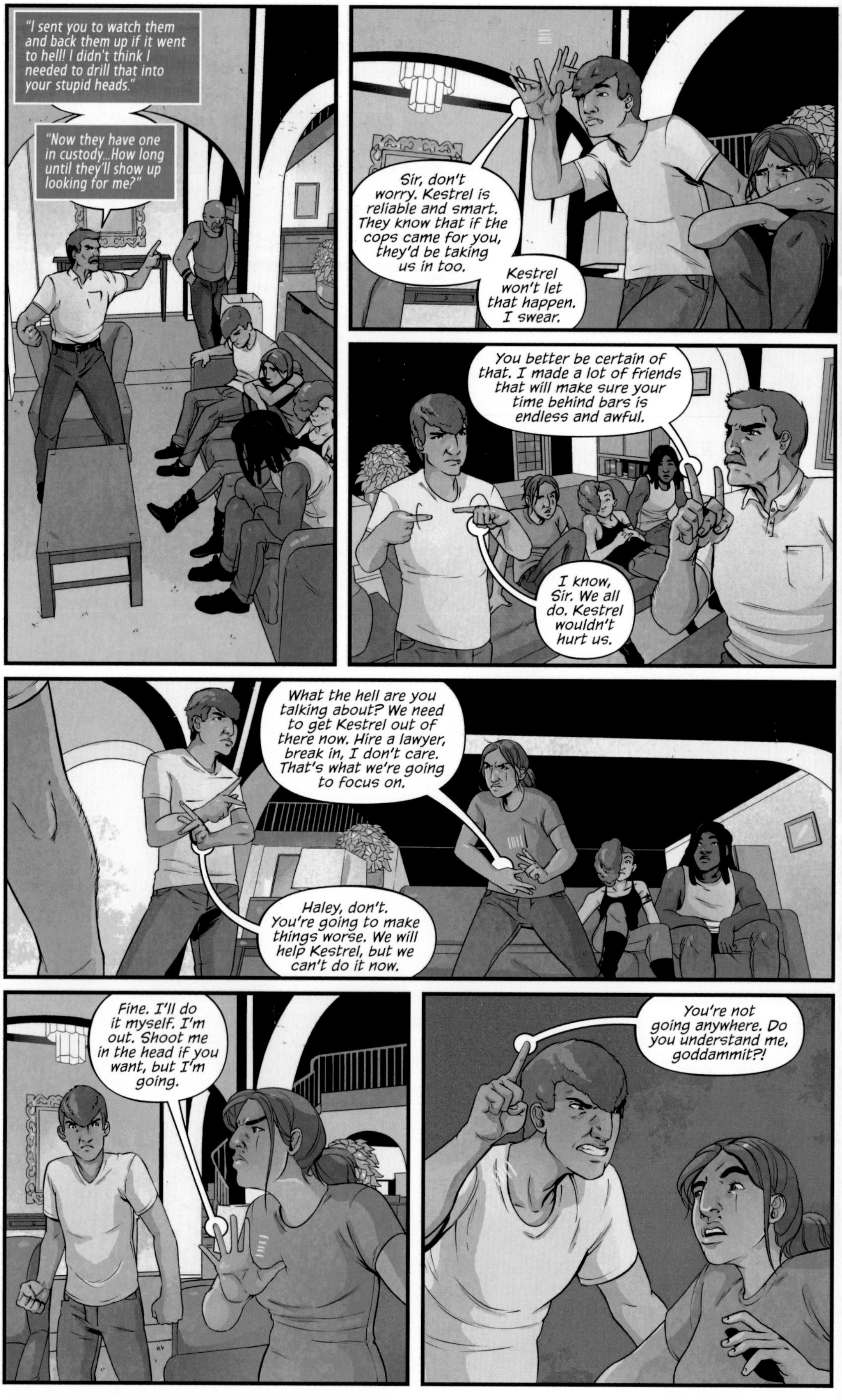
"I sent you to watch them and back them up if it went to hell! I didn't think I needed to drill that into your stupid heads."
"Now they have one in custody...How long until they'll show up looking for me?"
Sir, don't worry. Kestrel is reliable and smart. They know that if the cops came for you, they'd be taking us in too.
Kestrel won't let that happen. I swear.
You better be certain of that. I made a lot of friends that will make sure your time behind bars is endless and awful.
I know, Sir. We all do. Kestrel wouldn't hurt us.
What the hell are you talking about? We need to get Kestrel out of there now. Hire a lawyer, break in, I don't care. That's what we're going to focus on.
Haley, don't. You're going to make things worse. We will help Kestrel, but we can't do it now.
Fine. I'll do it myself. I'm out. Shoot me in the head if you want, but I'm going.
You're not going anywhere. Do you understand me, goddammit?!

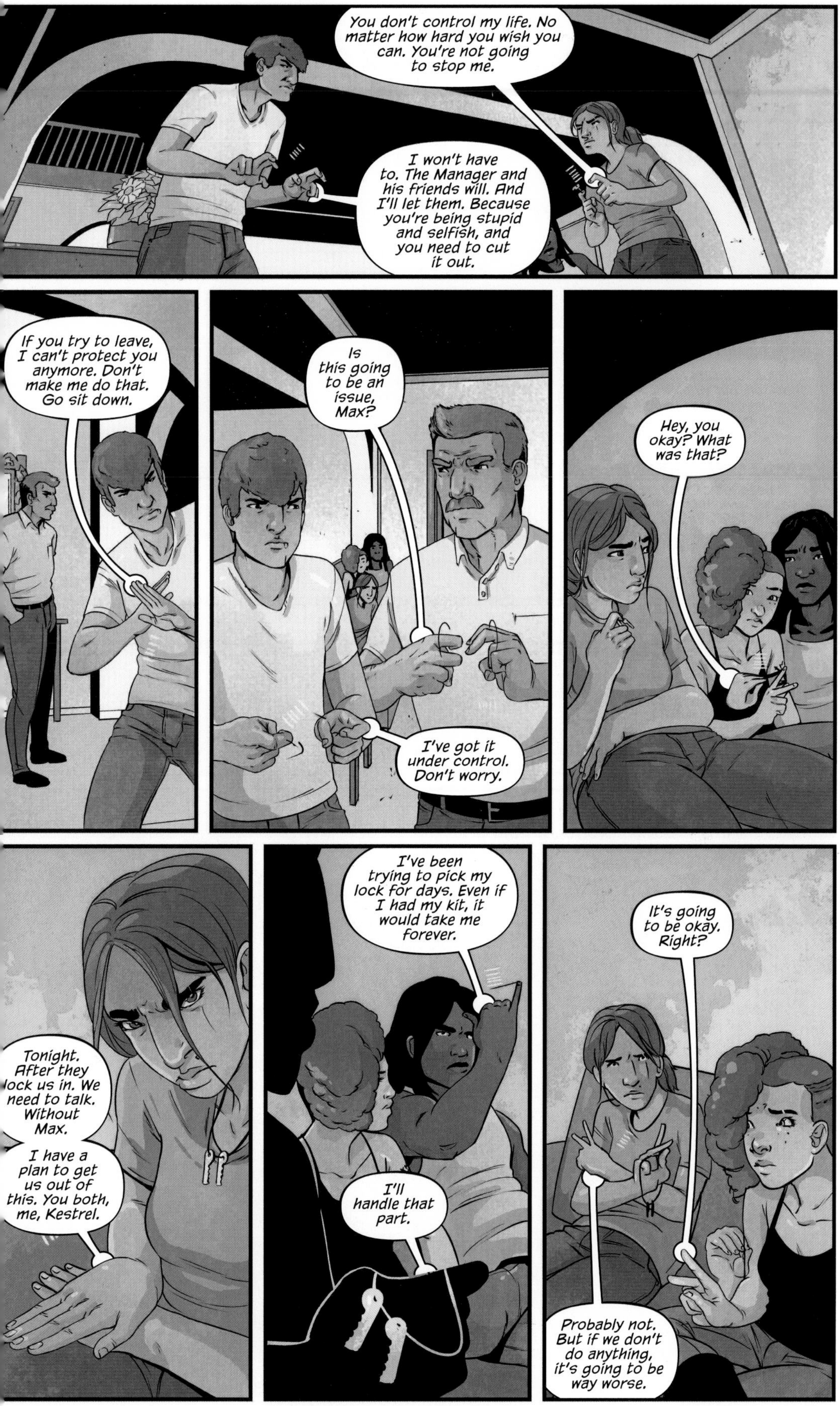
You don't control my life. No matter how hard you wish you can. You're not going to stop me.
I won't have to. The Manager and his friends will. And I'll let them. Because you're being stupid and selfish, and you need to cut it out.
If you try to leave, I can't protect you anymore. Don't make me do that. Go sit down.
Is this going to be an issue, Max?
I've got it under control. Don't worry.
Hey, you okay? What was that?
Tonight. After they lock us in. We need to talk. Without Max.
I have a plan to get us out of this. You both, me, Kestrel.
I've been trying to pick my lock for days. Even if I had my kit, it would take me forever.
I'll handle that part.
It's going to be okay. Right?
Probably not. But if we don't do anything, it's going to be way worse.

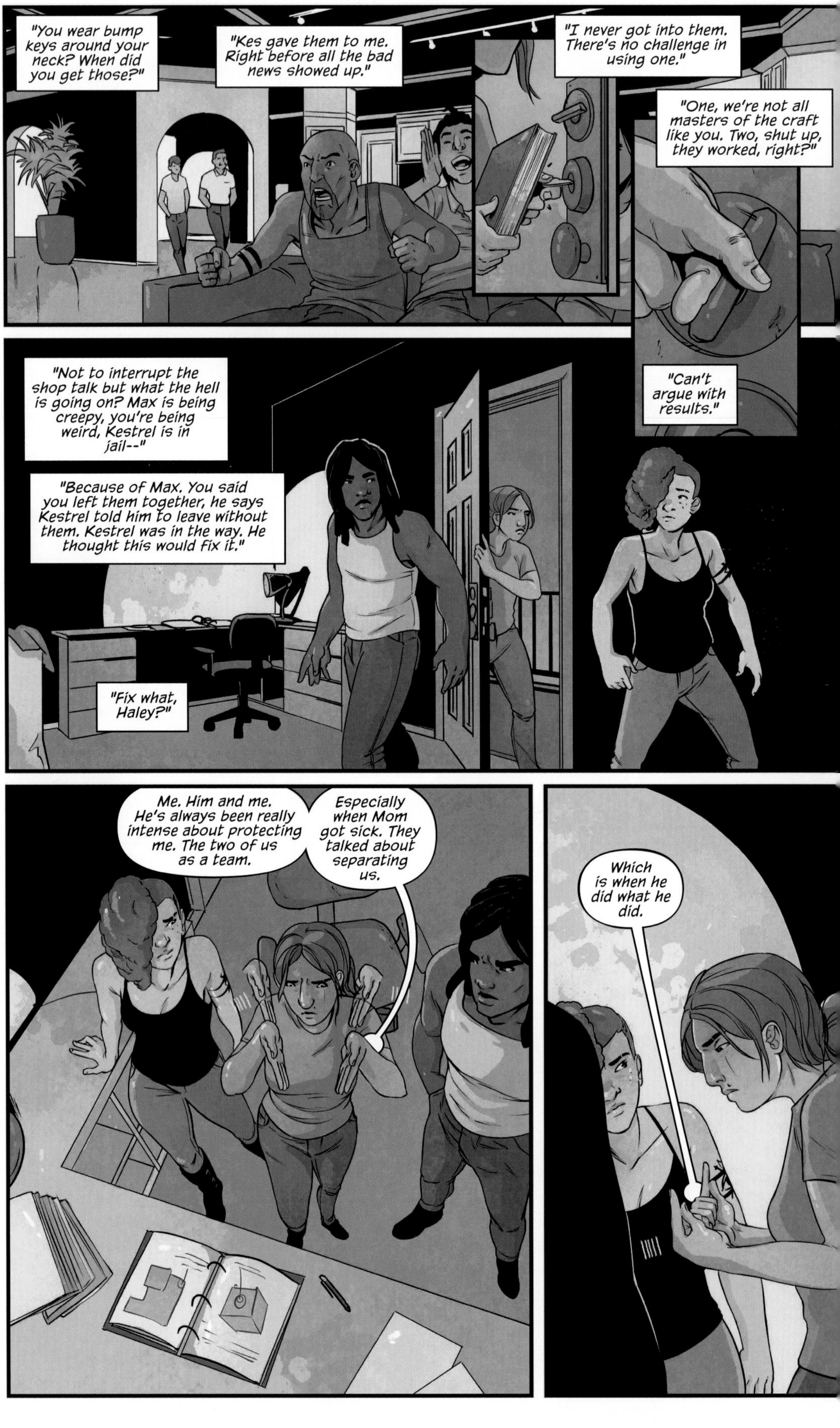
"You wear bump keys around your neck? When did you get those?"
"Kes gave them to me. Right before all the bad news showed up."
"I never got into them. There's no challenge in using one."
"One, we're not all masters of the craft like you. Two, shut up, they worked, right?"
"Can't argue with results."
"Not to interrupt the shop talk but what the hell is going on? Max is being creepy, you're being weird, Kestrel is in jail--"
"Because of Max. You said you left them together, he says Kestrel told him to leave without them. Kestrel was in the way. He thought this would fix it."
"Fix what, Haley?"
Me. Him and me. He's always been really intense about protecting me. The two of us as a team.
Especially when Mom got sick. They talked about separating us.
Which is when he did what he did.

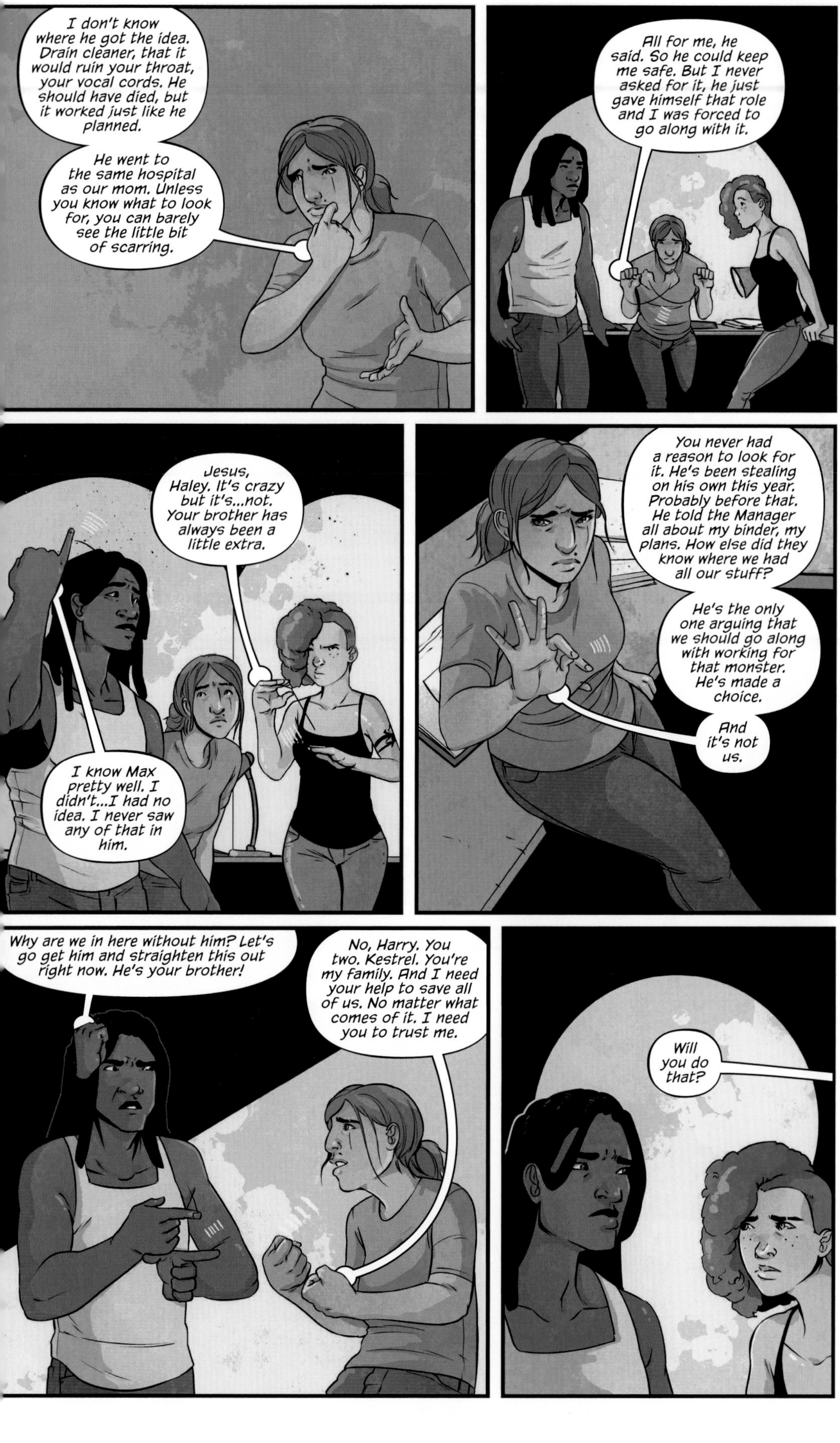
I don't know where he got the idea. Drain cleaner, that it would ruin your throat, your vocal cords. He should have died, but it worked just like he planned.
He went to the same hospital as our mom. Unless you know what to look for, you can barely see the little bit of scarring.
All for me, he said. So he could keep me safe. But I never asked for it, he just gave himself that role and I was forced to go along with it.
Jesus, Haley. It's crazy but it's...not. Your brother has always been a little extra.
I know Max pretty well. I didn't...I had no idea. I never saw any of that in him.
You never had a reason to look for it. He's been stealing on his own this year. Probably before that. He told the Manager all about my binder, my plans. How else did they know where we had all our stuff?
He's the only one arguing that we should go along with working for that monster. He's made a choice.
And it's not us.
Why are we in here without him? Let's go get him and straighten this out right now. He's your brother!
No, Harry. You two. Kestrel. You're my family. And I need your help to save all of us. No matter what comes of it. I need you to trust me.
Will you do that?

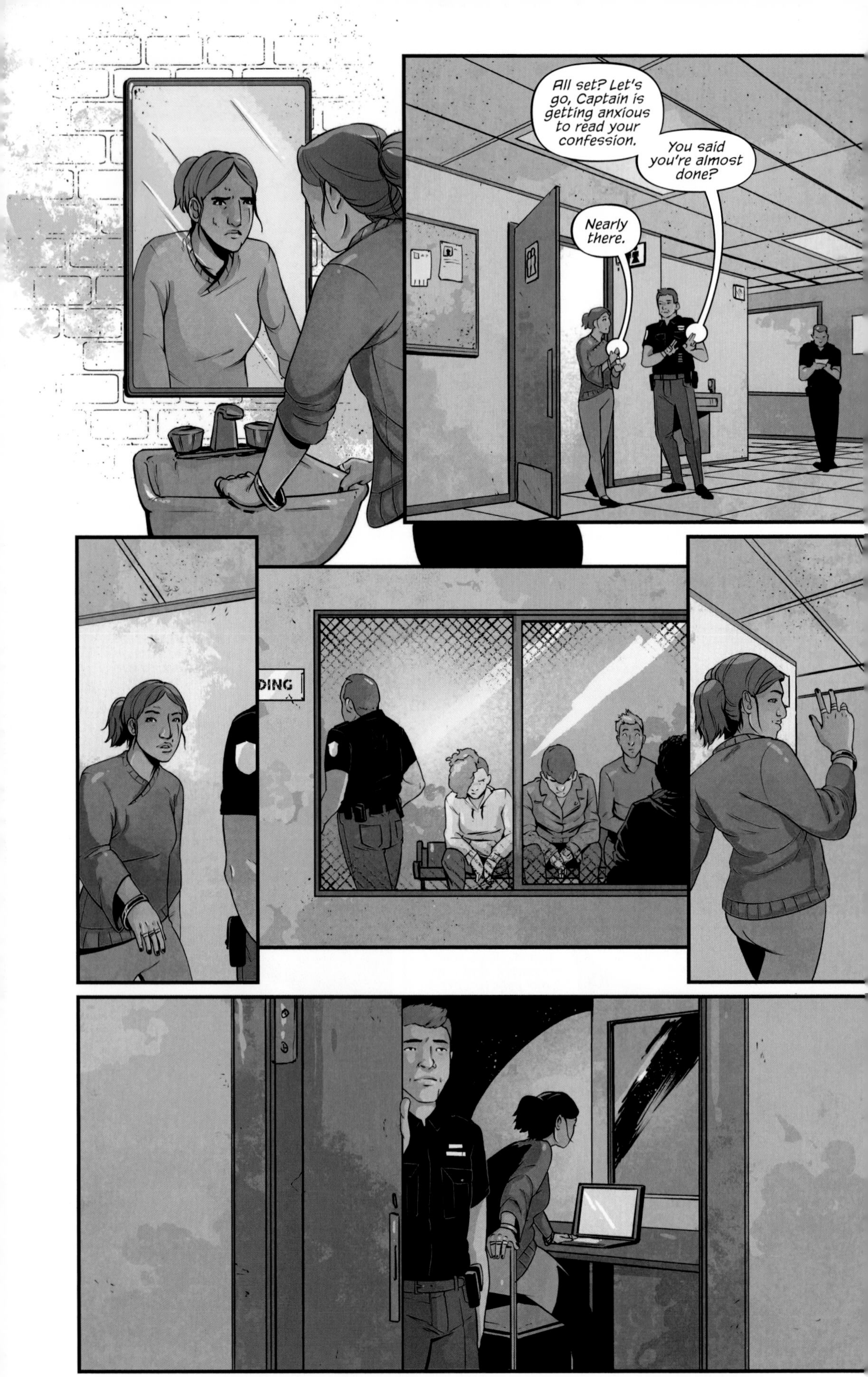
All set? Let's go, Captain is getting anxious to read your confession.
You said you're almost done?
Nearly there.
DING

CHAPTER SIX

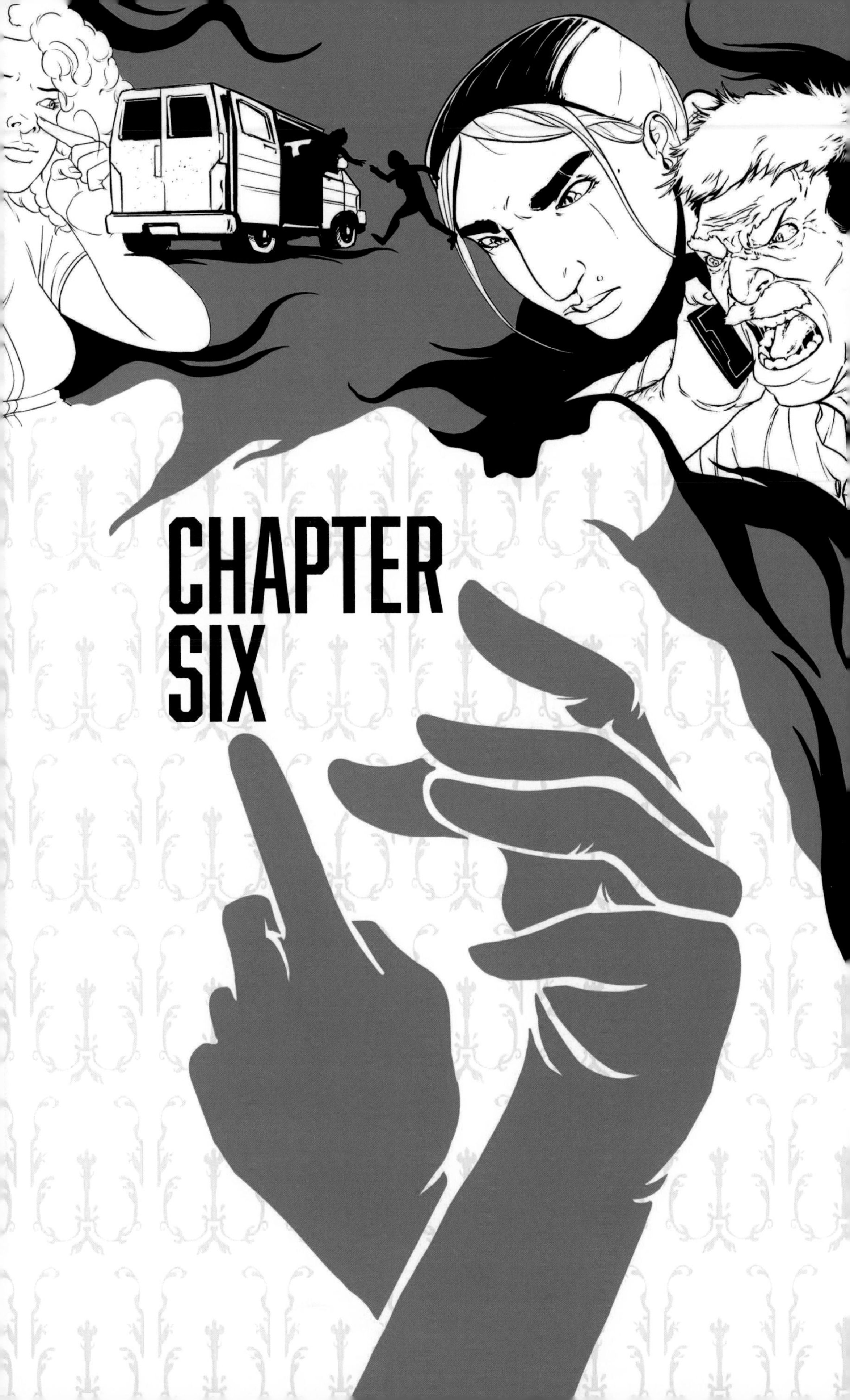

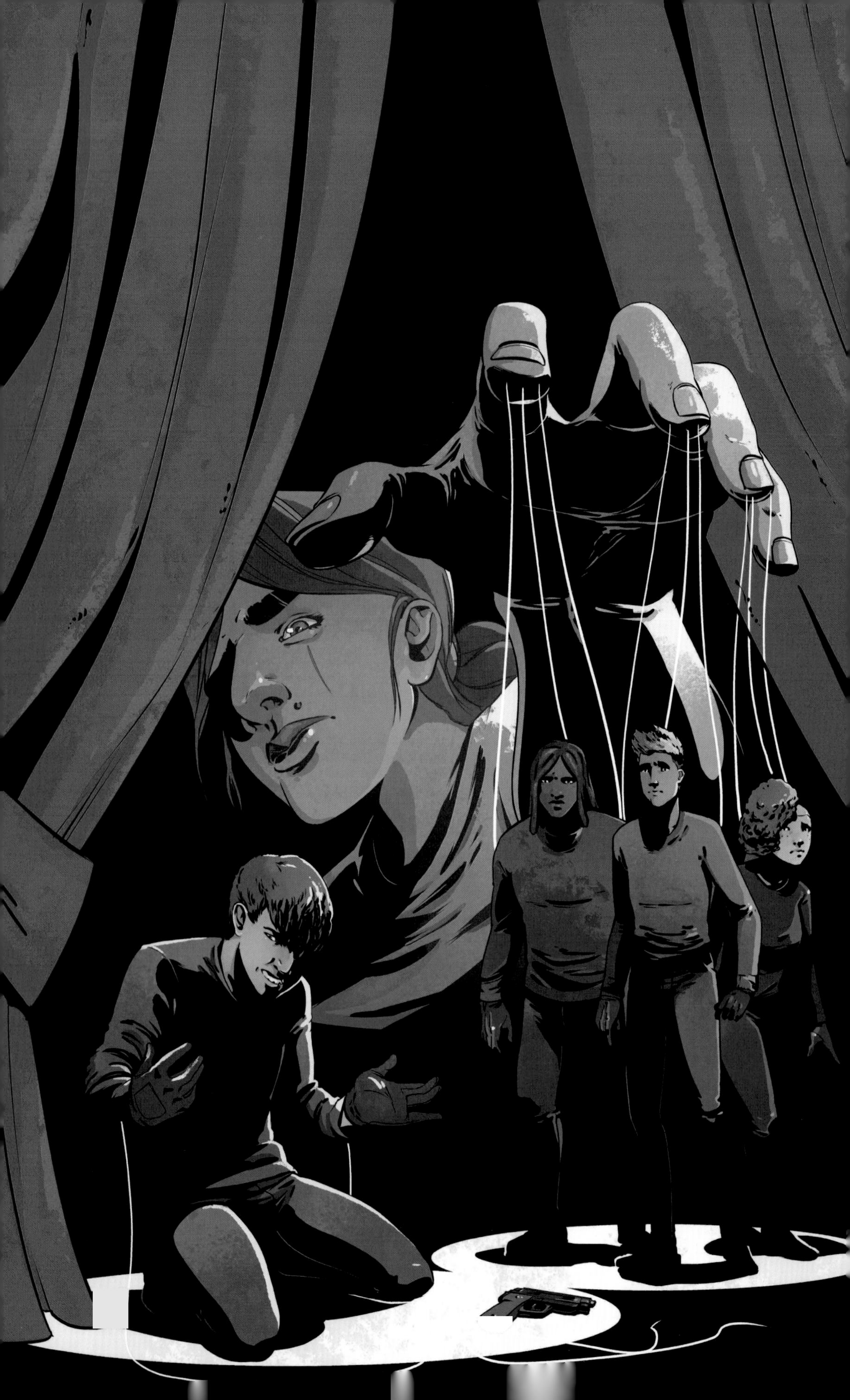

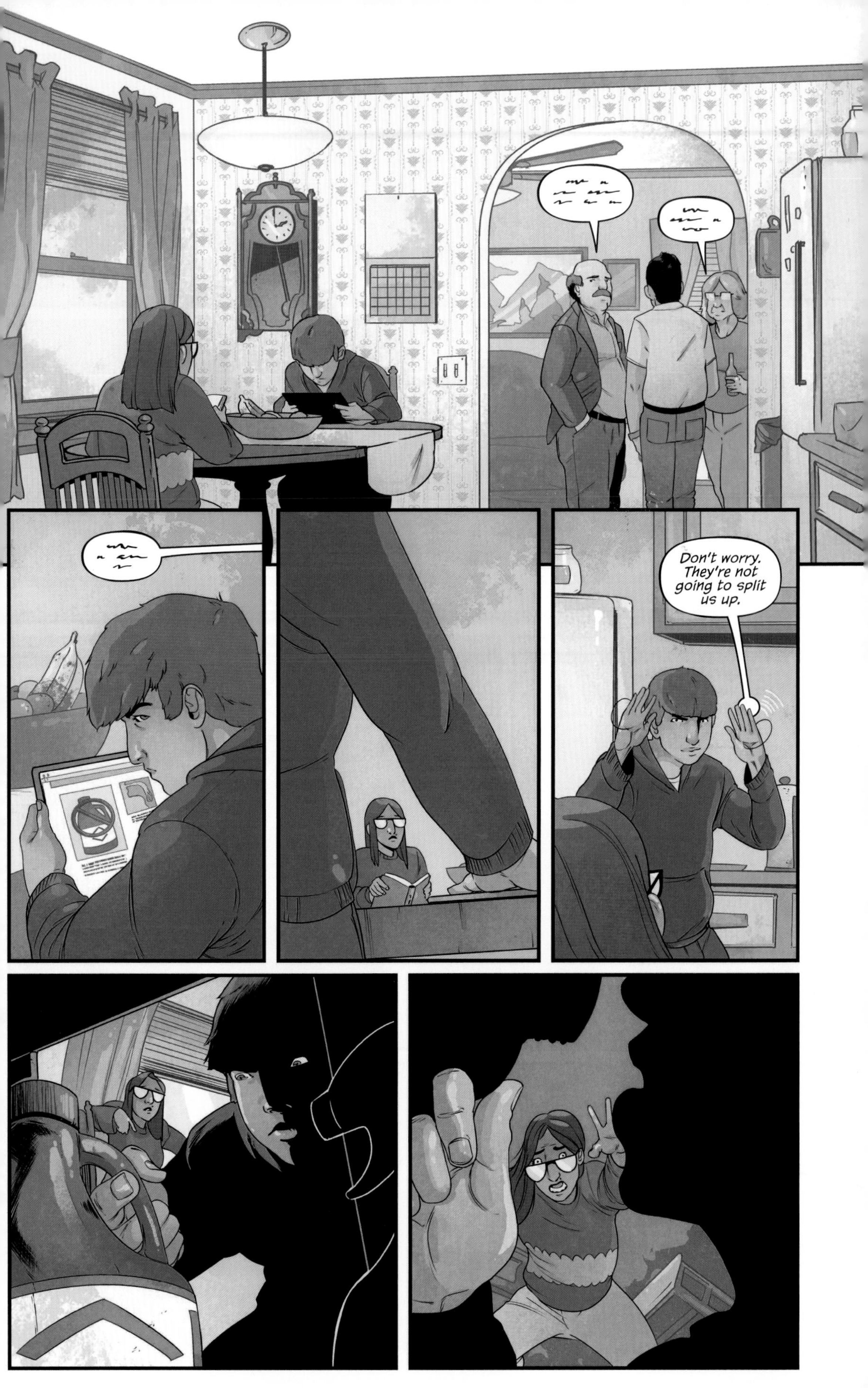
Don't worry. They're not going to split us up.

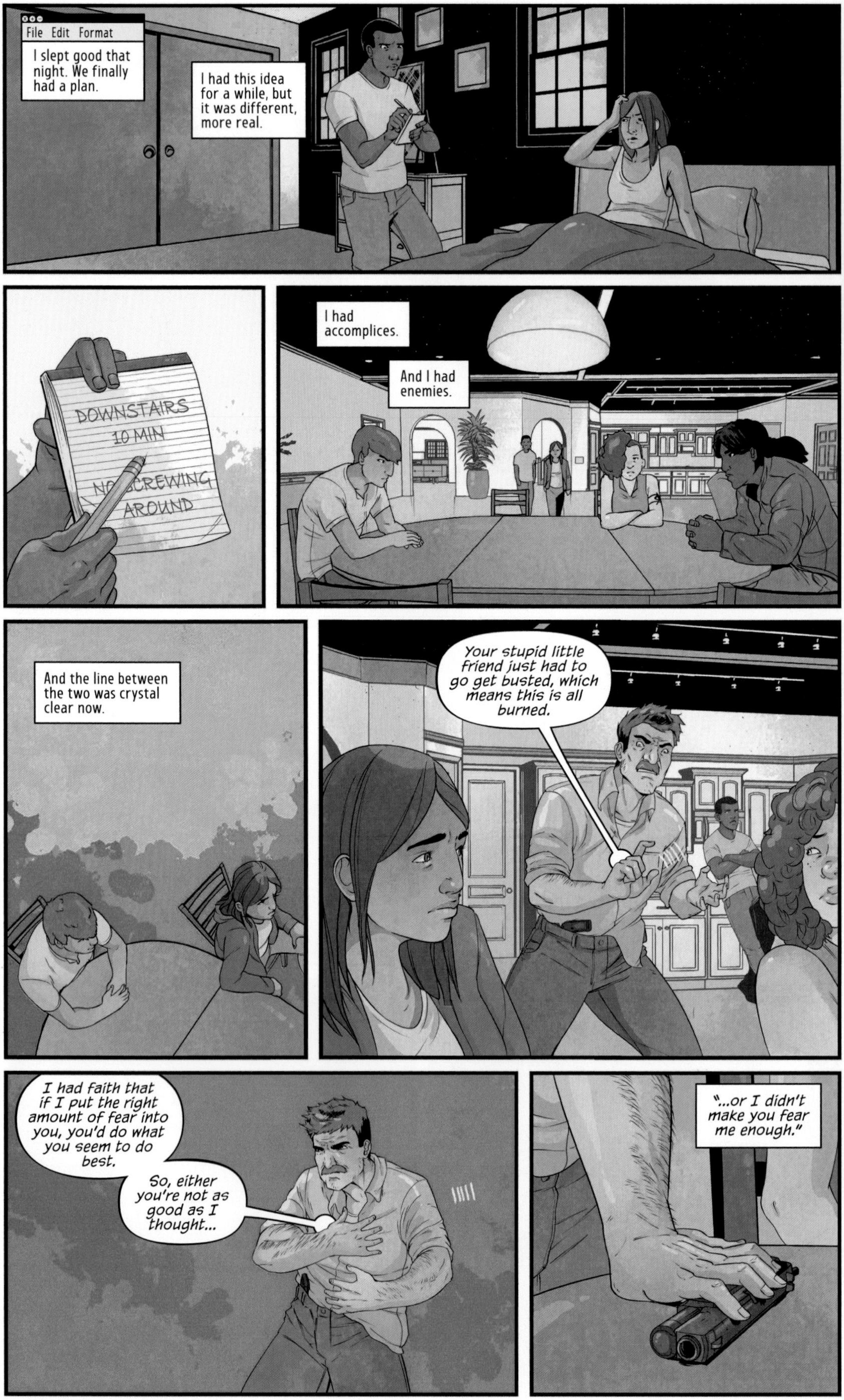
File Edit Format
I slept good that night. We finally had a plan.
I had this idea for a while, but it was different, more real.
DOWNSTAIRS 10 MIN
NO SCREWING AROUND
I had accomplices.
And I had enemies.
And the line between the two was crystal clear now.
Your stupid little friend just had to go get busted, which means this is all burned.
I had faith that if I put the right amount of fear into you, you'd do what you seem to do best.
So, either you're not as good as I thought...
"...or I didn't make you fear me enough."

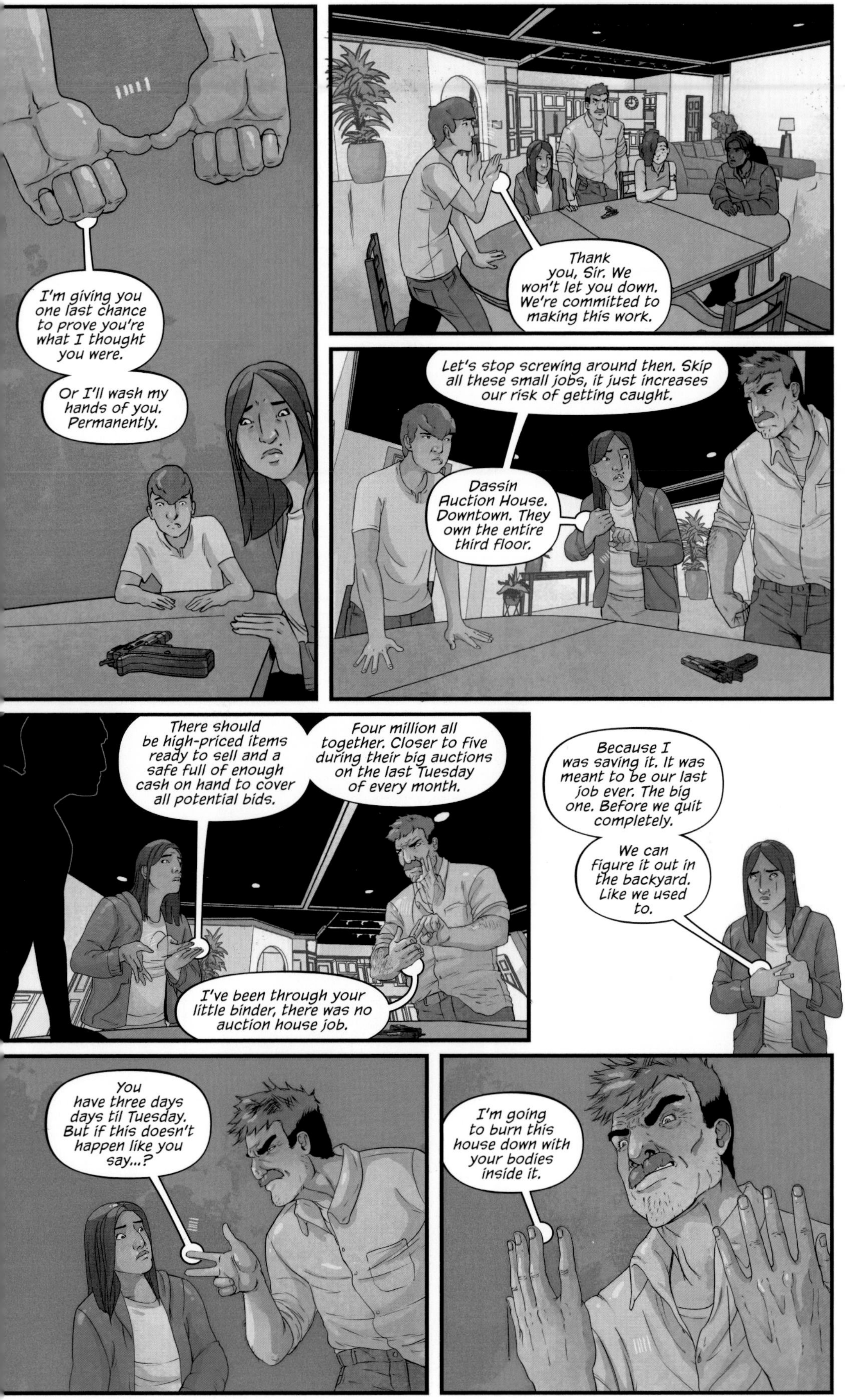
I'm giving you one last chance to prove you're what I thought you were.
Or I'll wash my hands of you. Permanently.
Thank you, Sir. We won't let you down. We're committed to making this work.
Let's stop screwing around then. Skip all these small jobs, it just increases our risk of getting caught.
Dassin Auction House. Downtown. They own the entire third floor.
There should be high-priced items ready to sell and a safe full of enough cash on hand to cover all potential bids.
Four million all together. Closer to five during their big auctions on the last Tuesday of every month.
I've been through your little binder, there was no auction house job.
Because I was saving it. It was meant to be our last job ever. The big one. Before we quit completely.
We can figure it out in the backyard. Like we used to.
You have three days days til Tuesday. But if this doesn't happen like you say...?
I'm going to burn this house down with your bodies inside it.

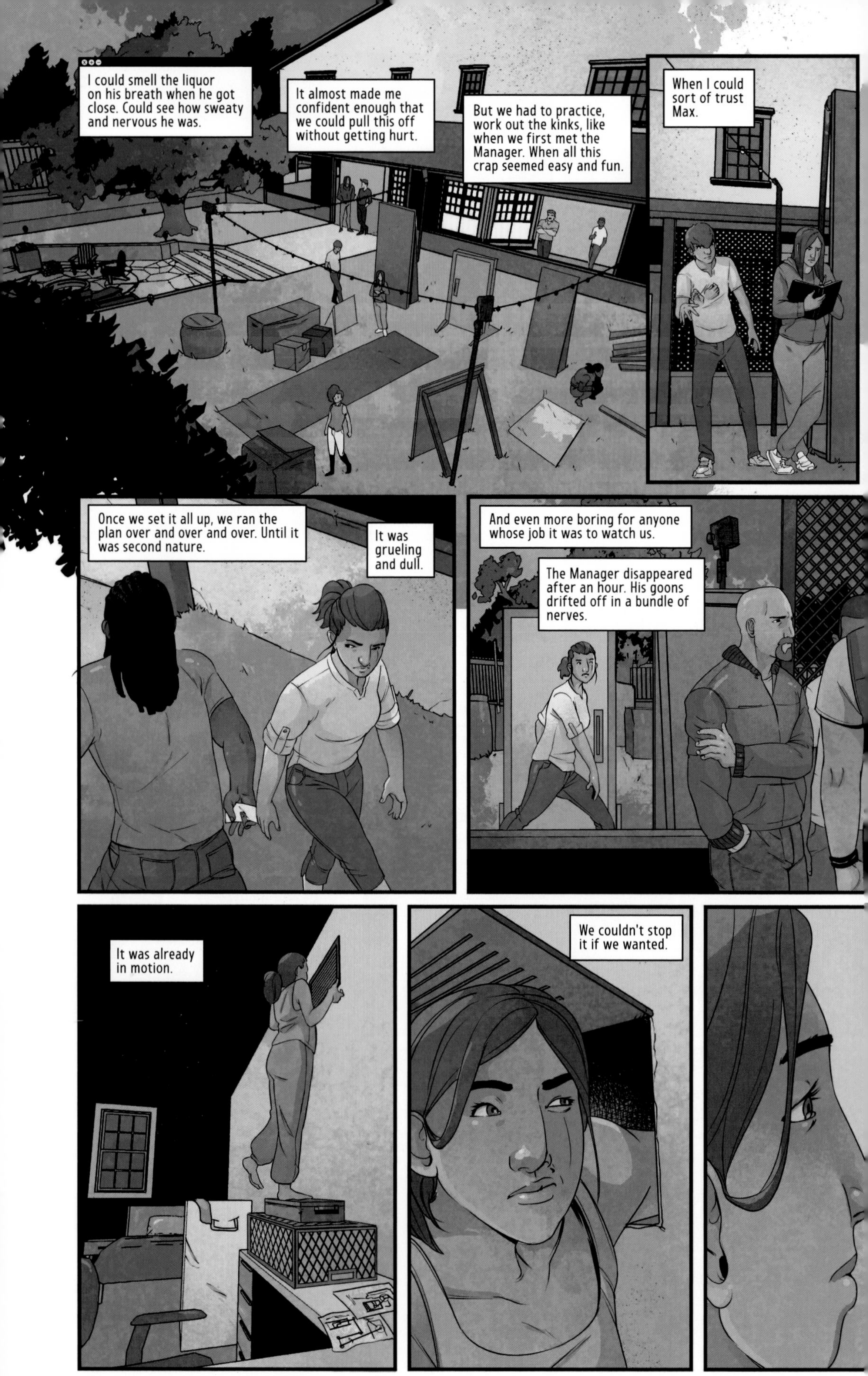
I could smell the liquor on his breath when he got close. Could see how sweaty and nervous he was.
It almost made me confident enough that we could pull this off without getting hurt.
But we had to practice, work out the kinks, like when we first met the Manager. When all this crap seemed easy and fun.
When I could sort of trust Max.
Once we set it all up, we ran the plan over and over and over. Until it was second nature.
It was grueling and dull.
And even more boring for anyone whose job it was to watch us.
The Manager disappeared after an hour. His goons drifted off in a bundle of nerves.
It was already in motion.
We couldn't stop it if we wanted.

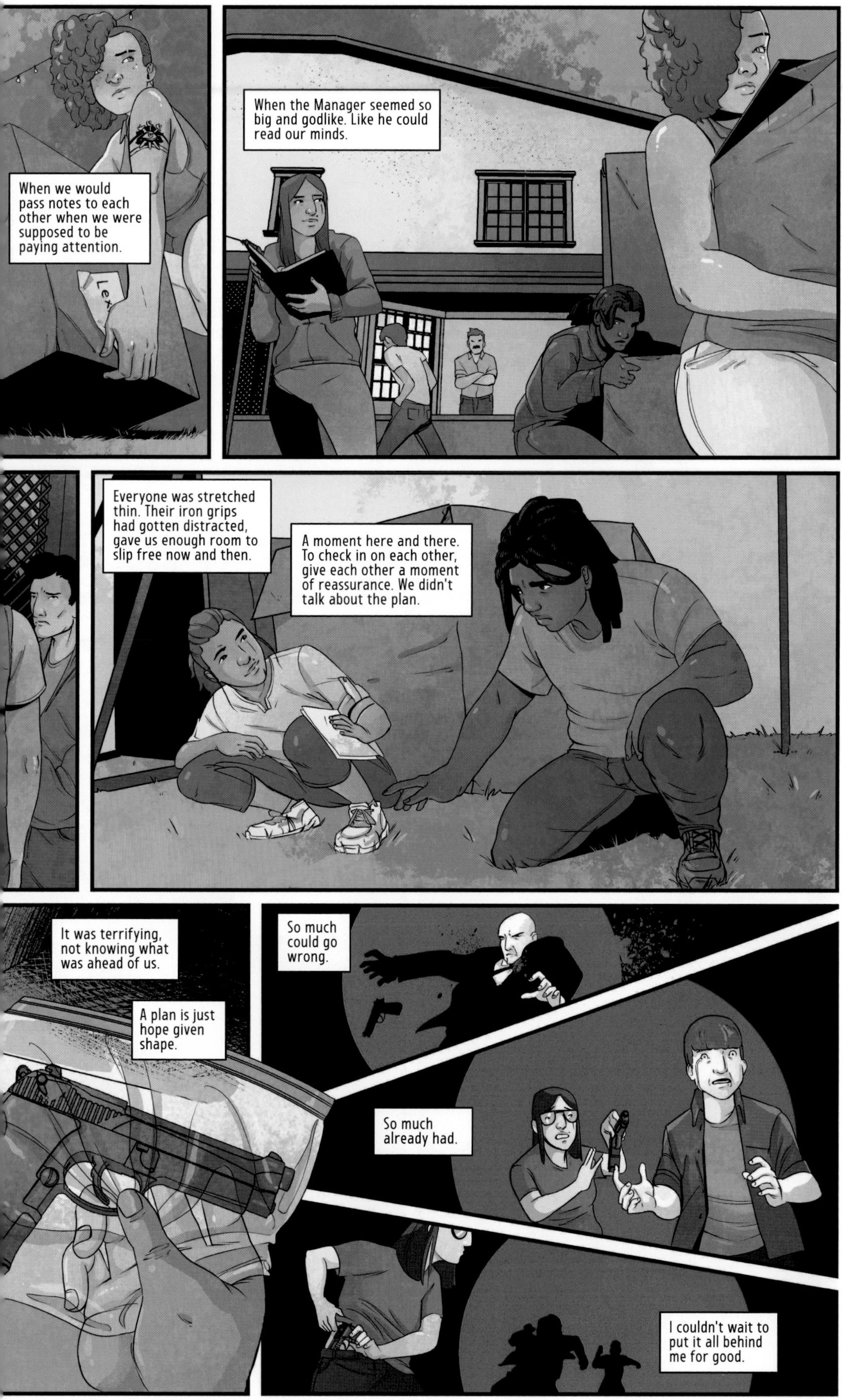
When we would pass notes to each other when we were supposed to be paying attention.
Lex
When the Manager seemed so big and godlike. Like he could read our minds.
Everyone was stretched thin. Their iron grips had gotten distracted, gave us enough room to slip free now and then.
A moment here and there. To check in on each other, give each other a moment of reassurance. We didn't talk about the plan.
It was terrifying, not knowing what was ahead of us.
A plan is just hope given shape.
So much could go wrong.
So much already had.
I couldn't wait to put it all behind me for good.

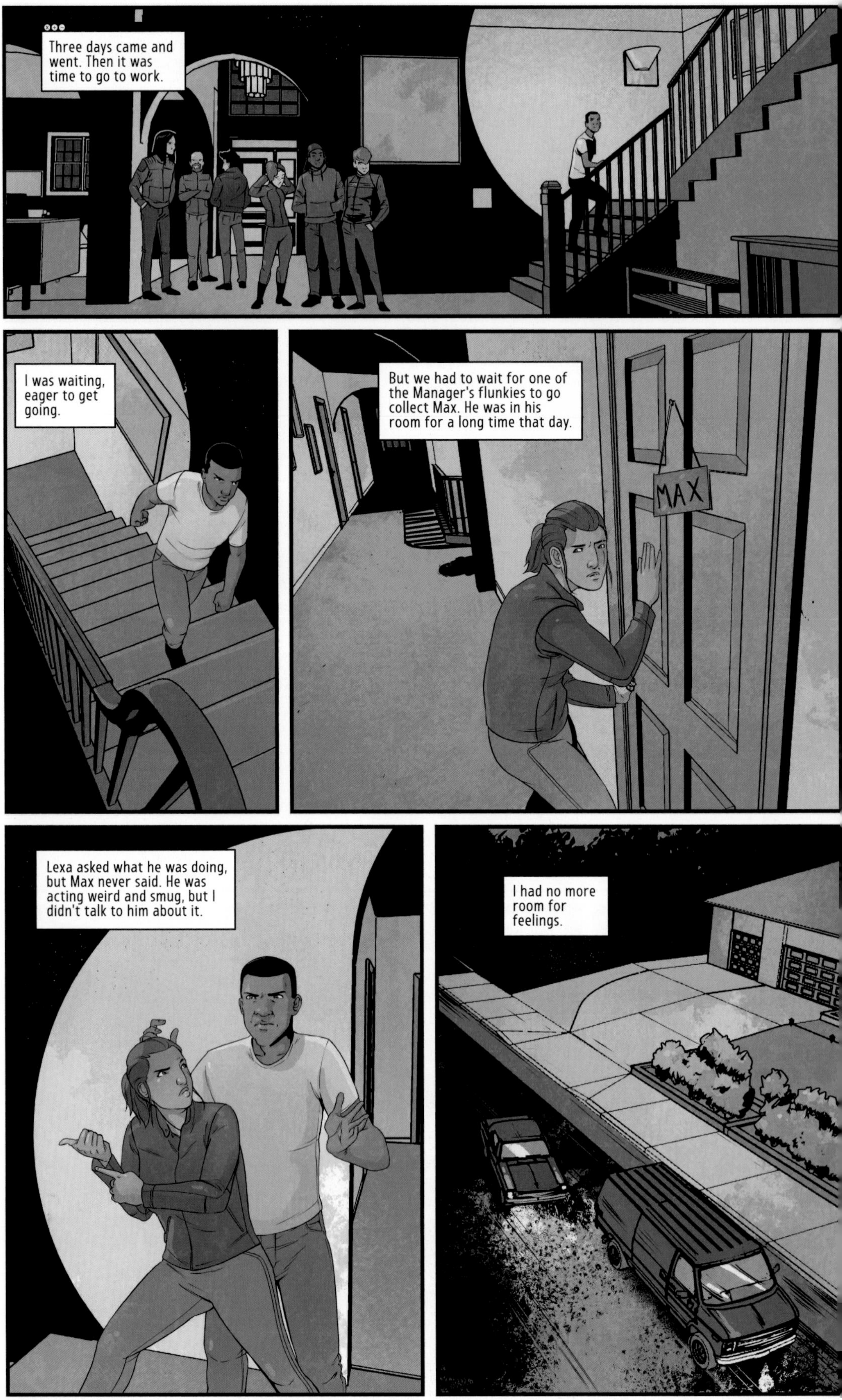
Three days came and went. Then it was time to go to work.
I was waiting, eager to get going.
But we had to wait for one of the Manager's flunkies to go collect Max. He was in his room for a long time that day.
MAX
Lexa asked what he was doing, but Max never said. He was acting weird and smug, but I didn't talk to him about it.
I had no more room for feelings.

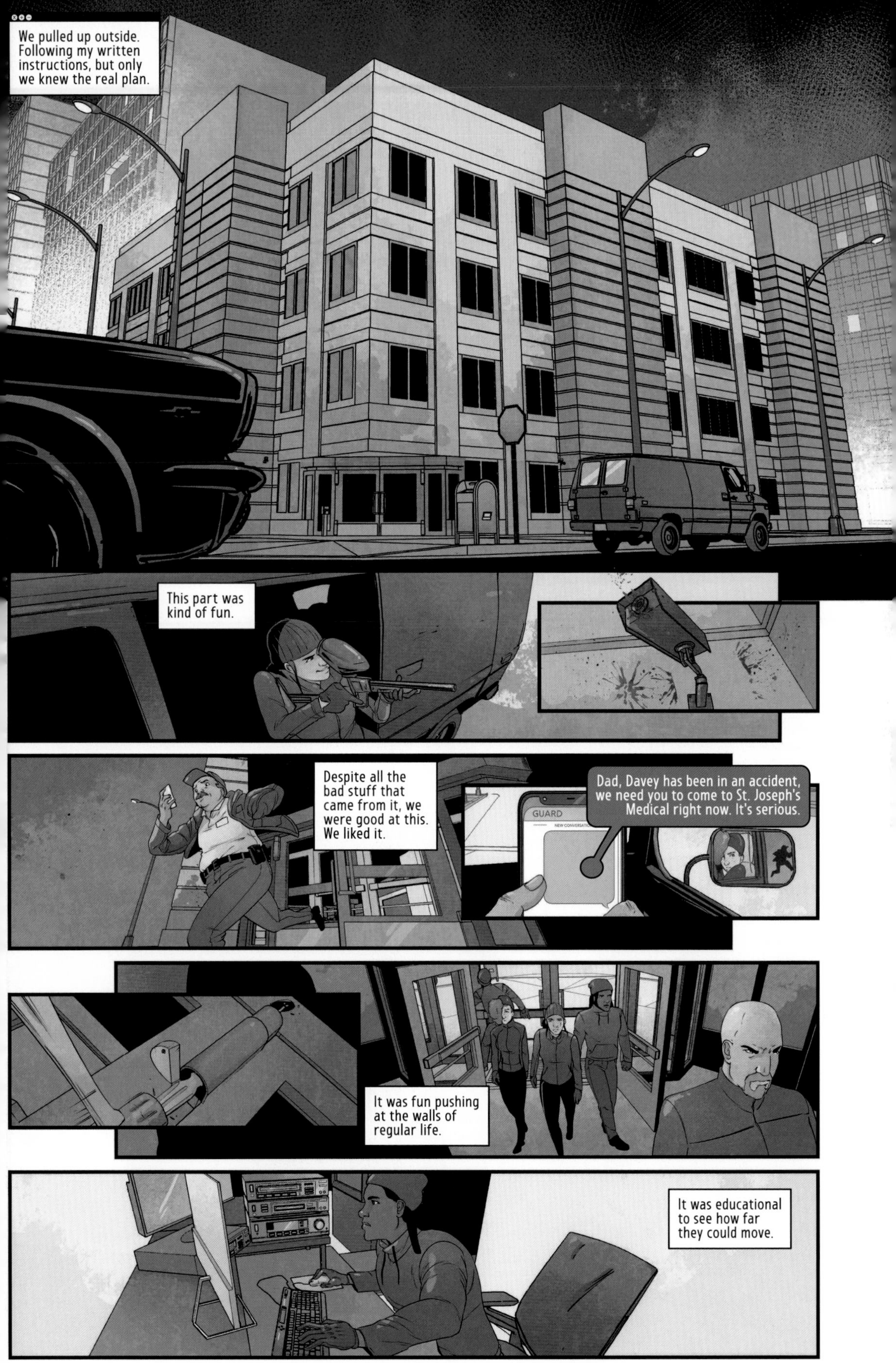
We pulled up outside. Following my written instructions, but only we knew the real plan.
This part was kind of fun.
Despite all the bad stuff that came from it, we were good at this. We liked it.
GUARD
Dad, Davey has been in an accident, we need you to come to St. Joseph's Medical right now. It's serious.
It was fun pushing at the walls of regular life.
It was educational to see how far they could move.

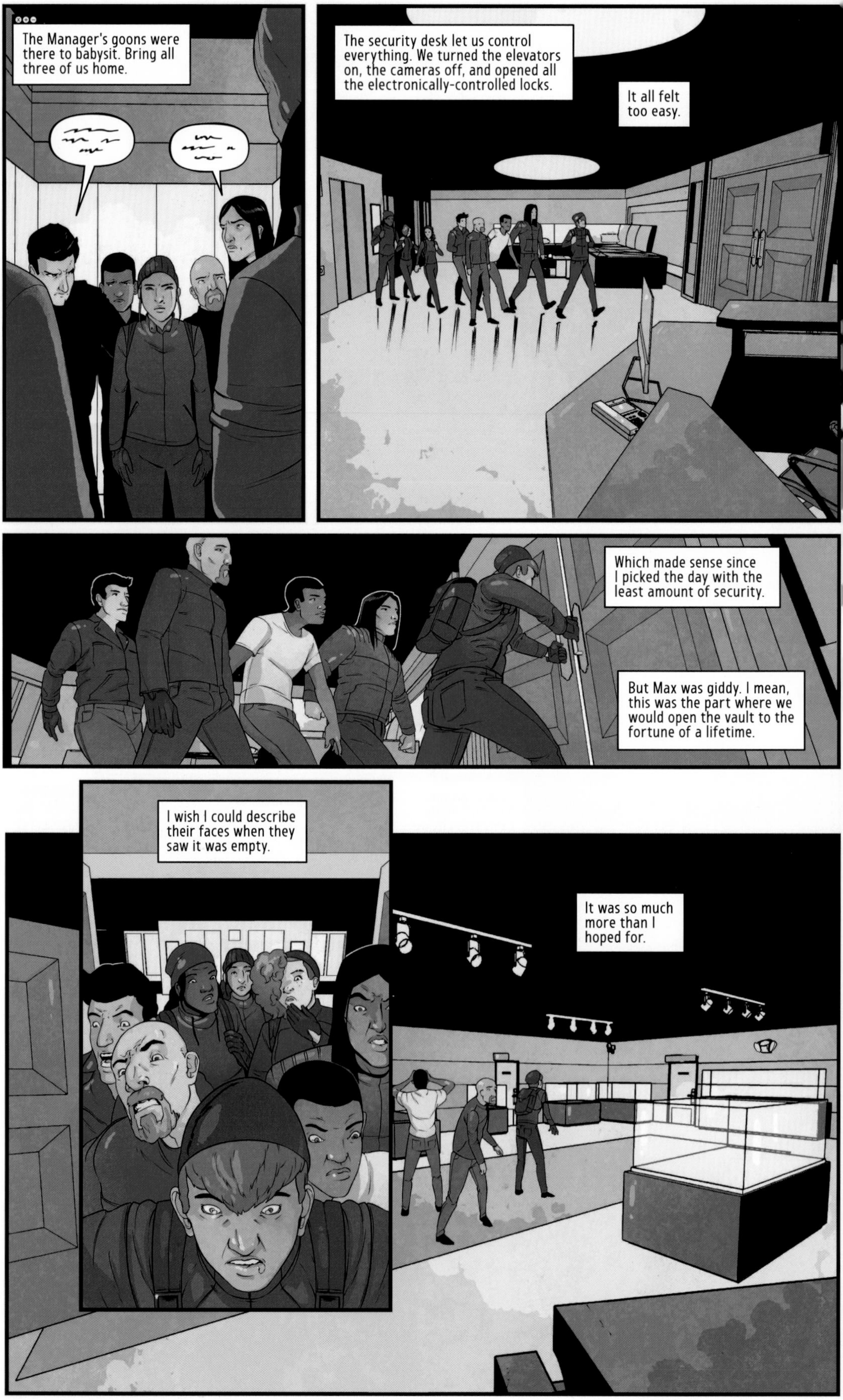
The Manager's goons were there to babysit. Bring all three of us home.
The security desk let us control everything. We turned the elevators on, the cameras off, and opened all the electronically-controlled locks.
It all felt too easy.
Which made sense since I picked the day with the least amount of security.
But Max was giddy. I mean, this was the part where we would open the vault to the fortune of a lifetime.
I wish I could describe their faces when they saw it was empty.
It was so much more than I hoped for.

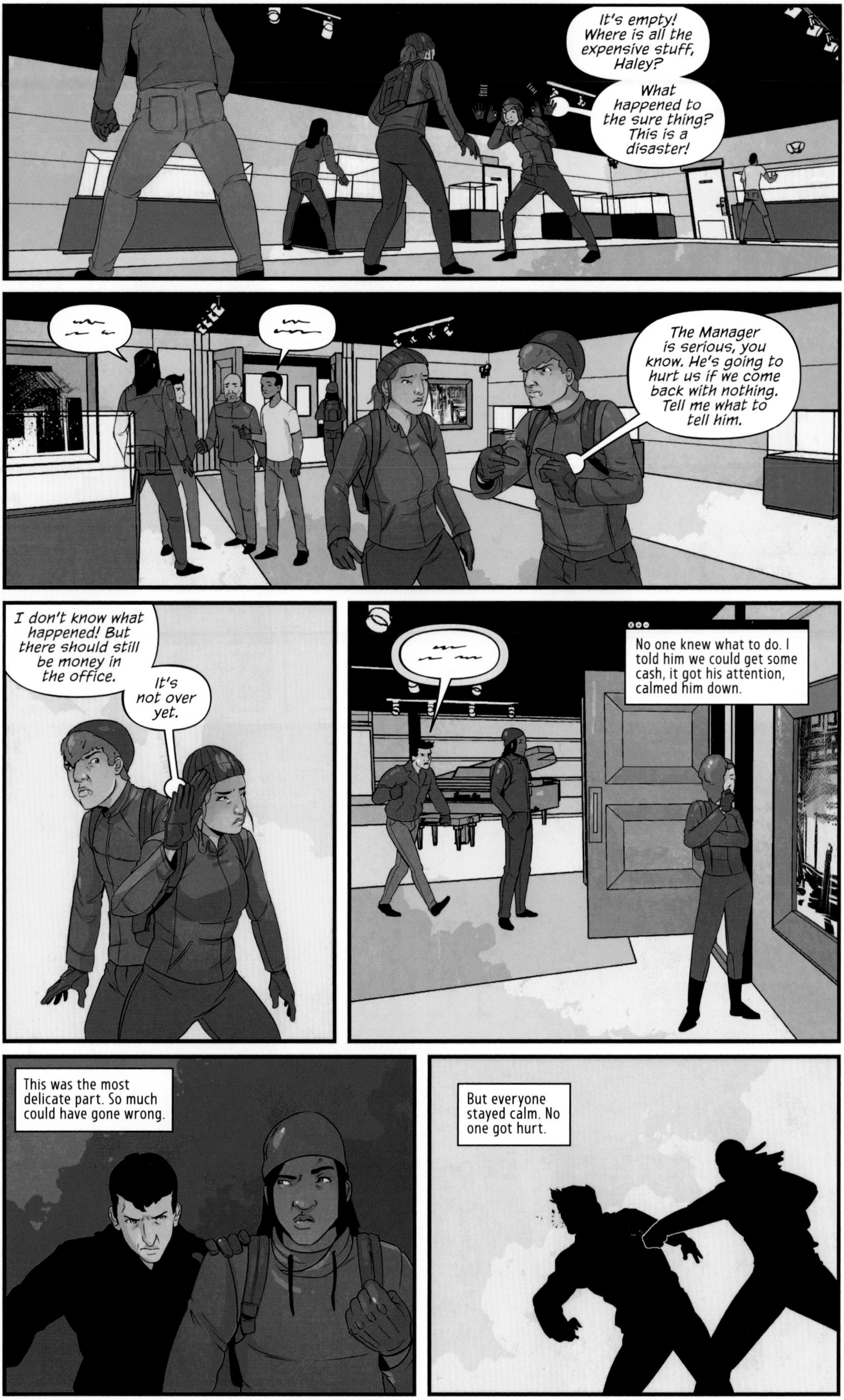
It's empty! Where is all the expensive stuff, Haley?
What happened to the sure thing? This is a disaster!
The Manager is serious, you know. He's going to hurt us if we come back with nothing. Tell me what to tell him.
I don't know what happened! But there should still be money in the office.
It's not over yet.
No one knew what to do. I told him we could get some cash, it got his attention, calmed him down.
This was the most delicate part. So much could have gone wrong.
But everyone stayed calm. No one got hurt.

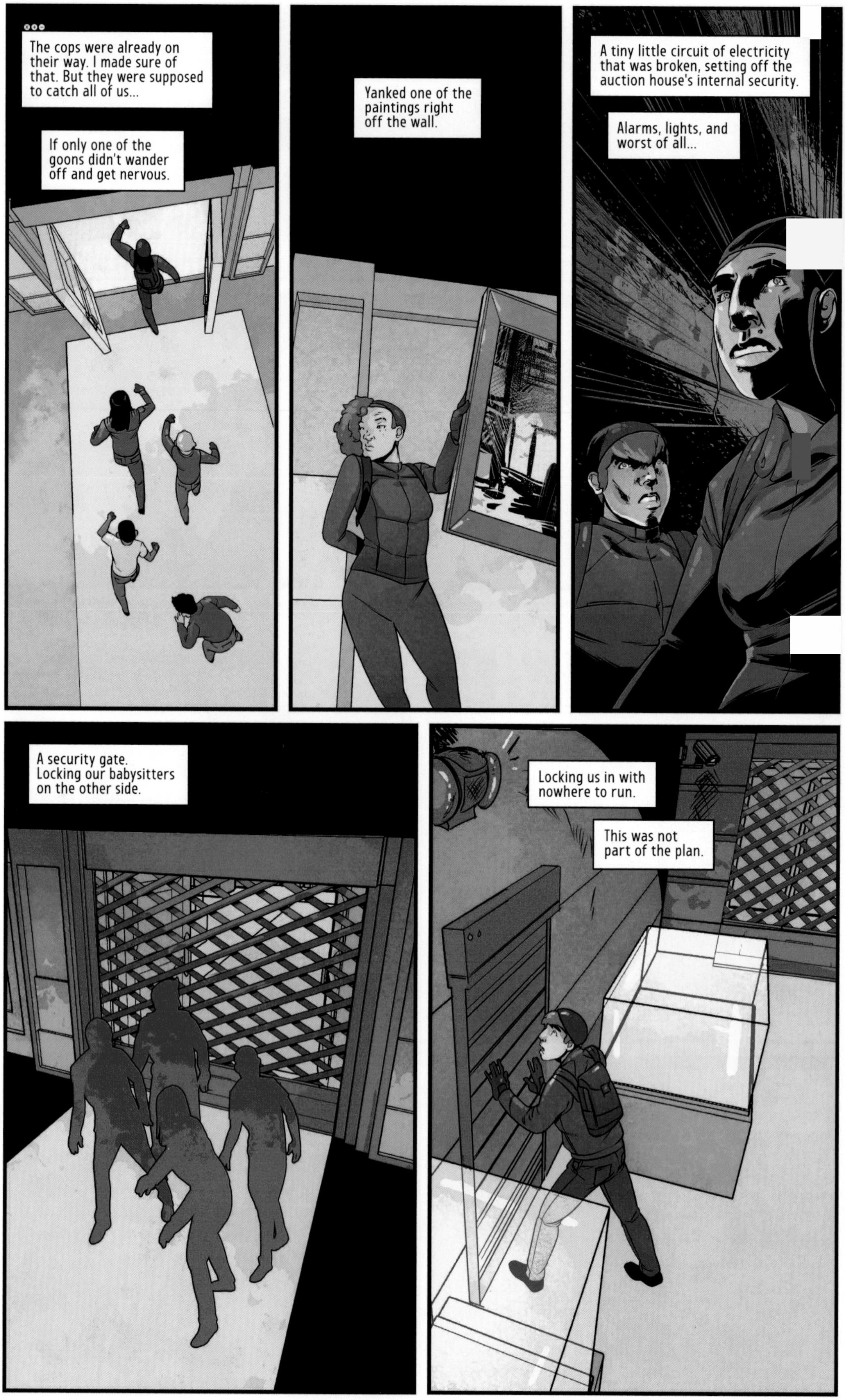
The cops were already on their way. I made sure of that. But they were supposed to catch all of us...
If only one of the goons didn't wander off and get nervous.
Yanked one of the paintings right off the wall.
A tiny little circuit of electricity that was broken, setting off the auction house's internal security.
Alarms, lights, and worst of all...
A security gate. Locking our babysitters on the other side.
Locking us in with nowhere to run.
This was not part of the plan.

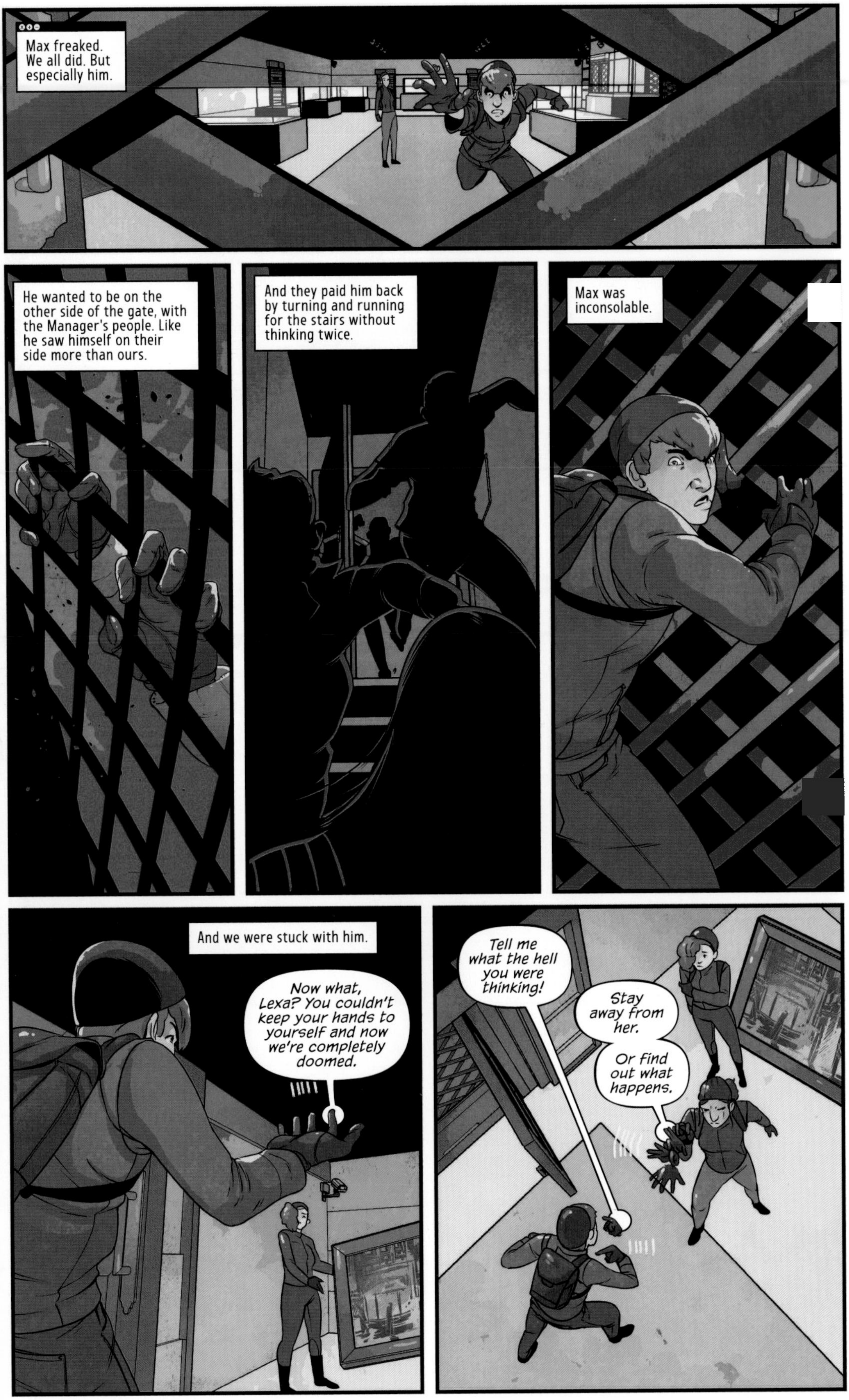
Max freaked. We all did. But especially him.
He wanted to be on the other side of the gate, with the Manager's people. Like he saw himself on their side more than ours.
And they paid him back by turning and running for the stairs without thinking twice.
Max was inconsolable.
And we were stuck with him.
Now what, Lexa? You couldn't keep your hands to yourself and now we're completely doomed.
Tell me what the hell you were thinking!
Stay away from her.
Or find out what happens.

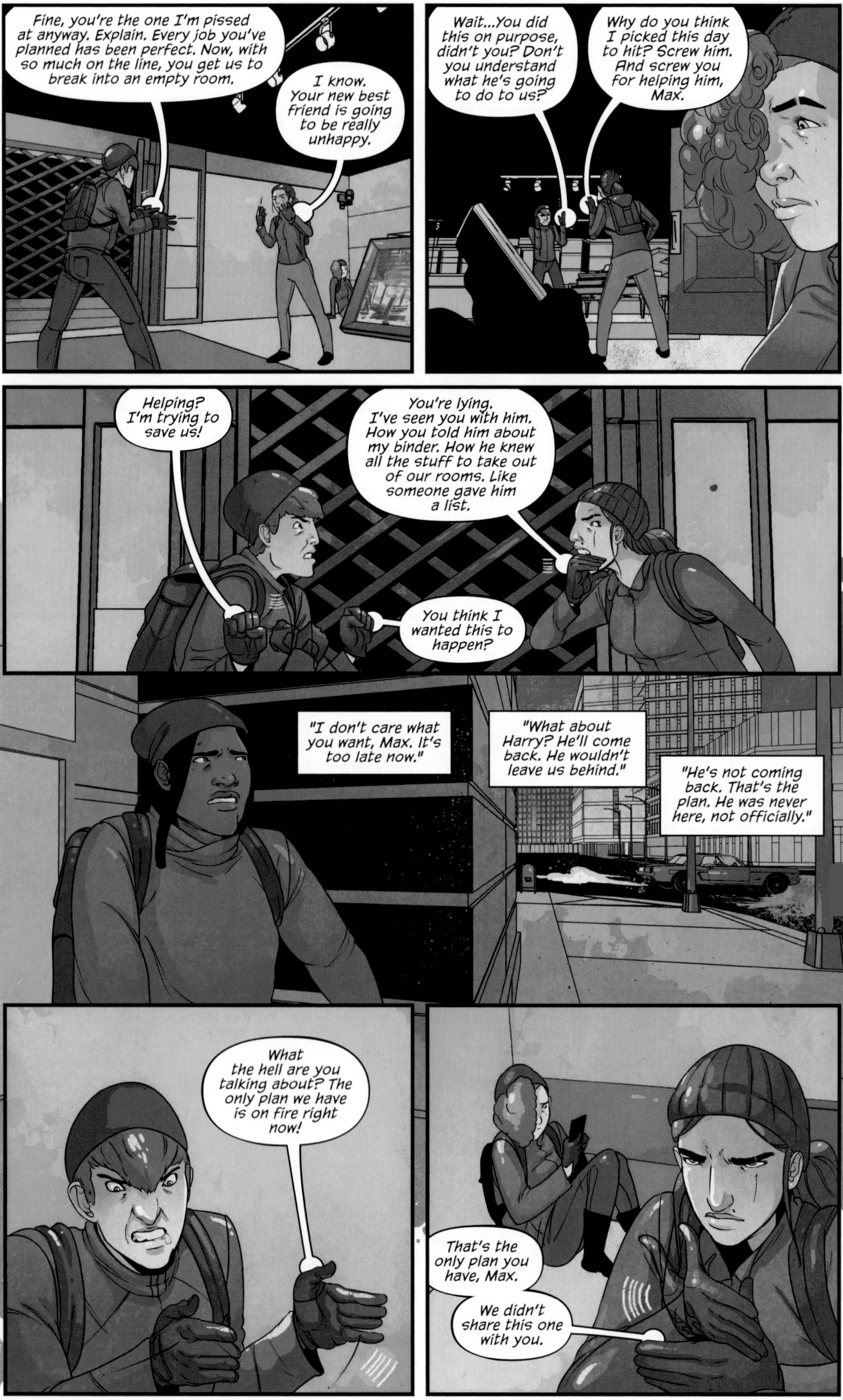
Fine, you're the one I'm pissed at anyway. Explain. Every job you've planned has been perfect. Now, with so much on the line, you get us to break into an empty room.
I know. Your new best friend is going to be really unhappy.
Wait...You did this on purpose, didn't you? Don't you understand what he's going to do to us?
Why do you think I picked this day to hit? Screw him. And screw you for helping him, Max.
Helping? I'm trying to save us!
You're lying. I've seen you with him. How you told him about my binder. How he knew all the stuff to take out of our rooms. Like someone gave him a list.
You think I wanted this to happen?
"I don't care what you want, Max. It's too late now."
"What about Harry? He'll come back. He wouldn't leave us behind."
"He's not coming back. That's the plan. He was never here, not officially."
What the hell are you talking about? The only plan we have is on fire right now!
That's the only plan you have, Max.
We didn't share this one with you.

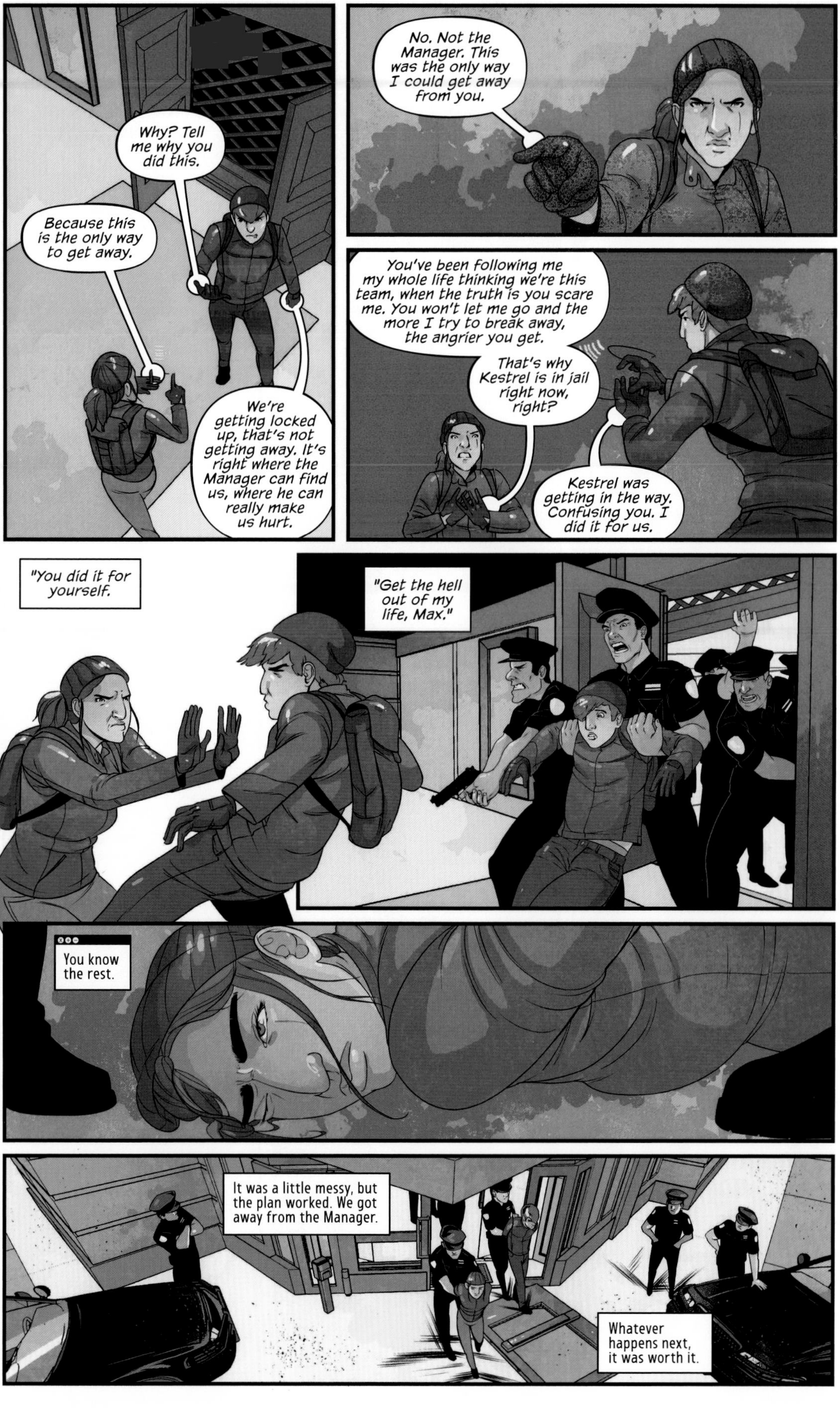

Why? Tell me why you did this.
Because this is the only way to get away.
We're getting locked up, that's not getting away. It's right where the Manager can find us, where he can really make us hurt.
No. Not the Manager. This was the only way I could get away from you.
You've been following me my whole life thinking we're this team, when the truth is you scare me. You won't let me go and the more I try to break away, the angrier you get.
That's why Kestrel is in jail right now, right?
Kestrel was getting in the way. Confusing you. I did it for us.
"You did it for yourself.
"Get the hell out of my life, Max."
You know the rest.
It was a little messy, but the plan worked. We got away from the Manager.
Whatever happens next, it was worth it.

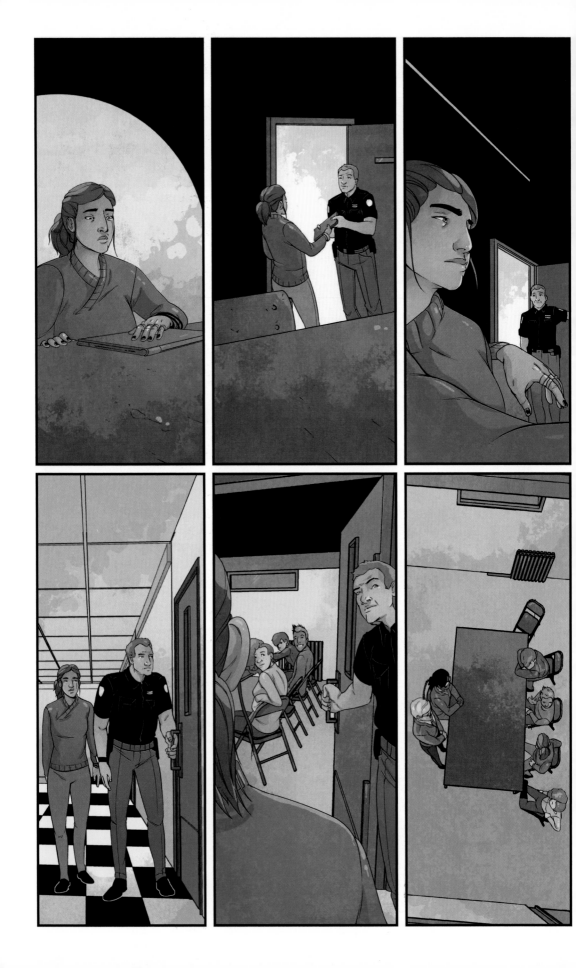

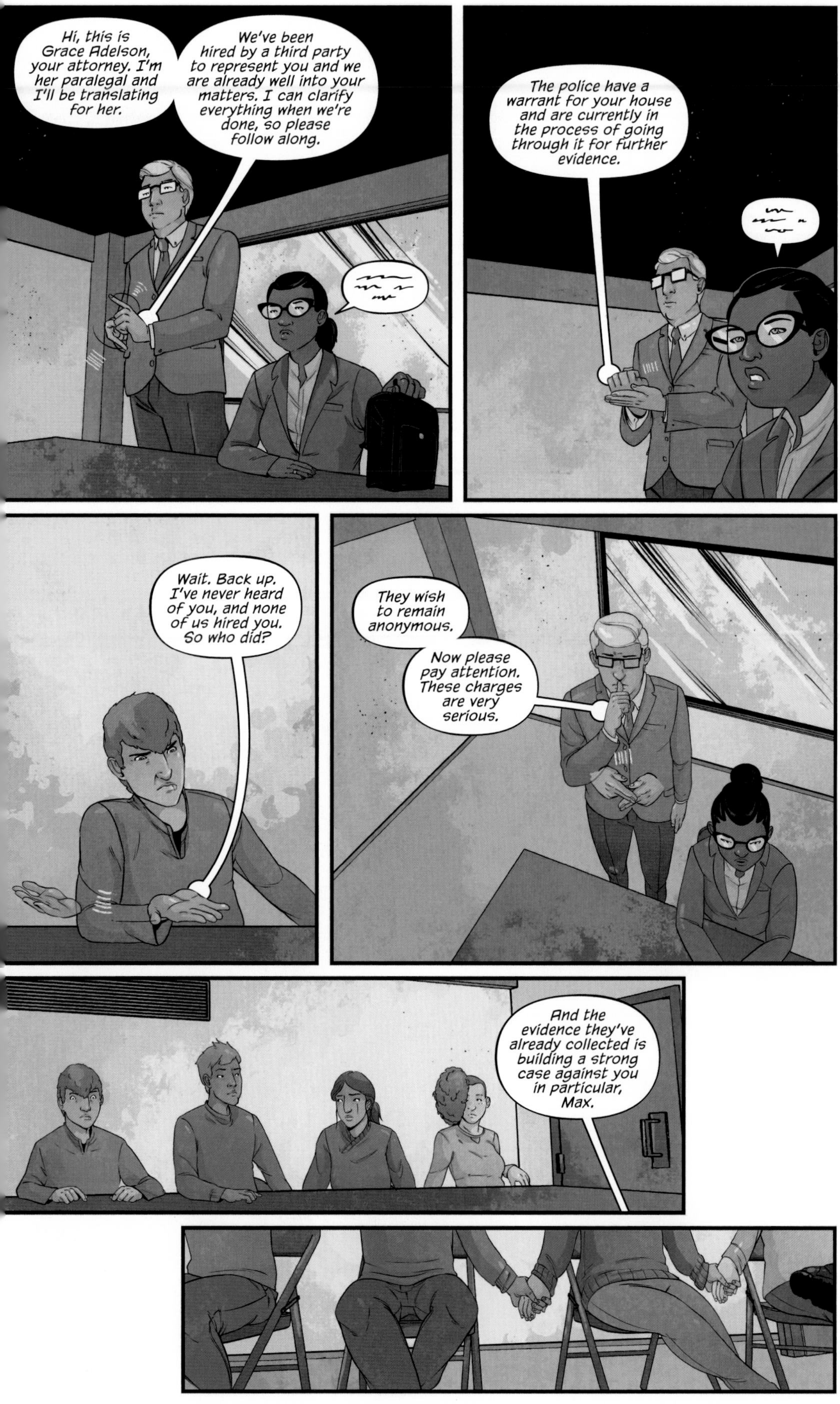
Hi, this is Grace Adelson, your attorney. I'm her paralegal and I'll be translating for her.
We've been hired by a third party to represent you and we are already well into your matters. I can clarify everything when we're done, so please follow along.
The police have a warrant for your house and are currently in the process of going through it for further evidence.
Wait. Back up. I've never heard of you, and none of us hired you. So who did?
They wish to remain anonymous.
Now please pay attention. These charges are very serious.
And the evidence they've already collected is building a strong case against you in particular, Max.

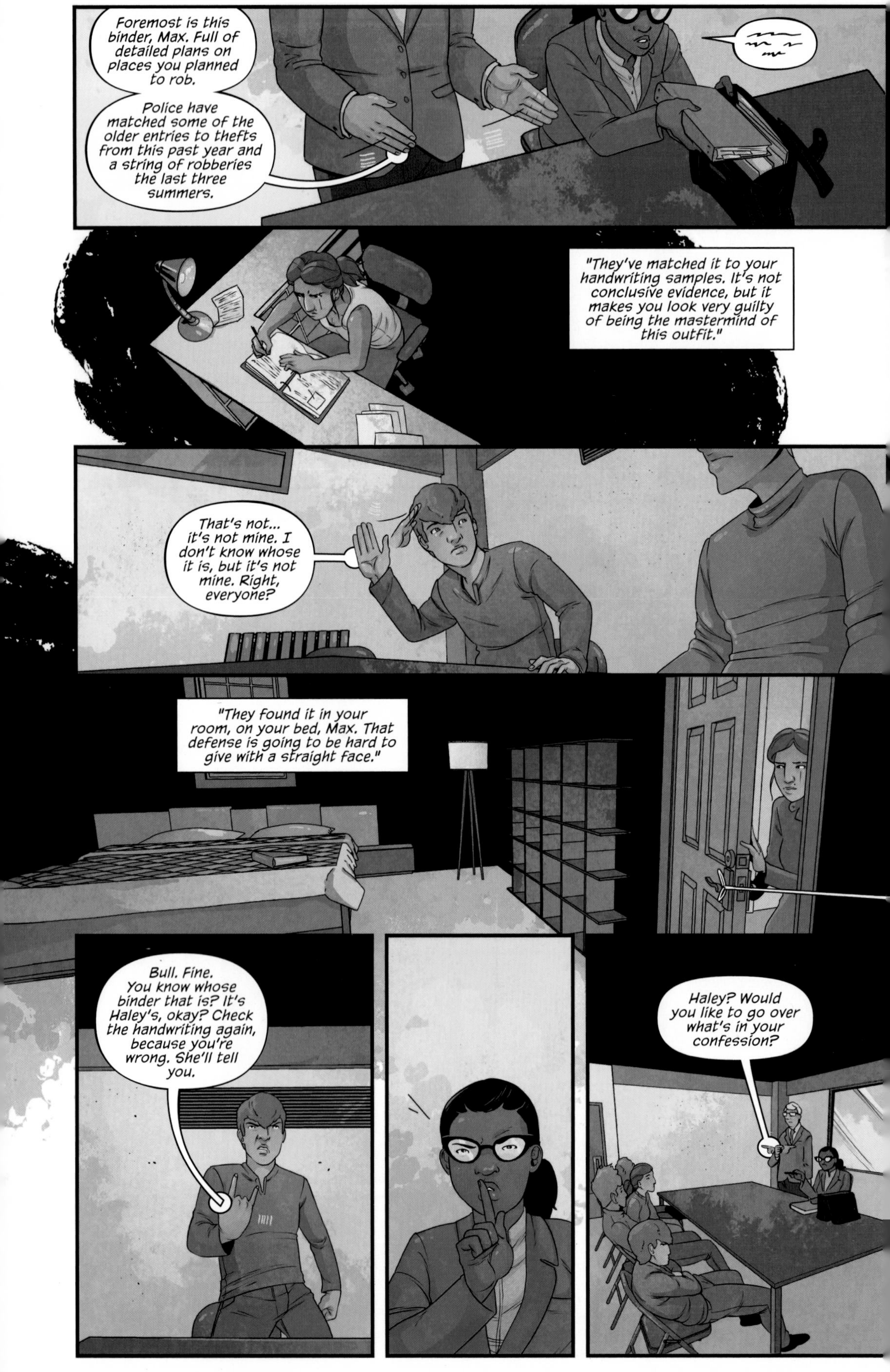
Foremost is this binder, Max. Full of detailed plans on places you planned to rob.
Police have matched some of the older entries to thefts from this past year and a string of robberies the last three summers.
"They've matched it to your handwriting samples. It's not conclusive evidence, but it makes you look very guilty of being the mastermind of this outfit."
That's not... it's not mine. I don't know whose it is, but it's not mine. Right, everyone?
"They found it in your room, on your bed, Max. That defense is going to be hard to give with a straight face."
Bull. Fine. You know whose binder that is? It's Haley's, okay? Check the handwriting again, because you're wrong. She'll tell you.
Haley? Would you like to go over what's in your confession?

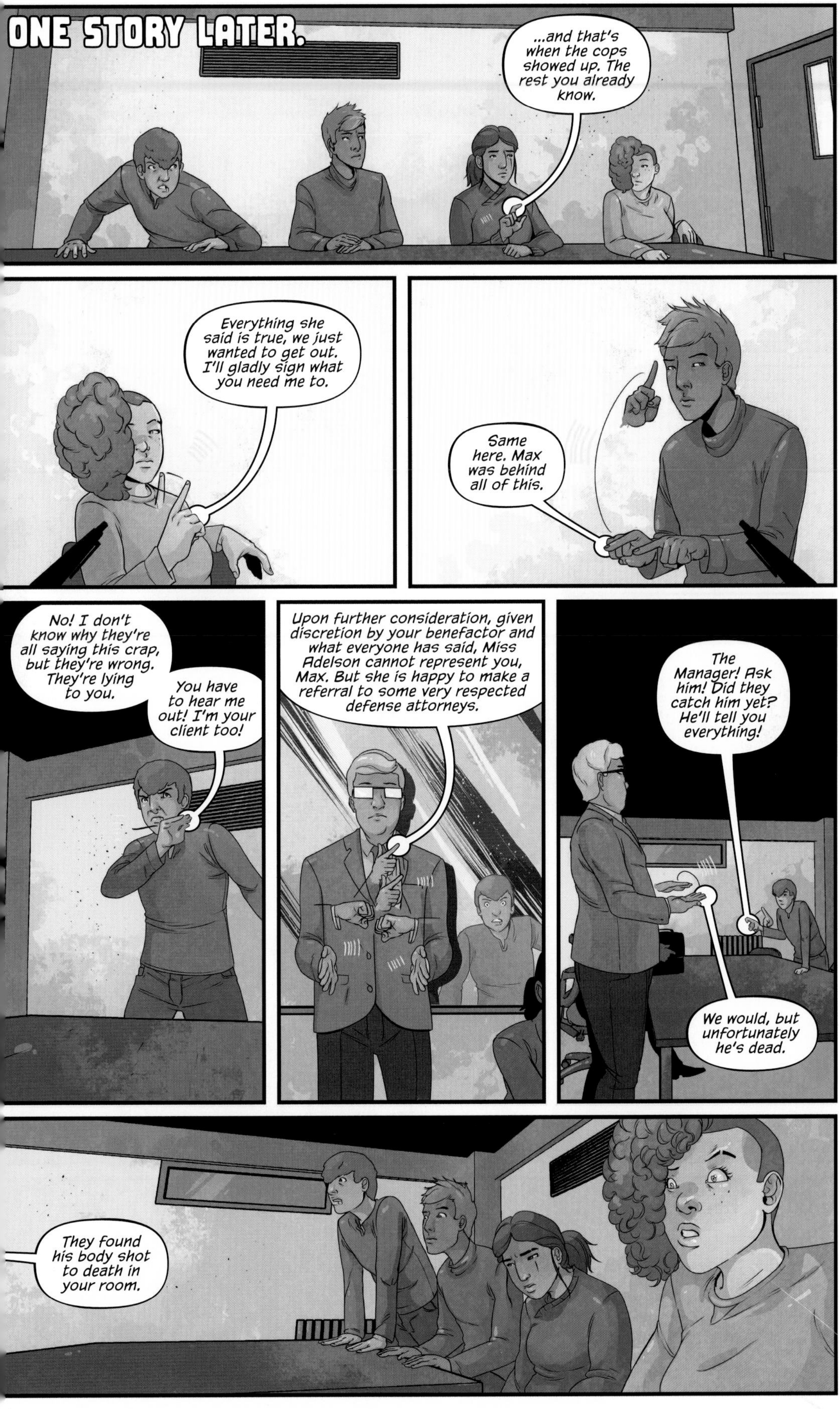
ONE STORY LATER.
...and that's when the cops showed up. The rest you already know.
Everything she said is true, we just wanted to get out. I'll gladly sign what you need me to.
Same here. Max was behind all of this.
No! I don't know why they're all saying this crap, but they're wrong. They're lying to you.
You have to hear me out! I'm your client too!
Upon further consideration, given discretion by your benefactor and what everyone has said, Miss Adelson cannot represent you, Max. But she is happy to make a referral to some very respected defense attorneys.
The Manager! Ask him! Did they catch him yet? He'll tell you everything!
We would, but unfortunately he's dead.
They found his body shot to death in your room.

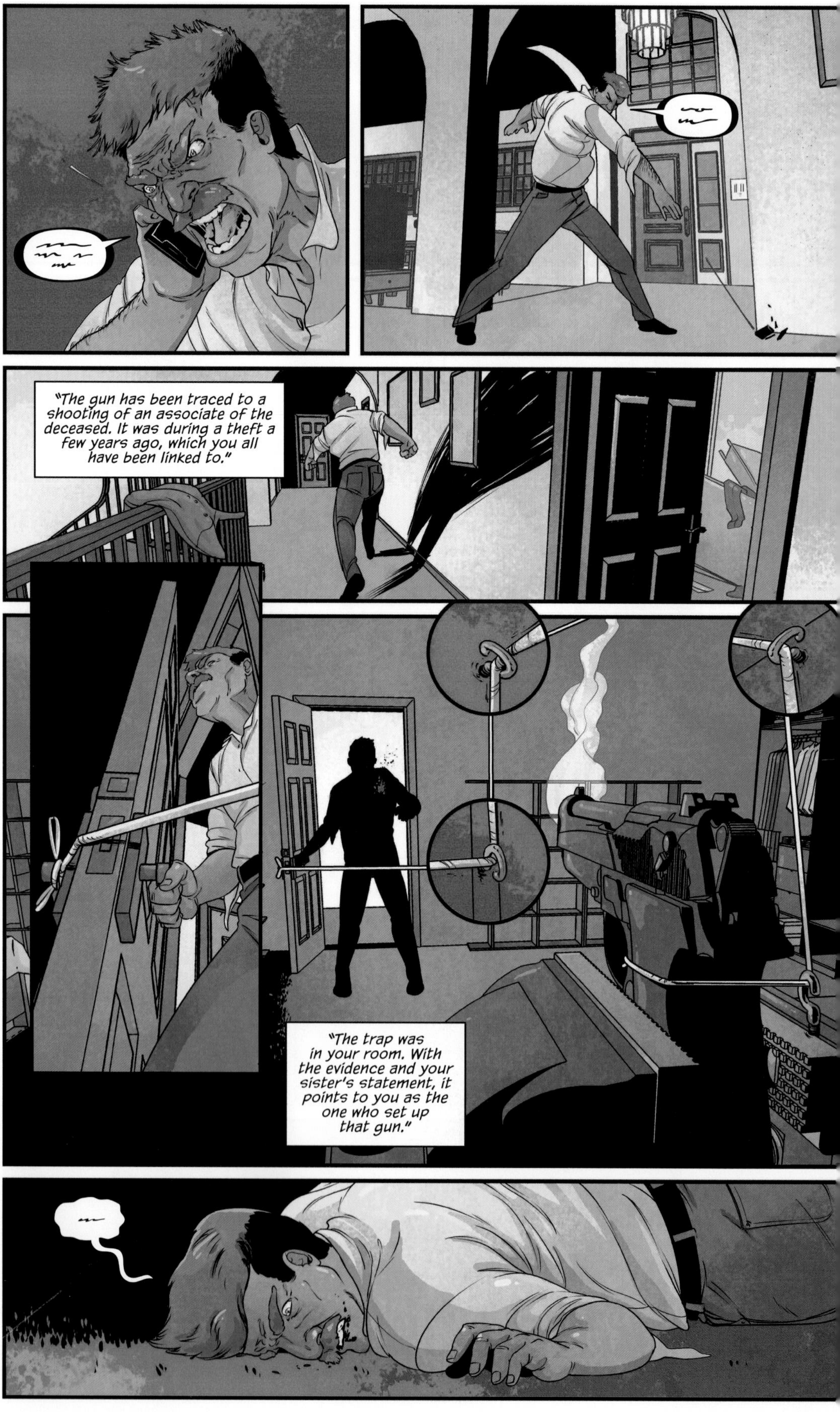
"The gun has been traced to a shooting of an associate of the deceased. It was during a theft a few years ago, which you all have been linked to."
"The trap was in your room. With the evidence and your sister's statement, it points to you as the one who set up that gun."

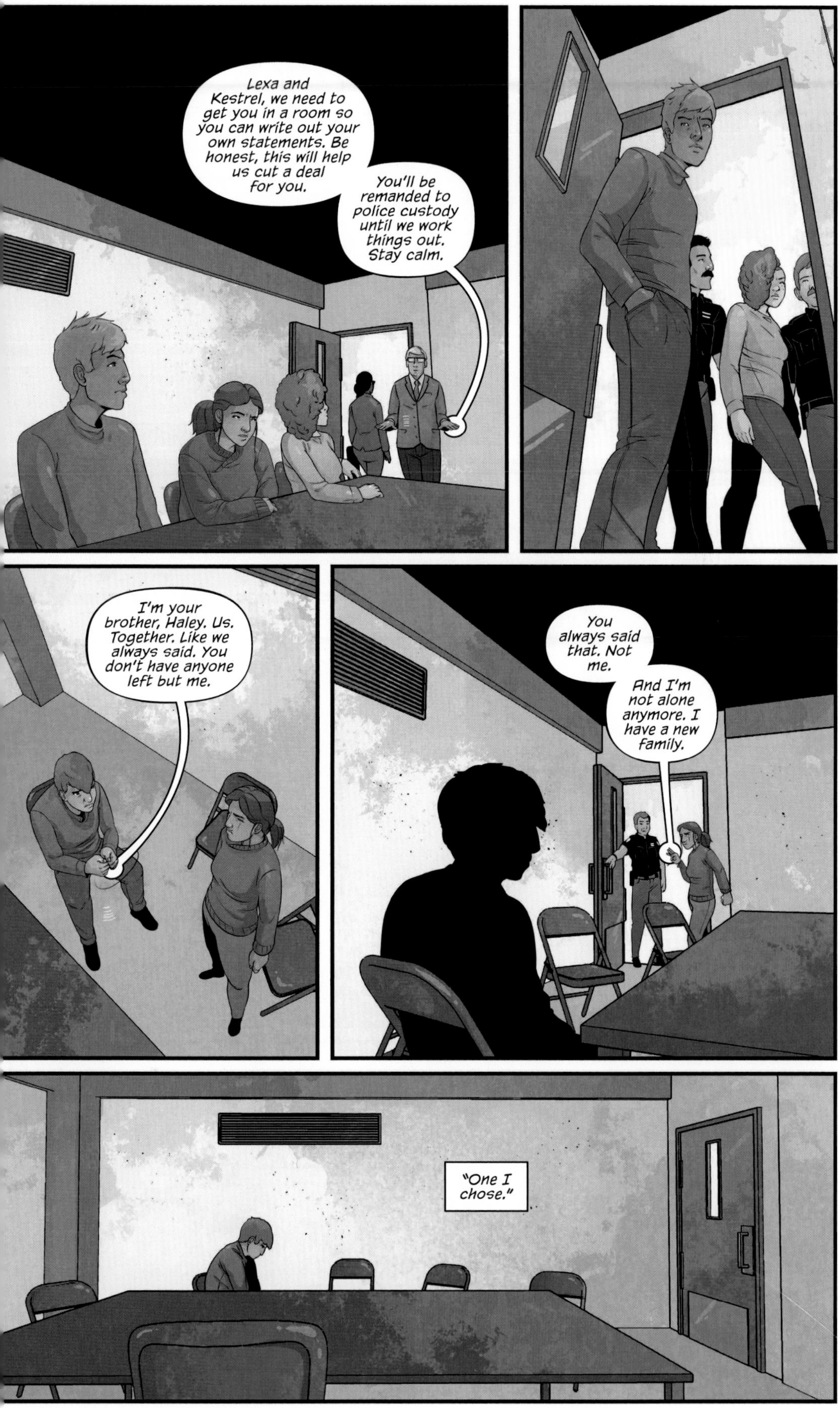
Lexa and Kestrel, we need to get you in a room so you can write out your own statements. Be honest, this will help us cut a deal for you.
You'll be remanded to police custody until we work things out. Stay calm.
I'm your brother, Haley. Us. Together. Like we always said. You don't have anyone left but me.
You always said that. Not me.
And I'm not alone anymore. I have a new family.
"One I chose."

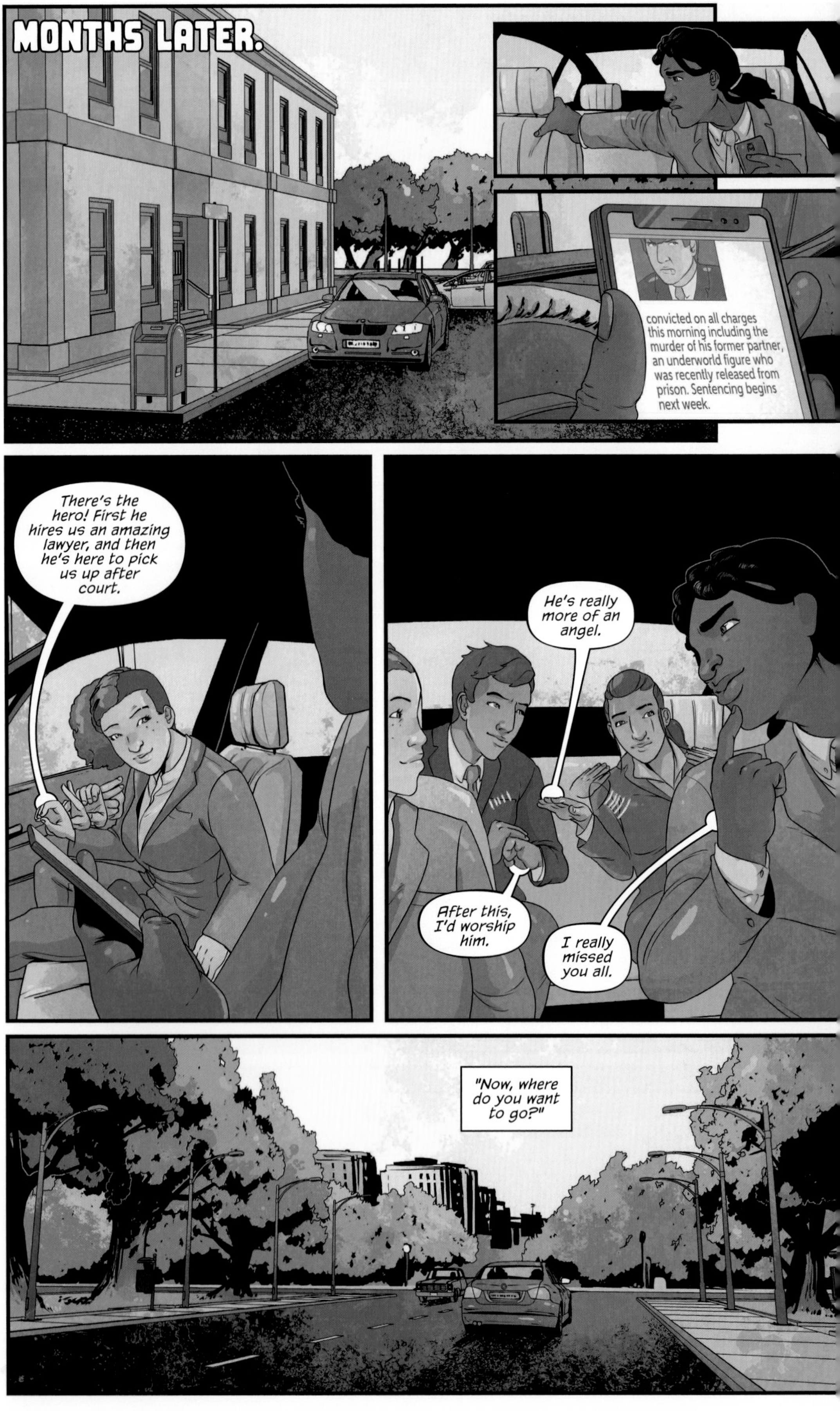
MONTHS LATER.
convicted on all charges this morning including the murder of his former partner, an underworld figure who was recently released from prison. Sentencing begins next week.
There's the hero! First he hires us an amazing lawyer, and then he's here to pick us up after court.
He's really more of an angel.
After this, I'd worship him.
I really missed you all.
"Now, where do you want to go?"

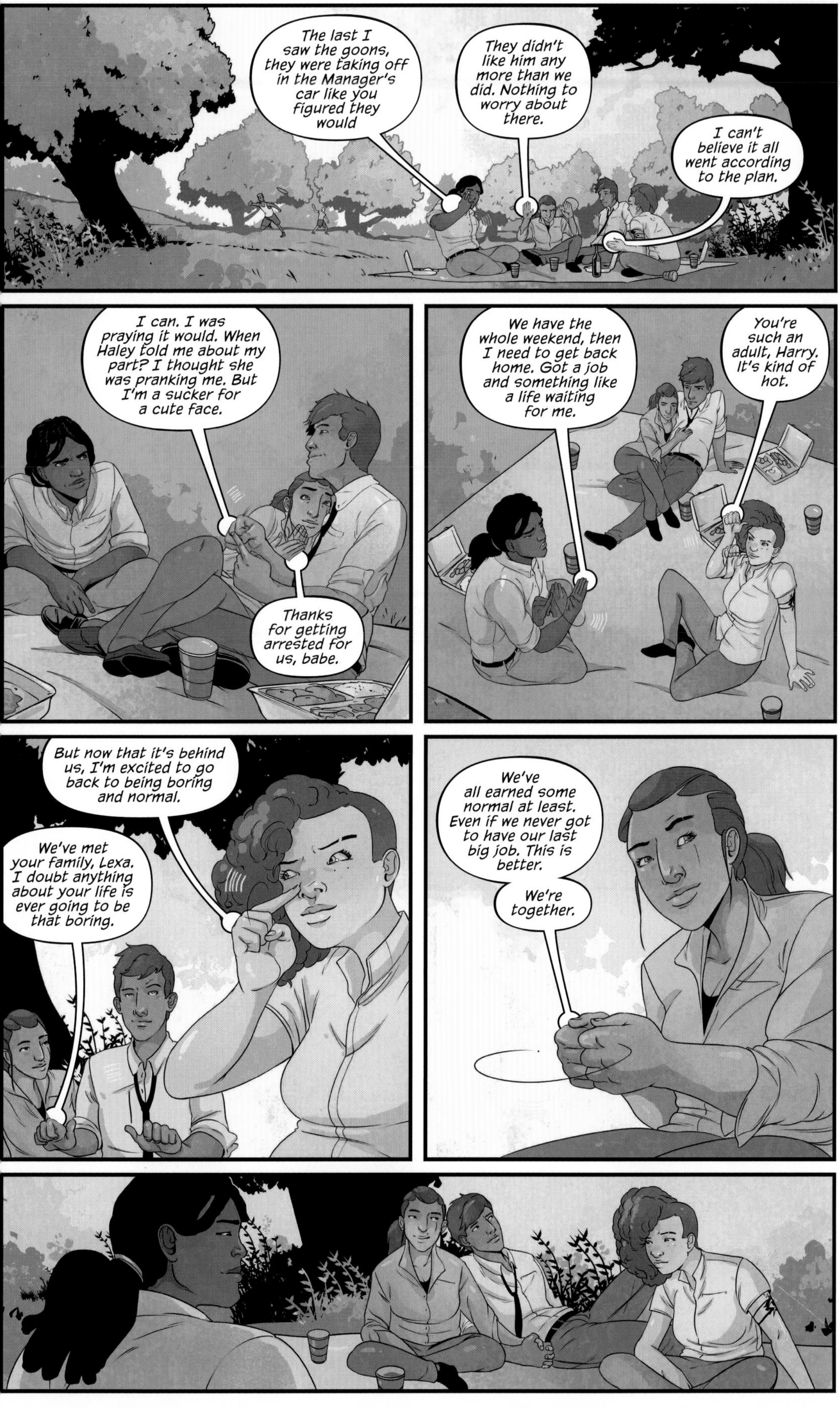
The last I saw the goons, they were taking off in the Manager's car like you figured they would
They didn't like him any more than we did. Nothing to worry about there.
I can't believe it all went according to the plan.
I can. I was praying it would. When Haley told me about my part? I thought she was pranking me. But I'm a sucker for a cute face.
Thanks for getting arrested for us, babe.
We have the whole weekend, then I need to get back home. Got a job and something like a life waiting for me.
You're such an adult, Harry. It's kind of hot.
But now that it's behind us, I'm excited to go back to being boring and normal.
We've met your family, Lexa. I doubt anything about your life is ever going to be that boring.
We've all earned some normal at least. Even if we never got to have our last big job. This is better.
We're together.

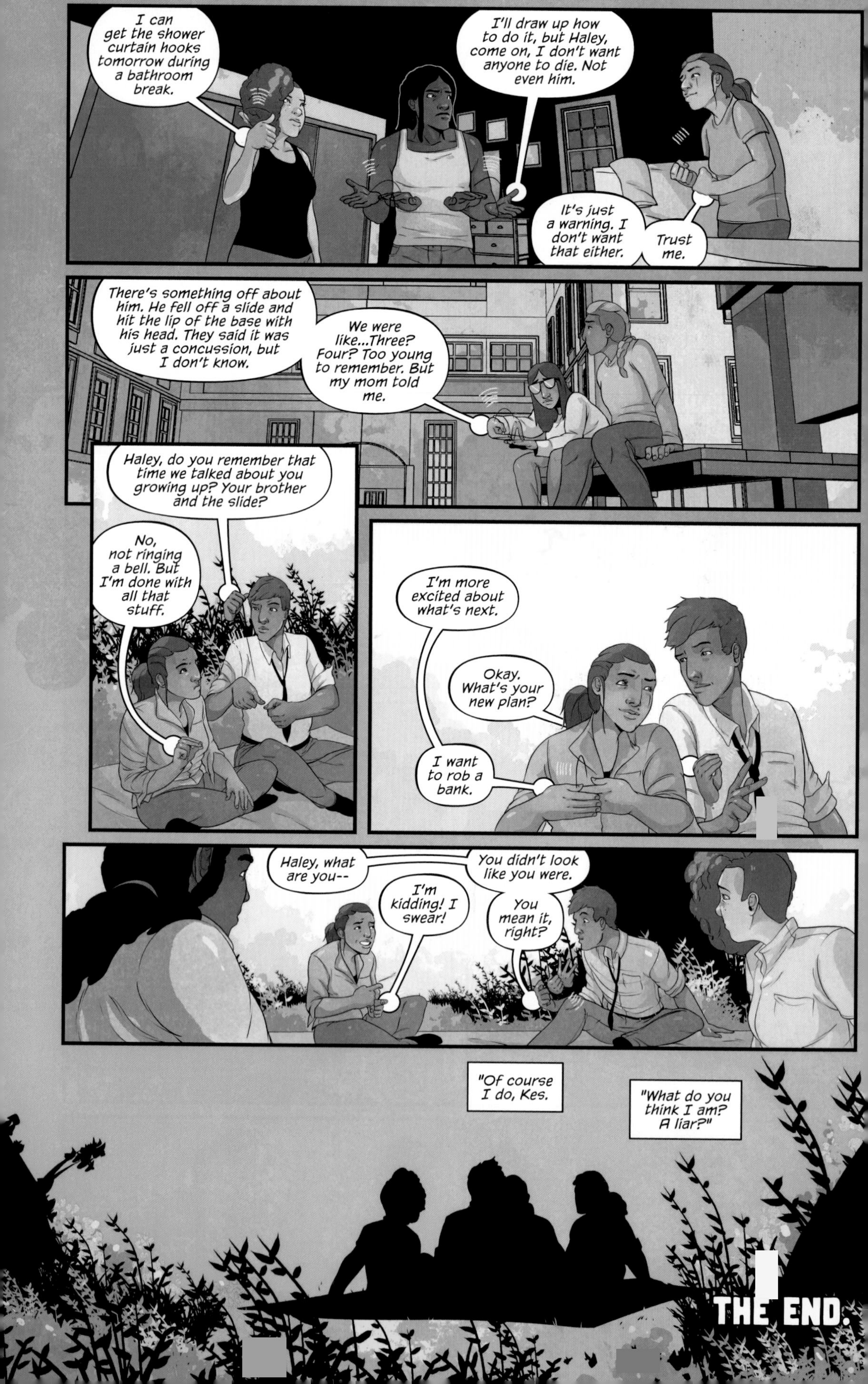

I can get the shower curtain hooks tomorrow during a bathroom break.
I'll draw up how to do it, but Haley, come on, I don't want anyone to die. Not even him.
It's just a warning. I don't want that either.
Trust me.
There's something off about him. He fell off a slide and hit the lip of the base with his head. They said it was just a concussion, but I don't know.
We were like...Three? Four? Too young to remember. But my mom told me.
Haley, do you remember that time we talked about you growing up? Your brother and the slide?
No, not ringing a bell. But I'm done with all that stuff.
I'm more excited about what's next.
Okay. What's your new plan?
I want to rob a bank.
Haley, what are you--
You didn't look like you were.
I'm kidding! I swear!
You mean it, right?
"Of course I do, Kes.
"What do you think I am? A liar?"
THE END.

CONCEPT ART

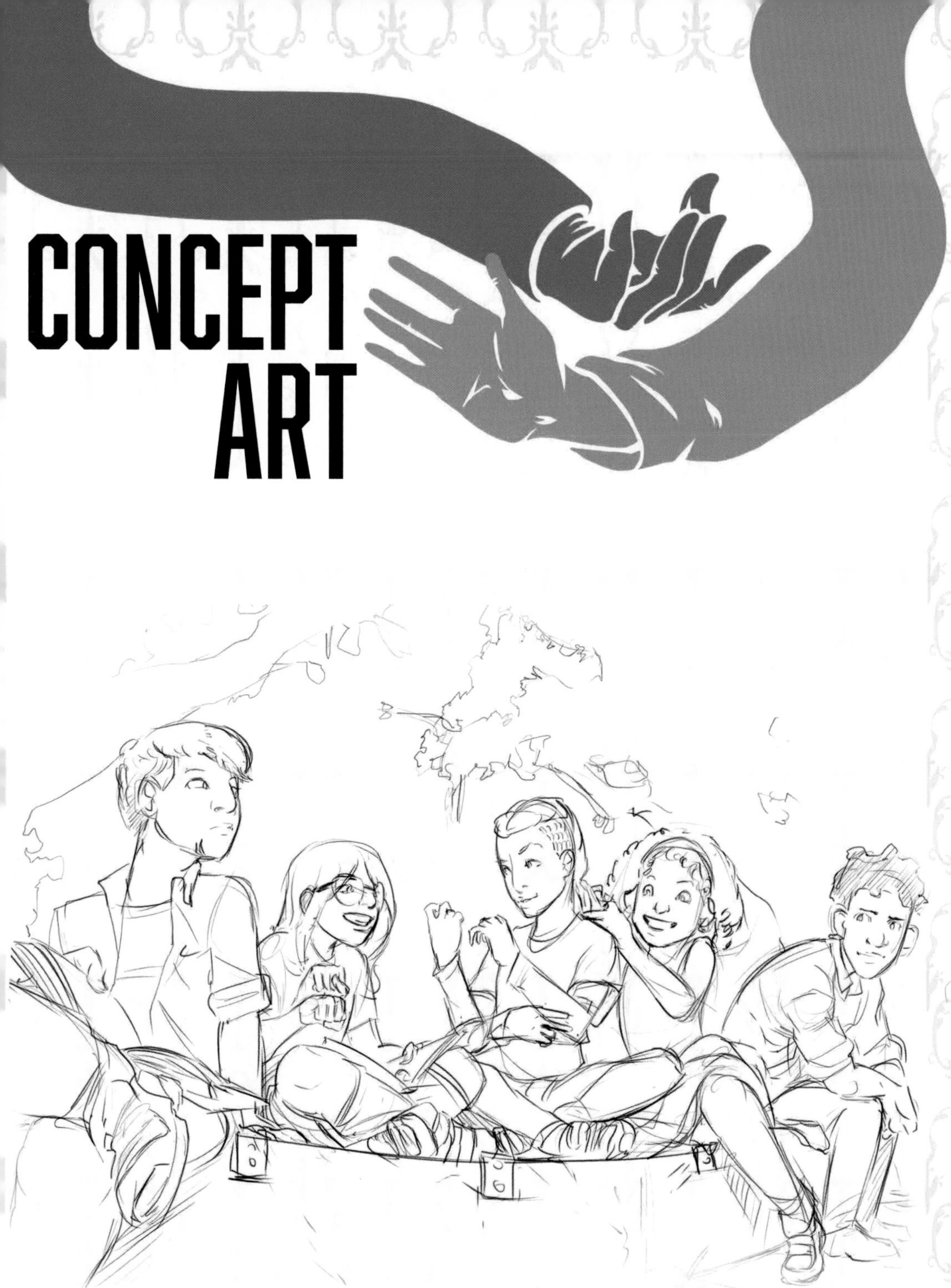

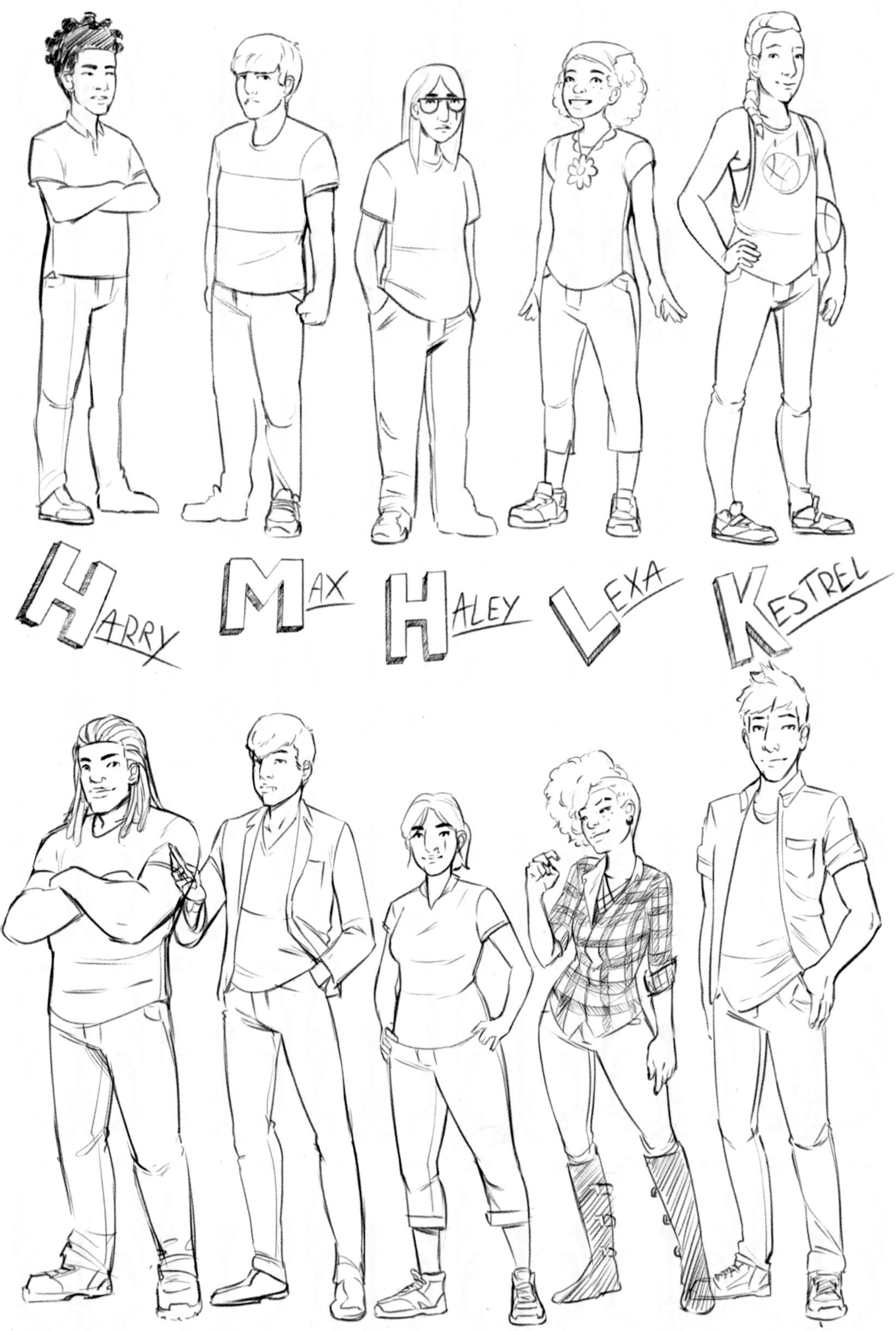
HARRY
MAX
HALEY
LEXA
KESTREL

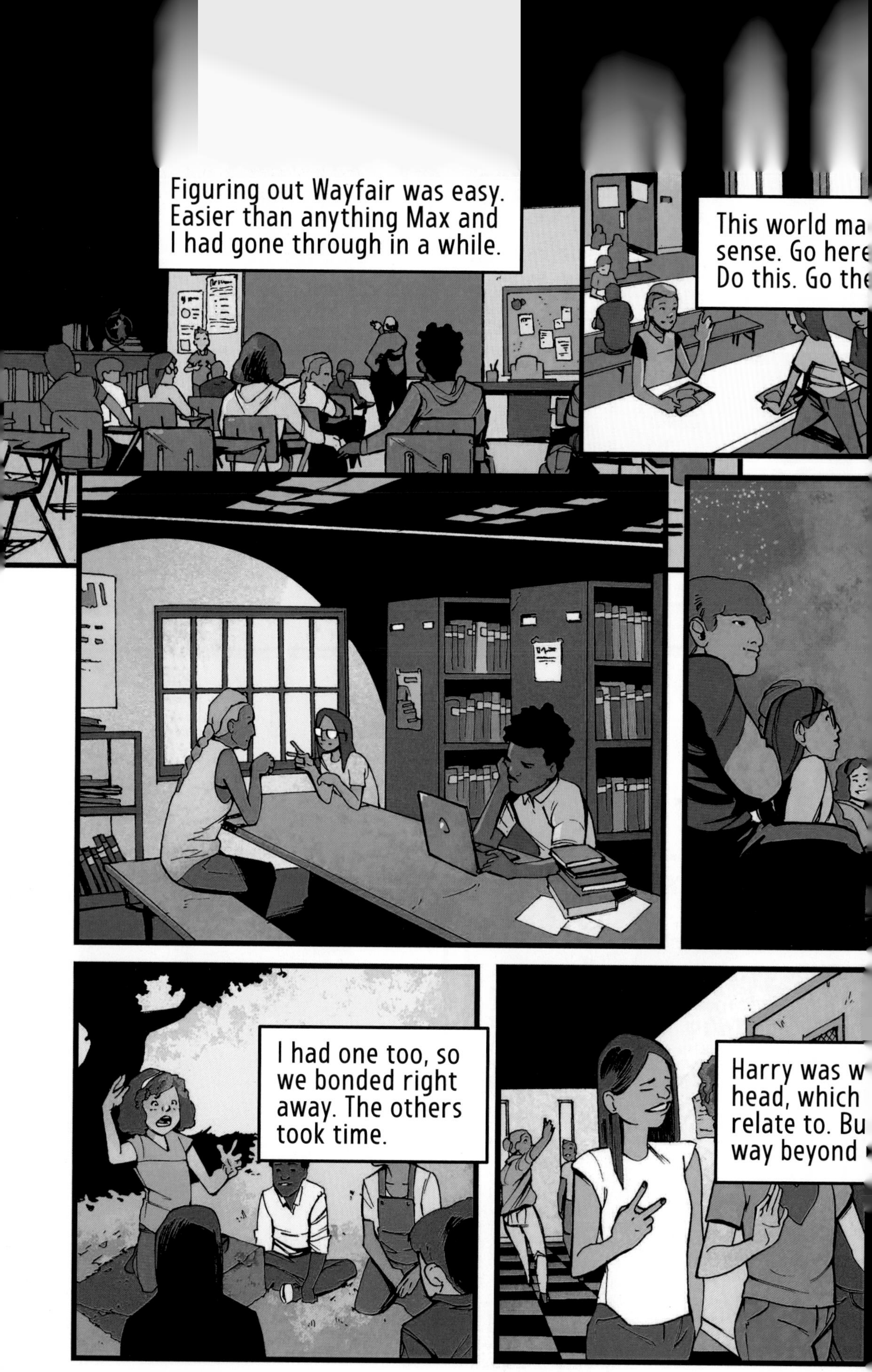
Figuring out Wayfair was easy. Easier than anything Max and I had gone through in a while.
This world ma sense. Go here Do this. Go the
I had one too, so we bonded right away. The others took time.
Harry was w head, which relate to. Bu way beyond

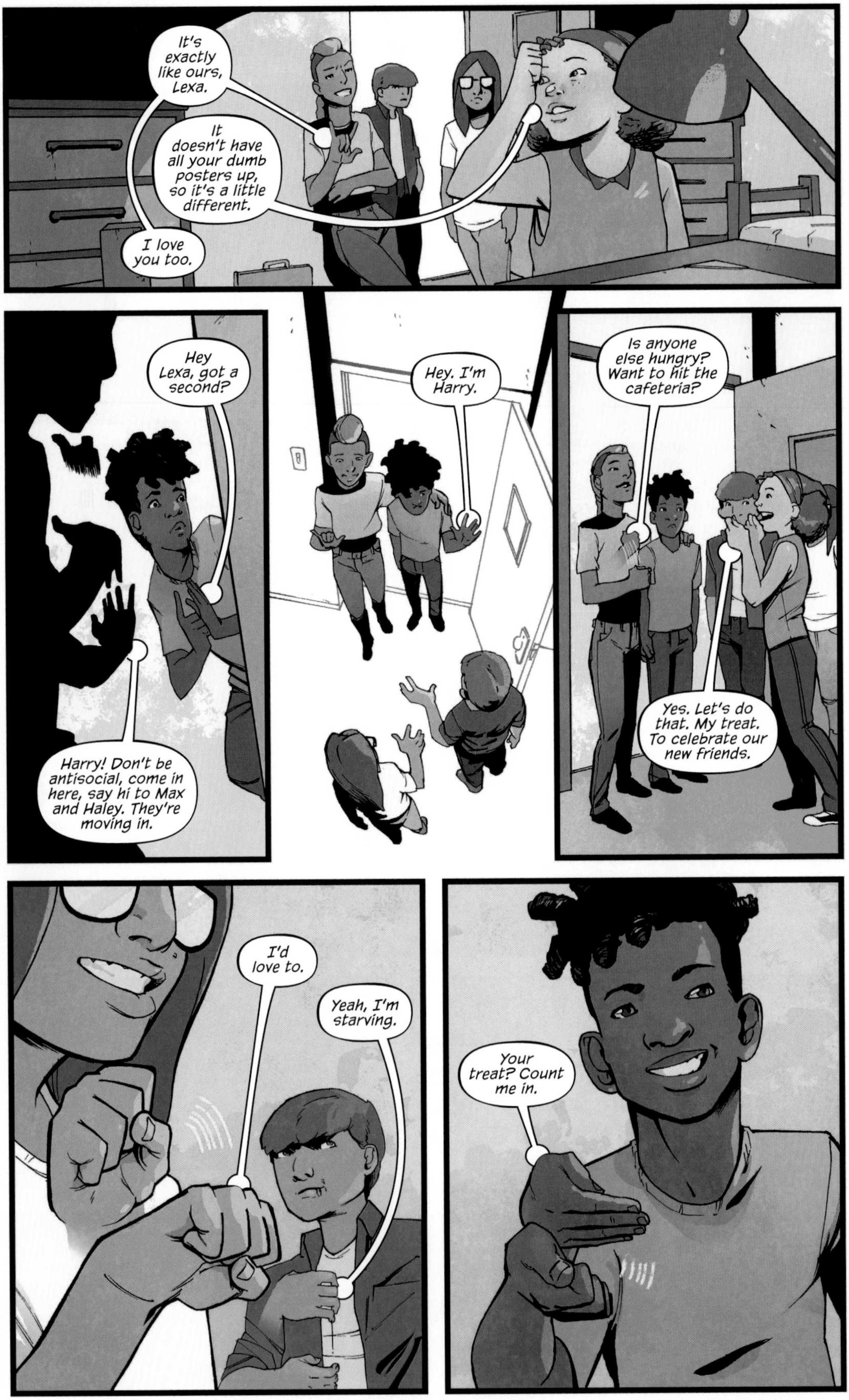
It's exactly like ours, Lexa.
It doesn't have all your dumb posters up, so it's a little different.
I love you too.
Hey Lexa, got a second?
Harry! Don't be antisocial, come in here, say hi to Max and Haley. They're moving in.
Hey. I'm Harry.
Is anyone else hungry? Want to hit the cafeteria?
Yes. Let's do that. My treat. To celebrate our new friends.
I'd love to.
Yeah, I'm starving.
Your treat? Count me in.

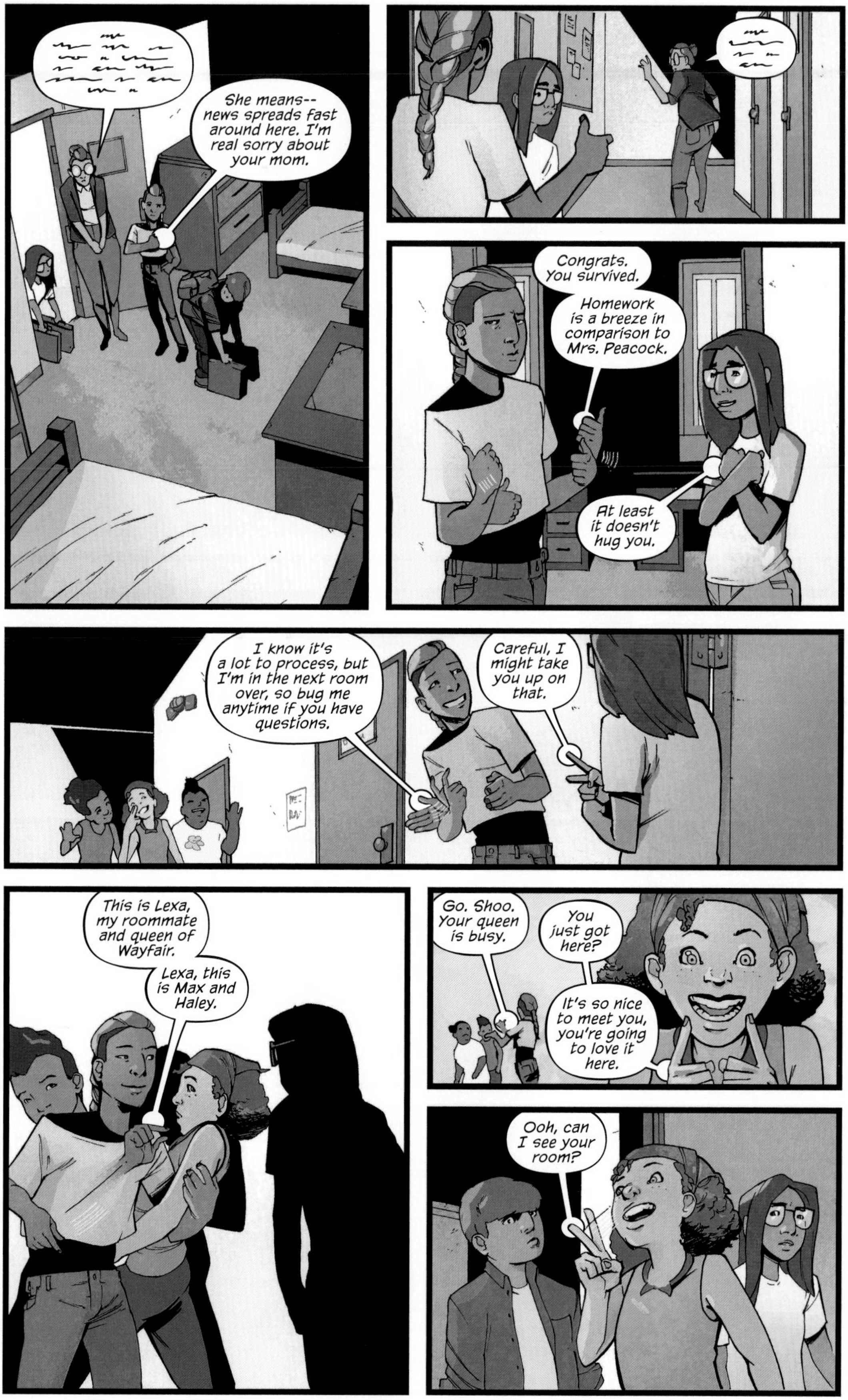
She means--
news spreads fast
around here. I'm
real sorry about
your mom.
Congrats.
You survived.
Homework
is a breeze in
comparison to
Mrs. Peacock.
At least
it doesn't
hug you.
I know it's
a lot to process, but
I'm in the next room
over, so bug me
anytime if you have
questions.
Careful, I
might take
you up on
that.
This is Lexa,
my roommate
and queen of
Wayfair.
Lexa, this
is Max and
Haley.
Go. Shoo.
Your queen
is busy.
You
just got
here?
It's so nice
to meet you,
you're going
to love it
here.
Ooh, can
I see your
room?

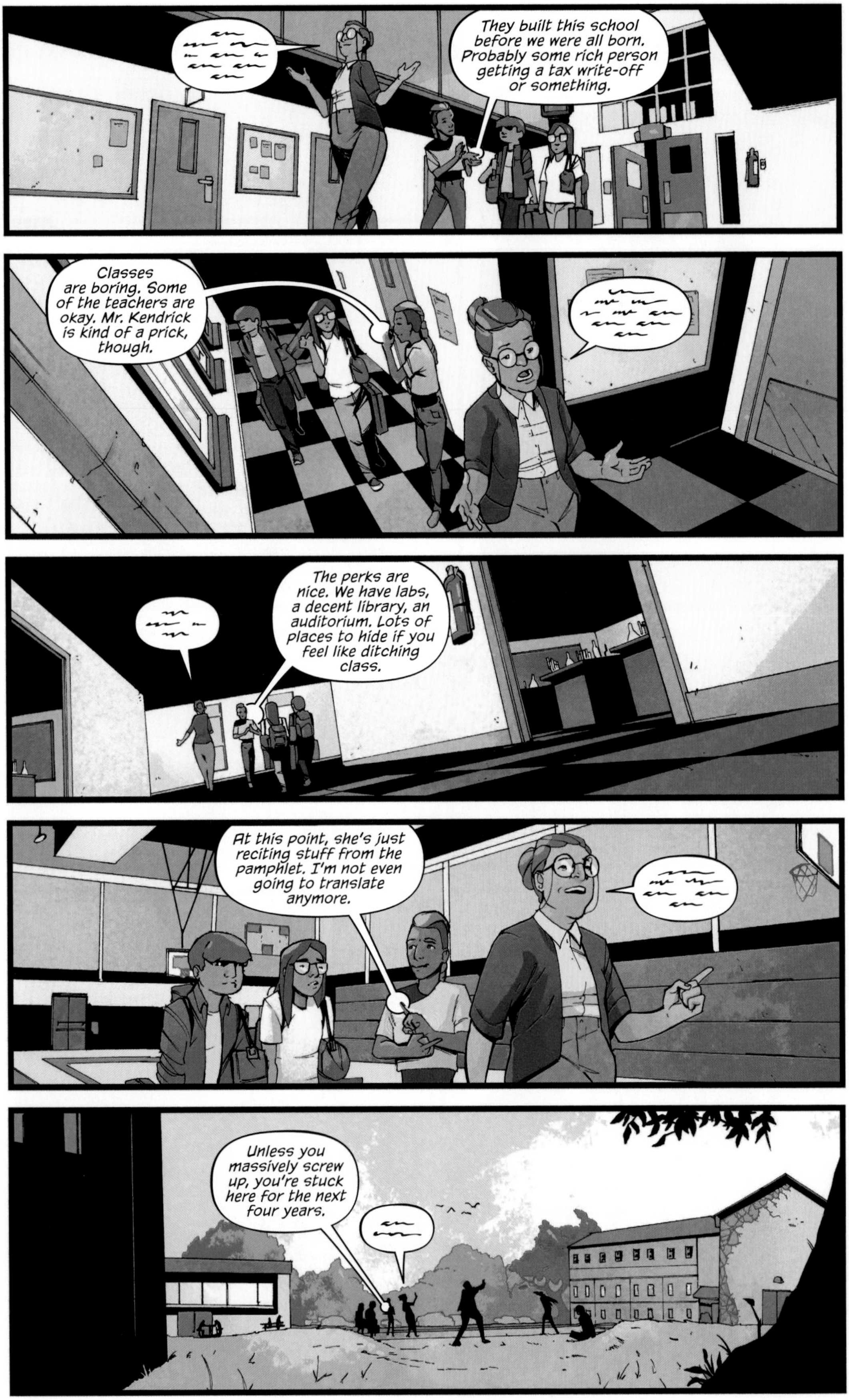
They built this school before we were all born. Probably some rich person getting a tax write-off or something.
Classes are boring. Some of the teachers are okay. Mr. Kendrick is kind of a prick, though.
The perks are nice. We have labs, a decent library, an auditorium. Lots of places to hide if you feel like ditching class.
At this point, she's just reciting stuff from the pamphlet. I'm not even going to translate anymore.
Unless you massively screw up, you're stuck here for the next four years.

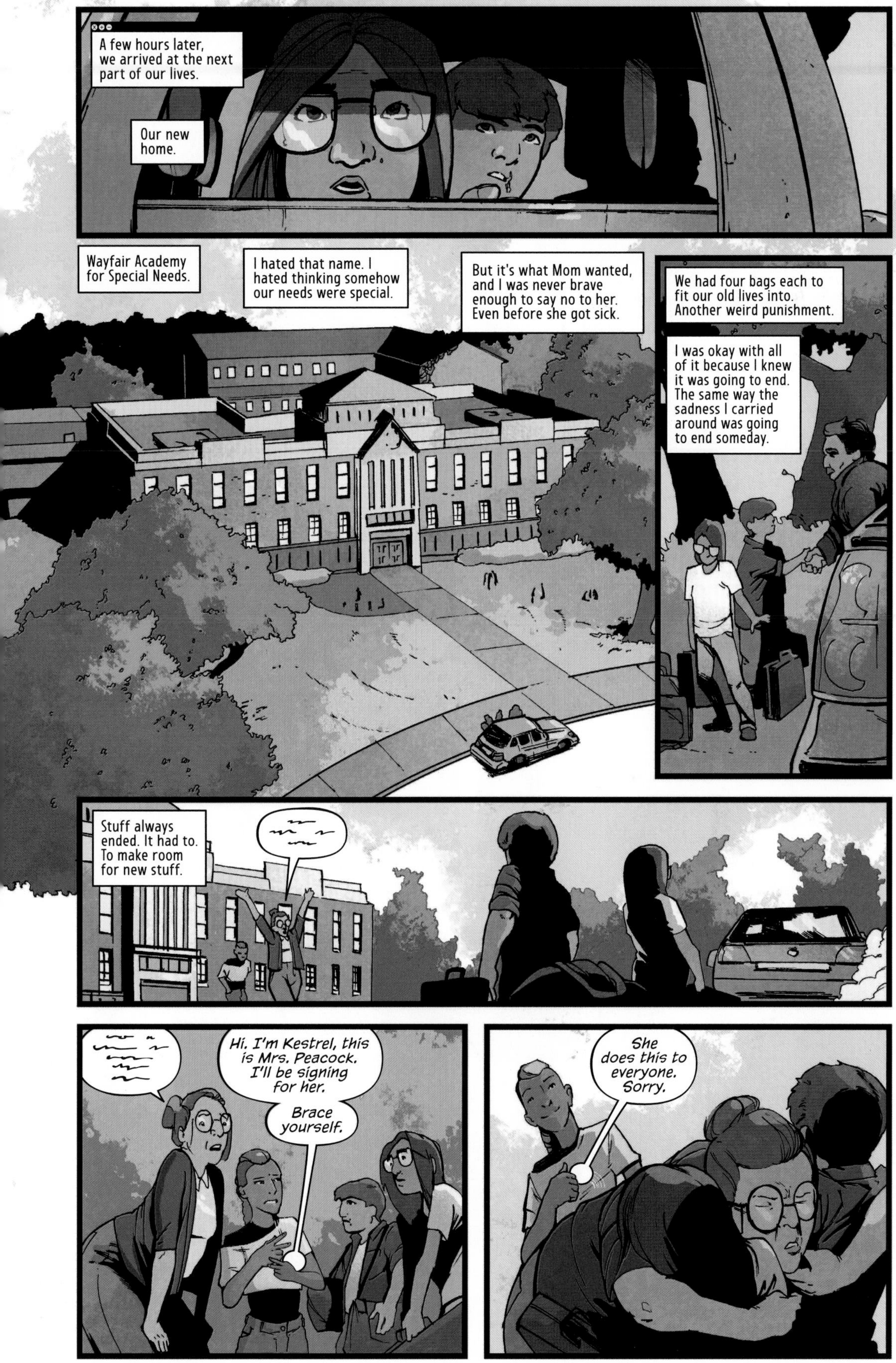
A few hours later, we arrived at the next part of our lives.
Our new home.
Wayfair Academy for Special Needs.
I hated that name. I hated thinking somehow our needs were special.
But it's what Mom wanted, and I was never brave enough to say no to her. Even before she got sick.
We had four bags each to fit our old lives into. Another weird punishment.
I was okay with all of it because I knew it was going to end. The same way the sadness I carried around was going to end someday.
Stuff always ended. It had to. To make room for new stuff.
Hi. I'm Kestrel, this is Mrs. Peacock. I'll be signing for her.
Brace yourself.
She does this to everyone. Sorry.

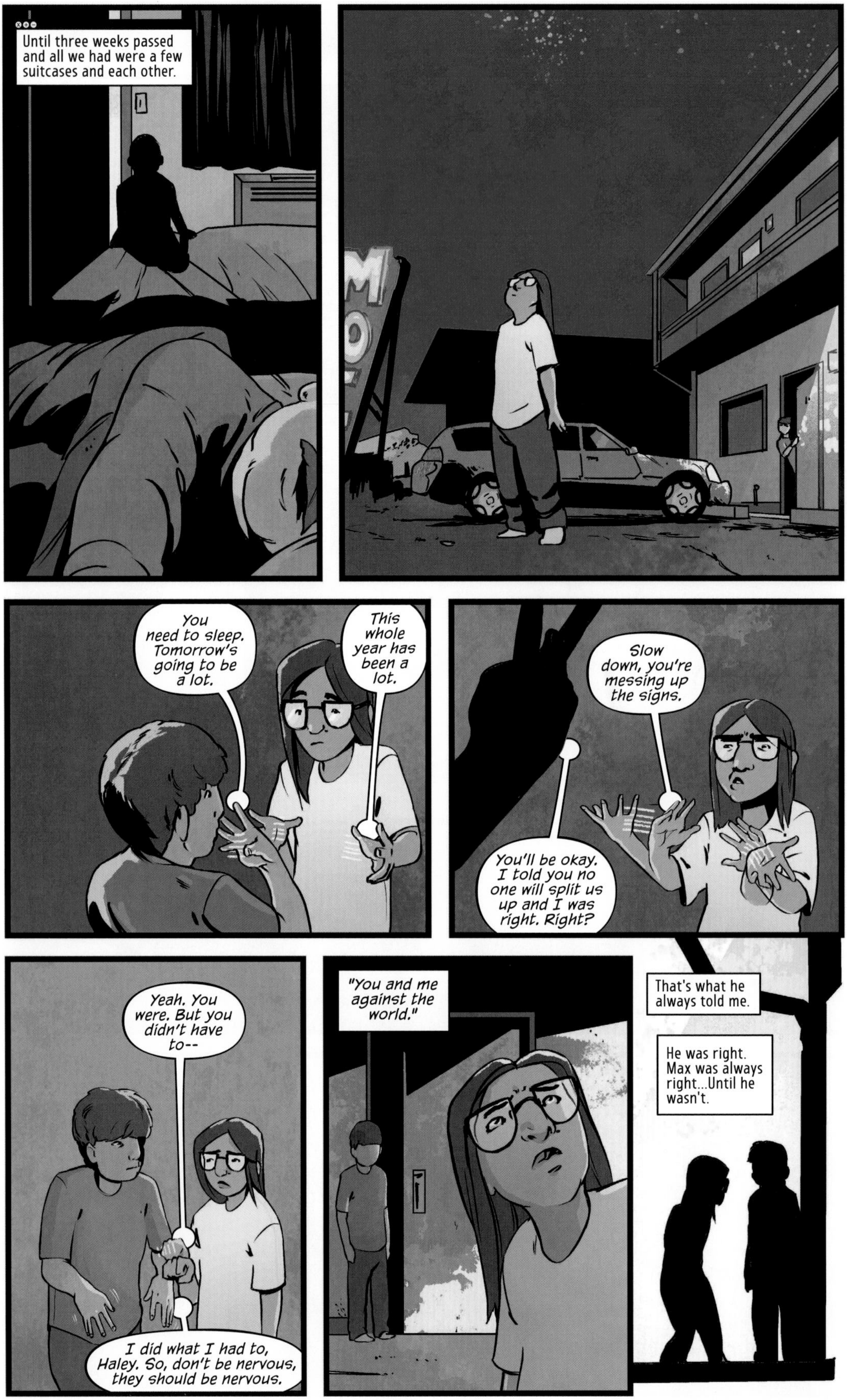
Until three weeks passed and all we had were a few suitcases and each other.
You need to sleep. Tomorrow's going to be a lot.
This whole year has been a lot.
Slow down, you're messing up the signs.
You'll be okay. I told you no one will split us up and I was right. Right?
Yeah. You were. But you didn't have to--
I did what I had to, Haley. So, don't be nervous, they should be nervous.
"You and me against the world."
That's what he always told me.
He was right. Max was always right...Until he wasn't.

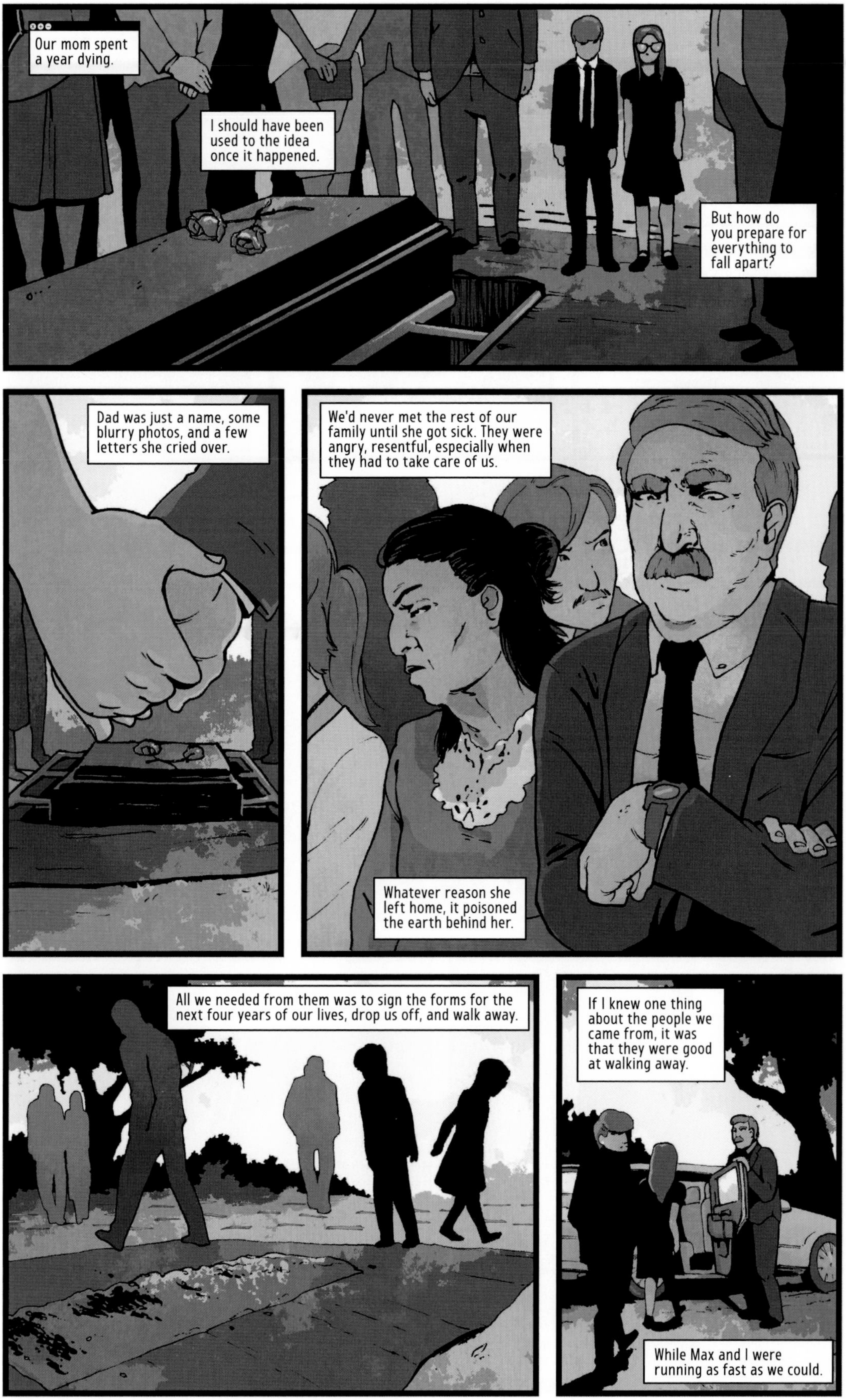
Our mom spent a year dying.
I should have been used to the idea once it happened.
But how do you prepare for everything to fall apart?
Dad was just a name, some blurry photos, and a few letters she cried over.
We'd never met the rest of our family until she got sick. They were angry, resentful, especially when they had to take care of us.
Whatever reason she left home, it poisoned the earth behind her.
All we needed from them was to sign the forms for the next four years of our lives, drop us off, and walk away.
If I knew one thing about the people we came from, it was that they were good at walking away.
While Max and I were running as fast as we could.

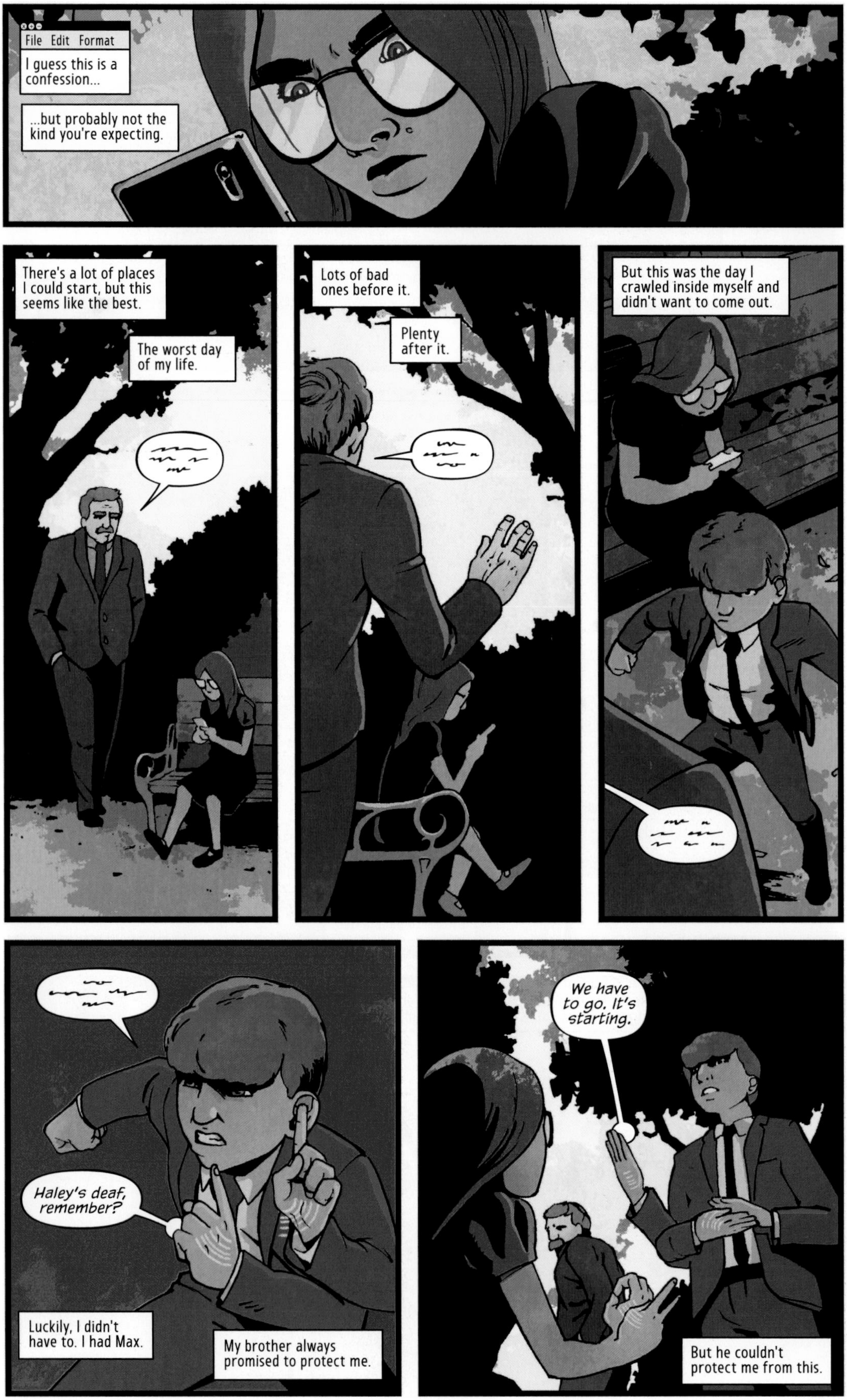
File Edit Format
I guess this is a confession...
...but probably not the kind you're expecting.
There's a lot of places I could start, but this seems like the best.
The worst day of my life.
Lots of bad ones before it.
Plenty after it.
But this was the day I crawled inside myself and didn't want to come out.
Haley's deaf, remember?
Luckily, I didn't have to. I had Max.
My brother always promised to protect me.
We have to go. It's starting.
But he couldn't protect me from this.

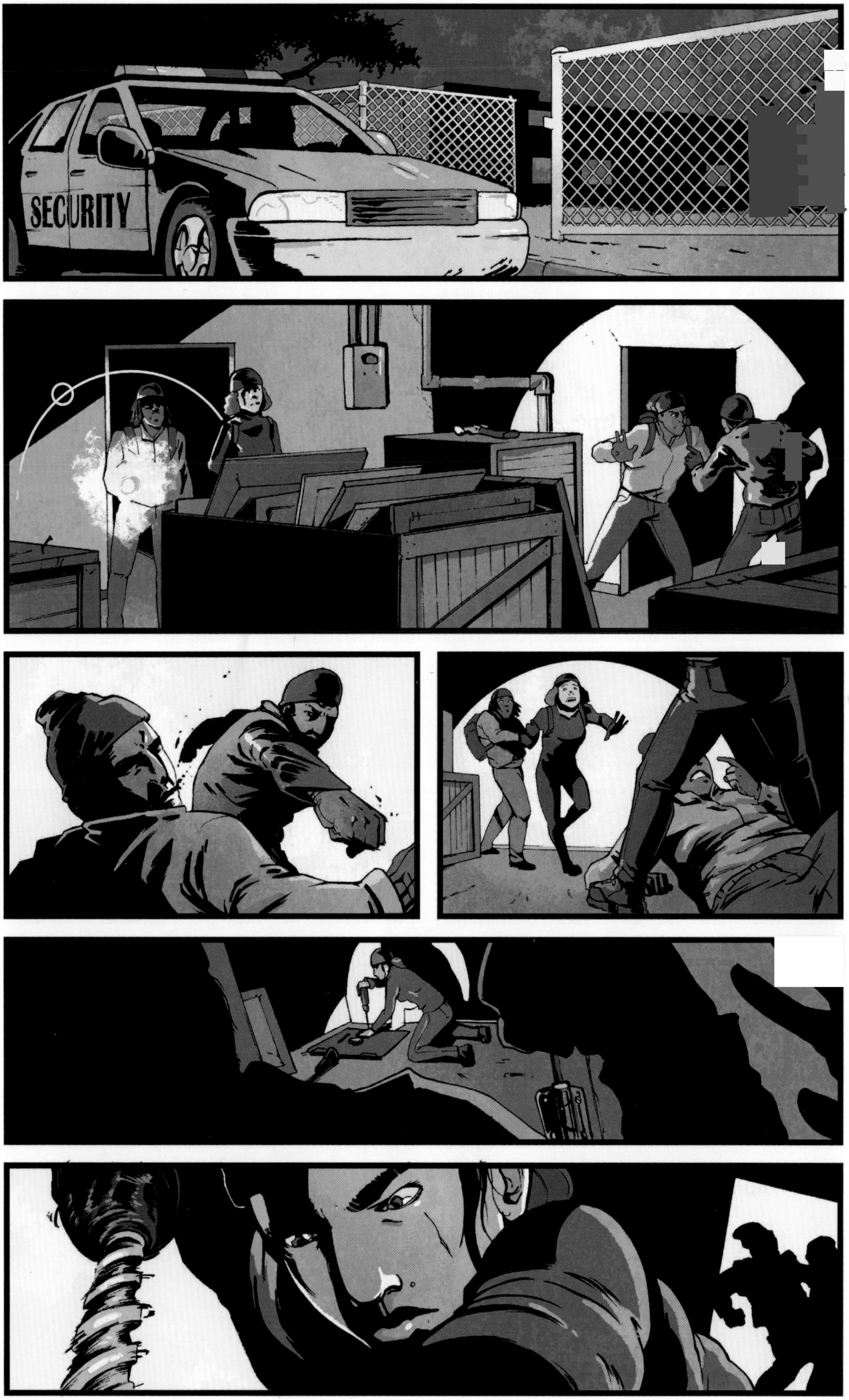
SECURITY

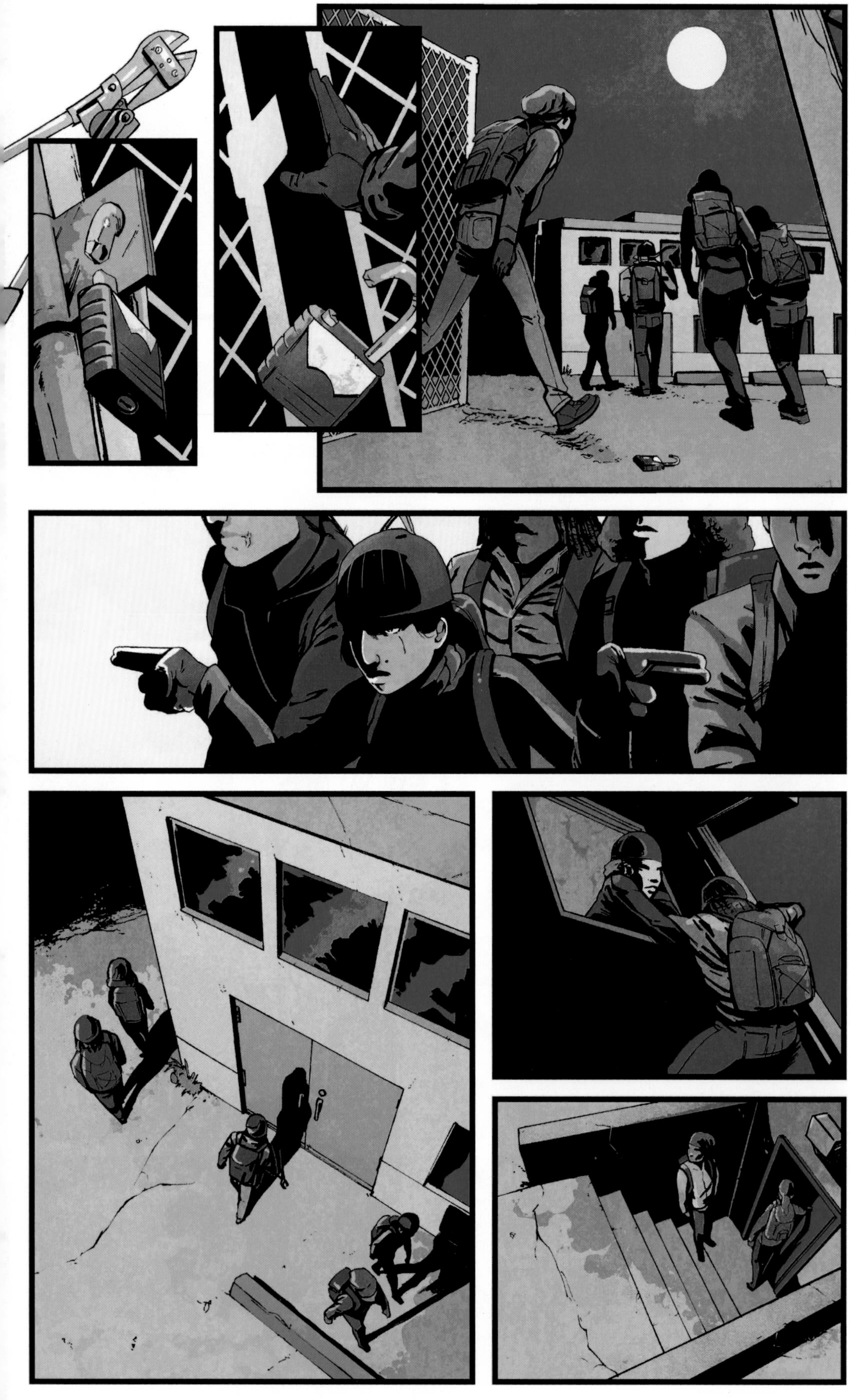

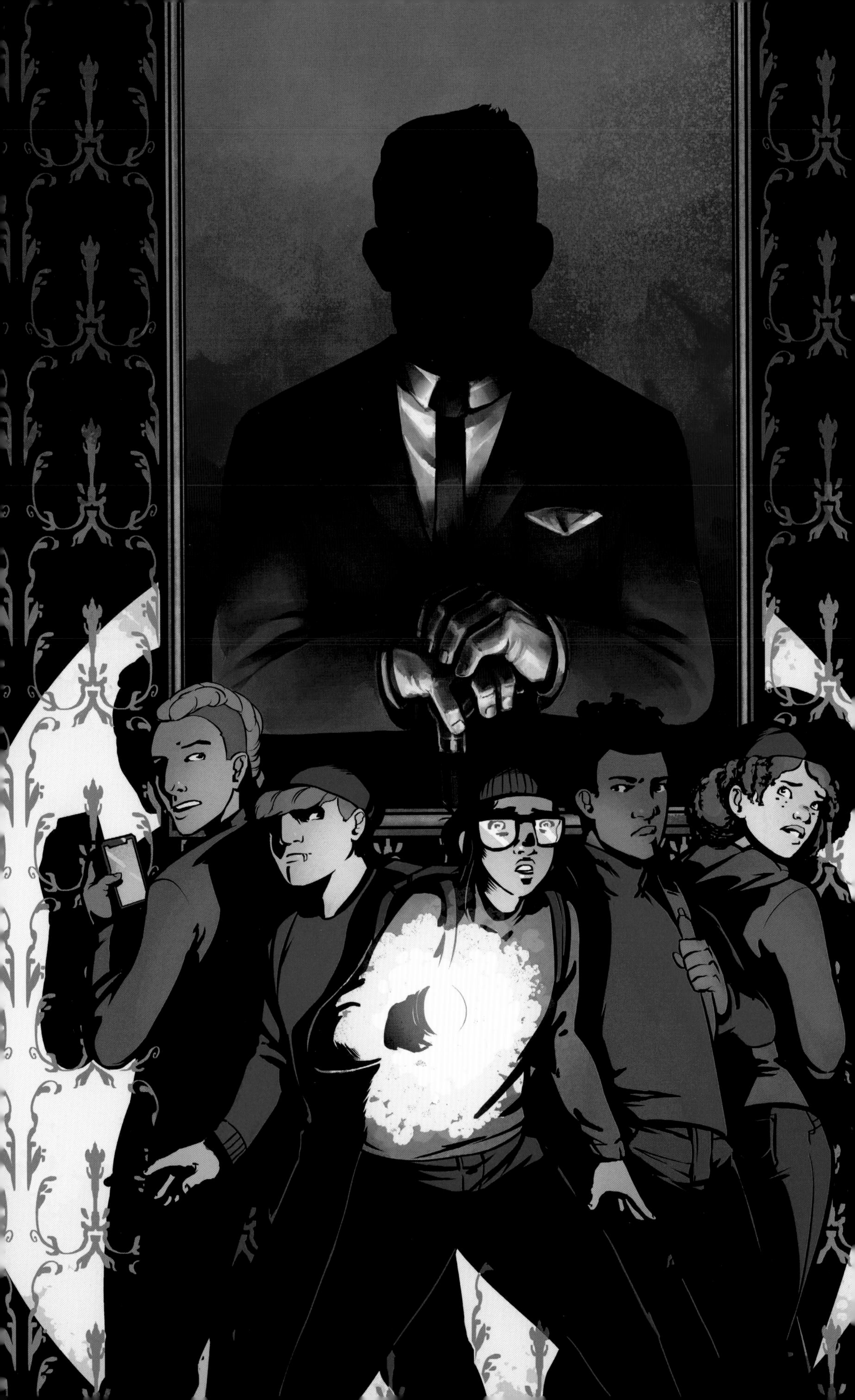

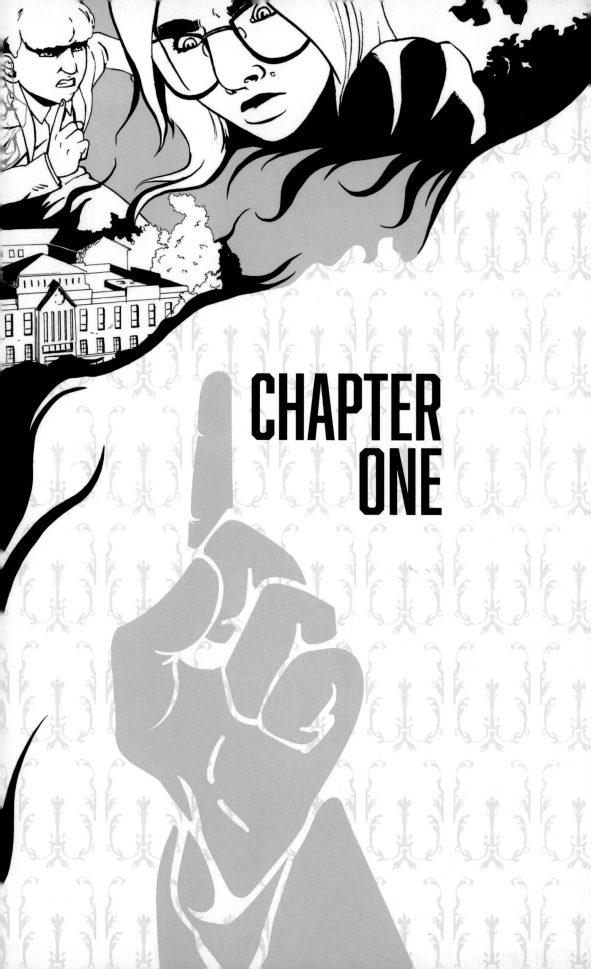

CHAPTER
ONE

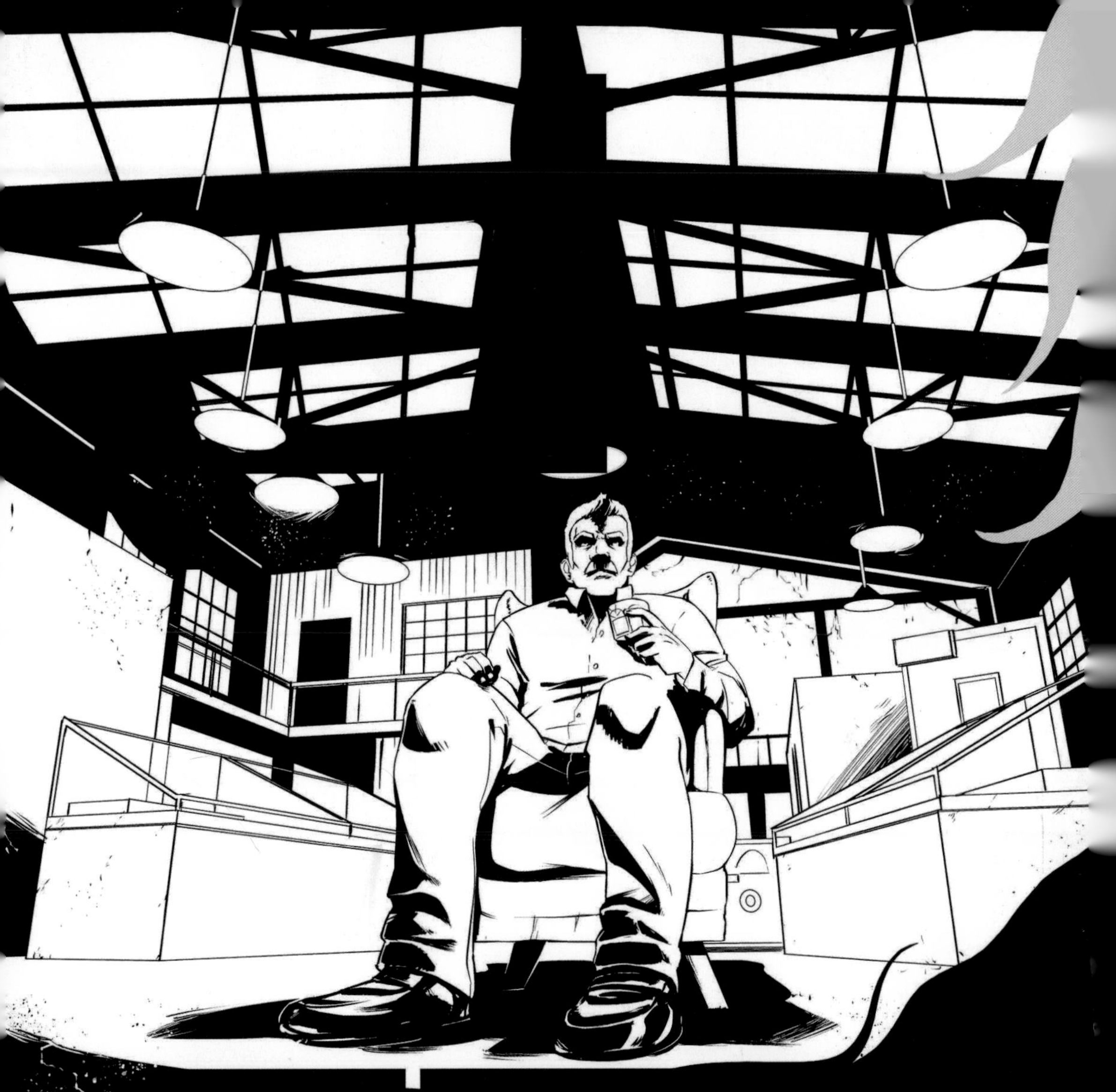

LAURA CHACÓN *FOUNDER* / MARK LONDON *CEO AND CHIEF CREATIVE OFFICER*
GIOVANNA T. OROZCO *VP OF OPERATIONS* / CHRIS FERNANDEZ *PUBLISHER* / CHRIS SANCHEZ *EDITOR-IN-CHIEF*
CECILIA MEDINA *CHIEF FINANCIAL OFFICER* / MANUEL CASTELLANOS *DIRECTOR OF SALES AND RETAILER RELATIONS MANAGER*
ALLISON POND *MARKETING DIRECTOR* / ASIA HIRSCHENSON *P.R. AND COMMUNICATIONS*
MIGUEL ANGEL ZAPATA *DESIGN DIRECTOR* / DIANA BERMÚDEZ *GRAPHIC DESIGNER* / DAVID REYES *GRAPHIC DESIGNER*
ADRIANA T. OROZCO *INTERACTIVE MEDIA DESIGNER* / NICOLÁS ZEA ARIAS *AUDIOVISUAL PRODUCTION*
FRANK SILVA *EXECUTIVE ASSISTANT* / STEPHANIE HIDALGO *EXECUTIVE ASSISTANT*

Pantomime™ published by Mad Cave Studios, Inc. 8838 SW 129th St. Miami, FL 33176. Contains materials originally published in single magazine form as Pantomime™ (2020-2021) #1-6.

First Printing. Printed in Canada. ISBN: 978-1-952303-09-8

MAD CAVE

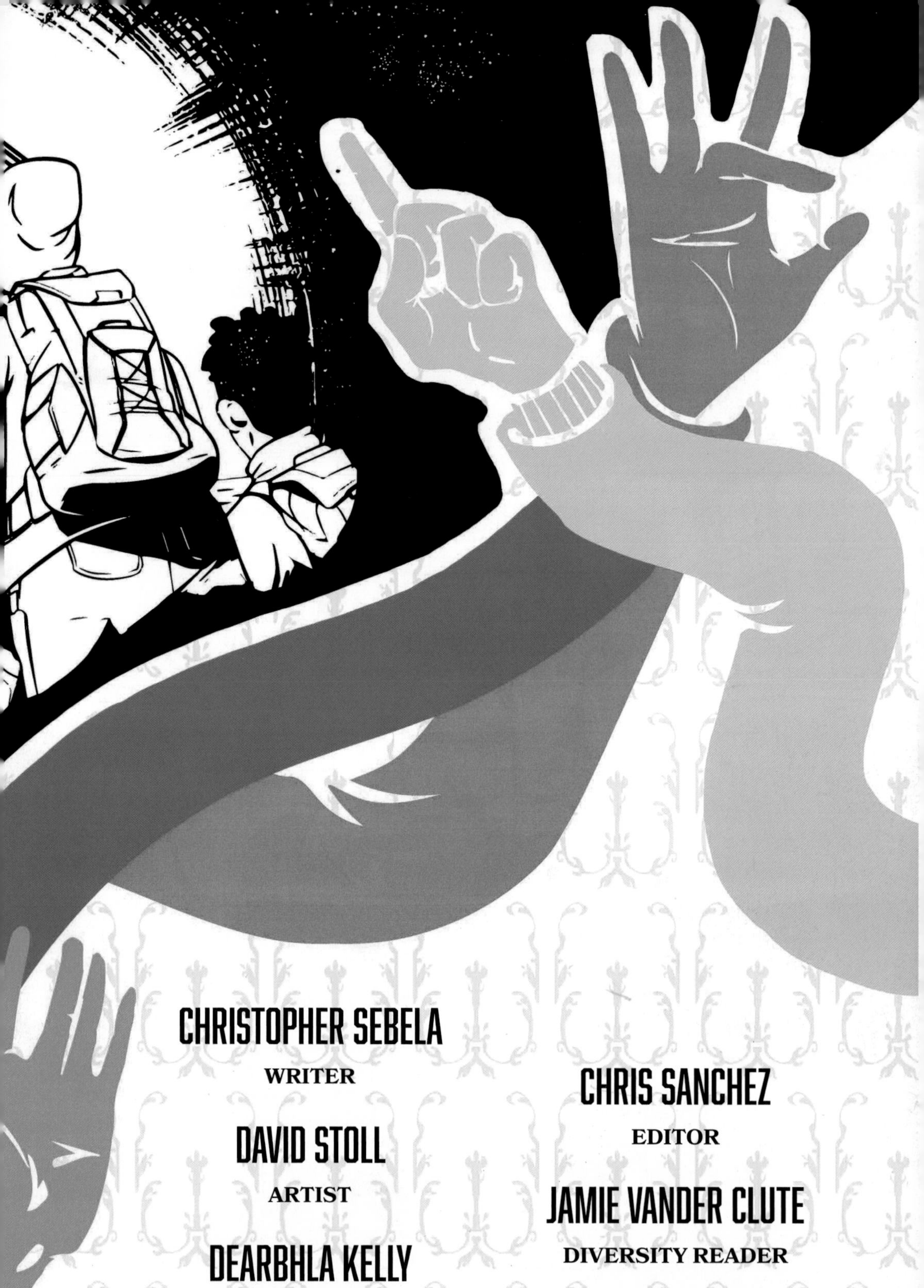

CHRISTOPHER SEBELA
WRITER

DAVID STOLL
ARTIST

DEARBHLA KELLY
COLORIST

JUSTIN BIRCH
LETTERER

CHRIS SANCHEZ
EDITOR

JAMIE VANDER CLUTE
DIVERSITY READER

DAVID REYES
BOOK AND LOGO DESIGN

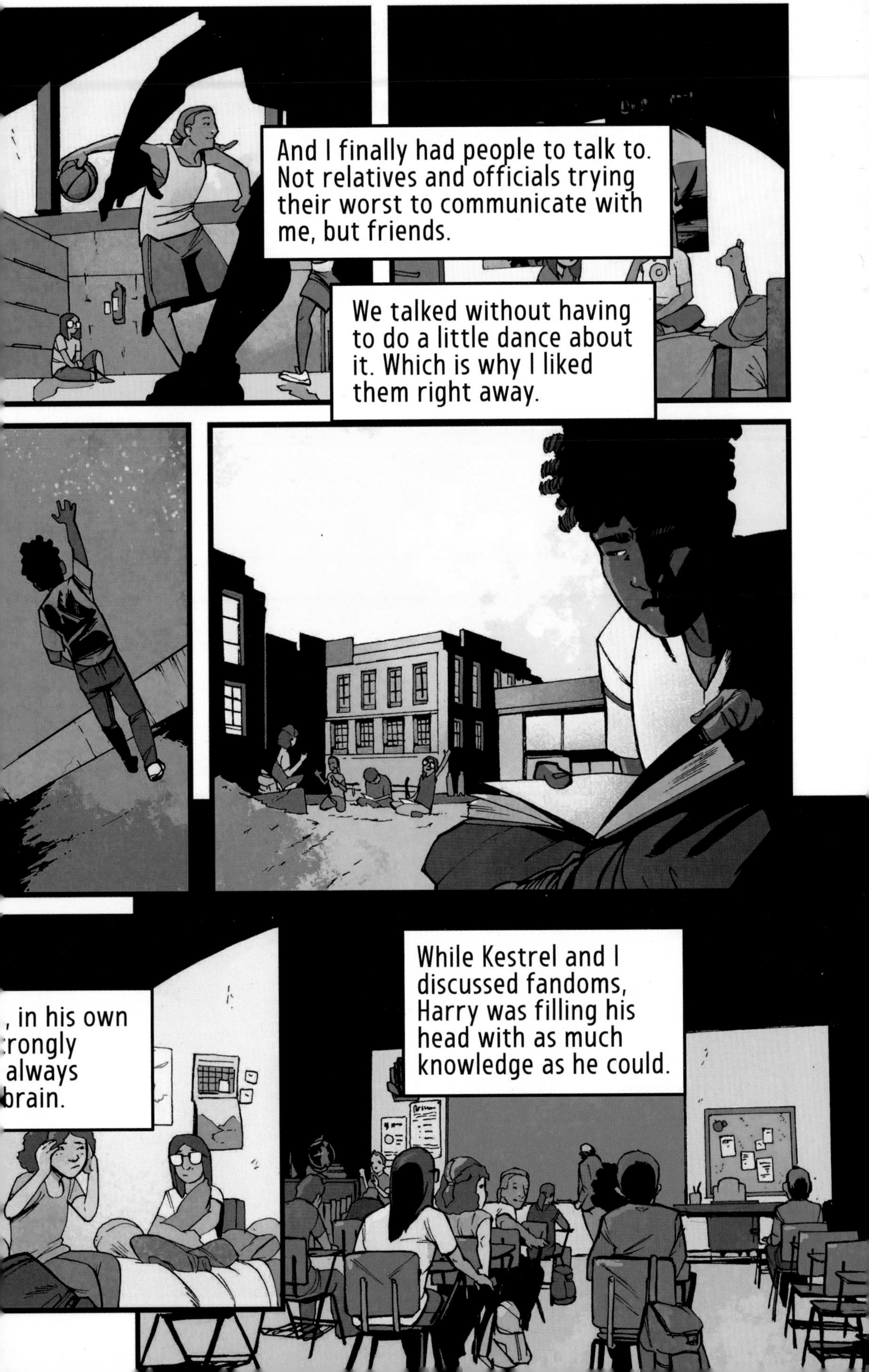
And I finally had people to talk to. Not relatives and officials trying their worst to communicate with me, but friends.
We talked without having to do a little dance about it. Which is why I liked them right away.
, in his own
rongly
always
brain.
While Kestrel and I discussed fandoms, Harry was filling his head with as much knowledge as he could.

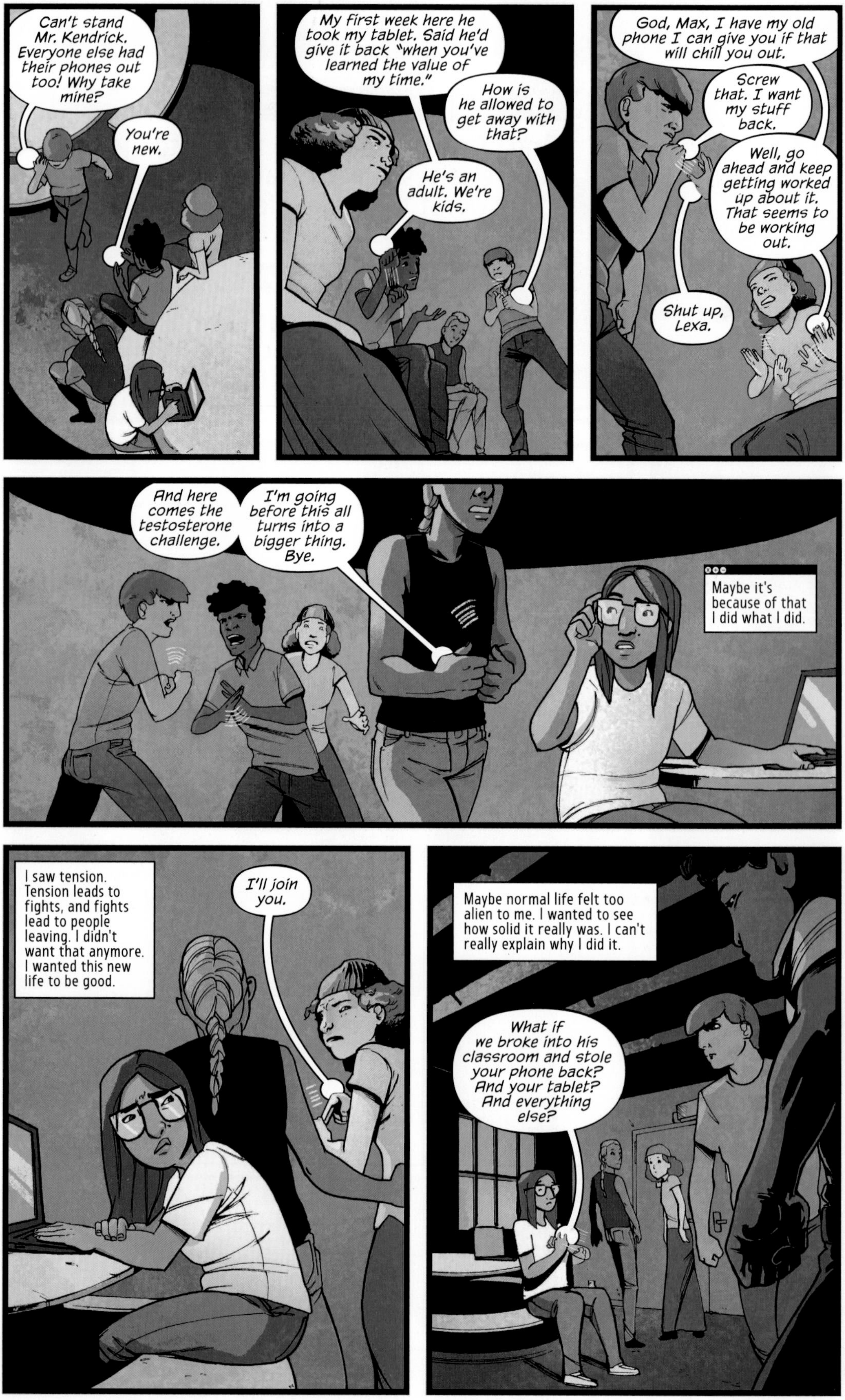
Can't stand Mr. Kendrick. Everyone else had their phones out too! Why take mine?
You're new.
My first week here he took my tablet. Said he'd give it back "when you've learned the value of my time."
He's an adult. We're kids.
How is he allowed to get away with that?
God, Max, I have my old phone I can give you if that will chill you out.
Screw that. I want my stuff back.
Well, go ahead and keep getting worked up about it. That seems to be working out.
Shut up, Lexa.
And here comes the testosterone challenge.
I'm going before this all turns into a bigger thing. Bye.
Maybe it's because of that I did what I did.
I saw tension. Tension leads to fights, and fights lead to people leaving. I didn't want that anymore. I wanted this new life to be good.
I'll join you.
Maybe normal life felt too alien to me. I wanted to see how solid it really was. I can't really explain why I did it.
What if we broke into his classroom and stole your phone back? And your tablet? And everything else?

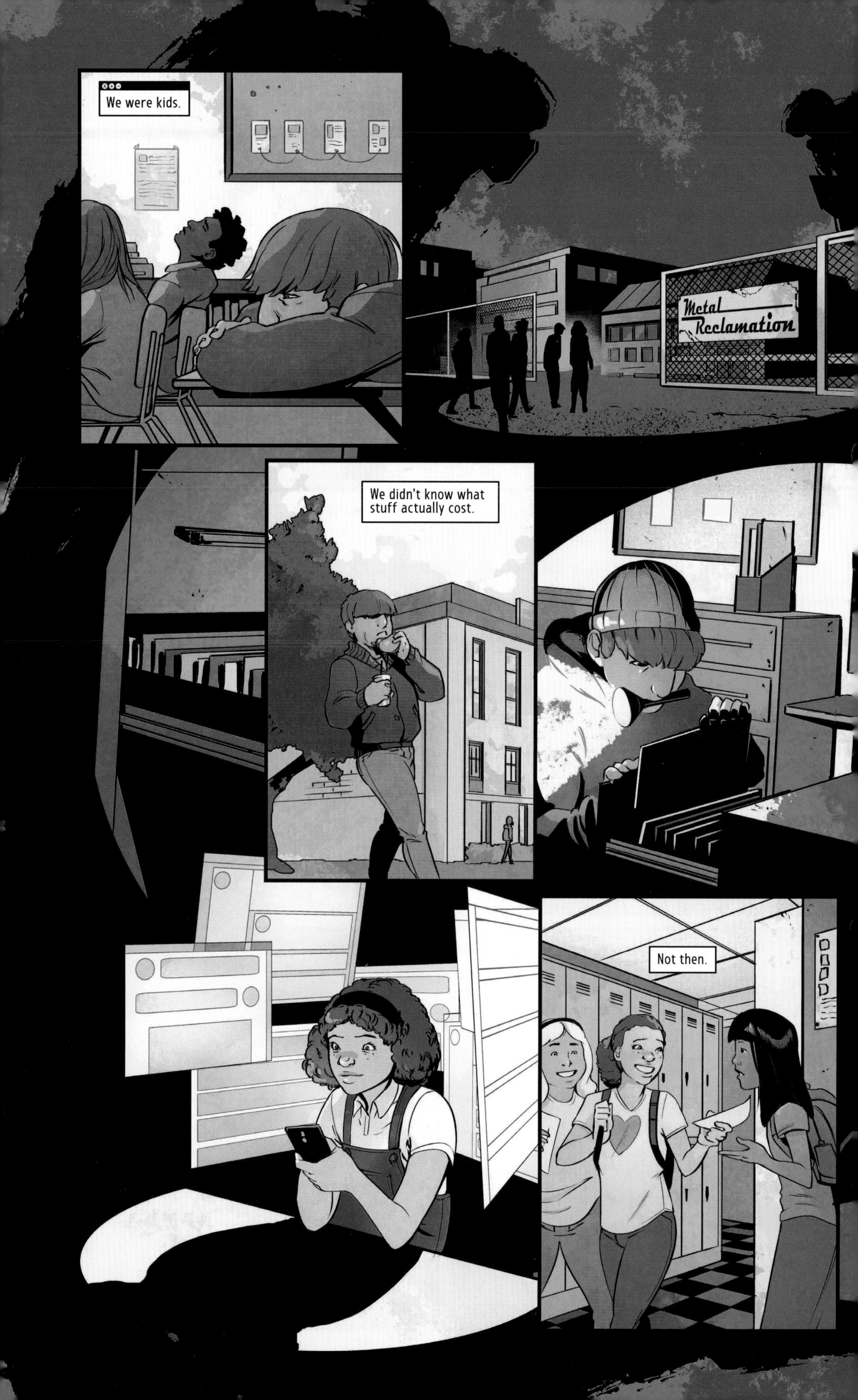
We were kids.
Metal Reclamation
We didn't know what stuff actually cost.
Not then.

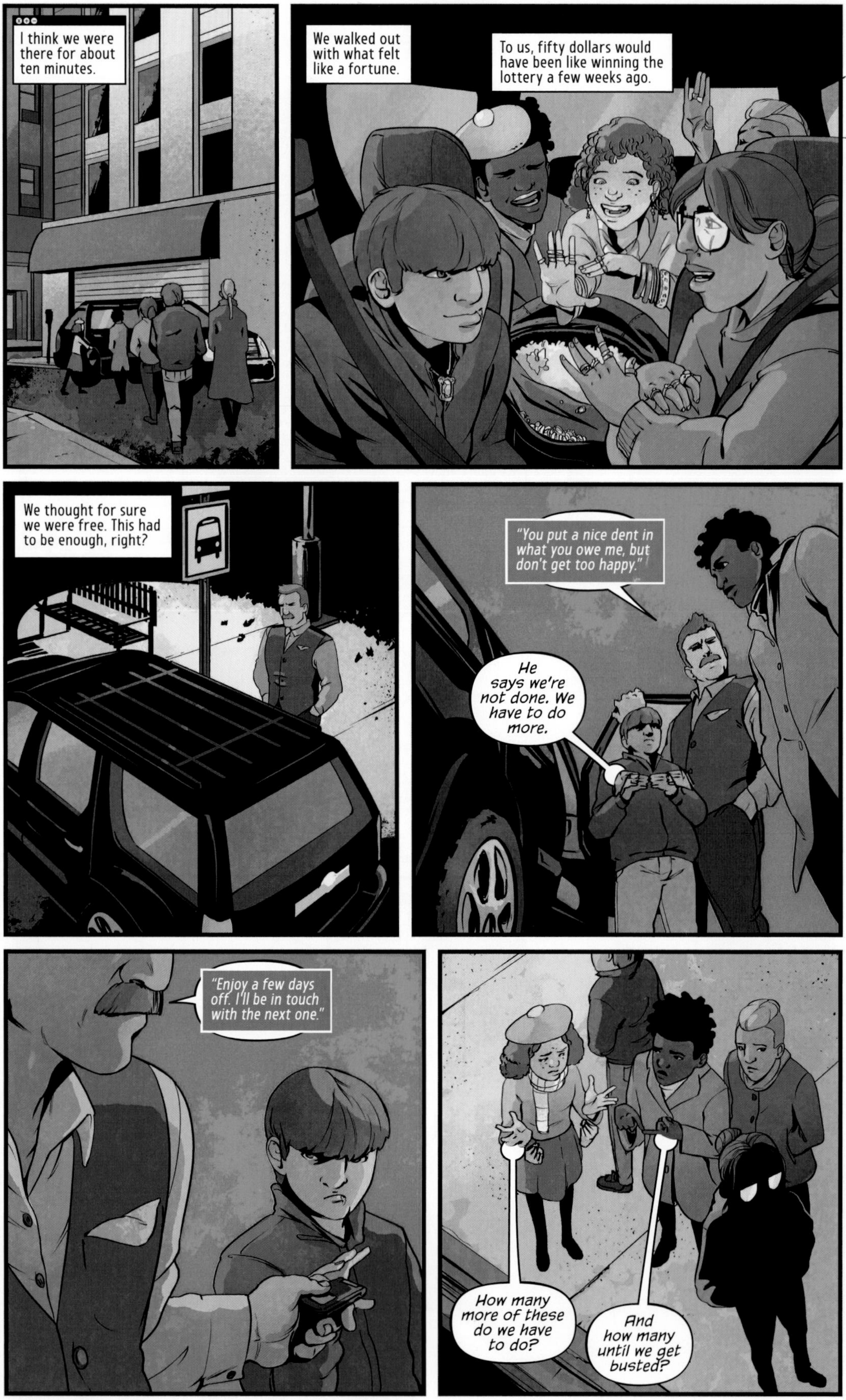
I think we were there for about ten minutes.
We walked out with what felt like a fortune.
To us, fifty dollars would have been like winning the lottery a few weeks ago.
We thought for sure we were free. This had to be enough, right?
"You put a nice dent in what you owe me, but don't get too happy."
He says we're not done. We have to do more.
"Enjoy a few days off. I'll be in touch with the next one."
How many more of these do we have to do?
And how many until we get busted?

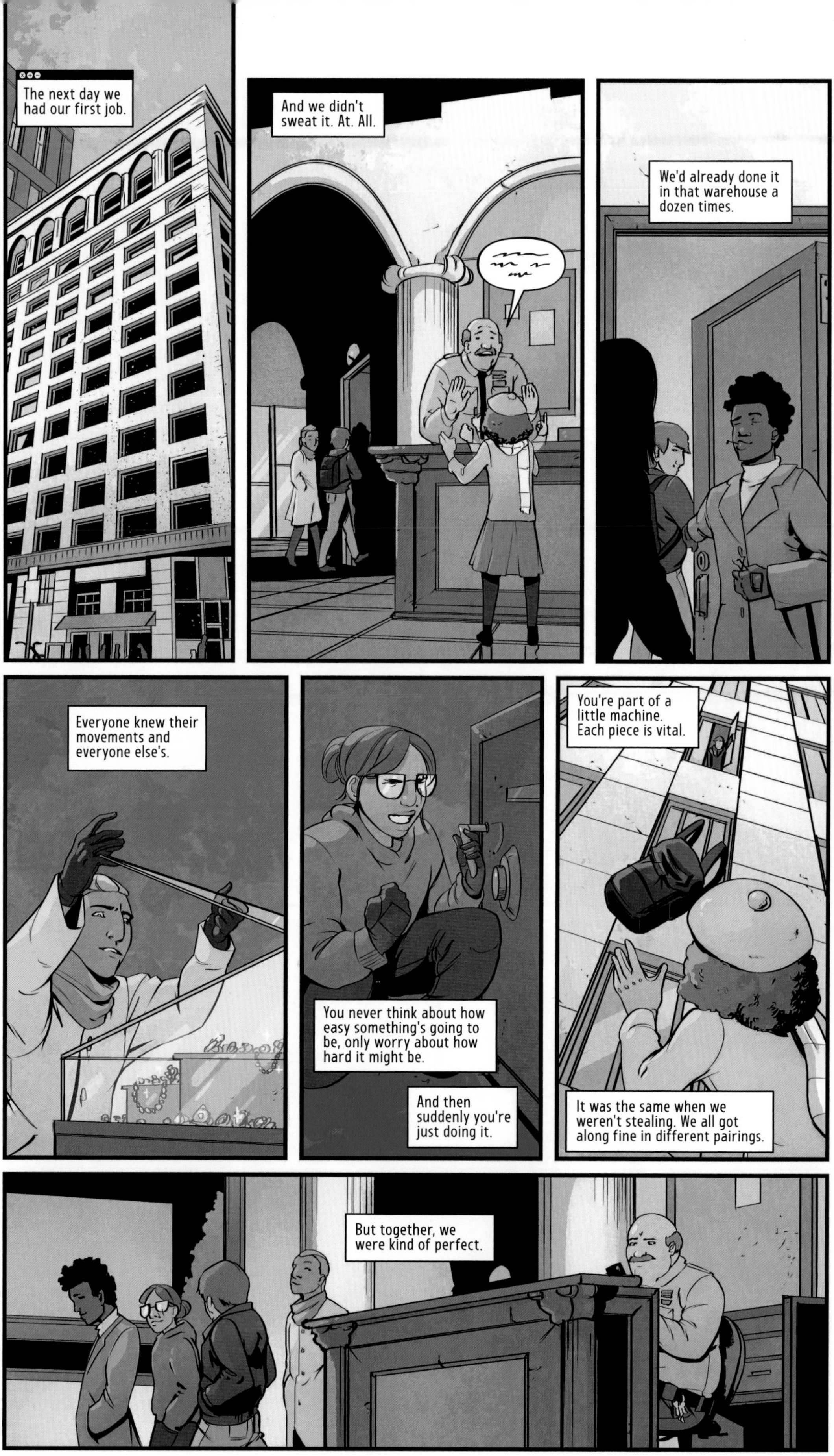
The next day we had our first job.
And we didn't sweat it. At. All.
We'd already done it in that warehouse a dozen times.
Everyone knew their movements and everyone else's.
You never think about how easy something's going to be, only worry about how hard it might be.
And then suddenly you're just doing it.
You're part of a little machine. Each piece is vital.
It was the same when we weren't stealing. We all got along fine in different pairings.
But together, we were kind of perfect.

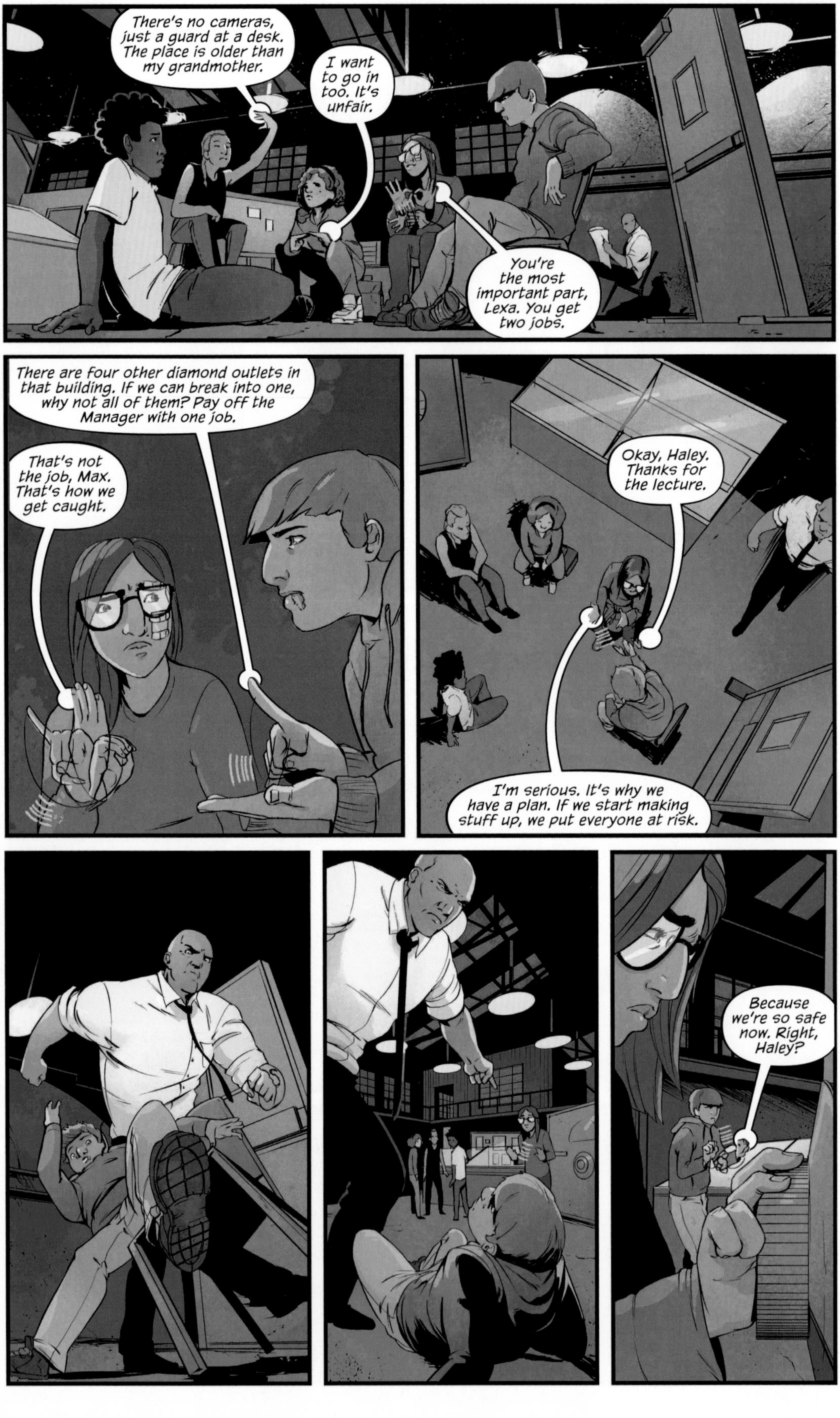
There's no cameras, just a guard at a desk. The place is older than my grandmother.
I want to go in too. It's unfair.
You're the most important part, Lexa. You get two jobs.
There are four other diamond outlets in that building. If we can break into one, why not all of them? Pay off the Manager with one job.
That's not the job, Max. That's how we get caught.
Okay, Haley. Thanks for the lecture.
I'm serious. It's why we have a plan. If we start making stuff up, we put everyone at risk.
Because we're so safe now. Right, Haley?

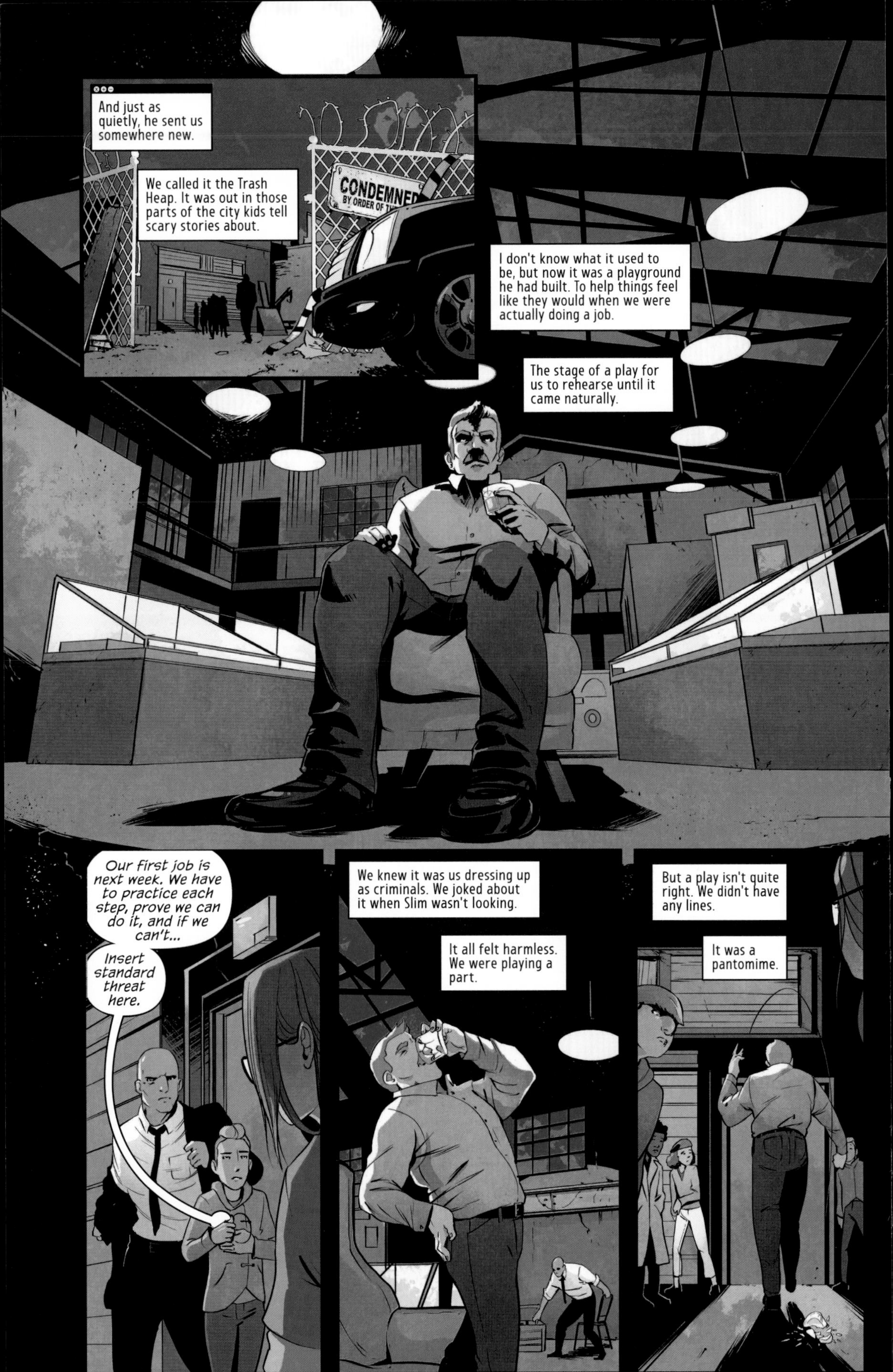
And just as quietly, he sent us somewhere new.
We called it the Trash Heap. It was out in those parts of the city kids tell scary stories about.
CONDEMNED
BY ORDER OF TH
I don't know what it used to be, but now it was a playground he had built. To help things feel like they would when we were actually doing a job.
The stage of a play for us to rehearse until it came naturally.
Our first job is next week. We have to practice each step, prove we can do it, and if we can't...
Insert standard threat here.
We knew it was us dressing up as criminals. We joked about it when Slim wasn't looking.
It all felt harmless. We were playing a part.
But a play isn't quite right. We didn't have any lines.
It was a pantomime.

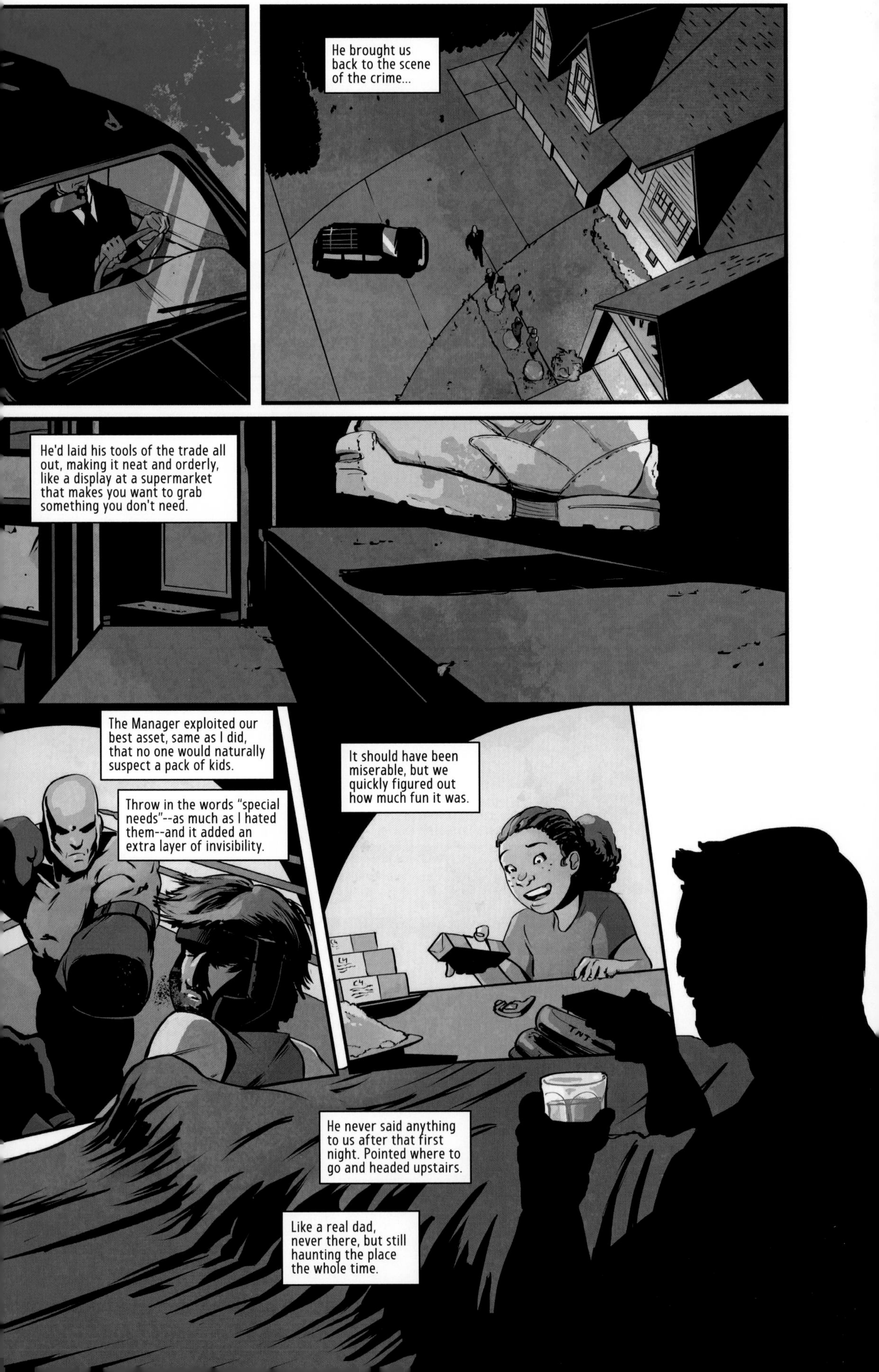
He brought us back to the scene of the crime...
He'd laid his tools of the trade all out, making it neat and orderly, like a display at a supermarket that makes you want to grab something you don't need.
The Manager exploited our best asset, same as I did, that no one would naturally suspect a pack of kids.
Throw in the words "special needs"--as much as I hated them--and it added an extra layer of invisibility.
It should have been miserable, but we quickly figured out how much fun it was.
TNT
He never said anything to us after that first night. Pointed where to go and headed upstairs.
Like a real dad, never there, but still haunting the place the whole time.

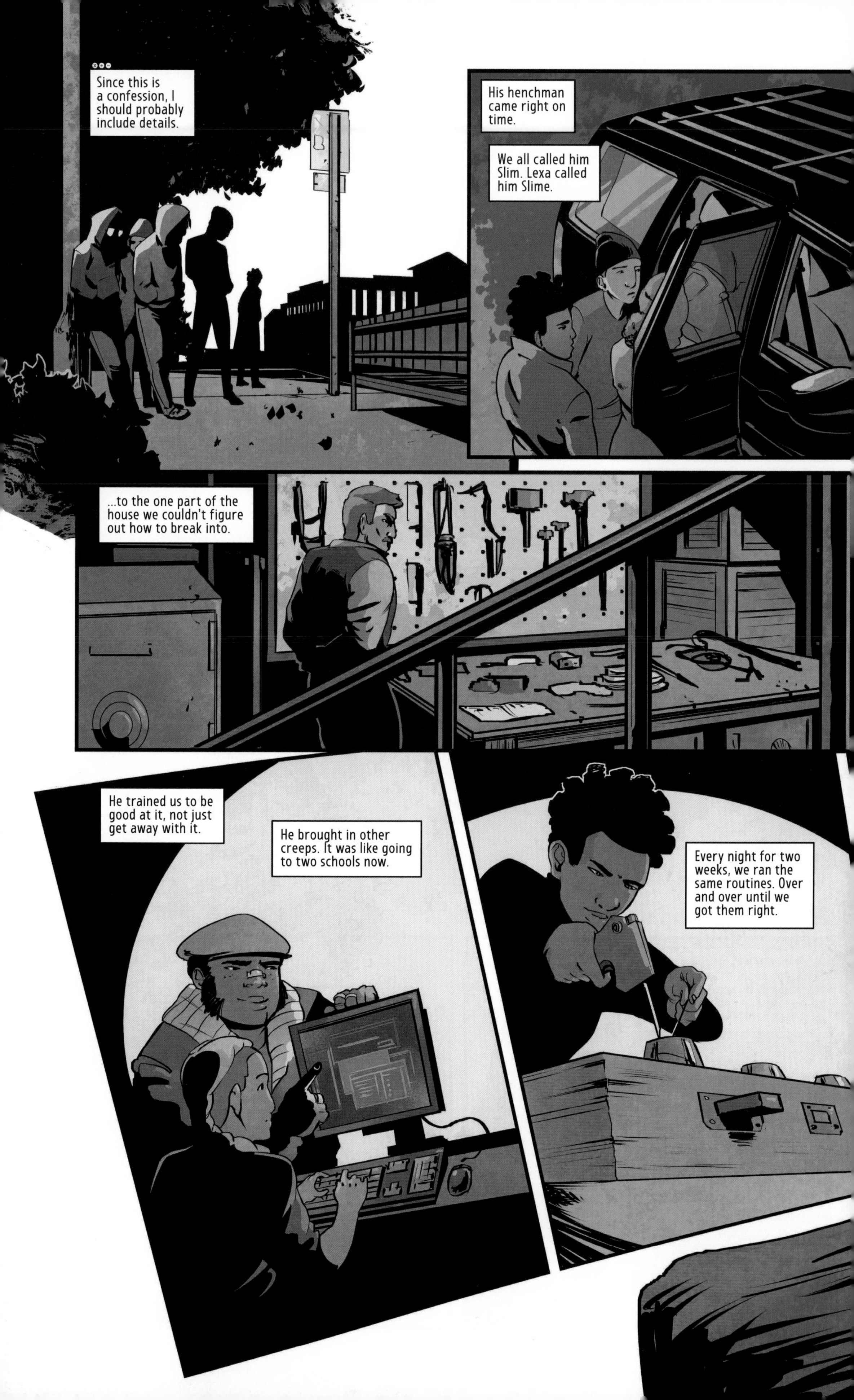
Since this is a confession, I should probably include details.
His henchman came right on time.
We all called him Slim. Lexa called him Slime.
...to the one part of the house we couldn't figure out how to break into.
He trained us to be good at it, not just get away with it.
He brought in other creeps. It was like going to two schools now.
Every night for two weeks, we ran the same routines. Over and over until we got them right.

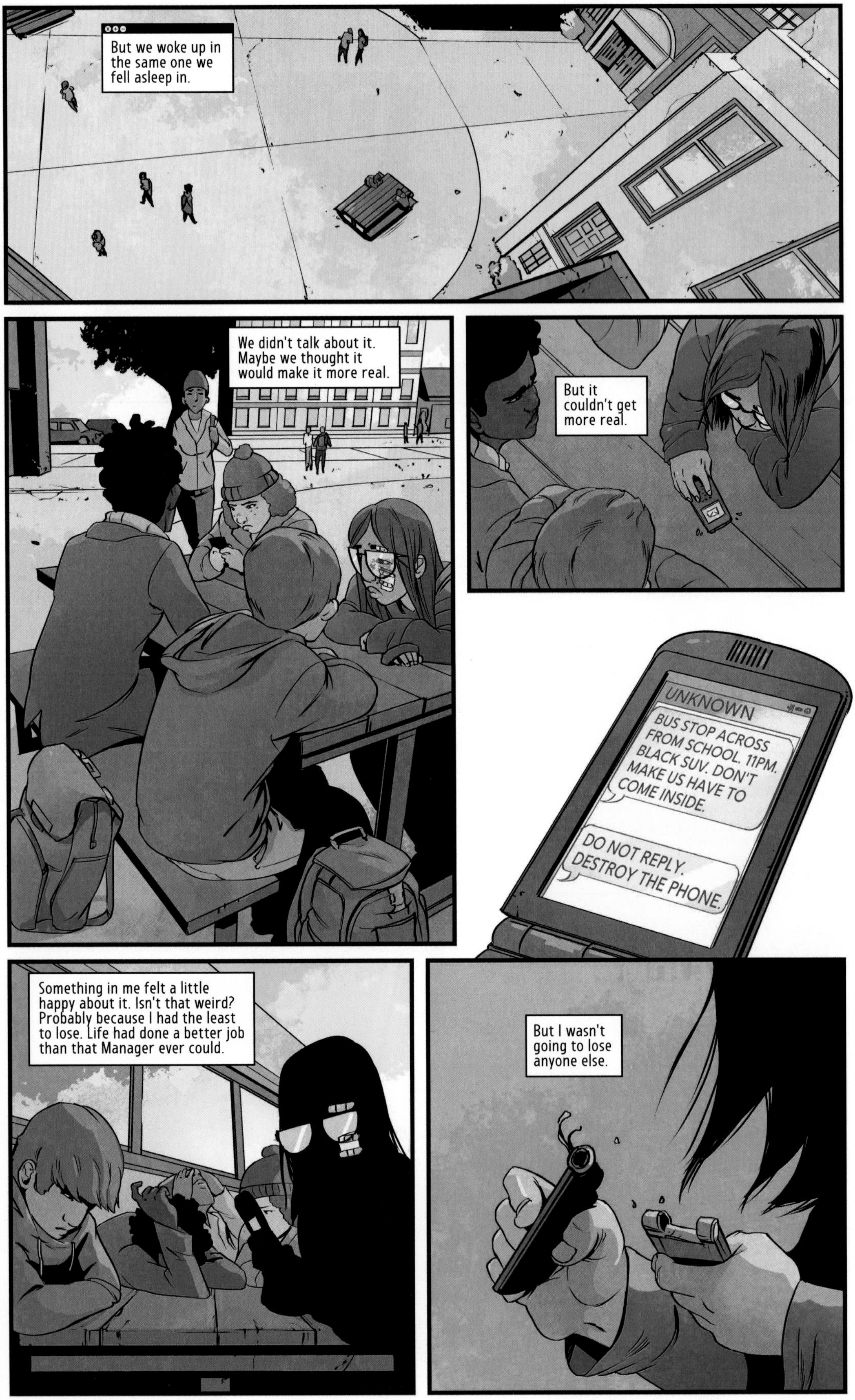
But we woke up in the same one we fell asleep in.
We didn't talk about it. Maybe we thought it would make it more real.
But it couldn't get more real.
UNKNOWN
BUS STOP ACROSS FROM SCHOOL. 11PM. BLACK SUV. DON'T MAKE US HAVE TO COME INSIDE.
DO NOT REPLY. DESTROY THE PHONE.
Something in me felt a little happy about it. Isn't that weird? Probably because I had the least to lose. Life had done a better job than that Manager ever could.
But I wasn't going to lose anyone else.

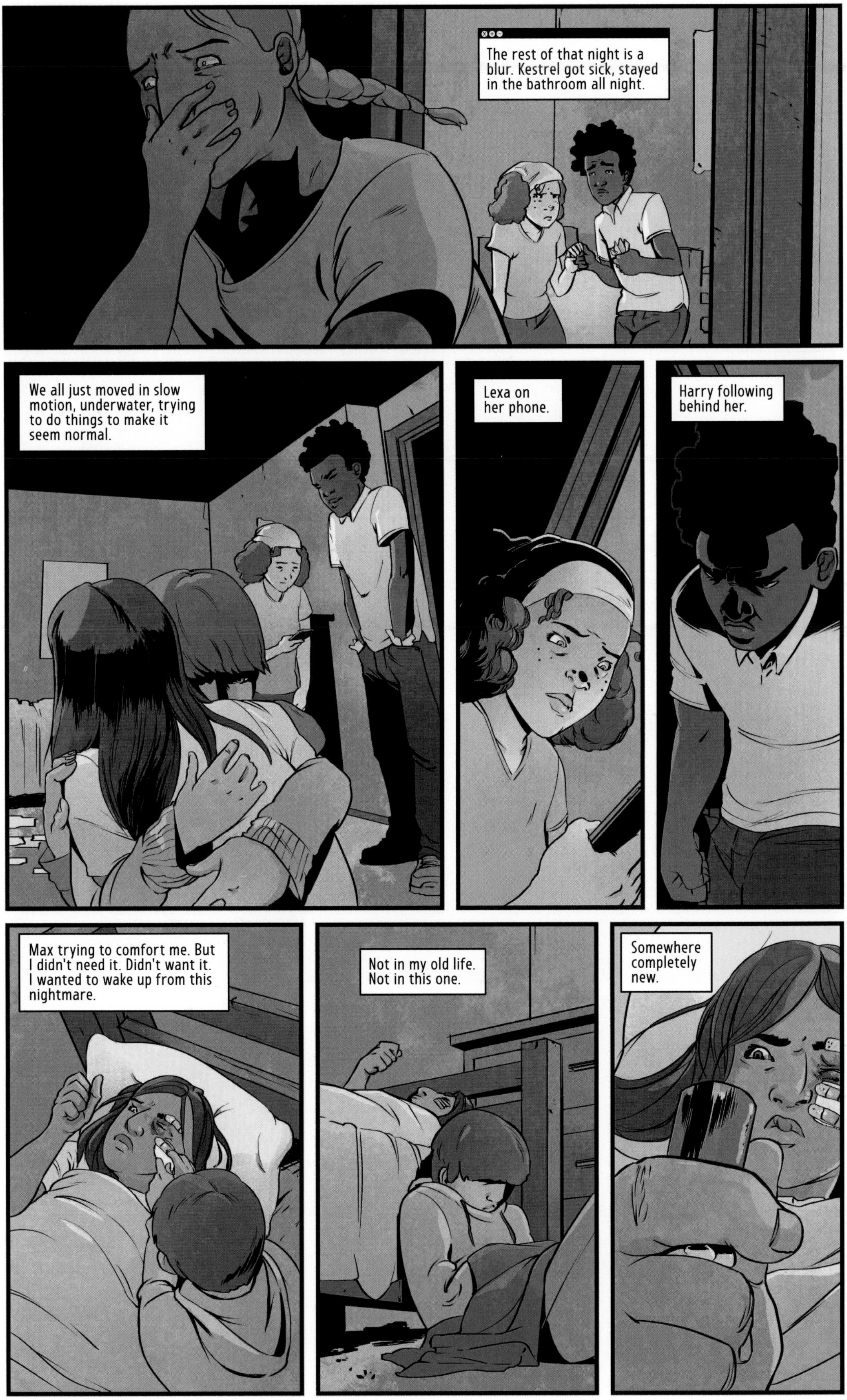
The rest of that night is a blur. Kestrel got sick, stayed in the bathroom all night.
We all just moved in slow motion, underwater, trying to do things to make it seem normal.
Lexa on her phone.
Harry following behind her.
Max trying to comfort me. But I didn't need it. Didn't want it. I wanted to wake up from this nightmare.
Not in my old life. Not in this one.
Somewhere completely new.

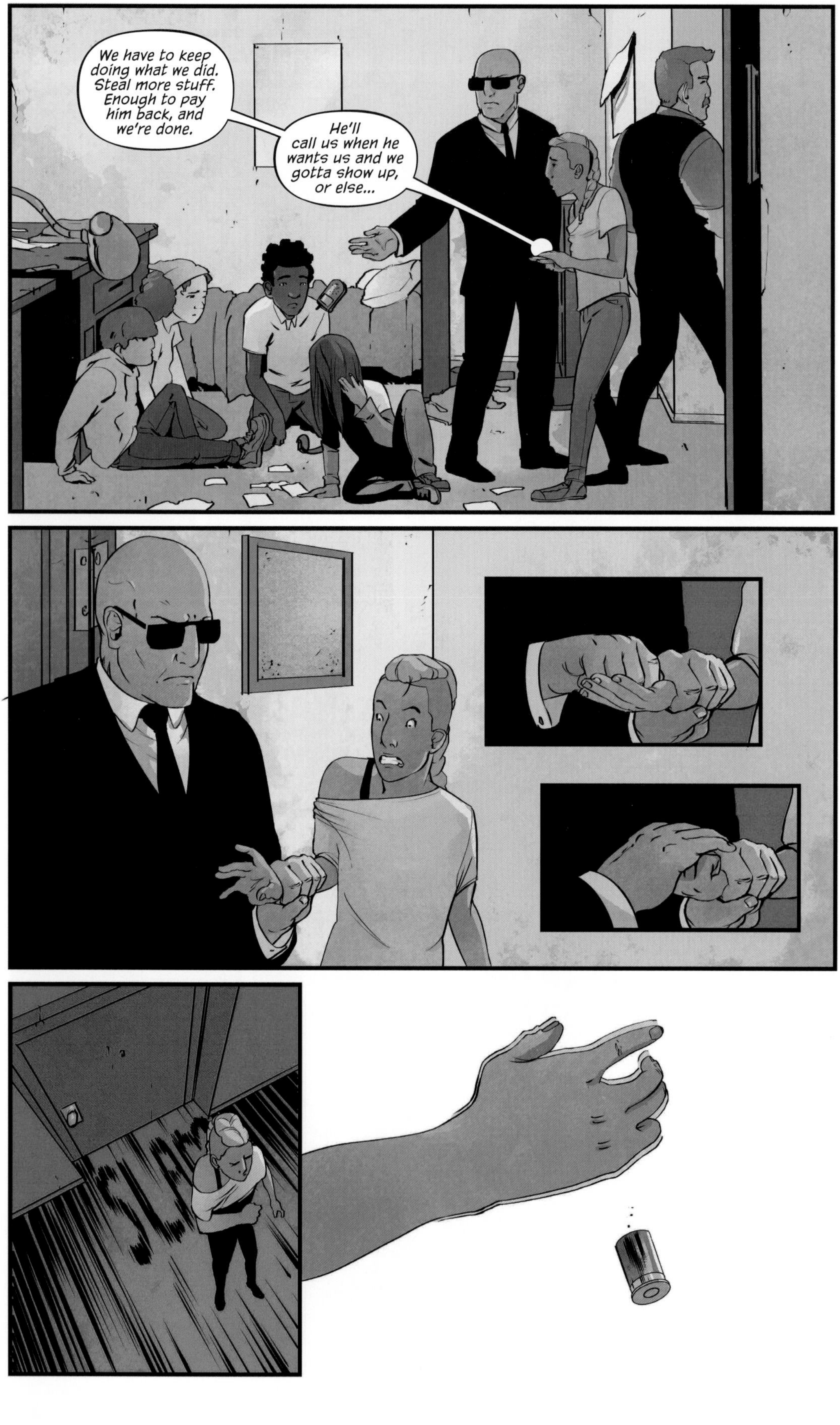
We have to keep doing what we did. Steal more stuff. Enough to pay him back, and we're done.
He'll call us when he wants us and we gotta show up, or else...

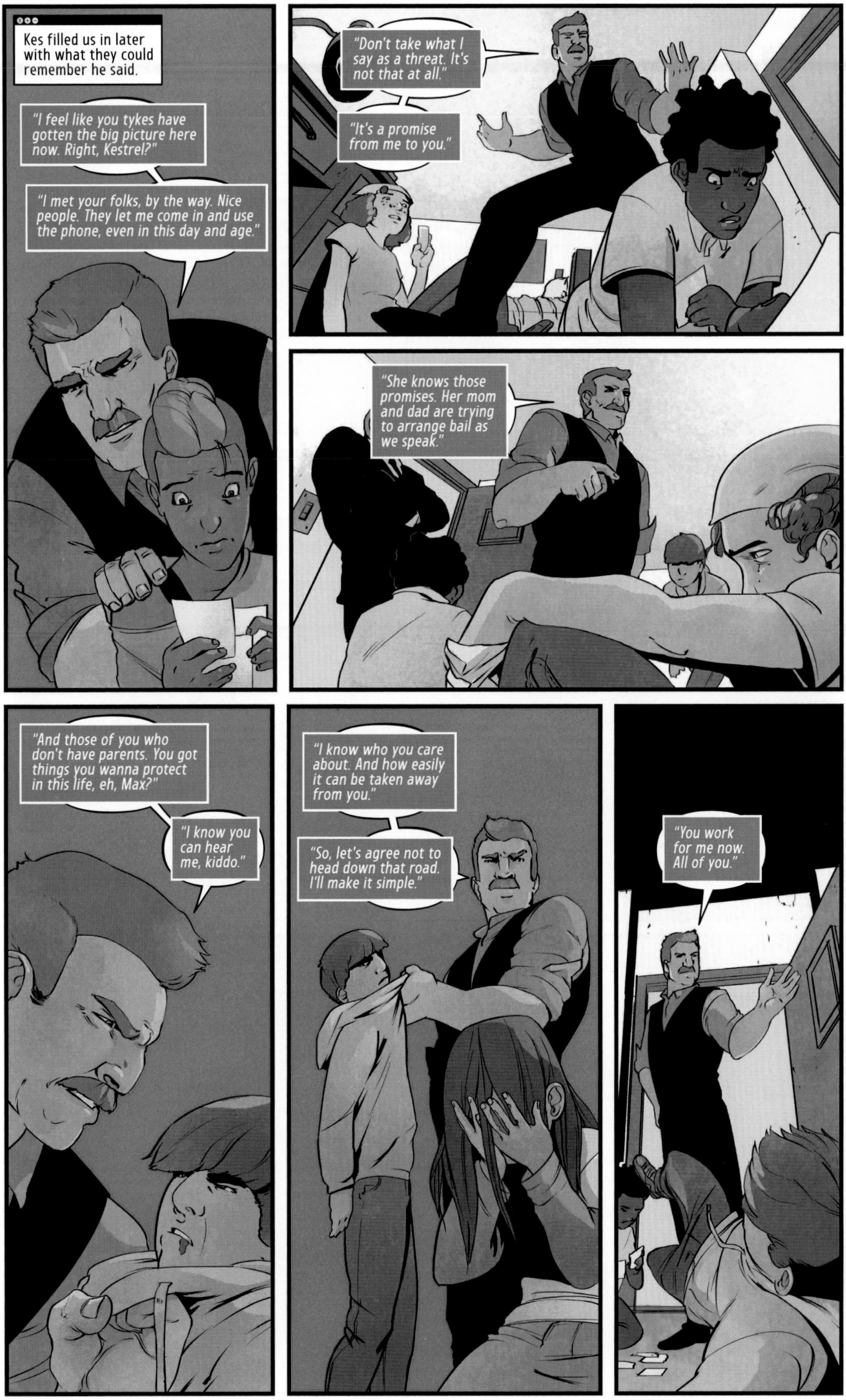

Kes filled us in later with what they could remember he said.
"I feel like you tykes have gotten the big picture here now. Right, Kestrel?"
"I met your folks, by the way. Nice people. They let me come in and use the phone, even in this day and age."
"Don't take what I say as a threat. It's not that at all."
"It's a promise from me to you."
"She knows those promises. Her mom and dad are trying to arrange bail as we speak."
"And those of you who don't have parents. You got things you wanna protect in this life, eh, Max?"
"I know you can hear me, kiddo."
"I know who you care about. And how easily it can be taken away from you."
"So, let's agree not to head down that road. I'll make it simple."
"You work for me now. All of you."

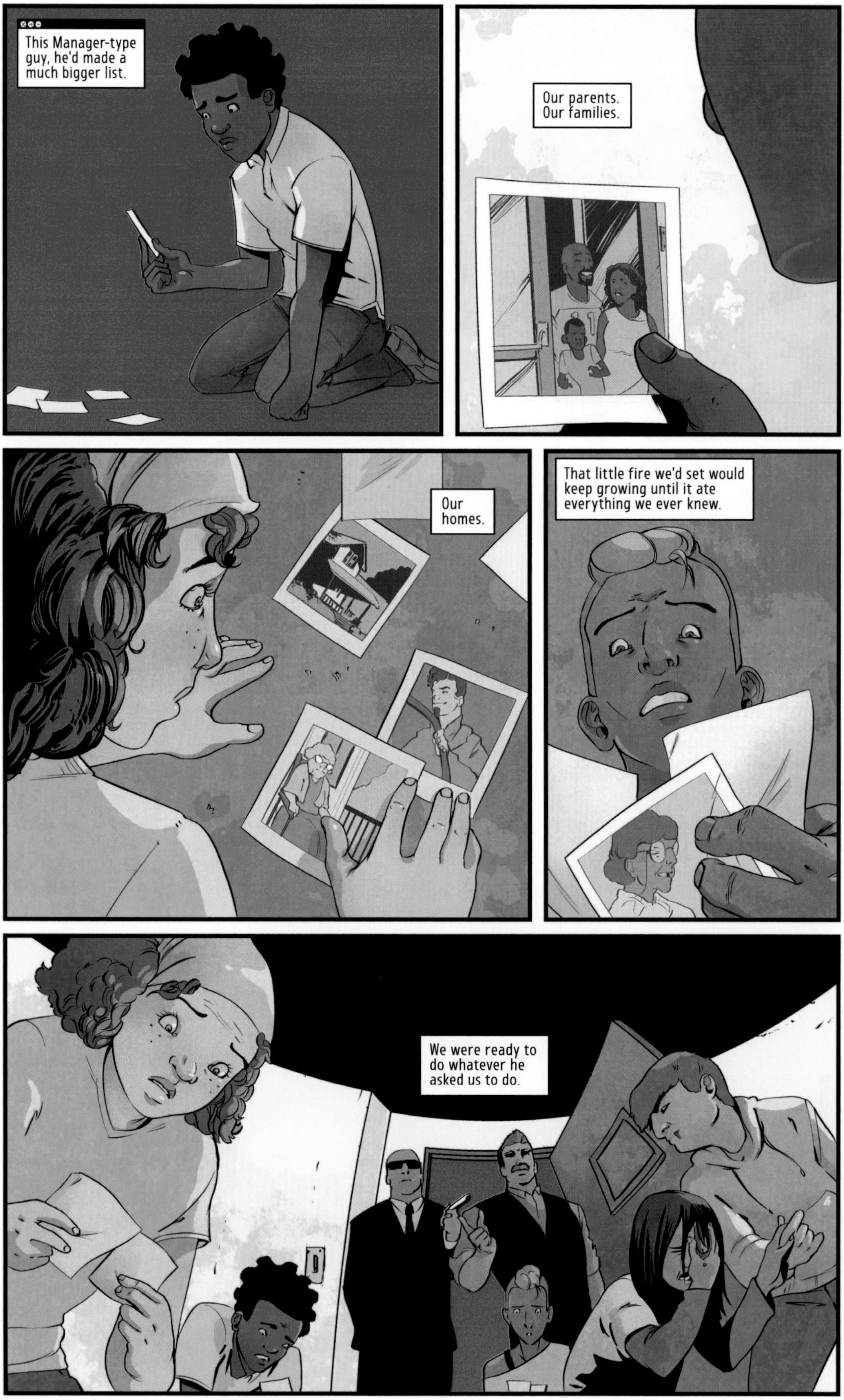
This Manager-type guy, he'd made a much bigger list.
Our parents. Our families.
Our homes.
That little fire we'd set would keep growing until it ate everything we ever knew.
We were ready to do whatever he asked us to do.

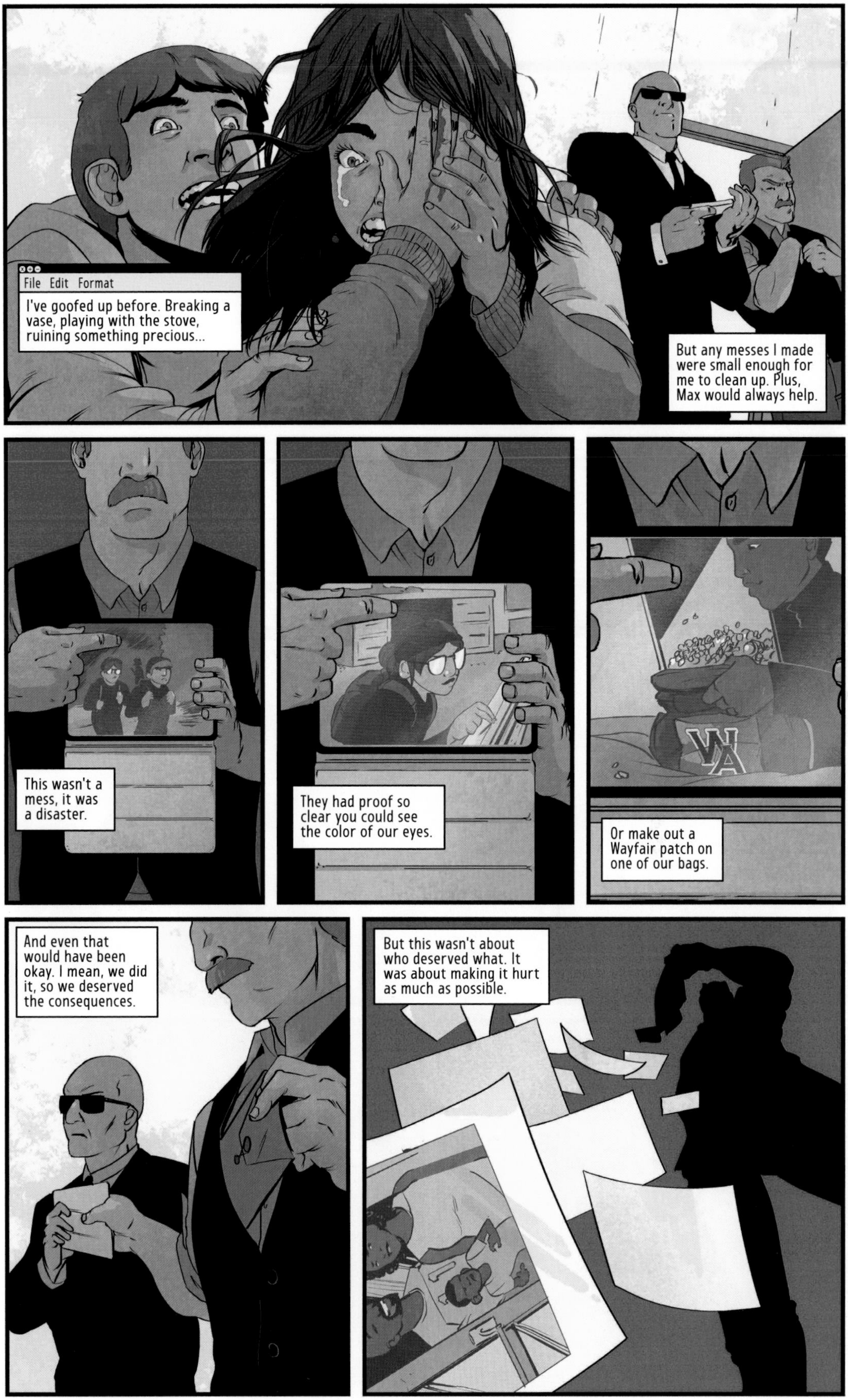
File Edit Format
I've goofed up before. Breaking a vase, playing with the stove, ruining something precious...
But any messes I made were small enough for me to clean up. Plus, Max would always help.
This wasn't a mess, it was a disaster.
They had proof so clear you could see the color of our eyes.
Or make out a Wayfair patch on one of our bags.
And even that would have been okay. I mean, we did it, so we deserved the consequences.
But this wasn't about who deserved what. It was about making it hurt as much as possible.

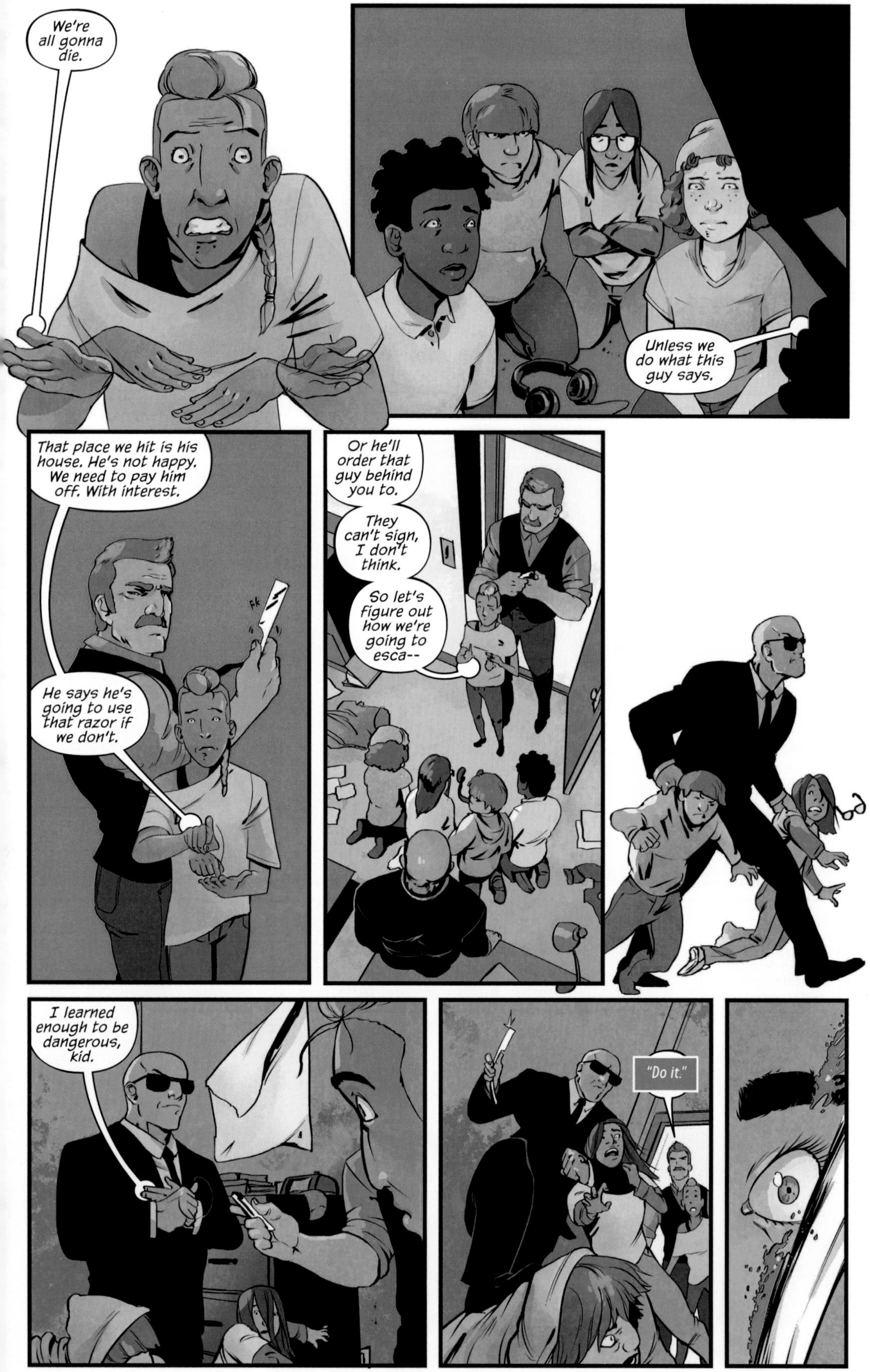

We're all gonna die.
Unless we do what this guy says.
That place we hit is his house. He's not happy. We need to pay him off. With interest.
He says he's going to use that razor if we don't.
Or he'll order that guy behind you to.
They can't sign, I don't think.
So let's figure out how we're going to esca--
I learned enough to be dangerous, kid.
"Do it."

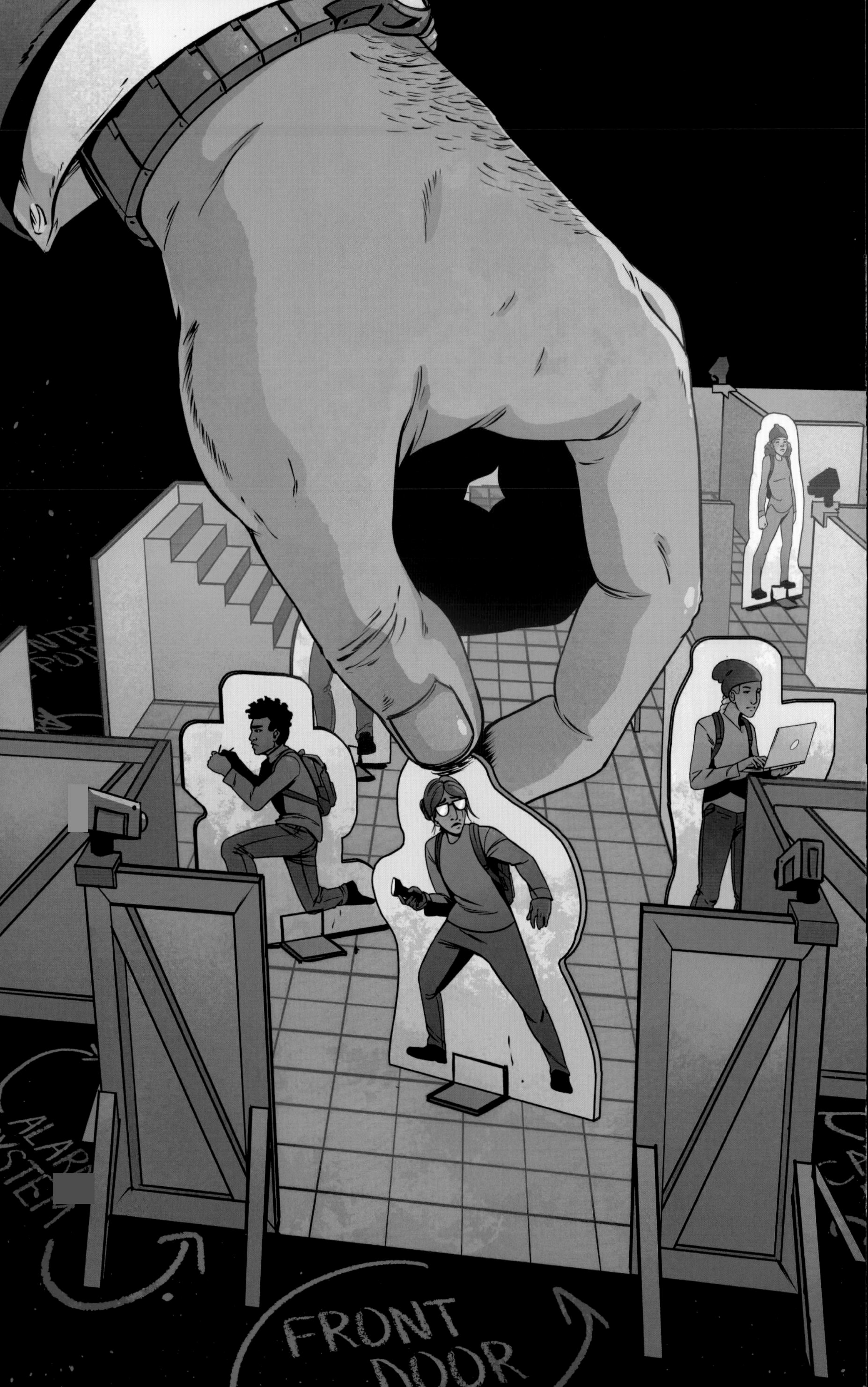
FRONT DOOR

CHAPTER TWO

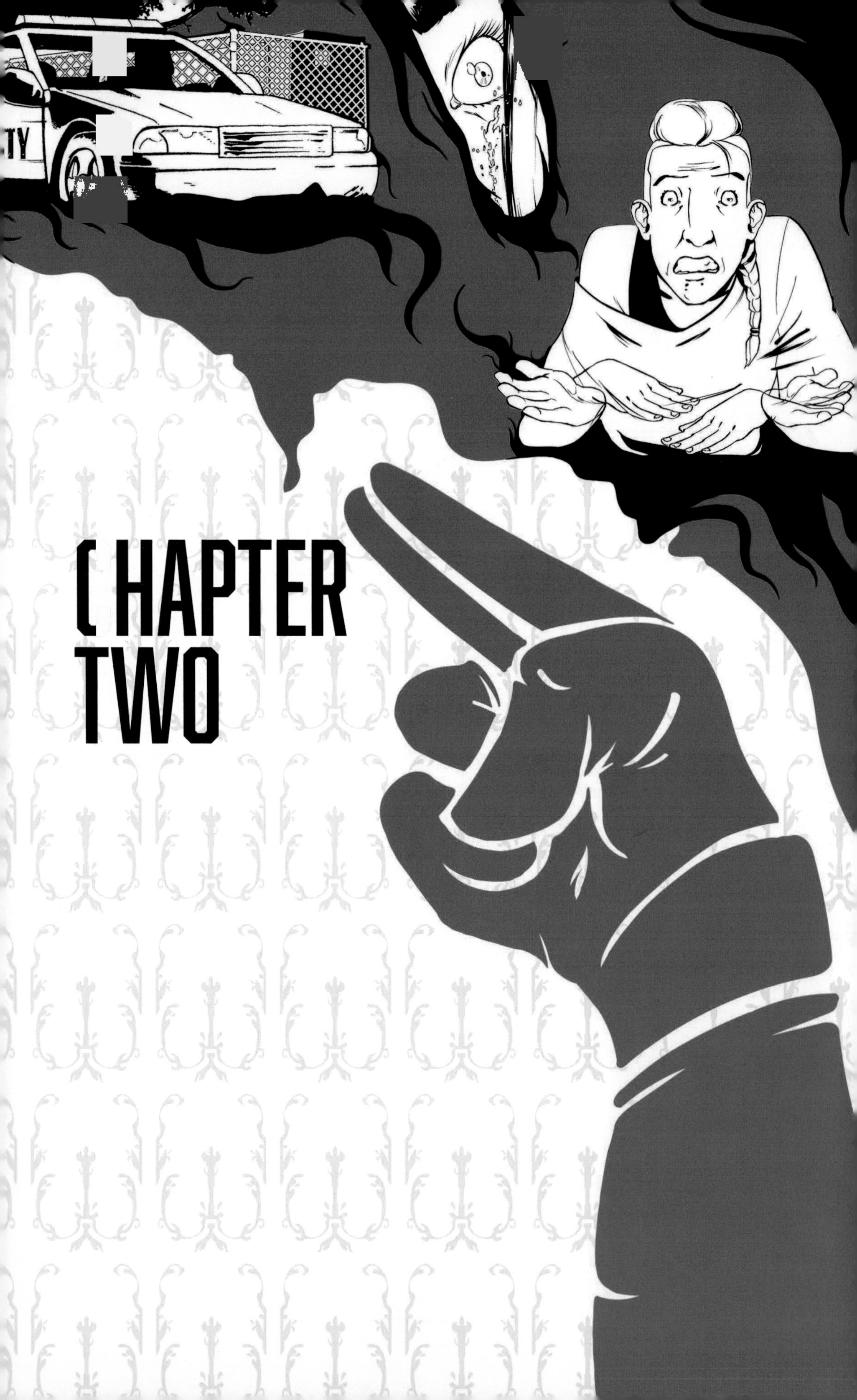

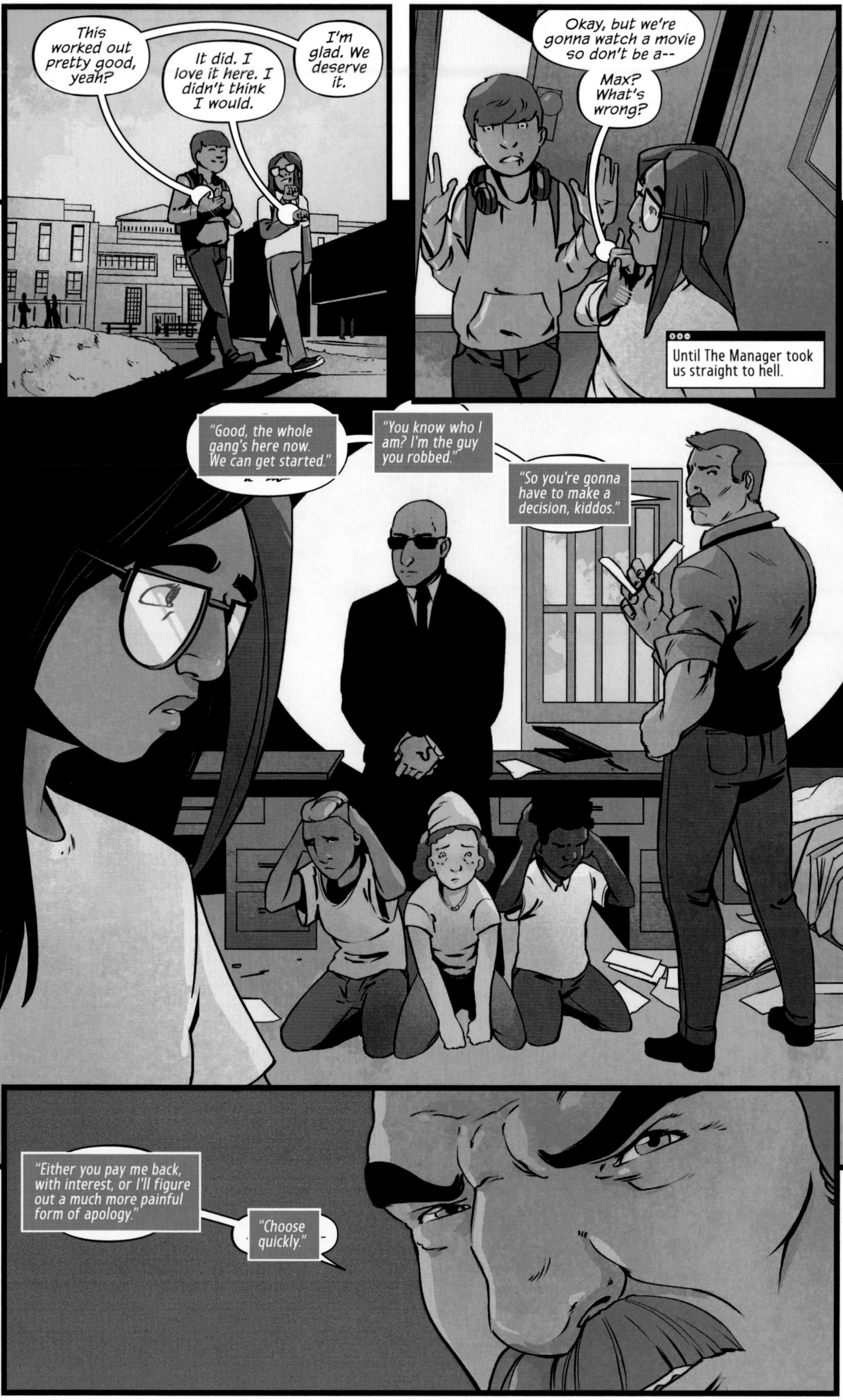
This worked out pretty good, yeah?
It did. I love it here. I didn't think I would.
I'm glad. We deserve it.
Okay, but we're gonna watch a movie so don't be a--
Max? What's wrong?
Until The Manager took us straight to hell.
"Good, the whole gang's here now. We can get started."
"You know who I am? I'm the guy you robbed."
"So you're gonna have to make a decision, kiddos."
"Either you pay me back, with interest, or I'll figure out a much more painful form of apology."
"Choose quickly."

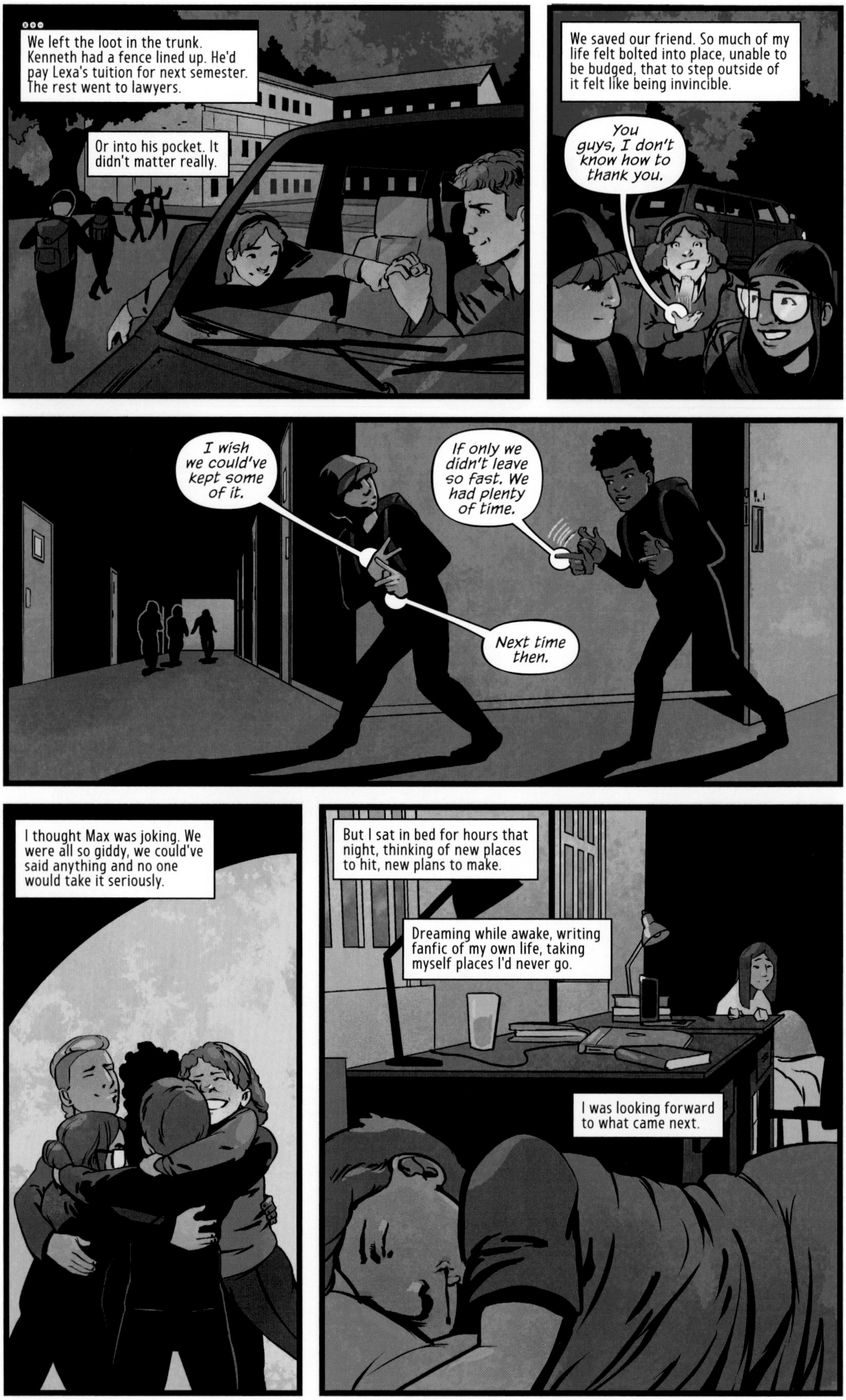
We left the loot in the trunk. Kenneth had a fence lined up. He'd pay Lexa's tuition for next semester. The rest went to lawyers.
Or into his pocket. It didn't matter really.
We saved our friend. So much of my life felt bolted into place, unable to be budged, that to step outside of it felt like being invincible.
You guys, I don't know how to thank you.
I wish we could've kept some of it.
If only we didn't leave so fast. We had plenty of time.
Next time then.
I thought Max was joking. We were all so giddy, we could've said anything and no one would take it seriously.
But I sat in bed for hours that night, thinking of new places to hit, new plans to make.
Dreaming while awake, writing fanfic of my own life, taking myself places I'd never go.
I was looking forward to what came next.

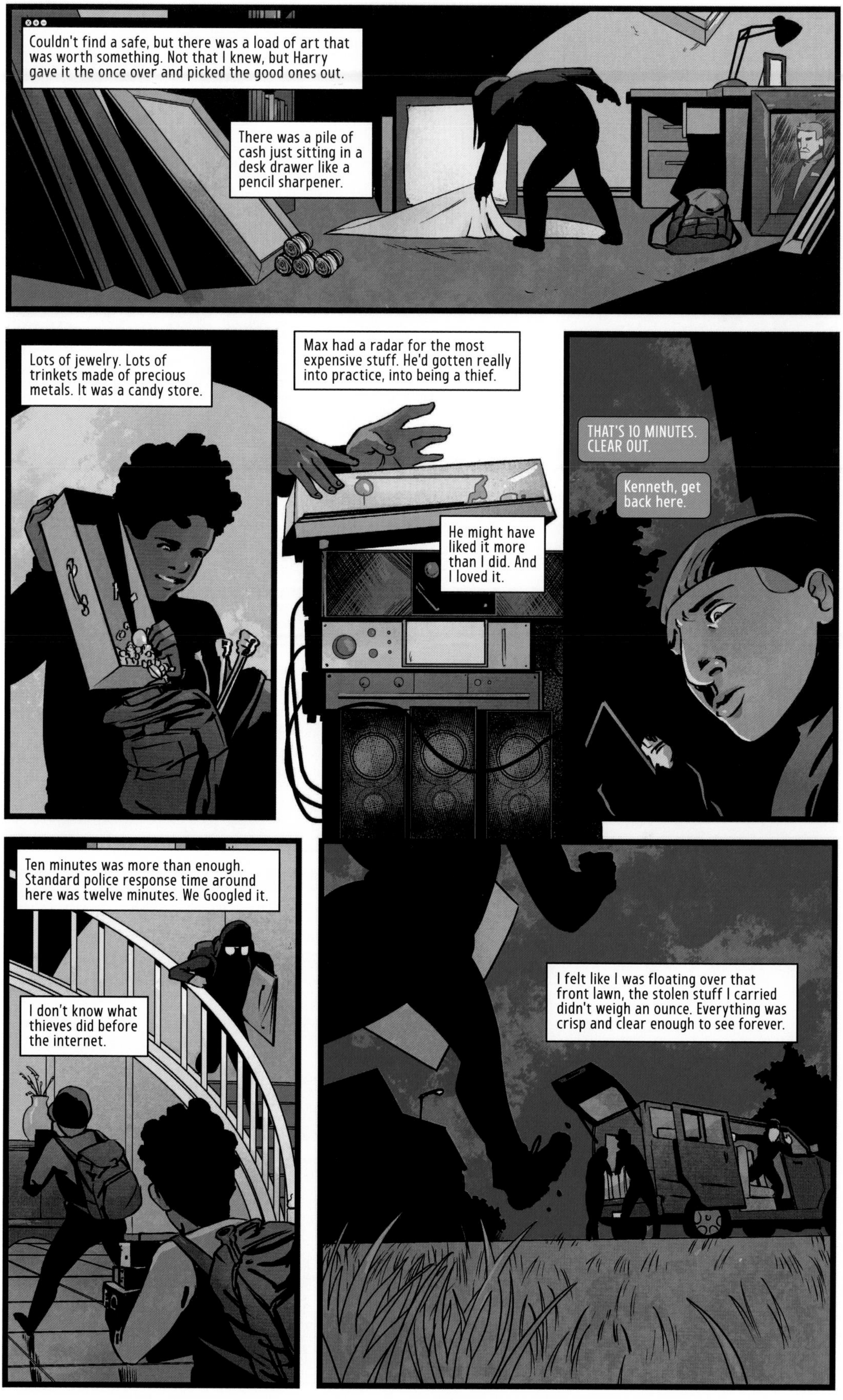

Couldn't find a safe, but there was a load of art that was worth something. Not that I knew, but Harry gave it the once over and picked the good ones out.
There was a pile of cash just sitting in a desk drawer like a pencil sharpener.
Lots of jewelry. Lots of trinkets made of precious metals. It was a candy store.
Max had a radar for the most expensive stuff. He'd gotten really into practice, into being a thief.
He might have liked it more than I did. And I loved it.
THAT'S 10 MINUTES. CLEAR OUT.
Kenneth, get back here.
Ten minutes was more than enough. Standard police response time around here was twelve minutes. We Googled it.
I don't know what thieves did before the internet.
I felt like I was floating over that front lawn, the stolen stuff I carried didn't weigh an ounce. Everything was crisp and clear enough to see forever.

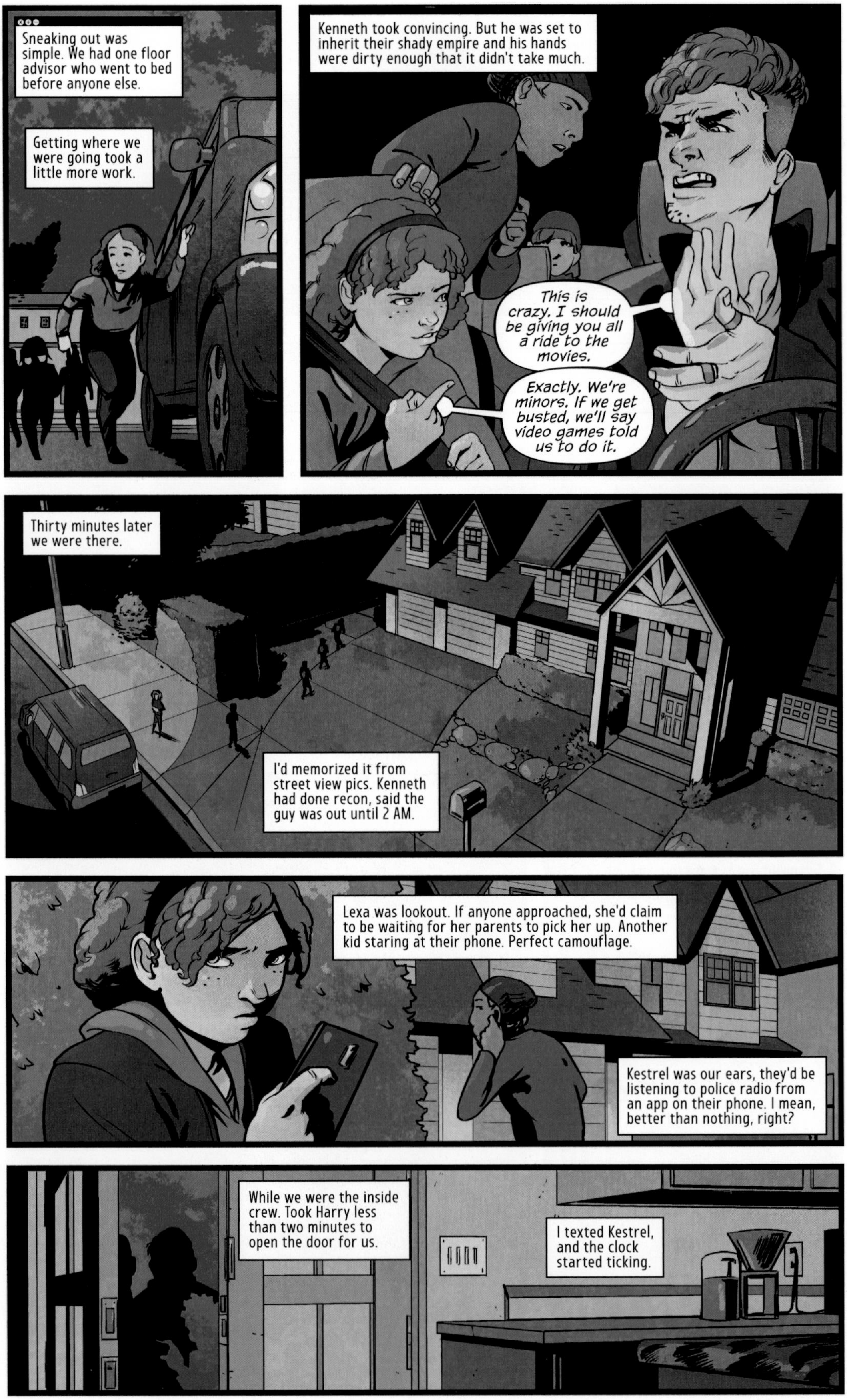
Sneaking out was simple. We had one floor advisor who went to bed before anyone else.
Getting where we were going took a little more work.
Kenneth took convincing. But he was set to inherit their shady empire and his hands were dirty enough that it didn't take much.
This is crazy. I should be giving you all a ride to the movies.
Exactly. We're minors. If we get busted, we'll say video games told us to do it.
Thirty minutes later we were there.
I'd memorized it from street view pics. Kenneth had done recon, said the guy was out until 2 AM.
Lexa was lookout. If anyone approached, she'd claim to be waiting for her parents to pick her up. Another kid staring at their phone. Perfect camouflage.
Kestrel was our ears, they'd be listening to police radio from an app on their phone. I mean, better than nothing, right?
While we were the inside crew. Took Harry less than two minutes to open the door for us.
I texted Kestrel, and the clock started ticking.

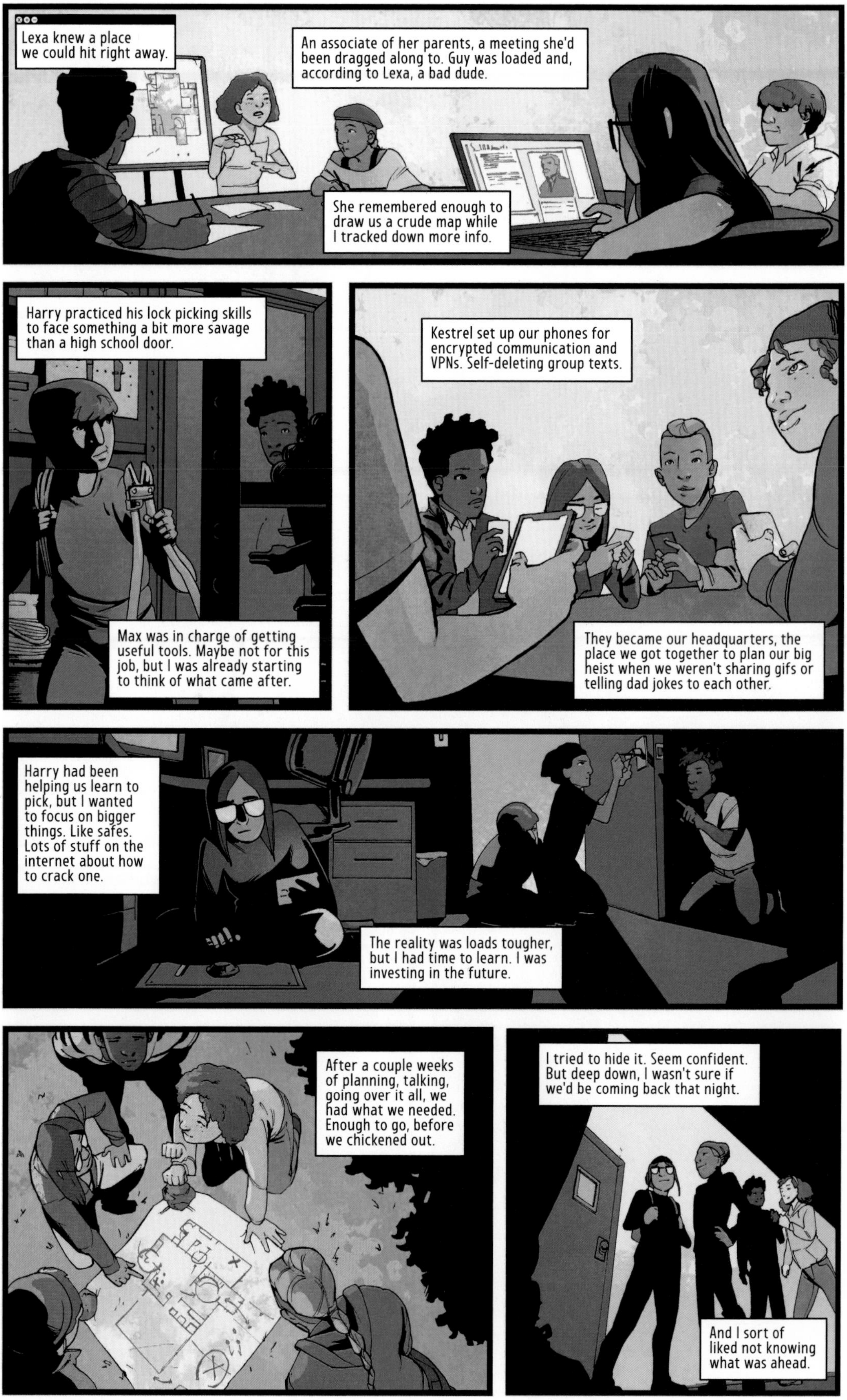
Lexa knew a place we could hit right away.
An associate of her parents, a meeting she'd been dragged along to. Guy was loaded and, according to Lexa, a bad dude.
She remembered enough to draw us a crude map while I tracked down more info.
Harry practiced his lock picking skills to face something a bit more savage than a high school door.
Max was in charge of getting useful tools. Maybe not for this job, but I was already starting to think of what came after.
Kestrel set up our phones for encrypted communication and VPNs. Self-deleting group texts.
They became our headquarters, the place we got together to plan our big heist when we weren't sharing gifs or telling dad jokes to each other.
Harry had been helping us learn to pick, but I wanted to focus on bigger things. Like safes. Lots of stuff on the internet about how to crack one.
The reality was loads tougher, but I had time to learn. I was investing in the future.
After a couple weeks of planning, talking, going over it all, we had what we needed. Enough to go, before we chickened out.
I tried to hide it. Seem confident. But deep down, I wasn't sure if we'd be coming back that night.
And I sort of liked not knowing what was ahead.

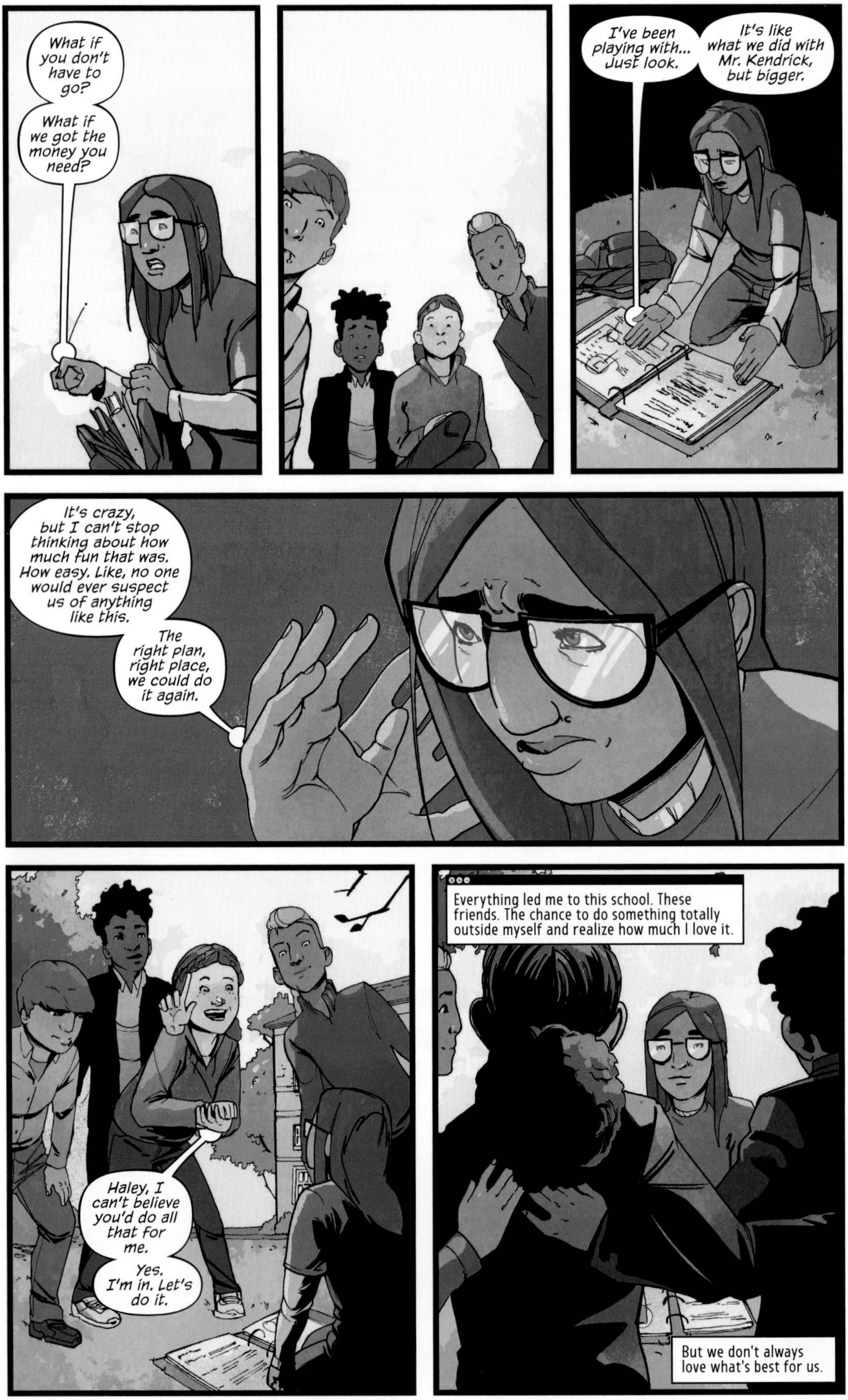
What if you don't have to go?
What if we got the money you need?
I've been playing with... Just look.
It's like what we did with Mr. Kendrick, but bigger.
It's crazy, but I can't stop thinking about how much fun that was. How easy. Like, no one would ever suspect us of anything like this.
The right plan, right place, we could do it again.
Haley, I can't believe you'd do all that for me.
Yes. I'm in. Let's do it.
Everything led me to this school. These friends. The chance to do something totally outside myself and realize how much I love it.
But we don't always love what's best for us.

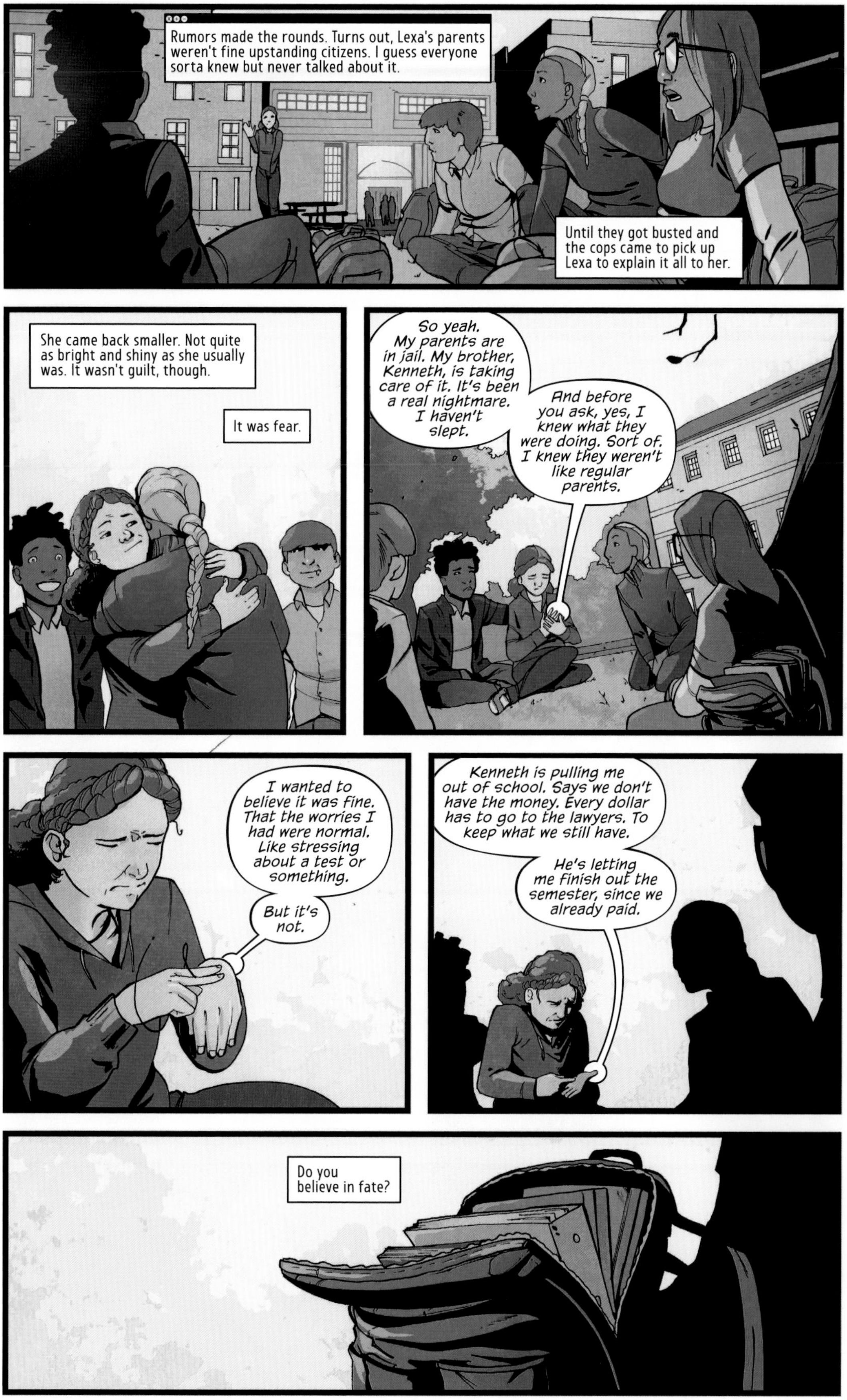
Rumors made the rounds. Turns out, Lexa's parents weren't fine upstanding citizens. I guess everyone sorta knew but never talked about it.
Until they got busted and the cops came to pick up Lexa to explain it all to her.
She came back smaller. Not quite as bright and shiny as she usually was. It wasn't guilt, though.
It was fear.
So yeah. My parents are in jail. My brother, Kenneth, is taking care of it. It's been a real nightmare. I haven't slept.
And before you ask, yes, I knew what they were doing. Sort of. I knew they weren't like regular parents.
I wanted to believe it was fine. That the worries I had were normal. Like stressing about a test or something.
But it's not.
Kenneth is pulling me out of school. Says we don't have the money. Every dollar has to go to the lawyers. To keep what we still have.
He's letting me finish out the semester, since we already paid.
Do you believe in fate?

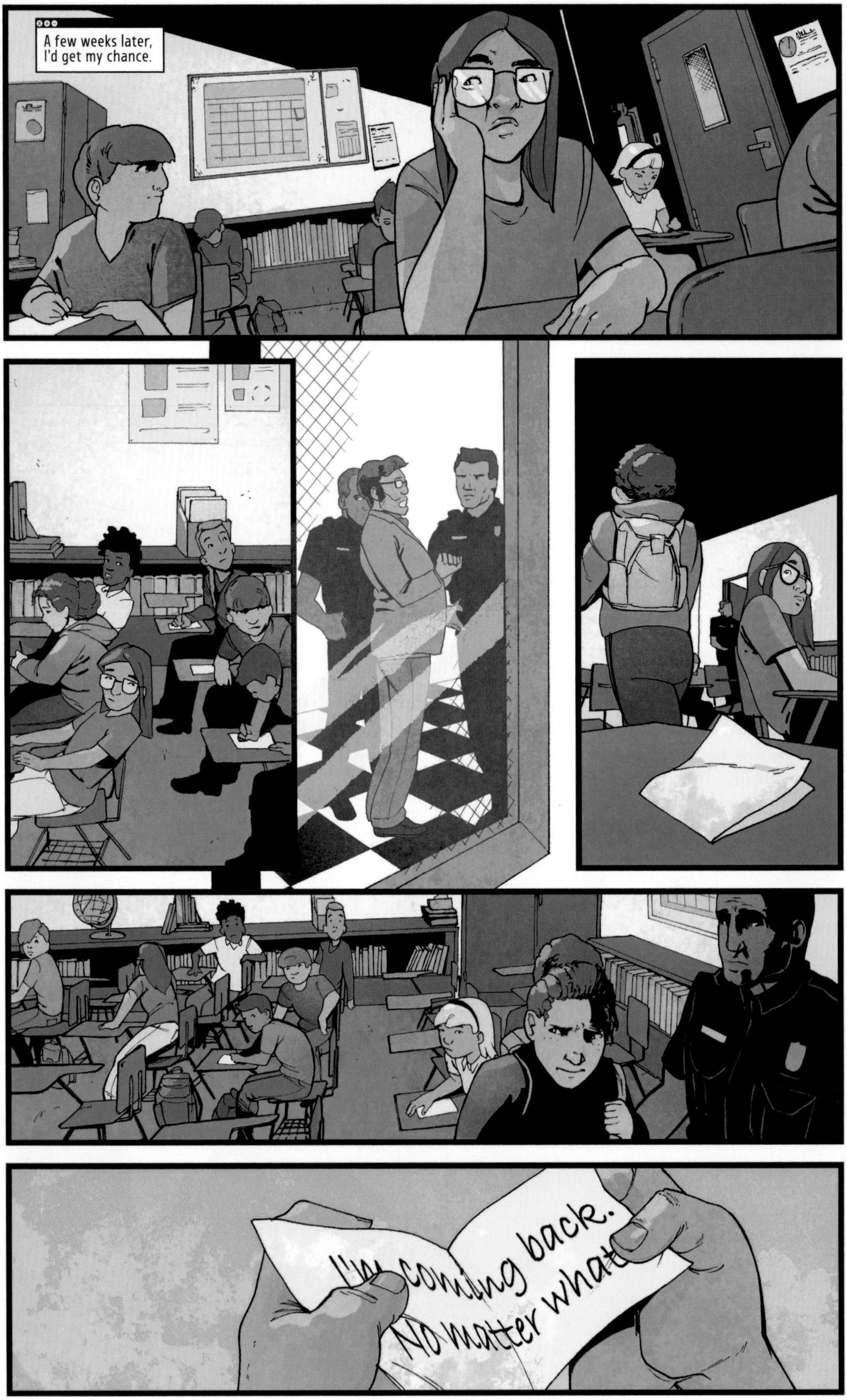
A few weeks later,
I'd get my chance.
I'm coming back.
No matter what

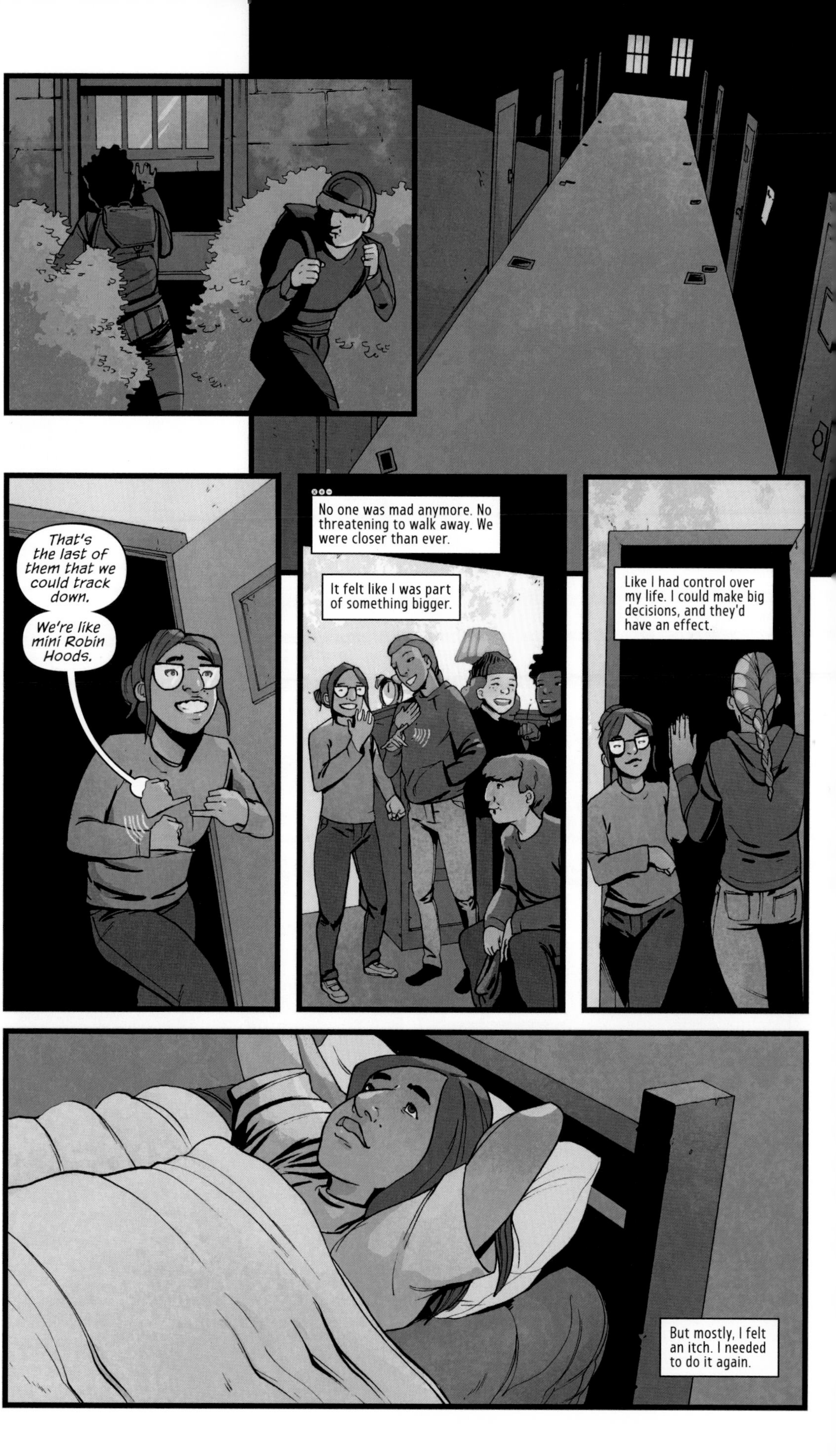
That's the last of them that we could track down.
We're like mini Robin Hoods.
No one was mad anymore. No threatening to walk away. We were closer than ever.
It felt like I was part of something bigger.
Like I had control over my life. I could make big decisions, and they'd have an effect.
But mostly, I felt an itch. I needed to do it again.

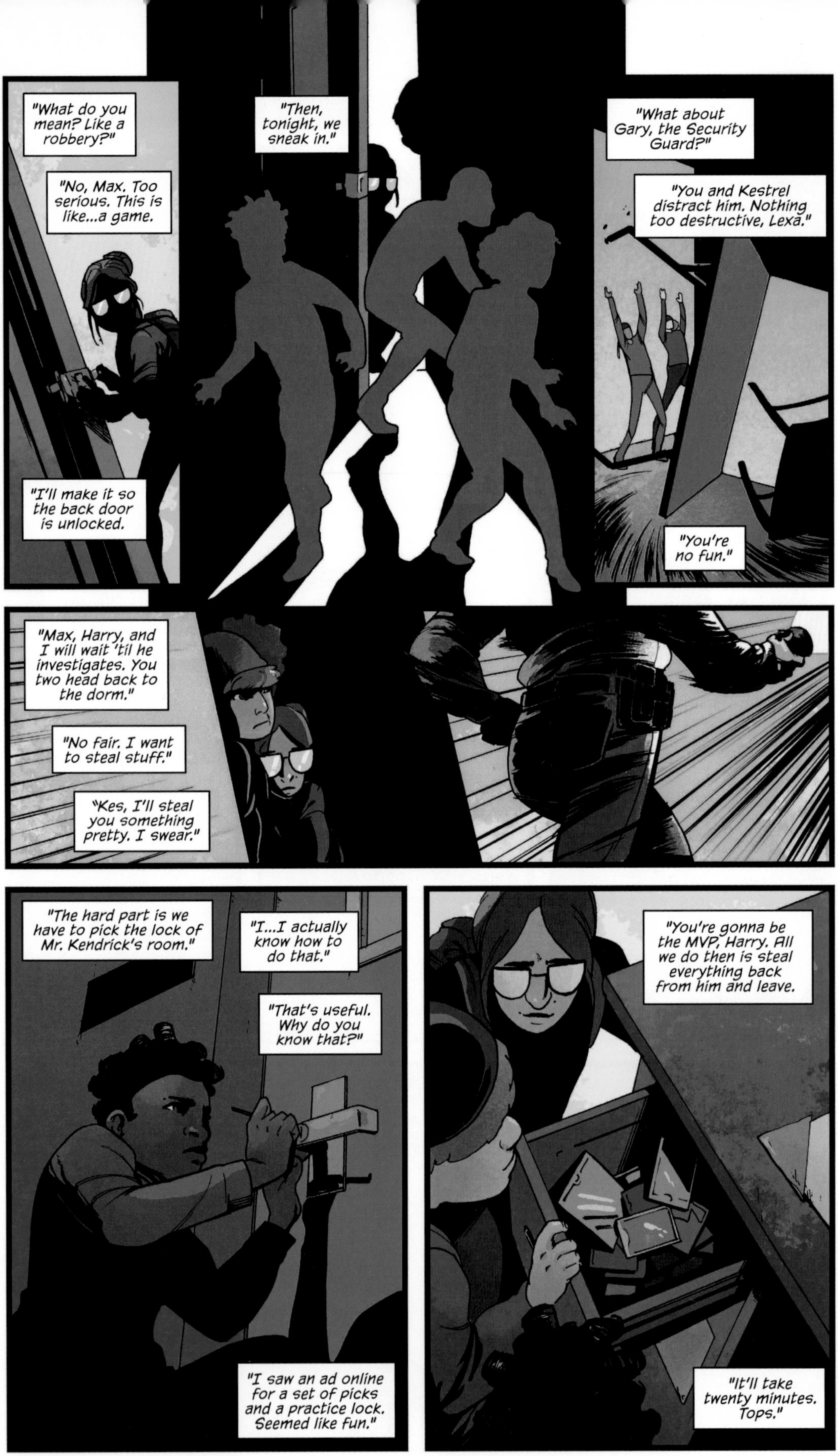
"What do you mean? Like a robbery?"
"No, Max. Too serious. This is like...a game.
"I'll make it so the back door is unlocked.
"Then, tonight, we sneak in."
"What about Gary, the Security Guard?"
"You and Kestrel distract him. Nothing too destructive, Lexa."
"You're no fun."
"Max, Harry, and I will wait 'til he investigates. You two head back to the dorm."
"No fair. I want to steal stuff."
"Kes, I'll steal you something pretty. I swear."
"The hard part is we have to pick the lock of Mr. Kendrick's room."
"I...I actually know how to do that."
"That's useful. Why do you know that?"
"I saw an ad online for a set of picks and a practice lock. Seemed like fun."
"You're gonna be the MVP, Harry. All we do then is steal everything back from him and leave.
"It'll take twenty minutes. Tops."

DISCOVER MAD CAVE COLLECTED EDITIONS

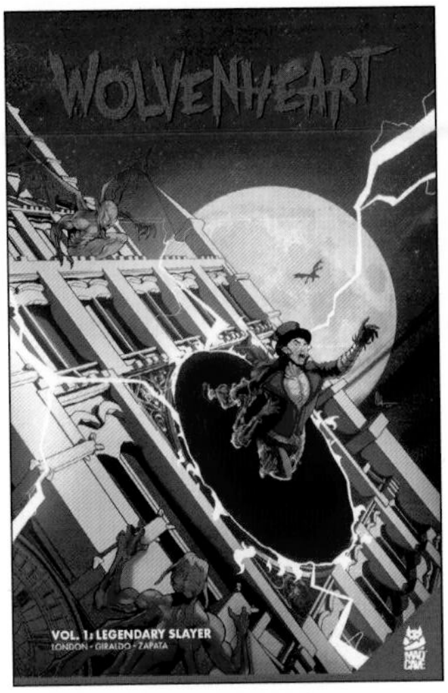
WOLVENHEART
VOL. 1: LEGENDARY SLAYER
LONDON · GIRALDO · ZAPATA

Wolvenheart Vol. 1: Legendary Slayer
ISBN: 978-0-9981215-8-1

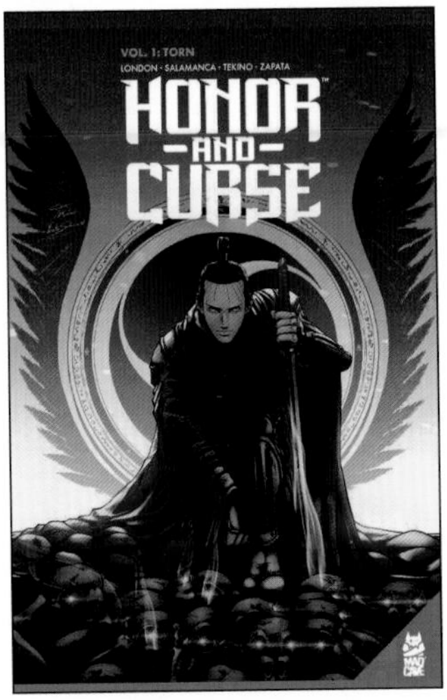
VOL. 1: TORN
LONDON · SALAMANCA · TEKINO · ZAPATA
HONOR
AND
CURSE

Honor and Curse Vol. 1: Torn
ISBN: 978-0-9981215-5-0

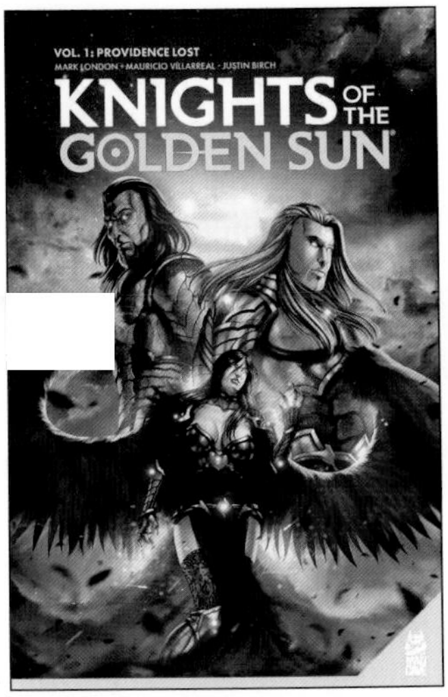
VOL. 1: PROVIDENCE LOST
MARK LONDON · MAURICIO VILLARREAL · JUSTIN BIRCH
KNIGHTS OF THE GOLDEN SUN

Knights Of The Golden Sun Vol. 1: Providence Lost
ISBN: 978-0-9981215-4-3

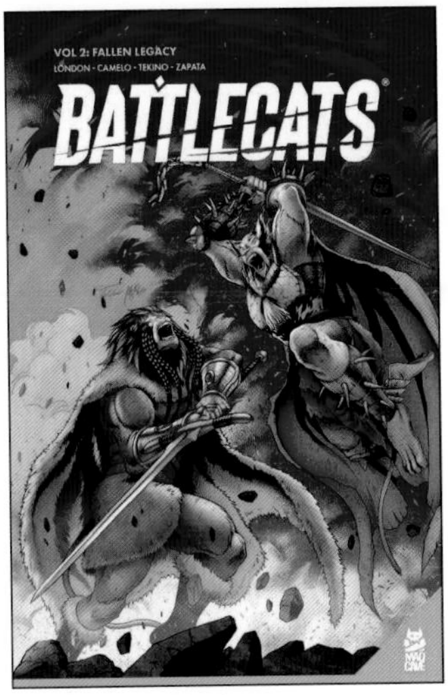
VOL 2: FALLEN LEGACY
LONDON · CAMELO · TEKINO · ZAPATA
BATTLECATS

Battlecats Vol. 2: Fallen Legacy
ISBN: 978-0-9981215-6-7

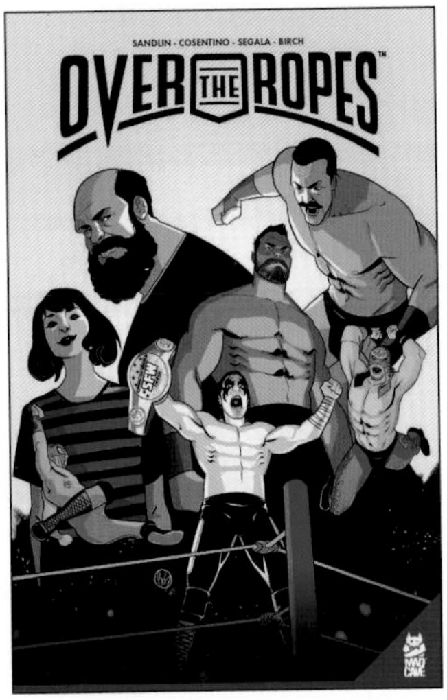
SANDLIN · COSENTINO · SEGALA · BIRCH
OVER THE ROPES

Over the Ropes Vol. 1
ISBN: 978-1-952303-00-5

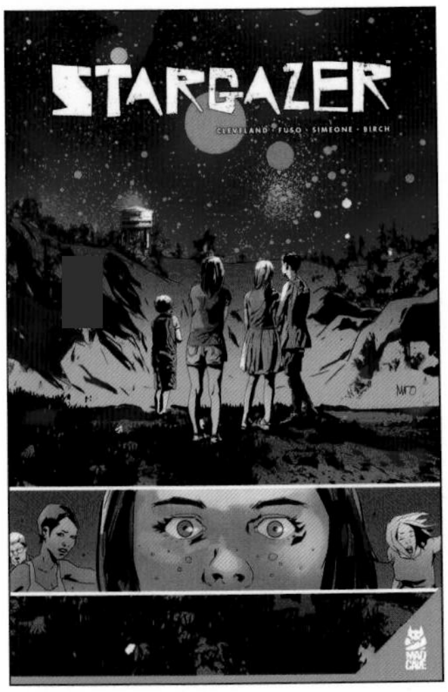
STARGAZER
CLEVELAND · FUSO · SIMEONE · BIRCH

Stargazer Vol. 1
ISBN: 978-1-952303-04-3

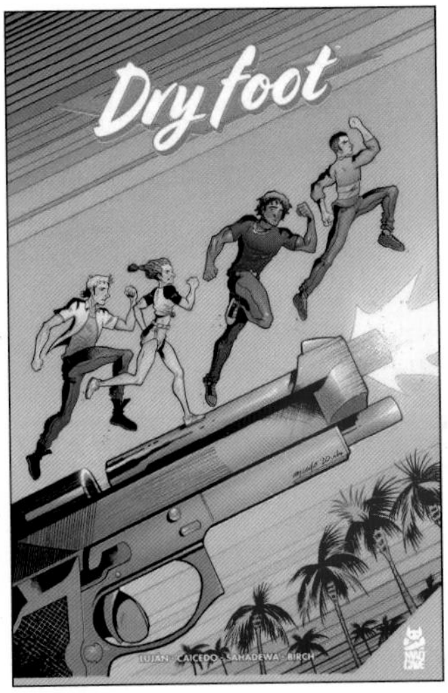
Dryfoot
LUJAN · CAICEDO · SAHADEWA · BIRCH

Dryfoot Vol. 1
ISBN: 978-1-952303-05-0

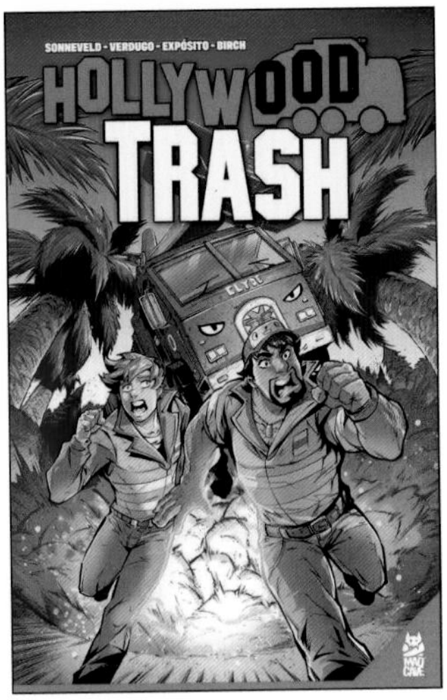
SONNEVELD · VERDUGO · EXPÓSITO · BIRCH
HOLLYWOOD
TRASH

Hollywood Trash Vol. 1
ISBN: 978-1-952303-08-1

PANTOMIME™